ALSO BY STEPHEN GREENLEAF

The Ditto List

Fatal Obsession

State's Evidence

Death Bed

Grave Error

BEYOND BLAME

SECOND PLACE

BEYOND BLAME

STEPHEN GREENLEAF

VILLARD BOOKS

NEW YORK

1986

β-2

Copyright © 1985 by Stephen Greenleaf

All rights reserved under International
and Pan-American Copyright Conventions. Published in
the United States by Villard Books, a division of Random
House, Inc., New York, and simultaneously in
Canada by Random House of Canada, Limited, Toronto.

Library of Congress Cataloging in Publication Data
Greenleaf, Stephen.
Beyond blame.
I. Title.
PS3557.R3957B4   1986   813'.54   85-40178
ISBN 0-394-54115-4

Manufactured in the United States of America

2   4   6   8   9   7   5   3
First Edition

This is a work of fiction.
The characters and events are entirely imaginary,
as is the institution entitled
the Berkeley Law School.

For Nana

And the Lord God planted a garden eastward in Eden; and there he put the man whom he had formed. And out of the ground made the Lord God to grow every tree that is pleasant to the sight, and good for food; the tree of life also in the midst of the garden, and the tree of knowledge of good and evil.

Genesis 2:8–9

The collective conscience does not allow punishment where it cannot impose blame.

Holloway v. United States, 148 F.2d
665 (D.C. Cir. 1945), cert. denied,
334 U.S. 852 (1948)

The defense of diminished capacity is hereby abolished. In a criminal action, as well as any juvenile court proceeding, evidence concerning an accused person's intoxication, trauma, mental illness, disease, or defect shall not be admissible to show or negate capacity to form the particular purpose, intent, motive, malice aforethought, knowledge, or other mental state required for the commission of the crime charged.

California Penal Code Section 25(a)
(Added by Initiative Measure,
approved by the people, June 8, 1982)

BEYOND BLAME

ONE

They were elderly, in their sixties at least, and like many older couples they radiated the warmth of siblings rather than the sparks of lovers. He was tall and stiff; she was short and stooped. His flesh was pasted right to bone; hers was tucked and pillowed. His eyes were blue and polished; hers were brown and melted. His clothes flapped and sagged; hers stretched as smooth and taut as second skin.

She had been the first to take a seat in my office, at my invitation. He had placed the spare chair snugly at her side before he followed suit. Now they were holding hands, looking at each other, exchanging the reassurances that, after forty years of marriage, do not make use of words. I knew why they were there, but their business was so delicate and disturbing I had to wait for them to tell me.

The woman had been elected speaker, but she was reluctant to begin. Her dress was blue and plain, with a pointed collar and white buttons up the front, and she fiddled with the top one until her husband nudged her arm. She nodded, placed her pocketbook on her lap, cleared her throat, and touched the tight bun she had made of her hair. There were streaks of steel through it, and doubtless through her heart as well. There would have to be, for her to have endured the past thirty days and remain as ordered as she seemed.

"We are here about our daughter, Mr. Tanner," Ingrid Renzel began, her strong voice clipped by the lingering chip of a Nordic accent.

When I didn't say anything, she glanced quickly at her husband. He nodded his approval and squeezed her hand. Fortified, she looked at me with renewed resolve. "We have practiced what to say, so you will understand our purpose, but it is difficult to know the proper words."

"Don't worry about the words. Just talk to me as you would to each other."

Her smile was unexpected, a bright new thing. "We speak Swedish to each other," she said, suddenly the imp, far younger than her years.

I grinned. "Better stick to English."

She quickly sensed that her expression was inappropriate and it vanished as suddenly as it had come, leaving her chagrined. "She was . . . she *is* . . . dead, Mr. Tanner. Murdered. Our Dianne—our daughter—was murdered in her home. In Berkeley. Last month. The twenty-first. It was a Friday. I . . ." She faltered into silence, her words outracing the plan she had hoped would carry her across the day.

"I read about it in the papers," I said to help her. "It was a terrible crime."

"Death . . . murder . . . is always terrible. But *this*. The police have pictures. We made them show us. The slashings. The wounds. So many, you would think she had been assaulted by a mob. Her flesh was ripped as though she were a *demon*. It was a monster's deed, Mr. Tanner. A monster killed our sweet Dianne. She is . . . was . . . our only child. It is a thing beyond our thought."

The requiem finally faded, leaving nightmare visions in its wake, and my own reluctance to hear more. Ingrid Renzel reached into her purse with her free hand and took out a blue print hankie and touched it to her eyes, which seemed to now stare inward, at the dark grotto where the grotesques she had just described would lurk forever.

I looked at her husband. Gunther Renzel had bowed his head and closed his eyes. The hand that didn't hold his wife's was curled into a fist that pressed like a pylon against his chest. He drew his breaths in rattling gasps, his aspect more indomitable than prayerful, as though he had usurped the redeemer's role and had damned the world that tortured him.

I asked Mrs. Renzel how I could help them.

She placed her hankie in her lap, twisting it into a shapeless snake that crawled between her fingers. "The police, they are working hard. They call, come to see us, tell us they are doing their best. We know that, and we are grateful. But there is so much crime, so many horrors, they have to share Dianne with many others. Although they are trying their best, they tell us they have learned nothing."

"These things take time," I said. "I'm sure—"

She interrupted with a forthright plea. "*We have no name.* Do you see? There is no one to whom to ask our questions; no one who can tell us why Dianne was stolen from us in this way. We want you to find this man, Mr. Tanner. We have asked people who know about such things and they have mentioned you to us. Will you assist us? Please? *Will you find a name for us?*"

I closed my eyes, as though that would cause her request to vanish. When it lingered, I opened my eyes and offered some excuses. "It might take a long while, Mrs. Renzel. Usually this kind of investigation is either over very quickly or it lasts for months. Even years. That is, usually the motive is obvious, or it's senseless. It could cost you quite a bit of money before it's over. My fee is forty dollars an hour."

I waited for a response and got the one I expected. "We are speaking of our daughter, Mr. Tanner. We will pay, whatever the amount. Gunther has sold his business. The night they came to tell us about Dianne, we were planning to buy her a gift with some of the money. A small red car. Now our gift will be to name the man who killed her. It will be the last thing we give her beyond our daily prayers."

Mrs. Renzel could seal the ducts no longer. She sobbed deeply and convulsively. A gel of tears varnished her rounded cheeks. Her husband tried to comfort her with murmurs and a long thin arm. While I waited for her composure to return I thought over what I knew about the case.

Dianne Renzel had been forty-one when she died. She went by her maiden name, but at the time of her death she was married to Lawrence Usser, a professor at the Berkeley Law School, a prestigious private school located not far from a more famous Berkeley institution—the University of California, and its law school, Boalt Hall. Usser was an expert in constitutional law and criminal procedure and had been a consultant in several notorious criminal trials over the past ten years or so. He and Ms. Renzel had a teenage daughter.

A Berkeley native, Dianne Renzel was a graduate of Berkeley High and the University of California. Over the past few years she had been active in many East Bay causes, and was a former member of the Berkeley City Council, the most turbid political body on earth, its most famous current aspirant none other than Eldridge Cleaver, its most abrasive recent controversy whether to pledge allegiance to the flag before each meeting.

Renzel had been a staff member of the Community Crisis Center which was located near the university campus. A month ago her husband had come home from the law school late on a Friday night and found his wife lying in their hillside home, naked and dying, slaughtered unspeakably by person or persons unknown. Luckily, the daughter had been spending the night with a friend. Sadly, Dianne Renzel had been dead on arrival at Alta Bates Hospital.

The police had released little information in subsequent weeks. Speculation in the press centered on rape or robbery as the motive, but neither of those was confirmed, at least as far as I knew. It was the kind of maelstrom I hate to get involved in, the kind of case that is never solved, not really, not in the sense that seeks both reason and remedy for subhuman behavior. But Gunther and Ingrid Renzel were the kind of people I could not easily say no to. By the time I was finished reviewing both the case and my compunctions, Mrs. Renzel was looking into my eyes again, waiting for an answer.

I cleared my throat. "I have to be frank with you, Mrs. Renzel. This kind of thing usually turns out to have been done by a junkie. A guy with his mind burned away by drugs, his moral sense erased by his need for money to finance his habit. Often the savagery is racially influenced as well. Finding a killer like that will be difficult at best, and it will be something the police are much more likely to do than I am."

"We do not care *who* finds him, Mr. Tanner. Only that he is found."

"The problem is, private detectives are like bloodhounds,

Mrs. Renzel. They need a scent. This case doesn't seem to have one."

"You don't know that, Mr. Tanner. Not yet. Not without talking to the police."

She had me there and knew it, so I cast about for more excuses. "Even if he is found, there's a real possibility it won't be of any help to you. You mentioned questions. A man like that won't be able to answer your questions in any way that's meaningful. You badly want this to make some kind of sense, Mrs. Renzel, and it's very likely that it won't make any sense at all. Plus, what he says won't help you learn to live without your daughter. I think you two should talk this over a little longer. It might be best to just forget about the murder investigation, to try to put the whole thing behind you. To—"

"We have talked of nothing else since that night." Gunther Renzel spoke for the first time since entering my office, in a voice as raw as a north wind, as crackling as warming ice. "Talking makes it worse. So now we must stop the talk; now we must act. We are asking you to help us. If you do not wish to, we have other names. I ask you to decide. We have no more time for you if you stand against us."

I held up a hand in quick disclaimer. "I'm not against you, Mr. Renzel. I just think—"

"Please. If you do not know that this is a thing a man must do, then you are not the one for us. So. What is your answer?"

His aqua eyes dared mine to match their unspoiled purpose. I tilted my chair away from their icy insistence. "Okay," I said, surrendering as I had known all along I would. "I'll look into it. If it seems like I'm wasting my time and your money, I'll let you know. If I develop any leads I'll follow them as far as I can, even if they tell me things about your daughter you won't want to know." I paused and looked at each of them. "Agreed?"

Their nods were firm and immediate.

"Can you point me in any direction at all? Did you know her life? Her friends and enemies?"

They exchanged a glance, then Ingrid Renzel answered. "From birth she was an angel. Everyone loved her; her playmates, teachers, everyone. It must still have been true; she was the same person. But since she married Lawrence she was so very busy. They were always doing, going, meeting, speaking.

It was as though there were a contest between them, to see who could do the most good deeds. These past years we saw Dianne only in passing, when she would drop off Lisa while they went to a music concert or a political meeting, or would stop in for cake and ice cream on birthdays and such. We can tell you very little about her recent years, Mr. Tanner. It's best you talk to Lawrence. But . . ."

"But what?"

Her eyes narrowed. "That Berkeley. There is such madness there. It is why we moved away, those people. But it was different for Dianne. She loved it so, and worked so hard to make it better, but they were always *at* her, the wild ones. The ones who do nothing for themselves, who look always to others to solve their problems, who destroy themselves on purpose, as though that would punish the power that made them what they are. Dianne could not be what they wanted her to be—she could not change either the world or their place in it. *No* person could." Ingrid Renzel sighed, as though the people she had just described were beyond both her experience and her theology. "So. Maybe one of them. The madmen. Maybe one of them blamed our Dianne for what he was, or destroyed her for being less than God."

I nodded because my own experience told me it made sad sense. "Do you have anyone specifically in mind?"

"No. We know no one."

"Who knew the most about her work at the crisis center? About any trouble she might have had there?"

Ingrid Renzel shook her head. "She never took us to her office. She was afraid we would try to make her quit, I think. To leave that place." She glanced quickly at her husband, indicating just which one of them had no use for personal crises or for organizations that existed to resolve them.

"Was she worried about anything at all that you know of?" I went on.

"No. But she never talked to me, not of such things. There must have been troubles, all lives have troubles, but . . ." She closed her comment with a shrug.

"Is there anything at all that came to your mind when you learned she had been killed? Anything that might suggest her killer?"

Mrs. Renzel shook her head. "What came to our mind was only grief, Mr. Tanner. You should talk to Lawrence. He is the one who can tell you who might have hated her so much."

"Have you told Professor Usser you're hiring me?"

She fidgeted. "No. We don't . . . no."

"Will he object?"

"It does not matter. She was our daughter. It is our sorrow as much as his." Her voice indicated that she was prepared to have to argue the point, if not with me, then with her son-in-law.

"Well, it's possible he might not be happy with me nosing around in his wife's affairs. He might not be very forthcoming if I just walk in off the street and start asking questions about his private life. Let's see. This is Thursday. Would you call him tonight? And tell him you've hired me and that I'll be calling him tomorrow? It might save a lot of time."

"Of course, though I can't promise you he will answer you. Lawrence has been . . . distant since that night. He seems to avoid us, perhaps because we are reminders of what he has lost."

"I understand. I'll bother him as briefly as possible. Now, is there anyone else I should see? Someone who might know if Dianne sensed any kind of danger before she died?"

Mrs. Renzel closed her eyes tightly, as though to extrude a useful memory. "A neighbor. There was a neighbor who was her friend."

"Name?"

"Phyllis, I believe. She has a daughter Lisa's age. They came to Dianne's house to borrow the vacuum sweeper once while I was staying with Lisa while Lawrence and Dianne were at the Ussers' cabin at the lake."

"The Ussers?"

"His parents."

"Do they live nearby?"

"In Piedmont."

"Would you call them as well? Tell them I'll be around to see them?"

She frowned. "I'd prefer not, Mr. Tanner. I'm sorry. We are not . . . comfortable with the Ussers. They do not wish to be disturbed by us, and we try not to disturb them." Ingrid Renzel started to add something, then stopped. "Please don't misunderstand, Mr. Tanner. We admire Lawrence very much. He is not responsible for the beliefs of his parents."

I nodded, embarrassed for her need to reveal social barriers, class distinctions, ethnic stereotypes, all the things that are supposed to have vanished but haven't, that seem even to be re-emerging.

Mrs. Renzel cleared her throat and spoke again. "It is embarrassing that we know so little about our daughter, Mr. Tanner. I had not realized until she died that we had drifted so far from her. Some of it is natural, I suppose. Parents and children, so hard for each to understand the other, so hard to meet on equal terms. But there was more. All her life Dianne worked to help the disadvantaged. After Gunther sold his business she was surprised at how much money we got for it, at the kind of home we could afford to buy, at the activities we had planned for our retirement. I think Dianne felt our profit was improper. I also think she came to feel that because we had money we had everything we wanted, when all we really wanted was to see much more of her."

Ingrid Renzel's grief seemed somehow to have doubled, the recollection of her daughter's life now more upsetting than the fact of her daughter's death. For both our sakes I hurried the interview to its end. "I think that's all I need for now, Mrs. Renzel. I can get anything else I need from Mr. Usser. Be sure to call him tonight. I'll talk to him tomorrow and look around and let you know."

"Lisa," she said simply.

"What?"

"Lisa. Dianne was troubled about her daughter, Lisa. There were many problems in recent months. Lisa fought her parents like a tiger. The language. The threats. It was a painful thing to see their love become buried under so much bitterness."

"What was the trouble, exactly?"

Ingrid Renzel shook her head. "Lisa has always been an unhappy child. Unable to enjoy what other children do. She seemed to feel that acting silly, having fun, was all too—how shall I put it?—*unimportant* for her. She was so serious and lonely that Lawrence and Dianne sent her to a psychiatrist. For a while it seemed to be working. Until a few months ago."

"What happened then?"

"I don't know. There are many reasons to be unhappy with the world, even for those as young as Lisa. I only know that Lisa began to behave badly, to disappear at times, to roam the streets in the middle of the night, to miss many days of school. The police were called at least once to find her. What worried Dianne and Lawrence most was that her new friends were crazies, like those Dianne saw at the center. They suspected she took drugs. They even suspected she once set fire to her father's study and broke a window in his automobile." Ingrid Renzel looked pained at the memory. "I believe Lisa was Dianne's biggest problem, Mr. Tanner. I believe she caused her mother much, much pain."

"That might be important," I said. "If you think of anything else about Lisa, let me know."

Ingrid Renzel nodded, gradually relaxing. The planes of her face slipped into a less concentrated configuration and she seemed another person. "Poor Lisa," she said softly. "Who will be her mother now that our Dianne is dead? Who will love her no matter what she does?"

I said the only thing I could think of to say: "Maybe you can be that person, Mrs. Renzel."

She shook her head. "We are too old. Too old, and too afraid."

She looked over at her husband. He frowned, then stiffened his back as if to disprove her statement. She smiled at him with affection, then looked away. Her eyes sought whatever it was that lay beyond the window and above the clouds. "My dear sweet Lord," she murmured. "What sins have we committed, that we should be cursed to live longer than our only child?"

TWO

The Renzels departed under a cloud of bereavement, leaving a dark gray tuft of it behind for me. I convened beneath it for a time, along with their daughter's ghost and my own reservations.

There were a lot of reasons not to get involved in the case. It was notorious, which meant the cops would be on edge and uncooperative because of pressure from the media, and the media would be determined to do what they do best—make everything they focus on seem more unseemly than it is. Plus, Dianne Renzel had been killed in Berkeley—Berserkley, the natives call it—that mix of intellectual frenzy and socioeconomic frustration that regularly boils over into the bizarre, and often into worse.

Berkeley isn't what it was fifteen years ago, but it's closer to what it was than any other place I know, so I viewed the prospect of wading through its frenetic scene with trepidation. But it was 1984. An Orwellian landmark, and also the twentieth anniversary of the day Jack Weinberg was arrested on the Berkeley campus for the high crime of collecting public funds for a political purpose. When a group of sympathetic students surrounded the police car and refused to let it haul him off, the Free Speech Movement was born. That struggle, in turn, was mother to the antiwar turmoil of the next ten years, a turmoil that touched us all and Berkeley most of all. How better to commemorate the anniversary than by solving a murder committed within strolling distance of Sproul Hall, where Joan Baez had sung and Stokely Carmichael had threatened and Mario Savio had convinced a surprising number of students that "there is a time when the operation of the machine becomes so odious, makes you so sick at heart, that you can't take part; you can't even tacitly take part, and you've got to put your bodies upon the gears and upon the wheels, upon the levers, upon all the apparatus and you've got to make it stop."

I was thinking back to the old days—to the demonstrations and sit-ins and love-ins and the rest—when Peggy took Ingrid Renzel's place in front of my desk, armed with a watering can and sponge. "Was that about that horrible Berkeley thing?"

I nodded. "Their daughter."

"It sounded just ghastly in the papers." Peggy closed her eyes and shuddered. "What are you going to do?"

"See if there are any motives lying around loose, I guess. If so, I'll check them out. If not, I'll bail out and let the police do their thing. My guess it was some kid shoved out of West Oakland by his habit and his rage. I told the Renzels that if that's what it looked like, I didn't have the resources to track him down."

Peggy shook her head. "I think you're wrong, Marsh. I think it was someone she knew. A stranger wouldn't have kept *hacking* at her like that. There was some kind of personal vengeance going on there, that's what I think." Peggy grimaced at her own morbidity.

"I hope you're wrong for a change," I said.

"I do too. For your sake."

Peggy eyed me for a long minute, then tried to change the subject. "Time to water the plants. You look a little dehydrated yourself, Marsh Tanner."

"How would you look if you'd just agreed to go looking for the man who slit Dianne Renzel's throat?"

"About like you," Peggy admitted, and wrinkled her face once again. "You must hate this job sometimes."

"It's not the job, it's just the world it comes in."

I looked toward the window. The shadows cast by the rays of sun that slanted through the glass made it seem like everything in the office was disappearing. Peggy emptied her watering can into a potted palm and dusted the philodendron with her sponge and went off to wherever she went after work to help her discard the hours she spent with me. I picked up the phone and called a lawyer.

Jake Hattie was the best criminal lawyer in town now that Jim MacInnis was dead and Hallinan and Garry were getting along in years, at least he was if you could afford him and could stomach his politics, which were to the dark side of Jesse Helms'. But that didn't matter much if you found yourself on the wrong end of an indictment, because when he was in court, Jake Hattie didn't truck with causes or crusades and didn't care about philosophies or propaganda, he just went to war for anyone who could pay his rates. Nine times out of ten, when all was said and done and the verdict had come in, his clients walked out the front door with Jake instead of the back door with the bailiff.

I'd done some work for Jake from time to time—locating witnesses, taking statements, testing alibis, searching records— and I thought he could give me some unbiased dope on Professor Lawrence Usser, husband of the late Dianne Renzel. I hadn't mentioned it to the Renzels, but when a wife is murdered, the best bet is that the husband did it: one third of all the murdered wives are murdered by their mates.

I got through to Jake after three different secretaries had made me say my name. "Hey, Jake. Marsh Tanner. Got a minute?"

"Sure, Marsh."

"Be right down."

I left my office, locked the door, went down to the alley, trotted around the corner and approached Jake Hattie's legendary digs.

Over the years, Jake's office had become his own best monument. Evolving daily, visible from the street through floor-to-ceiling windows, its current degree of vainglory exactly matched the man. The mahogany paneling and Tiffany lamps and crystal chandeliers set off everything from expressionist abstractions to art deco monstrosities. The law books and the furnishings were wrapped in calf. The tables were oak and walnut and were piled high with research material for Jake's latest book which, like all of Jake's books, was about himself.

The shelves on the wall were heaped with evidentiary souvenirs: murder weapons, fraudulent bank ledgers, falsely advertised ointments that cured baldness and small breasts, worthless stock certificates from uranium mines and oil wells, and framed legal documents that recorded not-guilty verdicts, divorce decrees and million-dollar personal injury judgments. A row of photos was autographed by the great and near-great, the holy and the profane. A stripper's G-string and a pornographer's book jacket lay near a safecracker's stethoscope and an arsonist's blowtorch. And all of it was arrayed beneath a giant oil portrait of Jake Hattie himself, presiding in a slightly skewed majesty from its place above the magnificent mantel and the roaring fire that, like Jake himself, blazed year round.

The same secretaries I'd spoken to on the phone guided me one by one to the sanctum sanctorum. When he heard us coming, Jake swiveled away from his rolltop desk and crossed the room to greet me. My lovely guide evaporated as silently as water after her employer blew her a kiss. She was so delighted by the gesture she must have been new. Jake went through secretaries the way the Pentagon went through money.

Jake was short and round, wore high-heeled black boots and three-piece black suits and a toupee that glowed like patent leather and almost worked but didn't. His portly physique and antique half-glasses made him look like a kindly chemistry professor until you noticed the glint of an assassin's cunning in his eyes and the three-inch monograms on all his clothes.

"Marsh. How's it happening for you?" He pumped my hand and slapped my back. Jake had never met a stranger, found fascination in the entire reach of humankind, which was probably why he was so good at what he did, which was to persuade jurors to believe him or at least to doubt the other guy.

"Tolerably, Jake," I said. "Yourself?"

"Crime still pays damned well, Marsh. Bought a little horse ranch last month. Up in Sonoma County. You'll have to come up some weekend. Always a spare girl or two around. Or bring your own. Always room for two more tits in the Rolls."

"I'll only come if I can keep away from the nags. Something bad always happens when I get on a horse."

Jake laughed. "I hate the bastards too. *Stupid* fucking animals. I only got in it for the tax dodge, but damned if I'm not about to make another bunch of money. Got a little two-year-old my trainer wants to take to the derby. A finish in the money will guarantee a million in syndication fees, maybe more. Or so he claims."

"The rich get richer, Jake."

"That does seem to be the way it works, doesn't it? Wish I could breed kids as well as I do Thoroughbreds. Youngest boy just joined the Moonies."

"Rough," I said.

"Yeah, hell. Now I got to change my will again. I got five kids and I've changed my will four times. Lucky for me Gary, the middle boy, he's too dumb to realize the world's fucked up so I got him working for me. What's on your inquiring mind, Marsh?"

"Lawrence Usser," I said.

Jake's bright countenance darkened several shades. He pointed me toward the leather couch then sat down at his desk, which had once been used by the younger Holmes, or so the story went. When we were comfortable, Jake spoke in his courtroom grumble. "Usser. Hmmm. The wife thing, right?"

"Right. Know anything about it?"

"Only what I read. The only thing that gets me over to Berkeley these days is the Big Game, so I haven't picked up on any bullshit. Looks like the papers aren't pressing and the cops aren't talking. Who's your client?"

I smiled. "An interested party."

"I amend my invitation. You'll have to supply your own woman and she'll have to sit on my lap all the way up."

I lowered my eyes. "I better have her bring a search party."

"Fuck you, Tanner. You get as old as me, *then* you can start making cracks about my waistline. You ain't Fred Astaire yourself, I might add."

"Touché," I admitted. "How about Usser? You worked with him once, didn't you?"

"Couple of times."

"And?"

Jake lit a cigarette. "Bright guy."

"And?"

"Lots of ideas; lots of energy."

"And?"

Jake shrugged.

"Come on, Jake. What's his problem?"

Jake chuckled. "Inscrutable, aren't I? Well, Larry's a humorless, inflexible, idealistic twerp, is about it, I guess. Intense as hell. Always certain he's on the side of right and justice, always impatient, always a little disdainful of the rest of us poor saps who have to do this kind of thing for a living."

"Nice guy."

Jake sighed a cloud of smoke. "He's not so bad, I guess, he's like a priest with a new religion. Always armed with the latest theoretical claptrap spouted by some professor who couldn't find a courtroom with a guide dog. Trouble is, all that theory is usually guaranteed to accomplish only two things—get the judge pissed off and cost the client a few hundred grand in defense fees. Larry's specialty is the insanity thing, you know."

"Right. I'd forgotten."

"I hate insanity pleas," Jake said.

"Why?"

"Because when you plead insanity you have to deal with shrinks. Ever had to rely on a shrink for anything, Marsh?"

"Nope."

"It's like relying on a Doberman—never know when they're going to turn on you and leave you bleeding. I've represented some real Wiffle balls in my time, Marsh, and every time I've sent one to see a psychiatrist he turned out to be goofier than my client on his worst day. Luckily, the legal insanity business is in recession, at least in this state."

"Why?"

"Remember the election of '82? Proposition 8?"

"Refresh my recollection. Lately I've tried to forget elections as soon as I see the results. Even before then, this year."

Jake grinned. "Not a Reagan man, huh, Marsh?"

"Nope."

"He's the best thing that's happened to this country since Roosevelt. Teddy, I mean."

"The best for you, maybe."

"Hey. I'm not my brother's keeper; I'm just his lawyer."

I laughed and Jake did too. Then he launched a lecture. "In 1982, the voters of this great state, in the exercise of their initiative powers, abolished the diminished capacity defense in criminal prosecutions. The law is probably unconstitutional as hell, since it amounts to a conclusive presumption of the capacity to commit a crime, but for the time being the chief generator of psychiatric evidence in the California legal system has been eliminated."

"Diminished capacity," I repeated. "That was when the defendant claimed he was too mentally disturbed to form the specific intent necessary to commit the crime. Or do I have it wrong?"

"No, that's it. If the diminished capacity defense prevailed, that meant the jury found no crime had been committed because the mens rea was lacking. Take a guy who steals a loaf of bread. If he was too nuts to form an intent to steal—if he thought he already owned all the loaves of bread in the world, for example—then he was not guilty of theft, of intentionally taking the property of another. Or, to use the example the Model Penal Code people use, if a guy believes he is squeezing lemons when he's actually choking his wife, then he isn't guilty of murder because he didn't knowingly cause the death of another person."

"So all that's out now."

"Right. The only thing left is the full insanity defense. In California we use a hyped-up version of the old M'Naughten rule, which means the guy may well have had the intent to commit the crime but he was so nuts the law says it wouldn't be humane to punish him for it. Sure he meant to steal the bread, but he stole it because God ordered him to. Get the distinction?"

I held up a hand in a gesture of surrender. "I'm getting flashbacks to law school."

"It's complicated all right. And since the Hinckley thing it's even worse. When a state court in Michigan ruled a while back that an insanity acquittee had to be treated like any person who had been civilly committed for mental illness, over sixty persons who had earlier been found not guilty by reason of insanity were immediately let out of the mental hospital because the state and their psychiatrists couldn't prove they were dangerous enough to hold. Well, surprise, surprise. One of them proceeded to commit rape; another murdered his wife. So in Michigan now the jury can find a defendant 'guilty but mentally ill.' Since Hinckley a bunch of other states have adopted that verdict too. The problem is, it amounts to abolishing the insanity de-

fense entirely, since it gives the jury what it thinks is an easy way
out. They *think* they've done something humane by finding him
guilty but mentally ill, but in reality the prison term is the same
as if he'd been convicted for the crime itself and the poor defendant doesn't get any more psychiatric treatment than the normal prisoner, which is none in seventy-five percent of the cases,
at least in Michigan. So the law's in a hell of a mess. Me, I blame
the shrinks. They keep claiming they can tell who's going to be
a danger to society and who's not, but they keep releasing guys
who commit some atrocity or other the very next day. If the
shrinks could get their act together it wouldn't be so bad. Actually, they should get out of the game entirely, admit they don't
know what the hell they're doing. Christ, Freud himself said
psychiatry couldn't predict future behavior. And the American
Psychiatric Association admits its members can't reliably antici-
pate future violence. But they keep giving it the old med school
try. The truth is, Marsh, if a jury is *really* frightened by the guy
—if he's a Manson, say—no way in hell they're going to find
him insane, no matter *what* the shrinks have to say, because
they're scared he'll be out on the street again and come looking
for *them.* Hinckley got off because he was only a danger to
presidents and Jodie Foster, not to jurors."

I shook my head. "From what I read, not many people are
happy with the state of the law—shrinks or lawyers, either one."

"Well, a few are, and Lawrence Usser is one of them. He's
one of the best guys in the country for wending his way through
the jargon. He knows his law and he knows his psychiatry. A
formidable opponent, as many a prosecutor has learned."

"Which cases were you and Usser on together?"

Jake leaned back against the desk, causing a stack of files to
teeter. "The first was that gang rape over in Mill Valley. Rich
college kids on speed and angel dust, banged the local home-
coming princess. Larry got his boy dumped down to simple
assault, two years' probation, on a plea of diminished capacity.
Showed the kid was so abused by his father over the years that
he became powerless to resist the demands of an authority figure, such as the kid who led the gang. That particular psychosis
they called a folie à deux. The jury bought the entire package
Usser offered them."

"How about your guy?"

"Oh, he walked, as I recall. Seems he only watched, or so twelve of his peers believed."

Jake Hattie shook his head in wonderment, whether at the mutability of the system of criminal justice or at his own impressive skills I couldn't be sure. "The other thing was the Nifton case," he said.

I remembered it. "The guy who followed that coed around for a year, begging her to go out with him, and finally stabbed her one night when she started necking with another guy on the porch in an effort to torment Nifton into leaving her alone."

"That's the one. A real jewel, that boy. But Usser and his pal Lonborg—he's the shrink Usser uses—convinced the jury that Nifton was so upset when the girl wouldn't pay any attention to him it created a 'transient situational disturbance' that rendered him incapable of conforming his conduct to the law. I didn't want Usser in on it with me, to be honest, but the local civil liberties group was footing the bill and they insisted, so I brought Larry in and I must say he did a hell of a job. After the verdict they sent Nifton to Napa State Hospital and six months later he made a PC 1026.2 showing that he was no longer a danger to himself or to others and now he's roaming loose out there somewhere, probably trying to convince some other sweet thing to let him in her pants."

"You've got a real cheery practice, Jake."

"Yeah, and guys like Usser make it worse. I go in there and try to make the jury understand what it was like, what the pressures were that drove my man to do what he did. And usually they *can* understand it. Hell, they have pressures too. They've all thought of blowing somebody's brains out at one time or another, smashing someone in the face, lashing out in one way or another. That's all murder is, usually. Lashing out. Getting rid of whoever it is that's driving you crazy. So okay. I've got my jury relating to slipping over the edge, to losing control, to doing something they wouldn't have done in ordinary circumstances. Then Usser and his buddy Lonborg come along, and start talking about 'transient situational disturbances' and 'psychomotor varients' and 'dysthymic disorders' and 'unipolar depressive reactions' and 'disassociative states,' and the jurors' eyes glaze over and I can't tell *what* the fuck they're going to do except get pissed off that all these eminent psychiatrists can't

seem to *agree* on anything. So I try to avoid Usser and his ilk
when I can. When I can't, I make sure he knows I'm in the case
to win, not to make the papers or the law reviews, not to reform
the world or even California. We get along, I guess. Haven't
seen him since his wife got killed."

"Know her at all?"

"Just to say hello to. Lovely. Sharp as a tack, I heard. Come
to think of it, she called me not too long ago. She ran some crisis
intervention thing. Wanted me to contribute, since my clients
have been known to precipitate a few crises in their day. I told
her the only charity I support is Uncle Sam, and him I support
both reluctantly and minimally, thanks to my accountant."

I left Jake Hattie to his memories and his practice and went
back to the office and called the only person I knew in the
Alameda County District Attorney's office. Her name was
Rhonda Stein. She was fifty-plus and had been a prosecutor
since her husband ran out on her two decades before and she
had to find work that would pay her kids' way through school.
Five years ago I'd testified for the defense in one of her cases,
and it was complicated enough that I felt sure she'd remember
me.

"Haven't seen you since that embezzlement thing," she said
after I told her who I was.

"I don't get over to the East Bay much. How's it going with
you?"

"Oh, overworked and underpaid, I guess. Or maybe it's vice
versa. I'm too old to keep track anymore." Her laugh was dry
and brief. I guessed it wasn't one of her better days.

"I'm calling about the Renzel case, Rhonda. Dianne Renzel,
married to Lawrence Usser, professor at the Berkeley Law
School. Killed in Berkeley last month. You know it?"

"Sure. Some. A real grisly one. Nightmare material."

"Can you tell me who's handling it for the cops? And maybe
put in a good word for me between now and tomorrow, so he
won't throw me out of town when I start asking questions?"

She paused. "Well, I can put in a good word, but I can't
guarantee it'll take. Bart Kinn is not a graduate of Dale Carne-
gie."

"That the cop?"

"Right. Detective lieutenant Berkeley P.D. Good officer, but a loner. Got a stare like Darth Vader and he hasn't got much use for female prosecutors, as he's told me more than once. I'd guess private eyes will get the same reaction."

"Who's handling it on your end?"

"Not much to handle at this stage, but Howard Gable's got the file."

"Good man?"

"Good lawyer," Rhonda said.

"And?"

"Maybe a little ambitious. Maybe a little more concerned with his won-lost record than he ought to be. Maybe a little too eager to send kids to jail. But if he files a charge he usually makes it stick. I guess that's all we can ask."

"You can ask a hell of a lot more than that and you know it, Rhonda. You've been giving more than that for years."

Her voice sounded tired and betrayed. "Yeah. Maybe. Anyway, as far as I know, nothing's broken on the case, but then Howard and Kinn both play it close to the vest. If I hear anything, I'll let you know. In the meantime, I've got my own corpses to worry about. Who's your client, anyway?"

"Off the record?"

"Sure."

"The dead woman's parents."

"Good. I've seen the pictures, Marsh. He really did a number on her."

"Any physical evidence at all?"

"Nothing that points in any direction. She was nude, ready for sex or ready for bed, they're not sure. No sign of forced entry, no sign of a struggle. They're guessing she knew the guy, and maybe had a thing going with him on the side, but I don't think they've nailed that down yet. The husband took it hard; Howard still has to hold his hand once in a while. That's about all I know."

"Thanks, Rhonda. If they zero in on anyone, I'd appreciate it if you'd give me a call."

"Okay."

"And let me know when I can take you to Spengers for some abalone."

"Spengers. Jesus, I haven't been there for years."

"Then let's do it."

"Right. Soon. But I warn you, abalone goes for more than gold these days."

"Hey. It's only money. I've got more of it than I can use."

Rhonda laughed. "And I've got Paul Newman waiting for me in my apartment."

THREE

On Friday morning I called the Berkeley Law School, only to learn that Lawrence Usser was teaching a class and unavailable. A woman with a breathy, anxious voice advised me to call again in an hour. Next I called the Berkeley Police Department. Bart Kinn wasn't in, either. No one seemed to know where he was or when he'd be back. This time a gruff, captious officer didn't give me any advice at all beyond the implied suggestion that I was a nuisance.

I called the law school again at eleven. I told the ethereal voice who I was and mentioned the Renzels and sounded official or at least officious. After a long wait and some background mumblings, Lawrence Usser came on the line.

His voice was abrupt, dismissive, strained, as though he'd just finished a long argument with an unreasonably stubborn adversary. I started to repeat the information I'd given his secretary, but he stopped me after three words. "I know who you are and what you want. Ingrid called me at home last night." He paused, then spoke before I could ask a question. "I'll be frank with you, Mr. Tanner. I tried to convince her to forget about it, to inform you your services weren't required."

"I take it she didn't accept your advice."

"No. She didn't."

Usser sounded both unnerved and saddened by the fact. His

voice cracked briefly, like an adolescent's. "Can I meet you somewhere today?" I asked. "For half an hour? I can be at the law school any time. Or wherever."

Usser hesitated. "I'm very busy. There's . . . Oh, hell. I might as well get it over with. I can just see Gunther's scowl if he learned I refused to see you. Let me check my calendar. Christ, I have students coming in, and a curriculum meeting, an adviser's conference at the law review. . . . Okay. Let's do this. Can you be over here in an hour?"

"Sure."

"I have to go over to the north side of campus on some personal business. You know the Shattuck Commons building?"

"I know the street, not the building."

"You can't miss it. Take Shattuck north from University until it begins to veer left. There'll be a triangular building on your right. It's fairly new. Pennants on top, a pasta shop on the ground floor. It's a block past Chez Panisse, if you know where that is."

"Nope. Sorry."

Usser seemed annoyed by my ignorance of the wellspring of nouvelle cuisine. "Well, there's a Bill's Drugs there," he went on, still exasperated. "And a Safeway. So you shouldn't have any trouble. I'll be having lunch at Rosenthal's Deli. That's in the little shopping area just south of the Shattuck Commons. Meet me there at noon. I can give you thirty minutes, if you have to have them."

Usser cut the connection before I could get a head start on my questions, leaving me as empty as a law student after an encounter with the Socratic method. I thought for a minute, then decided to get to Berkeley a little early. Lawrence Usser had some personal business to attend to. I thought I'd try to find out what it was.

I got there in twenty minutes, across the bridge, up the Nimitz, off on University Avenue, left on Shattuck. I found a parking place just south of the triangular building Usser had described, the one with flags on top and a weather vane in the form of an eagle, and got out and stretched my legs and looked around. What I saw were restaurants, bakeries, chocolate shops, meat markets, delicatessens—an array of enterprises devoted exclusively to stuffing the alimentary canal.

Berkeley has changed a lot since 1964. Food has replaced politics and sex as the major focus of both energy and ideology, and this area of the city was known as the "gourmet ghetto" because of its dependence on the new infatuation. Just for kicks I strolled down the street until I came to Chez Panisse. The menu was posted at the door. Vegetable soup, pan-fried quail breasts, walnut soufflé. Forty dollars per person, corkage not included. Feeling barbaric and amazed, I walked back to the Shattuck Commons, browsed in the bakery and bought some muffins for the morning, then meandered through the arcade until I found the nook that sheltered the building directory.

Most of the listings were retail businesses—toy store, shoe repair, copy service, travel agency. But there was one professional office and it belonged to A. Adam Lonborg, M.D. His specialty was psychiatry and he was the man Jake Hattie had mentioned as being an expert witness for Usser in one of the trials they had worked on together. I ambled back to my car, stowed the muffins, bought the new Ross Thomas novel at Black Oak Books, then went into Rosenthal's and asked for a table for two. They showed me to a booth beneath a poster advertising a public meeting to express sympathy with the Russian revolutionaries. Since it was Berkeley I checked to make sure the date was 1917 and not last week.

I was on Chapter 3 and my second Dr. Brown's strawberry soda when I heard my name. "Tanner? I'm Larry Usser."

He was tall and dark and delicately handsome; thin, precisely dressed, with wire-rim glasses and a grimly searching stare, as though he suspected me of stealing something from him. His cheeks were hollowed, his flesh sallow, his black curls tousled, suggesting he habitually warred with them. Behind the round rims of his eyeglasses his eyes were squeezed into a squint, as though he bore up under a congenital affliction. I was reminded of pictures of Mahler, taken at the height of both his genius and his torment, superficially stern, fundamentally fragile. I stood up and shook his narrow hand, then looked from Usser to the man who stood beside him.

"This is Adam Lonborg," Usser said. "A friend. Do you mind if he joins us?"

"Not at all."

Usser's failure to mention Lonborg's profession interested

me, as did the electricity that seemed to pass between the two men. Whatever its source, Lonborg was clearly the primary beneficiary of the current. He was forty, probably; blond, blatantly athletic even discounting the gaudy exercise suit he was wearing, as cheerful as if they gave out prizes for it. If Usser was annoyed at having to meet with me, Lonborg was extravagantly amused. His smile stayed long enough to descend from fellowship toward insult.

We squeezed into the booth and placed our lunch orders. The two of them sat across from me, looking like a losing coach and the star performer he was counting on to bring him out of it. Oddly, Lonborg was the first to speak, Usser's thoughts clearly unformed or in disarray. "Is it that you feel the police are unequal to their task, Mr. Tanner?" Lonborg began with a studied nonchalance. "Is that why you have inserted yourself into this matter?"

When I could ignore the scorn, I answered him. "I haven't inserted myself into anything but this booth. I've been asked to help. And what *I* feel isn't the question, is it? What my client might feel would be more pertinent, and what my client *knows* is the most pertinent thing of all—that the police have not made an arrest in the case as yet. So I don't see why you or anyone else would object to another pair of eyes and ears and legs joining the search for Ms. Renzel's killer."

I glanced at Usser to gauge his attitude. His eyes were lowered and his hands fiddled with the wine list without opening it. His forehead shone with sweat though the room was only tepid. He might not have heard a word I'd said, or he might have heard them all and been infuriated.

"My reason for opposing your participation," Lonborg was saying, "is simply that reviewing the events of that evening still another time will be very traumatic for Larry. He's only now beginning to adapt to his new reality, to manage his depression rather than yielding to it. Another grilling might set him back, perhaps permanently. I'm sure you can appreciate that. I'm trying to spare him a needless journey through the past. I'm sure you've encountered similar objections over the course of your . . . career, Mr. Tanner."

I met Lonborg's sassy grin with one of my own. "Yep. I sure have. But I've managed to track down a killer or two in my time, and each time I did do you know what? The victim's family was relieved as hell to have the case over and done with. So it *could* finally become history, something that *had* happened, not something that was still happening. I'm sure you've experienced similar reactions during the course of *your* career, Doctor."

Lonborg raised his thin blond brows, then glanced at Usser, then back at me. "You know who I am."

"Only by name and reputation. You've testified for the defense in some of Professor Usser's cases, haven't you?"

"In all of them, actually."

"Are you treating Professor Usser? Is that why he met with you this morning?"

Lonborg glanced at Usser once again, then held up a hand to silence him when Usser shook his head and started to speak. "That sort of information is totally confidential, Mr. Tanner," Lonborg cautioned.

"The fact of the psychotherapist-patient relationship is not confidential, Doctor. Not the last time I checked the law books."

Lonborg twisted his lips into the neighborhood of a sneer. "You seem to know your law, Mr. Tanner. Are all . . . investigators . . . amateur attorneys?"

"Some are and some aren't and some are professional, card-carrying members of the bar. Like me, for instance."

Lonborg bowed in mock respect. "Really? I'm impressed."

"No, you're not. You haven't been impressed since the day you bought your first couch."

"Oh, couches aren't considered therapeutically effective anymore, Mr. Tanner. There are several monographs on the subject if you care to consult them. It's felt such artificiality is contraindicated in its stimulation of transference."

"So what's the latest?" I asked, looking over his outfit. "Short pants?"

Lonborg clearly wanted to continue our little game, but Usser spoke for the first time since we'd sat down. "What do you want from me?" The question was resigned, agonized, reluctant. Lonborg started to object, but something in Usser's anguished eyes made him yield.

I cleared Lonborg from my mind, though not without difficulty, and turned my attention to Usser. He awaited my question the way he would have awaited the results of a biopsy. Clearly the man remained haunted by his wife's death, was leery of opening himself up to it. I decided to concentrate not on the murder but the murderer.

"It's been a month since your wife was killed, Mr. Usser. You must have thought about it a lot in that time."

Usser's eyes fell shut. "I have thought of little else. You can't possibly imagine what—" He forced himself to stop, to refrain from stirring the sediment of his grief. From the lines that streaked his face the effort took all his will. "Go on," he instructed finally.

"What I mean is, you must have thought a lot about who might have done it."

"Of course."

"What did you decide, if anything?"

"A dope addict," he said simply. "A junkie."

I nodded. "That was my first thought too. But let's put that possibility aside for a minute. If not a junkie, then who?"

His answer was a mumble, urged between clenched teeth. I told him I hadn't heard him.

"A madman," he repeated.

I hesitated, an idea forming as I took a sip of Dr. Brown's. "Are you thinking of someone in particular?"

Usser frowned, confused by my question or perhaps afraid of it. "What do you mean? There are many deranged persons in the world. The streets of Berkeley are full of them. The policy of the current experts in the field is to force these poor people to exhibit their illness in public whether they want to or not. Which merely makes them frightened of themselves as well as of the world they live in. I have no idea which one might have wandered into my house that night, pursuant to God knows what compulsion."

"I was just thinking," I continued calmly. "You've represented a lot of people that were unbalanced under almost any definition of the term. Maybe one of them might have a score to settle with you, or thought he did. Maybe he picked this way to do it."

"But who? I win almost all my cases."

"Almost?"

Usser shrugged and rubbed a palm across his face. "I'm not perfect and neither are my juries. And sometimes winning simply means they get to know they'll stay alive instead of residing on Death Row."

"So there are a few people out there who might have reason

to think you did less for them than you promised, or at least less than they expected you to do. Someone who spent some time in jail and thinks you should have prevented it from happening, for example."

"I suppose one or two of my former clients might feel that way."

"Give me a name."

Usser gestured helplessly. "I can't. Not off the top of my head. It's just so . . . preposterous . . . that someone would take out their animosity toward me on poor Dianne."

"Preposterous people are your specialty, aren't they, Professor?"

The question lay undisturbed for several seconds. Dr. Lonborg opened his mouth to say something, then abandoned the idea. When Usser showed no signs of speaking, I did what I usually do when given the opportunity—I asked another question: "Have you even considered the possibility that one of your clients did it?"

He shook his head, not meeting my eyes.

"Would you start considering it now? Would you go through your files this evening and see if any names pop out at you? And give me a list of everyone who ever made a threat of any kind against you, no matter how trivial it might have seemed at the time?"

"I don't . . . I'm so busy, I . . . ."

"I don't have to remind you that every day that passes makes the likelihood of finding your wife's killer that much smaller, do I, Professor? Or that if the killer's grudge was against you and not your wife, he might not be satisfied with what he's done to date?"

Usser lowered his head to his hands. "I can't believe we're talking like this. As though there's some . . . some *fiend* running around, trying to ruin my life." He shuddered briefly and Lonborg patted his shoulder to calm him down. The condescending gesture seemed to work. "I'll do what I can," Usser managed finally. "By this weekend at the latest."

"Fine. How about over at the law school? Anyone there have a grudge against you that he might have satisfied by murdering your wife?"

The question was blatant, but Usser let it pass. Finally he was thinking about the problem and not about its cause. "That's even more ridiculous than your other idea," he said.

"It doesn't seem so ridiculous to me. Some guy down at Stanford killed his math professor for giving him a C, and admits he might well kill someone else on the faculty if they ever put him on parole. It's not such a big jump from there to killing a professor's wife to punish her husband for failing him in class."

"I'm sure I know no one at the law school who's capable of that, even remotely." Usser glanced at Lonborg, who nodded approval of the answer. I doubted either of them was as naive as they were pretending to be. Still, madness is always denied, is somehow the last resort, as though all of us fear a personal psychotic stain from the mere acknowledgment of its existence.

"We've talked about you," I continued, "now how about your wife? Who might have been angry enough at her to do something like that?"

Lonborg couldn't restrain himself. "*Please*, Mr. Tanner. Surely even you must realize how terrible it is for Larry to think of Dianne in this context."

"It's all right, Adam," Usser said, then looked at me directly for the first time. "Dianne encountered some very disturbed people in her job, Mr. Tanner. She spent many hours at the crisis center, both day and night. Some of her clients were, well, capable of almost anything. I suppose if I were honest I'd admit that I think it might have been one of them, a client at the center who imagined Dianne had wronged him somehow, who inserted her into some paranoid fantasy and thought he had to kill her to save himself."

"Any names?"

"No. We didn't talk about our work that much at home. We tried to keep our professional and private lives separate. We weren't always successful, but we tried."

"Who would know the details of that part of her life."

"Her supervisor, I suppose. Pierce Richards."

"Anyone else?"

"I'm not sure. Various staff members, but there's such a high turnover down there, I'm not sure who's still available."

"All right. Now. How about her personal life, Mr. Usser? Anything going on there that might be helpful?"

"Come now, Tanner," Lonborg interrupted. "Enough surely is enough, even from you."

"Mr. Usser's a grown man, Doctor," I said. "If his wife was having an affair and it turned sour, I'm sure he realizes that information would be crucial in a case like this."

I'd asked my question indirectly, and Usser answered it by shaking his head. "We were very happy," he said softly. "Very, very happy. That's all I can say."

Usser was in tears. Lonborg was looking at me with acid eyes. I decided to give up. "Okay. I'll let you go. But keep my questions in mind, Mr. Usser. If anything comes to you, please give me a call. I'm in the San Francisco phone book. And one last thing. I'd like to talk to your daughter this afternoon. Can you tell me where I can find her after school?"

Lonborg immediately leaned over and whispered something in Usser's ear. From his look it was an urgent, vital something. Usser listened, then nodded. "You must leave Lisa out of this, Mr. Tanner," Usser said firmly. "I will not permit you to grill her about her mother's death."

"I'll be tactful," I said. "Sometimes it helps if they talk about it."

"No!" Usser thundered. "My daughter is a fragile child. She has been in therapy with Dr. Lonborg for several years. Every time she seems poised at a breakthrough, something happens to set her back. Dianne's death has been a major block to her development. Dr. Lonborg assures me it is not permanent, but I simply will *not* have you jeopardizing her treatment or driving her toward even more outlandish behavior by inflicting additional psychic injury. If you attempt to see her, I'll take whatever steps are required to ensure that she's left alone."

Usser's heated words caused heads to turn our way. He was so clearly upset that I willingly surrendered. "I'm sorry if I've disturbed you," I said to him. "But my clients have rights in this matter too. I'm sure you understand."

Usser didn't say a word. Lonborg draped an arm around his shoulder and patted him as if he were a tyke who'd lost his dog. I was out of the restaurant before I realized I hadn't ever gotten lunch.

FOUR

After leaving the delicatessen I trotted across Shattuck Avenue and used the pay phone at the Safeway, plugging my free ear with a finger to keep out the street noise. Bart Kinn still wasn't in. They thought he might be in court, testifying in a rape case. They had no idea when he'd be back.

At the Community Crisis Center they were certain Pierce Richards wouldn't be in till Monday morning. He was conducting a weekend retreat in Calaveras County and was already on his way. My third dime got me the D.A.'s office, where a secretary told me Howard Gable was waiting for a jury to come back, and then had a bar association meeting to attend, so he couldn't possibly see me till next week.

I decided I'd wasted enough dimes for one day. If I went back to the office and cleared the decks I could devote the next week exclusively to the Renzel case. And maybe by Monday there would no longer be a Renzel case; maybe something would break and I wouldn't have to reengage the stricken countenance of Lawrence Usser or the conceited smirk of his friend the shrink or the grisly details of his wife's demise.

It was becoming a heavy weight, my distaste for the Renzel case, and I couldn't quite figure it out. Maybe it was because I was afraid that whatever the truth turned out to be, it would not be the truth the Renzels wanted me to find. It might even be a truth they couldn't abide, a suggestion that their beloved daughter was in some portion of her life besmirched. But another part of it had to do with Lawrence Usser. He was precisely what I had once wanted to become, back when I had studied law—a brilliant scholar and a successful practitioner, a respected teacher and trial attorney, a blend of the poet and the pragmatist that makes men like Usser loom large and leave their tracks in history. Usser's life was one I might have lived myself had my dreams and my abilities joined hands, and now his life was badly chipped if not entirely shattered. I felt a bit of Usser's pain myself as my Buick took me back to my office on Jackson Square.

I signed off on the monthly statements Peggy had prepared, reviewed two new-business memoranda and the transcript of a deposition I'd given in a contract dispute, then glanced through the journals and newsletters that had accumulated during the week. Peggy had clipped an article from the morning paper about the San Francisco Police Department's new Automated Fingerprint Identification System. It reportedly allowed the police to identify prints in about twenty percent of their current cases, as compared to five percent before they got the computer. A police inspector was quoted, declaring that "this is not the time to commit a crime in San Francisco." Maybe he was right, but it didn't matter to me—all the crimes I was working on had been committed out of town.

Peggy left for the weekend—the Sonoma Inn with her boyfriend, Paul, a patent lawyer. Ruthie Spring called to invite me to a potluck supper, but I begged off. Ruthie's the widow of the detective who schooled me in the trade. She's a wonderful woman but she's also a vivid reminder of her husband, Harry, and just then I didn't want to think about Harry Spring or about how much I wished he was still around to occupy some of the endless evenings of my life. I put my feet on the desk and read another chapter in the Thomas novel while I waited for the traffic to dwindle and the bars to clear. After a quick beer at the Vesuvio I headed home.

The first thing on Saturday I went to the library. The Berkeley *Gazette* folded a year or so ago, so now the Berkeley news shows up in the Oakland *Tribune*. I got the microfilm reels for the day of Dianne Renzel's murder and for several days there-

after, threaded them through the reader and spun the first reel
to the day I wanted.

None of the news articles suggested a motive for the murder.
If there was any important physical evidence the cops had not
disclosed it. Apparently Ms. Renzel had been sexually active a
short time before she died, but although she was found naked
in the bedroom, and there were stains of sex on the sheets, rape
was not suggested. Her clothing was whole and draped on hang-
ers, her nightgown was on its peg behind the closet door, her
body smelled of expensive scents. As far as they could tell she
had suffered only stab wounds, not the customary bruises of
unwanted sex. All of which led the police to conclude that her
nakedness and her sexual activity were voluntary. I wondered
if that conclusion and its implications were disputed by her husband, who had evidently been away the entire evening, until the
moment he'd found her dying.

The strongest suggestion in all of the articles was that Dianne
Renzel was an exceptional woman. She had come out of SLATE
politics at the University of California in the early sixties, had
gone to Columbia and earned a Ph.D. in psychology and social
work, then had scampered through the minefield of Berkeley
politics to a position on the city council after she and Usser had
moved there from New York a dozen years ago. Her platform
had included rent control, free day care and a string of shelters
for runaways and transients. Some progress had been made on
all those fronts, but after a single term in office, Renzel had
declined to run for reelection, saying city politics were too removed from the true needs and concerns of citizens, that in the
future she would devote her energies to community action programs that more directly touched the lives of the people of
Berkeley.

She had culminated her social activism by becoming a co-
founder of the Community Crisis Center. A long list of co-
workers and clients of the center gave eloquent testimony that
Dianne Renzel would be sorely missed by the many who clung
precariously to Berkeley's slippery underside. She was, apparently, a genius at calming people down. Still, there were hints
that threats of violence to the center's staff were not uncommon,
that many of its clients were temporarily or permanently unbalanced to a degree that made assaults of various kinds an ac-

cepted part of the center's daily regimen and staff turnover a major problem. One of Dianne Renzel's colleagues had described her as "foolishly fearless."

After reading the articles about Dianne Renzel, I looked in vain for comments from her husband. Apparently he was keeping quiet. The only statement made on his behalf came from Adam Lonborg, who announced the day after the murder that Usser would have nothing to say beyond conveying his thanks for the many expressions of sympathy and condolence he had received, and informing well-wishers that a fund had been established at the crisis center in memory of his wife. The fund would be used to hire additional staff and to improve the center's hotline phone system. It would be administered by Pierce Richards, director of the center. At that point the articles became irregular and repetitive, so I went back to my apartment and spent the rest of the weekend with *Don Giovanni, Briarpatch, Tunes of Glory,* and a shamelessly lustful longing for a bawdy escapade.

On Monday morning my phone rang as I was preparing a schedule of the interviews I needed to conduct in Berkeley. It was Rhonda Stein. "You wanted me to call you if anything broke in the Renzel case," she said after we exchanged pleasantries.

"Right. So what happened?"

"Howard Gable left here about an hour ago. He's going to rendezvous with Bart Kinn and they're going to make an arrest in the case. All this is confidential, by the way. Until he's in custody."

"Sure, sure. So who did it? Some punk?"

"Guess again."

"Come on, Rhonda."

"Usser. The husband."

"What? You're kidding."

"Nope. No doubt about it."

"But why?"

"Why did we arrest him?"

"Why did he do it."

"I don't know for sure why he did it. Gable's being real careful with this one. No leaks, no pretrial prejudice of any kind."

"But what kind of evidence has he got?"

"I don't know. I *think* a witness turned up. I don't know who,

or what he was a witness to, but I think Howard got hold of
some testimony of some sort. You'll have to talk to him about it.
Or Kinn. But don't count on getting anything from either of
those guys. Besides, what difference does it make to you?"

I thought about it. "I guess it doesn't make any difference at
all, if you can make it stick."

"Oh, Howard will make it stick. We tend not to book Berkeley
law professors unless we can make it stick." Rhonda laughed
and I did, too, until I pictured Usser's tortured demeanor at
lunch three days before.

"What about the woman's parents?" I asked. "Do they know
about the arrest yet?"

"I doubt it," Rhonda said. "First things first and all that."

"Mind if I tell them?"

"Well, I don't know for sure that they've got Usser in custody
yet, so . . . wait a minute. Howard just walked by and gave me
the high sign. I guess you can go ahead if you want. Gable will
call them eventually anyway, but probably not for an hour or
so. If you hurry, you can beat the noon news."

"Thanks, Rhonda. Sounds like your people did a good job on
this one."

"We always do good work in this office, Marsh; the mutterings
of the defense bar notwithstanding. Maybe I'll see you in court
some day."

"You'll see me at Spengers next week. How about Thursday?"

"Thursday it is."

I hung up and found the Renzels' number and placed the
call. When Mrs. Renzel answered, I asked if her husband was
there. She told me he was. I told her I had some news they'd
want to hear. She put her husband on the second phone and I
told them the police had just arrested their son-in-law for the
murder of their daughter.

"Lawrence?" Mrs. Renzel blurted. "They have arrested Lawrence?"

"Yes. Within the past hour."

"He is in jail?"

"I'm sure he is. At least for now."

"They are saying Lawrence did this? They are saying he murdered our Dianne? In that way?"

"I guess they are."

"They are sure?"

"I suppose so, or they wouldn't have arrested him."

"Is he mad? Tell me. *Is he a madman?*"

Gunther Renzel's words raced through the wire like pointed, pronged projectiles. I didn't have an answer and I told him so, but his question pricked at me for hours.

FIVE

The late papers were full of the case. The theory seemed to be that on the night of the murder Lawrence Usser had come home earlier than expected, discovered hints of his wife's unfaithfulness, and in a violent rage stabbed her repeatedly with a pair of scissors, then fled the scene only to return an hour later and feign shocked discovery of the carnage. No specific proof of the theory was cited; nor had the murder weapon been recovered; nor was the identity of Dianne Renzel's paramour disclosed. The theory seemed only that at this stage, since the minor details of physical evidence that were revealed —most involving traces of his wife's blood on Usser's clothing— could be explained by Usser's version of the events as easily as by the cops'. Which seemed to support Rhonda Stein's hunch that a witness had turned up to make Howard Gable's case an easy one.

After the arrest the *Examiner* had interviewed several of Usser's colleagues at the Berkeley Law School and some of his peers at Stanford and the University of California law schools as well. All acknowledged that Usser was a controversial figure at the school, with at least as many enemies as friends, but all professed their shock and dismay at the arrest, all doubted Usser's capacity for such a deed, and all claimed ignorance of any reason for the crime. Usser himself was being held without bail pending arraignment. There was a suggestion that once bail was fixed he would have no trouble raising the premium on the bond, since his parents were importantly wealthy. At the conclusion of the story, the victim's colleagues were quoted as well. None of them knew of any particular problems between Usser and his wife. All of them were glad that an arrest had been made, since exaggerated rumors of violence at the crisis center were starting to jeopardize their funding.

A sidebar reviewed some of the high points of Lawrence Usser's career. He had grown up in a Chicago suburb and had attended New Trier High School while his father made a fortune in the advertising business. At Yale he was Phi Beta Kappa in psychology. At Harvard Law he was Coif and editor-in-chief of the law review. He had clerked a year for Justice Bazelon on the District of Columbia Circuit, then a year for Justice Douglas on the Supreme Court, then taught a couple of years during the SDS days at Columbia, where he met his wife. A year after their marriage, the couple had headed west to Berkeley, where ultimately Usser had become the youngest faculty member ever appointed to an endowed professorship at the Berkeley Law School. According to the article, Usser was popular with his students if not with certain factions of the faculty, and had published several seminal articles in his field, most having to do with the history, development and current controversy surrounding the use and abuse of the insanity defense.

Usser's public renown had developed as a result of a series of cases in which he had served as a consultant to the defense counsel: a black prisoner accused of the torture and murder of a white prison guard; a Chicano charged with the rape and dismemberment of his faithless girlfriend; a divorcée who had allegedly killed her two children to make herself more attractive to potential husbands; a Vietnamese immigrant who had garroted two teenagers who had been harassing him for months, assuming the Vietnamese was a helpless peasant rather than the former ARVN commando he actually was; plus the two cases Jake Hattie had mentioned—the gang rape and the obsessive suitor.

All the defendants had been found not guilty by reason of insanity or had been convicted of a lesser offense because the jury found they suffered from a mental disease that diminished

their capacity to commit the crime in question. Lawrence Usser
had played a large role in each of the defense teams, cross-
examining the prosecution psychiatrists, conducting the direct
examination of the defense experts and making the major portion of the defense summations. Usser's fees reportedly ranged
from nothing to the quarter-million dollars paid by the parents
of the young rapist in Marin County. The implication of all this,
at least according to the papers, was that Lawrence Usser helped
people get away with murder.

Usser had become a public personage, on a par with Bailey,
Belli, Kunstler and the like. He was in continuous demand, both
as a trial counsel and as a lecturer at trial lawyers' conventions
and jurists' workshops. He had written a book that was the bible
of attorneys pleading their clients not guilty by reason of insanity. And, after Hinckley had taken a shot at Reagan, Usser had
shown up on *Donahue* and *Good Morning, America* to explain the
definitions of legal insanity employed in various jurisdictions,
and to assert that the Hinckley jury had reached a humane and
conscientious verdict based on the facts in that particular case.

When I'd finished with the newspapers I tried to match their
strong suggestions of Lawrence Usser's guilt with the vision of
Usser I carried with me from our luncheon meeting the Friday
before, but I couldn't do it. Something had been flailing the
man, but I had come away from the delicatessen convinced that
Usser's demon was not his guilt, but rather a woeful purity. Still,
I'd been wrong in such assessments before, erring most often
on the side of innocence, so it would not be the first time I'd
failed to recognize a killer when he was sitting across from me.
But it would be the first time that the one across from me was
in so many ways a mirror image of myself.

I clipped the news articles for reasons not altogether clear
and carried them in my briefcase when I went to the office on
Tuesday morning. I'd poured my first cup of coffee and was
glancing through my calendar for the week when I heard the
door to the outer office open.

I double-checked the calendar. No one was scheduled for
another hour. Peggy wasn't due till one. I took a quick gulp of
Italian roast and went out to see who it was.

She was alone this time, dressed exactly as she had been when
I had seen her with her husband the week before. She nodded

silently at my greeting, followed submissively when I invited her into my private office, and refused my offer of a cup of coffee, all without altering her dreadful stare.

The chairs were where they'd left them and she took the one she'd occupied before. In the absence of her husband, Ingrid Renzel held her own hand and waited in stooped and prayerful silence till I had taken a seat. I asked what I could do for her.

"First, I have a question."

"Fire away."

"We have been told that when they arrested Lawrence, they took Lisa to stay with the Ussers. His parents. This morning I have talked to people at the Oakland City Hall. They say Lisa is to stay with the Ussers until this matter is resolved. They say if things are as they seem, and Lawrence does not return, Lisa will stay with them until she becomes an adult."

I nodded. "What's your question?"

She leaned toward me to fasten my attention on her mission. "Is there a way for us to get our Lisa back? Can we take her from the Ussers and bring her to live with us?"

Her eyes were wide with hope but I had nothing with which to satisfy it. "Don't you think the Ussers would be good foster parents?" I asked instead.

Ingrid Renzel paused to be certain of her words. "The Ussers are not like us, not like our Dianne. They do not live the way Lisa should live, the way she lived when her mother was alive. They travel, they go to parties, they have three different homes, one of them in Paris. We are afraid they would not *be* there for Lisa, not when they were needed. Lisa has been troubled, as I told you. She needs much love. Gunther and I have decided that we want nothing in life but to give it to her. As best we can."

Her expression compelled belief, but she was in the wrong place and I told her so. "You'll have to see a lawyer, Mrs. Renzel. To initiate a custody action yourself or to oppose a temporary order giving custody to the Ussers. Or to try to reach some informal agreement for shared or joint custody among all interested parties. Do you have a lawyer?"

"Gunther does. For the business."

"Good. Talk to him. He'll help you or can recommend someone who can. I don't practice law anymore, and I don't know many lawyers in the East Bay, so I'm afraid I can't help you on that one. But if you're worried about my bill, don't. I haven't run up much of a tab since Thursday. A couple of hours at most."

"We do not want you to stop working."

I frowned, surprised and wary. "Why? Don't you think he did it? I must say I was a little surprised myself when I heard about it, but . . ."

Her lips thinned. "The police would not have taken him if he was innocent."

Since I was no longer a lawyer I let her wish remain as truth. "Then I don't understand," I said. "Do you want me to help make the case against him? I have to tell you that in my judgment it would be a total waste of time. The district attorney's people seem confident they already have what they need for a conviction."

"They may think they have what they need, but they do not."

"I'm afraid I don't understand what you're talking about, Mrs. Renzel."

She adjusted her position and clasped and unclasped her hands. She seemed even more resolute than when she had asked me to find the man who'd killed her daughter.

"We received a phone call," she said when she was ready.

"From whom?"

"He would not say."

"When did you get the call?"

"Last night. At bedtime."

"What did he say?"

"He said that Lawrence had murdered our Dianne, as the police believe. He said that Lawrence would one day go to trial. And he said that Lawrence should be sentenced to death for what he did, that only such a sentence would be just."

She paused and wrung her hands, deeply distraught, as though the execution of her daughter's killer would be worse than even the crime itself. I asked her what else the caller said. The answer came at me in a rush of heated words.

"He said that although death *should* be the penalty, Lawrence would not die. He said that Lawrence was an expert on proving criminals insane, that he had done so for many others, and now he would do it for himself. He said that Lawrence had killed

Dianne because he knew he would get away with it, because he knew that he could prove himself insane and then after the trial could prove that he was sane again and be let free. He said they would do *nothing* to Lawrence, that he would *trick* them. He said that unless we stop them, Lawrence *will go without punishment for what he has done.*"

I was still evaluating what she had said when Mrs. Renzel spoke again. "Don't you see? Unless you stop him, Lawrence will go free and then my Gunther will try to kill him. He has sworn to it. After the caller hung up, Gunther went to get his pistol from the war. He put the bullets in it and sat with it in his lap for the rest of the night. If the court frees Lawrence, Gunther will track him down and kill him like an animal. That must not happen, Mr. Tanner. I must not bear two sorrows to my grave. *Please.* I must not, or God will not forgive me. You must prove that Lawrence *is not mad.*"

Her words sent rippling chills across my chest. I finished my coffee as my mind manufactured words of death and images of madness. "The phone call," I said finally. "It was definitely a man?"

"Yes."

"Young or old?"

"In between, I think."

"Accent?"

"No. He spoke slowly and . . . carefully. To be sure we understood."

"Was it familiar to you at all? Did anyone come to mind during the conversation?"

"No."

"Were there sounds in the background? Traffic, trains, whistles, ocean?"

"Laughter. And something ticking . . . a clock perhaps."

"What exactly did he say?"

"Only what I told you. That Lawrence was guilty and should be punished, but that he would trick the jury and they would let him go."

"That's quite a gamble on Usser's part, don't you think?"

She shook her head. "Lawrence is a brilliant man. I do not think he would see it as a gamble; I think he would see it as a game in which he was the superior player. I think he would see it as a game he would most certainly *win.*"

"Are you really worried that your husband will try to kill Usser if he's acquitted, Mrs. Renzel?"

"He will do more than try, Mr. Tanner. He will do it or die in the attempt. It is the way he resisted the Nazis during the war. And I am as frightened of that as I am of anything in this world. Or the next."

I sighed and ran a hand through my hair. My nerves were jangling already; the case had always had that feel to it, and now it was worse. Mrs. Renzel wanted me to immerse myself in madness, a milieu I dreaded more than murder. It helped only a little that this time the madman was already locked up.

"I'll have to think about this," I told her, reluctant to commit. "I mean, I'm not sure how I can help you. Proof that he was sane? What would that be? What if he eats a peanut butter sandwich every day? Is that sane or insane? A kid might say it's right on; Julia Child might say it's nuts. Insanity is basically a medical question, Mrs. Renzel. Psychiatrists for the defense and prosecution examine the defendant and testify to what they've found, and the jury flips a coin and decides which of them to believe. I just don't see what role I'd play in that process, to tell you the truth."

I was cynical and I was stalling and it irritated her. Her eyes narrowed and her lips pursed. "You could show Lawrence was doing his business—his teaching, his lawyering—as usual, could you not? You could show he paid his bills, mowed his lawn, washed his car? You could show he lived his life the way he always lived it, could you not, Mr. Tanner?"

"I suppose I could try."

"You could talk to the district attorney and see what he suggests? And the police? Perhaps they would welcome your assistance."

"Perhaps, but I doubt it."

She sighed. I had almost defeated her. "Are you saying you won't help us, Mr. Tanner?"

I sensed that Ingrid Renzel was begging for assistance for the first time in her life, that only murder had rendered her a supplicant, that I was the only one she would entreat. If I didn't help her, she would try to help herself. I didn't think I could let that happen. "I haven't decided anything yet," I told her. "I'll think about it tonight and let you know tomorrow. Is that okay?"

"If you prefer."

"But if I do go ahead, you'll be stuck with what I find. You understand that, don't you?"

She frowned. "What do you mean?"

"I mean that if I find Usser was a rational, premeditated killer, then so be it. But if I find evidence that he was nutty as a fruitcake, the defense will probably get wind of whatever I turn up and will probably call me as their own witness. In effect I'll be helping to do just what you've hired me to prevent: give him a defense. Are you willing to take that chance, Mrs. Renzel?"

Her lips stiffened. "It is nonsense to expect Lawrence to be found insane, Mr. Tanner. He is a brilliant man."

"Genius and madness are not that far apart sometimes, Mrs. Renzel. Philosophers from Aristotle on down have suggested they're two sides of the same coin."

She shook her head. "No madman could do what Lawrence has done with his life. And no madman could persuade our Dianne to love him."

I abandoned the debate, if not the task. "How did Usser and your daughter meet, Mrs. Renzel?"

"She went to law school for a year. In New York. She was in one of his classes. She hated law school so she dropped out and went into social work and psychology. He called her to ask why. They met to talk about it. And so on."

"As far as you know were they happy?"

"Yes, but who can tell? We saw them so little. I must be honest. Dianne did not confide in me. I think she came to believe I was not . . . *modern* enough to understand her life. If she meant I could not talk about her problems the way people do now—with the fancy words, the empty phrases, the slogans that mean nothing or anything—I suppose she was right. But because I do not understand the words does not mean I do not understand the problems. If she was having troubles with Lawrence, I wish she would have told me. Perhaps I could have helped. Perhaps I would have been able to do what the fancy words and fancy people could not."

"What's that?"

"Keep my child alive."

SIX

I struggled with the Usser case the rest of the day and night, between the phone calls, the mail, other clients and the rest of it, combating my conviction that it was not worth the trouble, that I could do nothing productive for the Renzels and nothing gratifying to myself by agreeing to Mrs. Renzel's request. But I kept remembering my talk with Jake Hattie about the nuances of legal insanity, my itchy meeting with Lawrence Usser and his pal the shrink, the mysterious bedtime phone call to the Renzels, and I decided that if the brilliant Lawrence Usser had deliberately murdered his wife and was going to try to walk away from it with the help of a phony insanity plea, I wanted to be there for a closer look. The first thing Wednesday morning I called Ingrid Renzel and told her I'd look into the case enough to assess whether I could be of any use to her. She thanked me with a profusion that embarrassed both of us.

"You're a little premature," I said to put a stop to it, more abruptly than I intended. "I'm not going to approach it quite the way you asked me to. I'm not going to look for evidence that Usser was sane when he committed the crime, mainly because I just don't know what kind of evidence that would be. Besides, the prosecution's psychiatrists will presumably be gathering that type of information themselves, with the help of the D.A.'s investigators."

"But . . . ?"

"What I *will* do is try to find out why he did it. If there's a clear motive, a discernible reason for Usser to have wanted your daughter out of his way, then I'll have gone a long way toward proving he was legally sane. If I can't come up with a motive that makes sense for Usser or for anyone else, then it'll be at least some indication that he wasn't. Does that sound agreeable to you, Mrs. Renzel?"

She hesitated. "I will talk to Gunther. But it appears satisfactory."

"Okay. Let me know if he objects. Otherwise, I'll talk to you when I know something."

I hung up and muttered a silent curse. Despite my fascination with the Usser case, my decision to get involved discomfited me, because insanity itself discomfits me. Predictability is lacking, and like the social fabric as a whole, my survival depends a great deal on predictability. The ones you can't peg, the ones who have drifted beyond pattern, inhibition, shame or fear, those are the ones who make me wish I'd taken up another line of work or had at least managed to stay out of their way.

Maybe my apprehension is testimony to the thinness of my own membrane, the tight, transparent drumhead that separates me from involuntary outrage. I'd make a good juror for Jake Hattie, because I'd lost my own grip once or twice, surrendered to the impulse to lash out, to vent rage until it was absorbed in the momentary mindlessness of violence. Once I'd wounded a particularly loathsome suspect who was less a threat to my safety than to my assumptions about evolution. Another time I beat on a mugger long after he had lost most of his consciousness and all of his resistance. Still another time I had said things to a woman who was both a friend and a client that neither of us has ever forgiven me for, because she had implied that my prudence was really cowardice, and in that instance she'd been right.

But despite such reasons for aversion, I had agreed to dive into the Usser case because those selfsame lunatics and my own collection of irrational outbursts are part of the mosaic that establishes the human mind as the most fascinating engine on earth, in its puckishness and its propensity the most fit subject of a lifetime's study. Which is why I do what I do, I guess, and

why I spent the noon hour in my car, crossing the Bay Bridge
from west to east again, this time on my way to a place that in
its own way is almost as fascinating as mental madness: the city
of Oakland.

"There is no there, there," Gertrude Stein is supposed to have
said about the place, but like most things she said, her meaning
was probably not the most obvious. Oakland labors under some
severe handicaps—some of them common to all major industrial cities and some unique, such as the tragic death of its inspiring young symphony conductor and the loss of its equally
inspiring professional football team. Oakland has suffered for
decades from the wet fog of arrogance that drifts its way from
the city across the bay, an arrogance less justified and therefore
more wounding with each day. But Oakland is fighting back. Its
downtown is in the process of renewal and its governors are
alert to the infections of the inner city and are more imaginative
than many in trying to cure them. Indeed, if you're an average
joe or jane, a working stiff just trying to make your way in the
world by doing a day's work for a day's pay, Oakland's probably
a far better place to live than San Francisco. San Francisco no
longer needs you; Oakland does. But it's not an easy choice. In
the past eighteen months, forty people had been murdered
vying for position in Oakland's freewheeling drug trade. One
of the killings occurred in broad daylight in front of an elemen-
tary school while a thousand children were in recess.

I left the bridge and took the Nimitz Freeway south to the
downtown exit, then headed for Fallon Street and the Alameda
County Courthouse. The entrance to the high white tower was
oddly placid compared to the first time I'd approached it, during one of Huey Newton's early trials. On that day the Black
Panthers had lined the steps like a museum exhibition of a
redneck's nightmares, armed and uniformed, disciplined and
disdainful, splashing an acid mix of awe and terror onto those
of us who scurried past beneath their razored stares. I haven't
heard much about the Panthers lately, but the way things are
going I expect them or something like them to reappear before
too long. The American dream is shrinking, leaving lots of people out. Sooner or later someone is going to offer them a different one.

The blue and gold elevator took me to the office of the district attorney, on the ninth floor. Through the small round hole in the high glass wall that protected the receptionist from me and everyone, I stated my business. The receptionist pressed some buttons, attended to her intercom, then told me that Rhonda Stein was in court and that Howard Gable was in room 920. After checking my ID she admitted me to the private offices and I walked down the empty marble hall until I found him.

When I tapped on his door, Gable looked up from behind some horn-rim glasses and a stack of *California Reporters*, each volume marked with slips of paper sticking like flat white tongues from the pages of the relevant appellate decisions. Gable was broad, not tall, with thick shoulders and a barely discernible neck. He wore a white shirt with the sleeves rolled up and the tie tugged loose. His arms were freckled, thick and hairless. His jaw was square and pink, his nose wide and flared, his expression harried but happy. His sandy hair was an inadequate veil across his pate. His blue eyes seemed to give off rays that would penetrate to essence. I resisted an urge to let my own eyes dodge away, instead let Gable's have their way with them. When he was finished with the inspection, I told Gable who I was.

He looked at me, frowned, then nodded. "Didn't Rhonda Stein say something to me about you?"

"Probably."

"The Renzels wanted you to find out who killed their daughter."

"Right."

Gable smiled. His face wrinkled in odd places, as though unaccustomed to the gesture. "But we beat you to it."

"Right again."

"So you're out of a job. Looking for work? Or maybe you just feel we made a mistake and arrested the wrong man."

From within their fleshy caves his eyes dared me to confirm the latter guess. His grin was the careful arrogance of an older brother whose sibling had just challenged him to fight for the very first time. I raised my hand and shook my head. "I don't have any problem with the arrest. Neither do my clients."

The disclaimer prompted Gable to relax. He took off his glasses and leaned back in his chair. "So why are you here?"

"The Renzels still want to hire me. But for a different job."

"Oh? What job is that?"

This time I was the one who managed an imperfect smile. "This may sound a little strange."

"That's okay. I hear strange things all the time. For instance, on Monday I heard Lawrence Usser claim he didn't kill his wife."

Gable folded his hands and placed them piously on what passed for his bible—the latest utterances of the highest court in the state. I leaned against the doorjamb to ease my aching feet. "The Renzels got a phone call Monday night," I began. "Anonymous. Male. Voice unknown to them. The caller wanted to talk about the Usser case."

"And?"

"The caller told them that Usser had definitely killed his wife, and that he deserved the death penalty. Then he said that Usser wasn't going to get the death penalty or any other penalty, he was going to get away with the whole thing by feigning an insanity plea. In other words, he told them Usser was going to beat the rap."

I was watching Gable closely. His face reddened and he seemed to freeze, as though my words were *Star Trek* weapons that inflicted something even more useful than death. "You can imagine how such a call might upset the Renzels," I added when Gable didn't speak.

Gable's cocky smile had been replaced by the slit-eyed stare of swift and brutal intelligence that is common to lawyers who are good in court and know it. "Is this a joke?" Gable demanded.

"Nope."

"This call thing is for real?"

"The Renzels aren't the kind of people who make up fairy tales or hear voices that aren't there."

Gable thought about it, then nodded. "So what's the story? Why the hell are you here? What does the phone call have to do with it?"

I gestured toward a chair. "You mind if I sit down? Since we're going to be here for another minute?"

Gable muttered an apology and I sat down and looked around. Like its occupant, the office was nondescript but for a single exception. In the corner was a table, homemade from studs and plywood, perhaps four feet square. On it was a miniature railroad, N gauge, complete with mountains and tunnels and streams and bridges and several yards of well-embedded track. Almost soundlessly, a train of gondola cars was being tugged up a mountain grade by a tiny steam engine blowing smoke. The railroad was the Union Pacific. The gondolas were full of rocks painted to look like gold.

Gable saw where I was looking. "Well, you've got to have something, right? To take your mind off it?"

"You're lucky yours is trains."

Gable shrugged away the digression. Out in the hall, the bureaucracy of justice made muffled noises, as though its plans were secret. Gable cleared his throat. "So like I said, Tanner. Where do you come in?"

I leaned back in my chair and folded my arms. "They want me to find proof the guy is sane. They want me to keep Usser from getting away with it."

"You mean they want you to work for us?"

"In a way."

"That's a switch."

"I suppose it is. But I've made it before."

Gable shook his head dubiously. "We've got our own investigators, as I'm sure you know. If Usser pleads insanity, our people can dig up whatever the shrinks think they need to establish capacity. What I'm saying is, I'm not sure how you'd fit into the picture."

"I had a little trouble with that myself. I told the Renzels as much. I told them I didn't know what kind of evidence makes a man look sane, told them your people could handle that project better than I could."

Gable opened his mouth but I hurried on. "What I also told them was that I'd try to come up with a reason for the crime. If Usser had a motive—if he was jealous of her, or if he would profit from her death, or if he was in love with someone else and didn't want to lose half his assets in a property settlement —then it seems to me that such a situation would go a long way toward showing he was sane. At least in the legal sense. If he loved his wife and I can't find anything to contradict that, then maybe he *was* nuts. That's the kind of thing I told the Renzels I would look for. Of course maybe you already have the answer." I raised my brows and gave Gable a chance to comment. He stayed quiet. "Maybe you can tell me exactly why he did it. Then I can resign the case and get back to one of my own distractions, the one that comes in a bottle straight from Perth."

There was silence for a time, during which I decided not to mention the rest of it, which was Ingrid Renzel's conviction that her husband would take matters into his own hands if Usser ever walked the streets again. I also decided Gable wasn't certain in his own mind why Usser had done what he'd been arrested for doing, which meant there was room for me in his case if he let me enter it.

"They don't just walk out the door, you know," Gable said finally. "I mean, even if he's found insane, in this state he has the burden of affirmatively establishing the restoration of sanity before he can be released. And even at the expiration of the time he would have served had he been convicted of the crime, we can still hold him if we can show he's dangerous to himself or to others."

"But even so," I said.

"Even so they sometimes walk a few months after the verdict's in," Gable agreed. The possibility that Usser would do just that seemed to make Gable more gregarious. "So what are your plans?"

"First, do you have any problem with me poking around in the case?"

"Don't know yet, to be honest. I've given some thought to this insanity thing, but not enough as yet. That's Usser's field, isn't it?"

"Right. The best in the country, Jake Hattie tells me."

Gable wrinkled his wispy brows and sat up straight. "Hattie? When did you talk to *him*?"

"Last week, after the Renzels first contacted me. Jake's worked with Usser a few times, and his office is near mine. I thought he could give me some background on Usser and his wife. Why?"

Gable's forehead rolled with puzzlement. "Usser hired Hattie to defend him, that's why."

"You're kidding. Jake?"

"Yep." Gable finally turned loose of his suspicion and leaned back in his chair again. "I've never been up against a hotshot like Hattie. Kind of looking forward to it."

Most prosecutors looked forward to opposing Jake a lot more when the case was beginning than they did when it was ending, but I refrained from pointing that out. "When do you think you'll decide whether you'll cooperate with me in the investigation?" I asked instead.

Gable grinned. "Who knows? When you screw up, probably."

I started to say something but Gable stopped me. "I know, I know, you've got a good reputation over in the big city. Of course, a decent reputation in Frisco can get you three to five in most other states of the union."

Gable's grin widened, and I guessed we had passed a barrier of sorts. Whether there were many more to get across remained to be seen. "So what's your first move?" Gable asked again.

"Talk to people. See if there were marital problems. Financial problems. And if I don't come up with anything, maybe I'll try to prove a negative."

"Like what?"

"Try to show that Usser demonstrated no signs of insanity up to the night his wife was killed. Try to show the guy was normal across the board."

"Lawrence Usser's anything but normal," Gable announced heavily.

"Crazy?"

"I didn't say that. I just said he wasn't normal."

I took a deep breath. "I hate to ask this, but are you certain he did it?"

Gable smiled a long thin smile. "Off the record?"

"Sure."

"I'm not as sure as I'd like to be. And I'm not as sure as I will be on the morning of trial. But I'm sure enough to take him off the streets, at least until some nincompoop of a judge sets bail. A motion I will oppose with vigor, I assure you."

"What kind of evidence do you have?"

Gable scratched his nose. "So far it's mostly negative. To borrow your term."

"Meaning?"

"Meaning there's no evidence anyone outside the house broke in, no evidence of a struggle, no evidence of rape or robbery. No evidence of anything that points to anyone but Lawrence Usser."

"What else?"

"Pubic hair."

"You found his pubic hair on her body?"

"Right."

I shook my head. "He was her husband, for Christ's sake. It could have been there for days."

"Maybe; maybe not. Our information is that they hadn't had relations for quite some time." Gable shrugged. "We've got more if we need it."

"Like what?"

"I don't see any reason to go into it."

"So how about motive?"

Gable's face went blank. "How about it?" he repeated. "I can assure you there was one."

"What was it?"

"No comment."

I debated whether or not to editorialize, then decided what the hell. "Sounds to me like you may have moved a little prematurely," I told him. "What if you don't get past the preliminary hearing?"

Gable managed a cocky grin. "We'll get him bound over, don't worry about it."

"But why'd you move so soon?"

"We had our reasons."

"Which were?"

"Confidential. We'll be ready when the time comes, Tanner. No sweat."

I wondered if the reasons were more political than criminological, given Rhonda Stein's label of Gable as ambitious. "Anything else you can tell me?" I asked.

"Nope."

"Got an eyewitness?"

"No comment."

"Can I get into the house?"

"What for?"

"Just to nose around."

"It's been sealed again, I think. The tech boys wanted to make another pass after we zeroed in on Usser. I can't give you formal permission, but if you find a key under the flowerpot on the porch, I guess it might get you inside. Just don't mess things up and don't let Bart Kinn catch you in there."

"He's the guy who has the case for the Berkeley P.D.?"

"Yep."

"Good man?"

"The best, when he wants to be."

"Put in a good word for me with him?"

"Kinn hates my guts," Gable said affably, as though it was a compliment.

I suppressed an urge to ask the reason. "When's the arraignment?"

"Tomorrow, if they don't ask for a continuance."

"You expect a plea?"

"Sooner or later."

"Which one?"

Gable gestured toward a stack of books. "Let me read you a little nugget I picked up on this morning." Gable pulled a tattered tome out of the stack and began to read. " 'It is not every kind of frantic humour or something unaccountable in a man's actions that points him out to be such a madman as is to be exempted from punishment: it must be a man that is totally deprived of his understanding and memory, and doth not know what he is doing, no more than an infant, than a brute, or a wild beast, such a one is never the object of punishment; therefore I must leave it to your consideration, whether the condition this man was in, as it is represented to you on one side, or the other, doth shew a man, who knew what he was doing, and was able to distinguish whether he was doing good or evil, and understood what he did.' " Gable closed the book and smiled. "Not bad, huh? Unfortunately that was written by an English judge, in the case of *Rex* v. *Arnold,* in the year of 1724. But precedent is precedent, right, Tanner?"

Gable's grin seemed almost giddy. I watched him for several seconds more. "You think it's possible Usser really is insane?"

"Sure he's insane. He'd have to be to do what he did the way he did it. But he's not legally insane. Legally, he's guilty as hell. And I'm going to see to it he pays the proper penalty."

"Death?"

"Oh, yes. Torture is a special circumstance in this state, and Dianne Renzel was definitely tortured. So I'm going to see to it that Lawrence Usser forfeits his life to the people of the State of California. I'm going to see to it he takes the pipe."

"No one's been executed in this state for twenty years."

Gable's face took on a slavering glow. "That's all right, Tanner. The people will be satisfied if Usser lives the rest of his life under the big black cloud of that possibility."

SEVEN

I should have gone to see the Berkeley cops after I left Howard Gable's office—to let them know I was in the area, to establish my bona fides, to genuflect, to wipe my feet before I stepped into the middle of their case—but I didn't do any of those things. If the Berkeley cops were like the cops in San Francisco, they wouldn't want me anywhere near the Usser case and particularly not anywhere near the house where the crime took place. They might, in fact, order me to stay away and put someone on my tail to see that I did. I decided not to give them a chance.

Often the scene of a crime is static, barren, impotent, a poor memorial to the status quo ante death. But once in a while a crime scene comes alive and begins to give off auras and vibrations, ghostly hints of what might have happened, even of who might be guilty of the offense. At such times you become wiser than you were, and I wanted to see if the Usser house would perform such services for me. After leaving City Hall I drove up Broadway, took a left on College and a right on Dwight Way, and approached the university just south of the law school and the football stadium.

The Ussers lived a short stroll from the southeast corner of the campus, on Hillside Lane. The map in my glove compartment indicated it was a tiny finger of a street, short, a dead end, apropos of nothing but seclusion. I found it only after a couple of wrong turns and one pass right by it because I thought the thick shrubbery on either side of the lane meant it was merely someone's driveway.

Hillside Lane went sharply uphill, doglegged to the right and ended almost as soon as it began in front of a matched pair of oddly proportioned stucco buildings that looked like a couple of two-story Mexican cantinas that had been airlifted across the Rio Grande, dropped in the middle of Berkeley and painted turquoise as an aesthetic afterthought. The Usser house was across from the cantinas on the uphill side, a three-story, sternly handsome brown-shingle residence, designed by Maybeck or one of his better imitators, surrounded by lush vegetation that screened most of its facade from outside eyes.

The windows were dark and leaded, the roof was shake, the front yard was a delicately landscaped ramp that rose from the street to the house in tiers of bright blooms and gleaming leaves that were sophisticated beyond the limits of my botany. The steep stone steps that led to the porch were more a ladder than a staircase. I turned around at the dead end, parked facing the way I'd come and surveyed the scene while feeling shrunken and a bit indecent in the shadow of the patrician home. When I looked for signs that it had sheltered both a murderer and his victim, I didn't find a one.

I was remembering again the abandoned, haunted look of Lawrence Usser, was trying to match him with his crime, when I heard a sound and looked behind me. A woman who must have come out of one of the turquoise cantinas was strolling down the center of the street.

She was spry and stately, her gray hair rolled into a tight braid at the base of her skull, her torso encased in a formless brown sweater, her legs in wide tweed slacks, her feet in shoes that were as sensible as shoes can get. The slim volume that she cradled before her eyes could only have been poetry or scripture.

I got out of my car. Her brown eyes flicked at me, then returned to her verse. "Excuse me," I said. "Could I ask you a question?"

She stopped and lowered her book and looked at me with a

gaze that had doubtlessly cowed many a pupil in its day and
many a man as well. "Yes?" Somehow, the word was trilled.

"Could you tell me if a woman named Phyllis lives on this
street? I believe she has a young daughter."

The woman frowned. "Phyllis what?"

I tried a rueful grin. "I forget her last name. That's the problem, you see. I—"

"What is the purpose of your question, sir? I'm not in the
habit of giving such information to strangers."

I squirmed beneath her rectitudinous gaze, and this time
didn't have to fake disquiet. "It's real embarrassing," I began.
"Phyllis and my wife are on this committee, you see—ACORN,
it's called. Action to Conserve Our Resplendent Nature? And
there was a meeting at our place last night—we live over on
Arch Street. I'm with the library, the city library, and anyway,
this woman Phyllis forgot her glasses and since I had to be over
here this morning, I said I'd drop them off but I didn't write
the address down so I forgot the number and—"

"I don't remember ever seeing you at the library."

"I work in the basement. Bindery."

"Really."

"Now about this Phyllis, I just need to—"

The woman gestured at the second blue cantina, the one that
caused the street to stop. "The woman who lives there is named
Phyllis Misteen. I know because her mail is frequently misdeliv-
ered to me. She is 10. I am 8. I am frequently persuaded that
mail carriers are no longer required to know the language. Now,
if you will excuse me? You may have made me miss my bus. I
intend to visit your office one day, by the way. To discuss certain
library policies that I find particularly reprehensible. What was
your name again?"

I made one up, apologized for detaining her, thanked her for
her help, and watched as she stuffed the little chapbook into the
elastic pocket of her sweater and strode off down the street with
a doughty, dauntless gait. I resisted the temptation to ask the
poet's name.

In the next minute nothing near me moved that wasn't blown
by the breeze off the bay. I leaned on the fender and sensed the
street, feeling very much alone.

The houses flanking Usser's were screened from me by

hedges. The slope directly behind the Usser house was undeveloped, a whistling glade of cypress and eucalyptus. The house
across the way was curtained and draped. My chances of getting
in and out unseen seemed about as good as they ever get in
their natural state, so I trotted up Usser's steps, not for the first
time wishing I looked like a vacuum salesman or a Witness.

The front door was polished walnut, its glass center panel
smoked and etched. The fine lines outlined a cheery sprig of
wildflowers that contrasted dismally with the official notice
tacked beside the door:

CRIME SCENE. CONTENTS UNDER SEAL.
ENTRY PROHIBITED. VIOLATION PUNISHABLE BY LAW.

The notice sobered me. Even though they'd had a month to
probe the place, and even though they had already arrested the
guy who'd done it, I respected physical evidence enough to be
leery of polluting the interior with whatever microscopic leavings I might unwittingly deposit if I ignored the warning and
went inside. I thought for a minute, then backed down off the
porch, turned and started toward my car, my retreat in large
part a reaction to being on foreign soil. If I was in San Francisco,
I would have already been inside.

The sound that stopped me was a muffled bump that was
quickly stifled. It came from somewhere behind the house. A
cat or dog. Garbage man. Meter reader. Felon.

Alert and nervous, I followed the narrow flagstone path along
the laurel hedge that flanked the house, brushing branches
away from my face. My shoe scraped noisily across a stone,
making me stumble, turning my heart into a flipping fish. But
nothing stopped me before I reached the yard in back.

The patio at the rear of the house was trimmed in poppies
and petunias and furnished in white metal. An ornamental olive
tree supported a finch feeder and a paper lantern. Somewhere
a wind chime tinkled in random tones that seemed to travel to
my ears through cotton. The little fish pond beside the patio
seemed empty of everything but a fibrous, chartreuse scum. By
the back door steps a plastic garbage can was on its side, spilling
refuse. I stood where I was and looked for what had dumped
it.

The sun was overhead and I was in its light. Sweat tumbled
down my temples and my ribs. My wool jacket seemed suddenly

an armored breastplate, stiff and weighted. I stayed where I was, though, because there was someone back there with me. I didn't know who or where he was, but he was somewhere near. It's a sense that serves the animals, a sense that evolution has blessedly left us with. I surveyed the yard again, this time alert for only movement. Nothing challenged me but a jay, typically brash and brazen.

There were only a few places he could be hiding. Behind the potting shed at the back of the lot. Or in it. Behind the back stairs. Behind a tree. Behind the hedge that surrounded the yard. Inside the house. I flipped a mental coin and crossed the patio on my way to the little shed. When I was halfway there, I heard a noise that made me turn.

He'd been crouched behind the stairs and he was running for the front. To get there he had to swerve toward me, to avoid an antique lamp post. When he did so, I took two steps and dove at him, an arm outstretched, grasping for a leg. I missed the leg but his foot caught under my wrist and he tripped. With a quick cry he sprawled across the flagstones and skidded face first for several yards, his feet flying high behind him. His speed was such that I was on my feet and standing over him by the time he slid to a stop and gathered his skinned legs and scattered wits.

He was just a kid, but he had chosen his clothes to be a constant clamor. His Levi's were slashed into tattered strips from the knee to the ankle. A chrome chain angled across his waist like a gun belt. One ear was pierced. From the lobe dangled a slender silver chain that was wound into a noose. A Japanese ideograph danced on the front of his black T-shirt like a spider's bloody web. On the shirt was a button that read WEIRD.

A blond streak divided his long black scalp like a roadway warning not to pass. He sat cross-legged and shook his head and brushed the dirt off his shirt with hands made lumps by fingerless leather gloves. I moved into the path of the sun, so when he looked up he could see me.

"I didn't do nothing," he muttered as I loomed over him like a thundercloud. His lip was bleeding and his wrist was scraped. He rubbed the latter across the former and made a scarlet smear on both.

"Why are you back here?" I asked him. "To steal something?"

He looked up at me and swore. "You creeps, you think everyone's a crook. I been back here a hundred times."

He seemed to think I was a cop. "Back here doing what?" I asked.

"None of your fucking business, swine. Why don't you just arrest me, huh? Then see what happens. My old man will have your ass." His lips curled into a bloody sneer.

"Are you a friend of the Ussers? Of Lisa?"

The curl momentarily left his lip. "You know Lisa?"

"Maybe."

"You bust her or something?"

"Why?"

He shrugged. "I ain't seen her for a while, is all."

"Why do you want to see her?"

"No reason."

"Come on. What's Lisa Usser to you?"

"She's got some stuff of mine. I need it back."

"What stuff?"

"Just stuff."

"You and Lisa friends?"

"We hang out sometimes," he said grudgingly.

"When did you see her last?"

He smiled his resistance. "I forget."

"Come on, son. You answer my questions and we'll wrap this up real quickly. You don't and you'll be seeing a lot of me for a long, long time."

It was a bluff and not a very good one, given the rules on detaining juveniles these days, rules I was certain the young man knew more precisely than I did, but it worked this time, I think because he wanted it to. "Okay, okay. The last I saw her was the night before it happened."

"You mean when her mother was killed?"

"Nah. When they picked up her old man."

"Were you here when it happened?"

"Nah. I just heard it was going to."

"Heard from whom?"

"I forget."

"Is Lisa your girlfriend?"

The boy shrugged and rubbed a hand through his two-tone locks. "The term is weak, man. We aren't each other's property."

"What's your name?"

He stayed silent, sullen again now that he'd decided I didn't know anything about Lisa. His chain belt made music with the wind chimes as he squirmed beneath my stare.

"You want to go downtown so we can run some prints? That'll tell me who you are." I was pushing it, but I'd begun to suspect the boy wasn't as streetwise as he wanted people to believe. There was too much life in his eyes, and too much warmth in his voice when he talked about Lisa Usser.

"Cal," he muttered finally.

"Cal what?"

"I trashed my surname, man. I'm just Cal."

"You live nearby, Cal?"

"I live where I am. Last night I lived in a van on Fifth Street. Tonight, who knows?" He laughed. "Hell, I crashed in that shed back there for two months one time. No one knew it but me and Lisa." Their secret made him proud enough to jut his chest.

"How about your parents?"

"You mean the people that fucked each other so they could fuck me over?"

"Right. Those people."

"What about them?"

"Where do they live?"

"Oh, Berkeley, Glen Ellen, La Jolla, Maui. You name it, they've lived there, so long as it's lily white."

"What does your father do?"

"Makes money; spends money; eats money; shits money."

"How about your mother?"

"Hits a white ball with a long stick, mostly; then rides after it in her cart and hits it again. Whatever else she does she does at Silverado; she split a year ago. The old man took it hard, losing his squeeze and his condo in the same month. What a bogus bastard he is." Cal's ersatz cynicism slipped away for a moment, leaving behind an earnest aura of concern. "Hey. Really. Do you know where Lisa is?"

I evaded the question with one of my own. "You know Lisa a long time, Cal?"

"We were in the same class at Berkeley High. Till her folks put her in that white bread school."

"When was that?"

"This term. They did it because of *me*, too; not because of that academic crap they laid on her." Cal thrust his narrow chest again. "They thought I was a bad influence. Hah. Lisa's the one that's out there in the zodiac, man. I just try to keep up." His demeanor softened once again. "Do they really think Lisa's old man killed Dianne?"

"Yep. What do you think? Could he have done it?"

Cal shrugged. "He's a prick. Thinks he knows everything in the world but he don't know what's going on under his own roof." Cal looked briefly at the big, silent house as if it were a dream that had not come true. "Old Larry is just another cog in the system, man. All this talk about civil rights and all, but he's still living high on the hog while the people eat shit. It took a while, but Lisa finally saw him for the scum he was. I just wish it had been the other way around."

"What do you mean?"

"Never mind."

I thought I knew. What I didn't know was what it meant, so I tried to pursue it. "Did you and Lisa's mother get along?"

"Dianne? She was adequate, I guess."

"How about Lisa?"

"How about Lisa what?"

"Lisa and her mother. How'd they get along?"

Cal shrugged.

"I heard they fought a lot."

"Yeah, maybe. Who the hell *doesn't* get freaky with their mom? Lucky for me mine wrote me off a long time ago. Berkeley's my old lady now, man. And I can suck her tit just fine."

Cal worked at making me believe it, but he was still too young, still too clean, still too eager to learn about Lisa to make me buy what he was selling. "Is Lisa at the Youth Authority, man?" he asked, his purpose still intact. "I called there but they wouldn't tell me shit. Fucking Nazis. Can I get up now?" he added, still alternating between bravado and a kittenish immaturity.

I gave him a hand and helped him to his feet. In the process I looked for needle marks on his arm, listened for sniffles in his nose, checked for dead space in his eyes. I didn't find any of those things, which was surprisingly heartening.

"You aren't a cop, are you?" Cal said when he was standing beside me.

"Nope."

"What're you doing here?"

"Looking."

"For what?"

"I'm not sure. Were you inside the house?"

Cal shrugged his head. "I was about to bust in when I heard you come up the walk. I figured you for a cop, so . . ." He shrugged his way to silence.

"What were you after?"

Cal looked past me, to make certain we were alone. "I scored Dianne some righteous grass a while back, and I figure it's still in there. What do you think? You think the pigs found it? I could sure use some bud."

I shrugged. "They search pretty well when it's a homicide. You say you got it for Lisa's mom, not Lisa?"

"Right."

"You get any other drugs for her?"

"Blow. But only once. Said she wanted to check it out, to see what all the fuss was about."

"Lisa know about this?"

"Nope. Just between me and Dianne. She was a clean lady, man. Too bad she had to beam up."

Cal said it as though her fate had been ordained. I looked at him and decided it was just an expression, as empty as most speculations about death. "You have any idea why Usser would kill her, Cal?"

I had tried to sneak the question in, but it's import didn't seem to register. Cal only shrugged, his interest clearly elsewhere.

"Did Lisa ever say anything about her parents having problems? Fights or anything?"

"Hell, they fought all the time. He was always giving orders like someone died and they appointed him the Dalai Lama. Dianne got bummed out by it, man. I could tell."

"Did she do anything about it? Like threaten divorce?"

"Naw. But Lisa thought she was getting it on with someone."

"Who?"

"Don't know. Lisa didn't either. We were thinking about tailing her, you know, about the time it happened. I . . . I kind of miss Dianne, you know? If she *was* getting it on it was only fair.

I mean, old Larry dicked everything that moved, just like my old man."

"You know any names?"

"Nah. Chicks at the law school mostly, I guess. They were always over here, hanging out, like Larry-babe was giving out free brain candy. Where is Lisa, anyway, buddy? Huh? She needs me, I know she does."

"Why?"

"She gets all agitated sometimes. I'm the only one can calm her down."

"She on dope? An addict of some kind?"

"Nah. Grass, that's all me and Lisa do. Bud and brandy, man, makes it mellow out."

Cal paused, fidgeted, was bothered by his answer. "What else?" I asked him.

"Ah, since she went away to that school she started hanging around with some real psychotics. The fucking Maniac and the rest."

"What maniac?"

"That's the guy she runs with now. Calls himself the Maniac. He's got this bunch of airheads he leads, calls them the Psychotics. A fucking *jailbird*, is what he is. I heard he offed a guy but I don't know if it's true. He's got Lisa taking some heavy shit, is the problem. Crank. Crystal. Then 'ludes to slide down off it. She gets real strung out now, like her brain keeps pumping about a million megabytes into her day and night, and sometimes she can't process it." Cal glanced up at the Usser house, then spoke in tones thick with admiration. "Lisa's something else, man. When she's on line she really computes, but sometimes she totally zones out. If it happens on the street it can get her in trouble. There's some real assholes out there, you know? I need to be there with her. Know what I mean?"

I thought about telling Cal that Lisa had gone to stay with her grandparents, but I decided I didn't know enough of the situation to decide whether uniting the two of them would be a good idea. Instead, I told Cal I didn't know anything about her, but if I heard anything I'd let him know. "How can I get in touch with you?" I asked him.

"Just come down to Fifth Street. Or ask at Hell House."

"Where?"

He was about to explain when some alien sounds drifted back to us. Someone was coming up the front steps, more than one person. Cal and I exchanged looks. "Fuzz," he whispered.

"Probably."

"There's a way out of here," he said, "but you got to crawl on your belly." He glanced at the back hedge, then looked at me inquiringly.

I was flattered by his invitation, but I shook my head. "You go ahead if you want. Or you can stay and I'll just tell them you came by to see if Lisa was here."

"It's okay with you if I split?"

"Sure."

"The cops around here fuck you over if you're punk, so I'll see you, man. If you see Lisa, tell her to come see me at the van."

"Where's that?" I asked, but Cal was gone, trotting to the hedge, dropping to the ground, low-crawling through an invisible gap in the tangled, twisted vines.

EIGHT

They were on the porch, a black man and a white woman. He was tall, as bright and straight as a polished pole. She was small, prim and powdered. Both were dressed stylishly and immaculately, both carried themselves with an imperial detachment, both were a bit disdainful of and disconcerted by their companion. When they heard me climbing the steps behind them, they seemed relieved to have something to contemplate besides each other.

He let me get within touching distance before he spoke. "You have business here?"

His question came packed in a sonorous baritone; hers was asked only with her wide gray eyes. "My name's Tanner," I said, looking first at the woman and then the man. "I'm a private investigator from San Francisco. Howard Gable of the D.A.'s office in Oakland might have mentioned me to you. That is, if your name is Kinn."

"I'm Kinn," he said. His smudged eyes measured me, labeled me, let me know who was boss and who was not.

The woman started to speak, then stopped, then began again. Her hand rose to her throat and fiddled with the pearls in her necklace. Below her linen jacket her pink polka-dot dress rustled lightly in the wind. "I'm Carlotta Usser," she managed finally. "My son and his . . . my son lives in this house." She glanced apprehensively at Kinn, as though she feared he would dispute her. When he said nothing she looked back at me. "Do you have something . . . *official* to do here?"

"I've been asked to look into the case," I said.

"By whom?" Her slivered brows rose in hopeful inquiry. She clearly thought I was there to help her son. What I had to do was defer her realization that I was there to do just the opposite.

"My client's identity should be confidential for now," I answered affably. "At this point I'm just gathering information."

"But are you on our side or not?" Mrs. Usser blurted. In the next moment she was wishing she could retract her question and reestablish the aura of quiet confidence that she had so carefully marshaled, that had gotten her through the hours since her son had been so shockingly hauled to jail. But it was too late; the task too formidable. She was his mother and she was scared as hell.

"What do you want here?" Kinn asked me, the question as forbidding as his sunless face.

"To look around inside. And to talk to you if you've got the time."

"The scene is under seal."

"Come on. She was killed a month ago. Usser's been living here ever since. You're not going to find anything you didn't find the first time you came out."

"The first time we came here we weren't building a case against Lawrence Usser."

"Look. You're obviously on your way inside. Can't I just follow you around?"

Kinn frowned impatiently. "She needs some things for the girl," he explained, gesturing toward Carlotta Usser. "We'll be in there five minutes, max."

"That's fine by me." I thought of adding a broad hint that I was on Kinn's side in this one, not the suspect's, but I decided to hold my tongue. Kinn looked like a man who believed his side was an army of one, always and forever.

Kinn hesitated a minute, perhaps remembering his conversation with Howard Gable, then muttered an oath, then shrugged. "Don't touch anything. Don't drop anything. Don't go anyplace I don't lead you. And the same goes for you, ma'am," he added.

"This is my son's house, Lieutenant," Mrs. Usser bristled. "I don't feel it's necessary for you to—"

Kinn gestured toward the notice by the door. "As long as *that's* up there, this house is *mine*. So do as you're told and we'll get along fine. Ma'am." He concluded the lesson with a burlesque bow.

Carlotta Usser's eyes swelled. "My son is *not guilty*, Mr. Kinn. Don't you understand? He's a brilliant, brilliant man. He could *not* have done what you say he did. You *must* believe—"

"It's not important what I believe, ma'am. He'll have his chance. With Jake Hattie as his lawyer he'll have a better chance than most. So just relax, ma'am. It'll all be straightened out sooner or later."

"But—"

"Lady, just let me do my job, huh? Save the rest of it for the judge."

Mrs. Usser hated to give it up, but Kinn turned his back to her and pulled out a key with a tag on it and unlocked the front door. We entered as silently as we would have entered a catacomb.

The foyer was dark, but subtly varicolored from the light passing through the stained glass panel above the door. To the right a staircase rose to the second floor. Beneath it was a bicycle with a flat tire. We followed Kinn into the living room, past an empty coatrack and a marble-topped table displaying a bouquet of dried flowers. Along the way I almost stumbled over a painted milk can with three umbrellas and a cane growing out of it.

The living room was large but dark, with wide wood trim around the draped windows and matching wooden frames around the prints and drawings on the walls. The furnishings were thick and masculine, the rug oval and egg-colored, the walls a beige print wallpaper. Books and magazines were abundant, many of them strayed from the bookshelves that flanked the fireplace and fallen into clusters beside the matching swivel rockers and the corduroy-covered couch.

The stereo along the far wall looked new and expensive. The upright piano in the back was suitable for honky-tonk. On the floor beside the fireplace was a painted plaster pig with a matchbox on its back. Over the mantel was an oversized replica of the

Declaration of Independence. Beneath it a bronze bust of Jefferson gazed approvingly on a photograph of Martin Luther King. But the handsome décor and the honorable ideals were coated with a layer of dust, as though the house had already decided Usser's guilt and had sentenced him to stay away for a long, long time.

Kinn came to a stop in the center of the room and asked Mrs. Usser where she wanted to go. "Lisa's room," she said.

"Upstairs? At the back?"

Carlotta Usser nodded, and we trooped along in single file, a small squad on a secret mission, back the way we'd come, up the hardwood stairs, down the runnered hallway, past the paisley wallpaper and the Audubon prints, halting at the entrance to the small bedroom at the very back of the house.

As Mrs. Usser began her search and Kinn kept his eye on her, I wandered around the room. The windows looked out over the back patio and garden and the little potting shed at the rear of the lot. As I looked down on the patio I noticed the trellis that climbed the back of the house and supported bougainvillea. I wondered how many times Cal had climbed it or Lisa had descended, bent on secret trysts. I wondered what they did, where they went, how angry and alienated they really were, whether they were like the ones you see frequently on the news, untethered to anything but rejection and rebellion, supposedly made hopeless by the specter of the bomb. I surveyed the outdoor scene for several seconds more, but saw no sign that Cal had returned to spy or plunder, so I turned my attention to the interior.

If civil rights was the religion of her parents, music was Lisa's orthodoxy. Rock posters mocked the bourgeois room—Billy Idol, Eurythmics, Judas Priest, Cyndi Lauper, Twisted Sister, Ratt. A two-foot stack of record albums was further testimony to Lisa's worship of punk and heavy metal. On the mirror above the desk were ticket stubs and other souvenirs of concerts at venues such as the Greek Theater and the Oakland Coliseum, and clubs like the Keystone and the Mabuhay Gardens. In the center of the mirror was a photograph of an outrageous and sullen someone who signed his name as Jello.

If memory served, Jello Biafra was the lead singer in a local punk band that called itself the Dead Kennedys. I didn't know anything about their music, but I guessed that Lisa Usser could have formed no more provocative alliance than with persons who blasphemed that name.

Though she was obviously at odds with her parents, and was susceptible to the simplistic anarchism of pop-song philosophers, Lisa's room was not entirely a bleak, depressing den. There were signs of another, more tranquil Lisa—Cal's school picture was taped to the mirror next to Jello's, beside a name tag indicating that Lisa had been a Humanities Symposium participant at some time or another, and above a schedule of her classes written in a baroque blue script. A trophy topped by a golden tennis racket rested on the corner of the desk, beside a volume entitled *World's Greatest Love Poems.* I opened the flyleaf. It was inscribed to Lisa from Cal, and expressed Cal's wish that he had written each of the poems for her.

The rest of the room was tattered and untended, as though Lisa forbid repairs. The beanbag chair was leaking plastic pellets; the carpet bore several singes from discarded cigarettes. At one place on the wall Lisa had evidently begun a tempera mural and abandoned it after a few messy minutes. A dominant species on the floor below, books were endangered here. The reasons might have been the color TV that was next to the compact stereo that was next to the video disc player that was next to the cordless phone that was next to the tiny Walkman that was next to the bed, which was a thin pallet in the center of the floor, covered with a camouflage net from army surplus.

As I completed my inspection, Mrs. Usser reached into her handbag and drew out a sheet of paper. She read the list with her tongue between her teeth, then went to the stack of records and picked out three or four, then to the closet and emerged with clothing that included some plastic shoes that laced up the leg in the fashion of ancient Rome and a pair of Levi's faded to the color of the sea and patched in the rear with a piece of cloth that somehow bore the face of Beethoven.

The final item she collected was a little cedar box on a shelf beside the bed. I wondered if it contained the stash Cal had come to reclaim. As she was about to stuff it in her handbag, Kinn motioned for her to show it to him. She started to object but finally didn't, handing the box over without a word. Kinn raised the lid, then laughed disparagingly and handed it back. "Fake fingernails," he said. "Purple ones. Christ on a crutch."

Mrs. Usser put the box in her bag and gathered a few more

scraps of clothing off the floor and folded them neatly and tucked them under her arm. Then she gestured toward the pallet. "Would one of you carry that to the car for me? Please? It's the blue Cadillac."

Kinn made no move beyond a smile of chilled reproach. I rolled the pad and cover into a floppy bundle and dragged it down the steps and out to the car. By the time I got back to the house, Mrs. Usser was coming down the steps to meet me, ready to leave.

"I'd like to talk to you and your husband about all this some- time," I said to her.

The lady frowned from the step above me, which put our eyes on the same level. "What about? I don't even know why you're here, young man."

"I'm just trying to get some facts about the case."

"Are you trying to find who really killed Dianne? Is that it?"

There was enough hope in her voice to float a stone. "I guess you could say that."

Mrs. Usser brightened. "We're incensed, of course, that the police think Lawrence guilty. They have no proof at all, need- less to say. It's so *unlike* them to make a mistake like this. I wonder what's behind it?"

"I'm sure I don't know."

"Lawrence has his enemies, of course. Anyone who accom- plishes so much so quickly in life makes enemies. My husband did, and now Lawrence."

"Who are some of your son's enemies? Do you know?"

She shook her head. "I'm not good with names. My husband could tell you, of course. Carlton and Lawrence are very close. I know that some men at the law school have been upset at some of the things Lawrence has been doing. I remember a discussion Lawrence had with my husband about it one night; the jealou- sies, the envy. I believe one of the men opposing Lawrence was named Greenberg, or something like that. A Jew. You know how competitive they are. Jews have been envious of Lawrence ever since he was at Yale. Then there were his law trials, of course. Why, Lawrence has had to hear the most *awful* things from the families of those victims. They are naturally upset, I understand that, but it's hardly Lawrence's fault, after all. I . . ."

Mrs. Usser fell silent and looked at her watch. "My. I must be

off. The garden club is coming at three. We are transplanting
tuberous begonias. This evening would be convenient, I believe,
Mister . . . ah . . ."

"Tanner."

"Yes. My husband will be home then. Perhaps you could come
by about seven. We're on Wildwood Drive in Piedmont." She
gave me the number. "It's quite easy to find."

"Will Lisa be there as well?"

A cloud dropped over Carlotta Usser's face, as shielding as a
purdah. "Lisa. I'm afraid I don't know *when* she will be available.
Lisa is, well, a handful. Her adjustment has been difficult."

I nodded in understanding.

"Do you have children yourself, Mister, ah . . ."

"Tanner. No. I don't. But I know it's hard to keep up with
kids these days. To understand why they do the things they do."

"Yes. The awful music. The clothes. She puts *thumbtacks*
through her ears, Mr. Tanner. And wears a necklace made of
rat bones. At least that's what she says they are. They couldn't
possibly *be* rat bones, could they? Surely they're imitation, something cooked up by those little Japanese."

"Probably," I agreed, not quite suppressing a smile.

"We're doing the best we can with Lisa, of course," Mrs. Usser
prattled on, "but we are old now, and, well, it will be better
when Lawrence is released. She's a lovely child, but she lacks
. . . direction. Lawrence will take care of it. He's brilliant, you
know."

"So I've heard."

"Well, thank you so much for carrying Lisa's bed to the car,
Mr. Tanner. Why she prefers that horrid *pad* to the beautiful
Simmons we bought her is beyond me."

I smiled with more sympathy for Carlotta Usser than I knew
I had. Kids. A subject beyond my expertise, beyond the expertise of almost everyone, if you believed your eyes and ears.
Difficult anywhere, raising kids in Berkeley would be akin to
raising orchids on the Gobi.

NINE

When Carlotta Usser and her Cadillac had disappeared, I trotted up to the house and went inside. Bart Kinn wasn't in the living room so I went back up the stairs. Kinn had left Lisa's room and was standing in the doorway to the large bedroom at the front of the house, motionless, contemplative, a stern sentinel guarding a weapon he doesn't understand.

Kinn didn't say anything even after I joined him. "This where it happened?"

Kinn nodded wordlessly. When he didn't offer anything further, I glanced around the room.

As the newspapers had suggested, it was neat, almost frilly, distinctly feminine in contrast to the thick masculinity of the floor below. The bed was king-sized and contemporary, the headboard containing built-in reading lamps, bookshelves and a radio. The coverlet was fringed, the pillows plump. The remaining furnishings were an eclectic mix, doubtlessly assembled one by one over the years of the marriage, as financial circumstances allowed. All were well-worn and looked well-traveled except for the two new upholstered wicker chairs that faced each other in the front dormer. The crystal decanter on the table between them was half full of what looked like fine brandy. The little nook was so cozy and intimate I couldn't see how Usser could bear any longer to look at it. But maybe it was just for show. Maybe he and his wife hadn't exchanged a single word across their crystal snifters. And maybe I'd never know whether they had or not.

I asked Kinn where the body had been found. He pointed to the floor beside the foot of the bed. I looked for stains or other signs of carnage but saw nothing at first glance. Kinn sensed my search. "He replaced the carpet and the bedding first thing. And painted the walls."

I looked closer at the bed. "How about that line on the bedpost and those spots on the box spring?"

Kinn's grin twisted. "Yeah, well, it spattered a little when she rolled off the bed. Not that it did her any good." Kinn breathed deeply. "Man, there was enough blood in here to float a boat. I can still smell it. And the bastard still *sleeps* in here," Kinn added, the music of dismay finally breaking through the rock-hard monotone of his professionalism.

Kinn lapsed into silence again, but if anything his eyes intensified their scrutiny. Somewhere a clock ticked off the seconds and made time itself seem ominous, the room seem incendiary. "You look like you're still trying to decide what happened in there," I said.

He took a moment before he answered. "I know what happened. I don't know why."

The conversation was where I wanted it to be. "Isn't motive a part of your case?"

"With a husband and wife there's motive for a dozen murders."

"So what was it with Usser? Jealousy? Did he catch her sleeping with the milkman and lose control when he confronted her and she admitted it?"

Kinn grumbled a basso curse. "That's a pretty long line you're fishing with, Tanner."

"You can't keep the elements of your case secret forever, Kinn. It'll all come out at the preliminary hearing anyway. Why don't you given me a preview? Maybe I can help you out."

"And maybe you can fuck things up even more than they are already."

Kinn's discontent grew more obvious by the minute. He was bothered by the quality of the investigation, maybe even by its results; so bothered that he didn't care who knew it. "You have any doubt that Usser did it?" I asked.

Kinn shrugged. "Doesn't matter if I do or don't. The D.A.'s filed the charge."

"You think Gable's got enough to make it stick?"

"Maybe. Maybe not."

"You still investigating? You still looking for more?"

"I look for more till they're locked up. Sometimes after that. Not just Usser. All of them."

"Why'd Gable move on Usser so soon, if his case is thin?"

Kinn shrugged again. "Gable doesn't consult with me about strategy."

"If Usser didn't do it, who did?"

Kinn eyed me disgustedly. "I never said Usser didn't do it."

"But you don't think Gable's got a case."

"I didn't say that, either." Kinn chastened me with a baleful stare. "Man, you come on like a reporter, you know that? Twisting everything, till it says what you think it ought to say."

"Sorry." I shifted gears. "Was I close? About Ms. Renzel and the milkman?"

Kinn cocked his head. "We're still checking that out."

"Anything so far?"

"Some. Me, I don't think it matters. Even if she had someone she was screwing, and even if Usser caught her at it, I don't think he'd give a shit. That's just my personal opinion."

"Why wouldn't he care?"

"People in glass houses, man, and like that."

"A cocksman?"

"Full time."

"Anyone in particular?"

"We're making a list."

"Any of them think they were in line to succeed the late Ms. Renzel in that bed over there?"

Kinn shrugged. "It's possible."

"Like who, for instance?"

"You get names, you get them from Gable. But if you're any good at your trade, you'll run across one or two of them before long. The man cut a wide swath."

"You sound as though you know Usser pretty well."

"Had him in class a couple of years ago, back when I thought being a lawyer beat the hell out of being a cop. Back when I thought how much money you made had something to do with how smart you were."

Kinn looked as if he expected me to object to his implication. When I let his comment stand it seemed to make him voluble. "What was Usser like?" I prompted.

"He got off on me being a cop, for one thing. Always having me tell the class how it really was out in the street." Kinn chuckled at the memory. "Then, after I'd tell them how some deal went down, how we finally made a case against some snot ball who lived off whores and sold kids dope, Usser would pipe up and say it didn't matter how warped the guy was, that the law couldn't concern itself with special cases, that it only applies to crimes, not criminals."

"You thought he was naive?"

"Hell, everyone's naive. You think those almighty judges know what goes down on the streets? Or the defense lawyers? They live in caves, man, like all civilians. Come out by day to earn their bread making Walt Disney rules for their Walt Disney world, then hole up at night behind Mr. Yale and Mr. Cyclone and hope no one breaks in and takes all the jewels they earned by being ignorant." Kinn eyed me closely, as if to gauge whether I was worthy of hearing truth. "Ever notice all the fancy cars around these days?" he asked finally. "Mercedes? BMW? All that shit?"

"Sure."

"Why you think there's so many of them?"

"People want to advertise their money?"

"Naw. That's the old days. Today people who spend twenty, thirty grand on a car want it to do one thing."

"What?"

"Get them the fuck through the ghetto without breaking down. The wheels give out in the wrong part of town and you're deep in a world of the extremely pissed off. People willing to pay Mr. Mercedes and Mr. Maserati a whole lot to keep that from happening." Kinn laughed. "Usser's got one, you know. Big BMW. Even the great Lawrence Usser don't want no vapor lock down in West Oakland." Kinn sighed, shook his head and looked back into the bedroom. "What the hell you want to know, Tanner?" he asked, his sarcastic argot replaced by a weary resignation.

"Whether Usser was insane."

Kinn gave me his look again. "He used some scissors on her," he said carefully.

"I read about it."

"You read what he did with them?"

"Not precisely."

"You want to know?"

I sighed. "Not really. But maybe I better."

Kinn looked back into the room. "Those babies must have been honed as hell, 'cause he cut off about everything she had that was loose. Hair. Ears. Tip of her nose. He cut off her tongue and shoved it up her cunt. He even cut her nipples off. Not the whole thing, just the little pointy part. Nipped them off like rosebuds."

There was nothing to be said until time and memory diluted all his words, redefined them so Kinn and I could shed their deepest meanings. "A sane man do that?" Kinn asked finally.

I thought about it. "Maybe. If he was trying to make someone think he wasn't."

Kinn met my glance. "Insanity plea. Yeah, I've thought about it. The guy knows his law, and he's buddies with a lot of shrinks. For sure he's defended enough corkscrews to pick up on the vocabulary." Kinn took yet another look at the bedroom, as though this was one of those times it had begun to speak to him. "But if he was trying to make it look like he was nuts, why'd he wipe away the prints, hide the murder weapon where we can't find it, stuff his bloody handkerchief away in the back of the closet?"

I shook my head. "I don't know."

"And why'd he try to wipe off the mirror?"

"What mirror?"

"That one." Kinn pointed to the oval mirror above the dressing table that was against the far wall.

"What was on it?"

"All kind of stuff. Religious, sort of. But bent. 'Death Is Redemption. Slay the Sinner, Slay the Sin. Free the Flesh. Sainthood Is Slaughter.' Shit like that, written in lipstick, then wiped off with a towel. Lucky for us, he didn't do a very good job. Now, why would he try to erase all that, Mr. Private Detective, if he was trying to pretend he was stone cold loco?"

I shrugged and smiled. "Maybe to get you to ask that question."

"Okay. You sound like a fucking lawyer yourself, always with an answer. So what about the sex?"

"That doesn't seem so hard to explain," I said. "She and Usser started making love, and sometime along the way she said something that set him off."

"That's not how it was."

"The papers said she'd had intercourse before she died."

"Yeah, well, what they should have said was that there were signs of sexual activity. The sign was semen. But it was on the outside, not in. How we figure is, he beat off on her. When she was dying, the guy stood there and whacked his pud and squirted his jazz all over her. Now you tell me. A guy do that to his wife? Doesn't seem that way to me," Kinn answered before I could. "To another broad, maybe. But not the wife."

I could only keep silent. Kinn began to fidget, then looked at his watch. Before he could order me away I gestured toward the bedroom. "Care if I go in there?"

"You won't find anything."

I waited.

"Hell, go ahead," Kinn said. "We only resealed it after Gable decided to move on Usser. We didn't find anything the first time and we didn't find anything this time, either. I'll be downstairs looking at the books."

Kinn went off toward the stairs and I went into the murder room, stepping softly, as though I trod on fragile facts.

There was a lot to look at, but the first thing that caught my eye was a photograph, formal, framed in gold, that leaned against the wall atop the headboard shelf. It must have been Lisa, and contrary to what I'd heard about her, this was a vibrant, laughing child, with long dark hair and flashing black eyes and a smile that would have sold a lot of toothpaste or persuaded you to drive a Ford. I went over for a closer look.

If there was trouble in her, if she had become as rebellious and defiant as Mrs. Renzel said, then this picture had been taken before all that boiled over. I wondered if Usser kept it there because it was the way he wanted her to be rather than the way she was.

I picked it up, conscious that I was violating Bart Kinn's orders. The girl stared at me as though I had an answer to a question we both shared. She seemed about to speak, to ask a favor or to give one. I put the portrait back in place and won-

dered if she had ever smiled that smile since the day her mother
died. Then I began to look for signs that her father had coldly
planned the deed.

The bed was covered with a quilt and pillowed with fat blue
cushions trimmed in lace. The nightstands on either side contained facial tissues, aspirin, Vaseline, Desenex, a Rex Stout
mystery, a Rosellen Brown novel, and a box of tampons that,
given the fact and circumstance of Dianne Renzel's death, had
now become pathetic.

The dressers on either side of the room were stuffed with the
expected items in unexpectedly sexy designs—bikini and plung-
ing and see-through and the like—all of it newish and expensive. After flipping through some argyle socks and eelskin belts
and Dean's sweaters and Bali bras, I probed the corners and
found nothing extraordinary, with two exceptions—in the back
of one bottom drawer were five hundred dollars in uncashed
traveler's checks and a .32-caliber revolver, complete with
leather holster, a box of cartridges and a trigger guard locked
in place. I assumed the police had checked out the gun and
decided it had nothing to do with the crime. Or maybe Usser
had bought it afterward, to help ward off nightmares.

On my way to the closet I stumbled over various pairs of
athletic shoes and a pair of wool sweat socks stained and stiff
from dirt and sweat. Inside the closet were more athletic shoes
and a cardboard box marked GOODWILL that was half full of
things I supposed were Dianne's. In addition to the clothing
there were tennis rackets, ski poles, backpacks, bike helmets,
and other paraphernalia of an active western Yuppie. I patted
my way through the clothing in the closet and found nothing
but a stray dollar bill, several matchbooks and handkerchiefs,
and a pocket calculator lying forgotten in one of Usser's sports
coats that hung way in the back. The shoes in the deep end of
the closet were a historical record in themselves, which made
them the most interesting things in the room.

I probed and poked and peeked and pried for five more
minutes, but in the end I concluded that if there had ever been
anything illuminating in that room, the police had already con-
fiscated it. I abandoned my search and trotted down the stairs
and joined Bart Kinn in the den.

All four wall were books, tier upon tier of them, books of all shapes and sizes, colors and bindings, subjects and styles. In the center of the room, a Queen Anne desk was piled high with papers and magazines, law journals and psychiatric publications, each of them splayed and awry as though laid waste by the whirlwind of Usser's brilliant mind. The credenza behind the desk held a Kaypro word processor, a Sanyo VCR, an Adler typewriter and an Aiwa cassette player. Next to the VCR were some prerecorded movies—*The Big Sleep, Patton, The Right Stuff, Reds*—as well as five or six blank tape cartridges. Beside the credenza a Sony video camera rested on a bright chrome tripod. My guess was that Usser had used the video equipment in his practice, to tape depositions and evidentiary matter that was immobile. The end of the credenza was a charred, black scar. I assumed it was the leavings of the fire that Lisa had tried to start.

After my quick inventory I looked back at Kinn. "Nice place," I said.

"Yeah."

The brief word contained a lot of awe. I wondered what Kinn's intellectual ambitions were, whether he had realized all or any of them, whether he had given most of them up, the way he had given up law school, the way I had given up learning Spanish and reading Proust, and given up the law as well.

"Care if I look up close?" I asked.

Kinn shook his head. "As far as I know, nothing happened in here that had anything to do with it."

I went to the nearest wall and looked at random book titles. The shelves farthest from the desk were novels, Russian and European mostly, classics known to all, though a few Wambaughs and Puzos and Micheners were hiding in there too. Next to the novels were a few pop psychology and spiritualist tracts, the kind that cater to our need to believe that we can somehow make it better than it is. A volume entitled *The Astral Light* was so stained and tattered it looked to have been read daily, as prayer or penance.

Next came brief sections on music and sports, a larger one devoted to biographies of men like Einstein and Jefferson, Lincoln and Huey Long, and then a single shelf of poetry, a lot of Keats and Whitman, Eliot and Baudelaire. Below the poets were the philosophers—Santayana and Buber, Heidegger and

Nietzsche, Kant and Hegel and Spinoza. And then the law books took over.

There were hundreds of them; thousands, maybe. Biographies of Darrow and Marshall, Stryker and Brandeis. Legal philosophy from Holmes and Pound and Cardozo, sets of Wigmore in cloth and Greenleaf in calfskin, hornbooks on subjects from civil procedure to real property, and textbooks old and new— Casner and Leach, Prosser and Smith, Halbach and Scoles, Louisell and Hazard. And law reviews, legal newspapers, Congressional Records and legal directories; loose-leaf services and three-ring binders and soft-covered advance sheets. It was very impressive to a former lawyer like myself, and maybe forbidding or maybe enticing to a layman like Bart Kinn. I looked at Kinn again, then looked where he was looking.

Just above the credenza, where Usser could reach them with an easy cast of his arm, were several shelves devoted to psychiatry and the law. Most prominent of the volumes was the *Diagnostic and Statistical Manual* of the American Psychiatric Association. But most of the books addressed a more specific subject: *The Insanity Plea, The Mark of Sanity, The Reign of Error, The Madness Establishment, The Myth of Mental Illness, Insanity Inside Out, Murder and Madness, The Criminal Mind, Psychiatric Justice, The Responsibility of Criminals, The Powers of Psychiatry, Manufacture of Madness.* And dozens more, an entire array discussing the jagged line between legal sanity and insanity, undoubtedly containing enough data and examples and case studies to support a script capable of fooling the most expert shrink, to say nothing of a jury of people who had never heard such terms before.

I looked at Kinn once more. His face was set in a dark fury. He seemed to have suddenly made up his mind that Usser was a fraud, that he was doing what the phone call to the Renzels had suggested he would do. I was more than halfway to that conclusion as well.

After we exchanged glances, Kinn backed out of the room. I started to follow him when my glance fell, entirely by accident, on a potted orange tree in the corner behind the door. There was something sticking out of the dirt at the base of the tree, something shiny. I went over and looked at it, then started to pick it out of the dirt, then stopped myself. "Hey, Kinn. Come in here a minute."

In a second he was at my side. I pointed to the object without saying a word. "Son of a *bitch*," Kinn said, then told me he'd be back in a minute. When he returned, he had a pair of tongs and a plastic bag. He plucked at the object with the tongs and finally loosened it enough to raise it out of its shallow grave.

The shiny thing was a pair of scissors, of course; the murder weapon. "These fuckers weren't here a month ago, I can tell you that," Kinn said as he put the scissors in the plastic bag. "He must have ditched them somewhere and went to get them later."

I didn't say what I was thinking, which was that a lot of things in that house didn't make much sense.

TEN

Kinn bid me a gruff good-bye, then stood in the street and waited for me to drive away. I did what he wanted me to do, but only briefly. After a left and a right, I stopped in the shade of a eucalyptus tree, waited ten minutes and drove back to the Usser house.

The main reason I returned was to see if Cal showed up again. Cal gave off hints that he knew more than he was saying, about the Ussers, perhaps even about the murder. All kids give off those hints, of course, at least to those of us who aren't parents ourselves and therefore aren't used to that reluctant, suspicious style, but given the circumstances I wanted to talk with Cal again, about what he knew and about what his girl-friend Lisa knew as well.

When Cal hadn't shown up five minutes later, I got out of the car and strolled up the Usser steps again. When I didn't hear anything abnormal I ambled to the back yard, watched and waited, then ambled back to the front again. No one saw me, as far as I could tell. It was one of those streets where privacy is as guarded as if it were illegal.

I considered staking out the back yard but I wasn't in the mood. It was too early in the case for a stakeout—as far as I'm concerned it's always too early in the case for a stakeout—so I trotted down the steps to the street and walked to the house at the end of the block, one of the turquoise cantinas. I knocked on the door, rang the bell, then knocked again.

Only then did I notice the sign: NIGHT WORKER. PLEASE DO NOT DISTURB. I gave myself a mental kick in the pants and retreated. When I was halfway to the street, I heard a door squeak open. A voice, languid and irritated, tossed a question at my back. "What is it you want?"

I stopped and turned. The woman on the front stoop wore a gray sweat suit, the old kind with elastic at the ankles and a drawstring at the waist, and incongruous blue silk house slippers. The red babushka atop her head was gnarled in the shape of hair curlers.

She was panting and she looked exhausted, as though she'd just finished a long run. But I had the feeling she hadn't run anywhere in years. "I'm sorry I knocked," I said. "I didn't notice the sign until it was too late."

She didn't let me off the hook but she didn't curse me, either. "What do you want?" she asked again.

"My name's Tanner. I'd like to talk to you about Dianne Renzel."

"Dianne's dead." Her voice was a match for the condition she described. Her eyes were as flat as paired decals.

"I know she's dead," I said. "I'd like to talk to you about why."

"Why she's dead?"

"Yes."

She frowned. "Who are you? I mean, *what* are you? I've already talked to the police."

"I'm a private investigator."

She showed interest for the first time. "Who hired you? Lawrence?"

"I can't tell you who hired me," I said, then took a shot at bettering my chances of learning something. "But I can tell you that Lawrence Usser did not."

"Honest?"

"Honest."

I could hear her sigh from where I stood. It blended so nicely with the breezy wheezes in the branches overhead, it seemed the city itself was weary with my presence. "You might as well come in, I guess," she said finally, and crossed her arms across her chest and waited for me to join her on the stoop. When I reached her side she stepped aside without a word and allowed me to precede her through the door.

The house was cool and dark, the shades pulled, shutters closed, the evergreens that grew beyond the windows scratching softly at the panes and masking the queer house even further. In contrast to the Usser house and its numberless signs of intellectual and physical activity, this one had an abandoned feel, as though its occupants were ghosts that left no traces and had no needs.

From what the Renzels had said, there should have been a teenage girl living there, but the only evidence of such a being in the living room was a framed color photograph propped on top of the end table beside the couch. The girl in the picture was lissome and listless, dressed in the tawdry beads and feathers and leathers of the avant-garde, a sharp contrast to her vivacious friend across the street. Her lips were burnt orange, her hair a frothy pink, her eyes twin bags of glitter. A single incisor, blackened for some outlandish purpose, was exposed by the reach of her carefully calibrated yawn. She was so disdainful of the photographer I assumed it must have been her mother. I wondered if she was persuasive as well, so much so that she had convinced her neighbor Lisa to change her ways and adopt an exasperating style.

I looked away from the photograph and back to my hostess. She wore no makeup and no jewelry, and I guessed she wore nothing beneath the sweat suit. She motioned toward the chair and took one herself, wearing the look of cautious expectancy of those who live alone and believe they have come across someone who will talk to them. "I'm Phyllis Misteen," she said.

"Marsh Tanner."

"A private eye."

"Right."

"I didn't know they made them anymore."

"I don't think they're made; I think they're born."

I smiled more than the axiom warranted. Phyllis looked like she wanted to do likewise but couldn't summon the strength. I started to apologize again for waking her but she waved it away. "You didn't wake me. No one wakes me anymore. I suppose it's because I so seldom find myself asleep."

"Does it have anything to do with Dianne Renzel?"

Her smile was small and pained. "That didn't help matters any, that's for sure. Dianne was my best friend. But—" She stopped, as though her thought had veered.

"What is it?"

"I was just thinking how different that term 'best friend' becomes as you grow up. In high school my best friend was Connie Waitley. I saw her ten hours a day, at least. Now I call Dianne my best friend and I didn't see her ten hours a month."

"But her death isn't why you're losing sleep."

"No. Not usually. What I'm losing sleep over is my daughter. Sherry." She glanced quickly at the photograph, then looked as quickly away from it, as though it was too bright to behold without a filter.

"What happened to her?"

"She ran away." Although short, the sentence didn't end before there was a break in the voice that uttered it.

"When?"

"Two months ago."

"I'm sorry."

"So am I. I'm sorrier than I ever thought I could possibly be. Unfortunately, it doesn't seem to make any difference. Sorriness does not seem to be rewarded in this world."

Her voice edged toward a self-mocking hysteria. I asked the first question that came to mind. "Is there a Mr. Misteen?"

"I'm sure there is. Somewhere. He ran away too. In 1972, when Sherry was five and I was frantic. That one I'm not sorry about at all."

She wiped her brow, then twisted the sleeve of her sweatshirt between fingers that had begun to spot and swell with age. "Everyone but me thinks Sherry's dead," she said, so softly I almost didn't hear. "I can tell from the way everyone avoids the subject, the way they do when someone gets fired or gets cancer. But she *isn't* dead. I can prove it."

"How?"

"I get these calls."

"What kind of calls?"

"From kids. Not from Sherry, but from people she knows. Street people."

"What do they say?"

"That Sherry needs clothes, or food, or money. They tell me

what to bring and where to leave it and I go there and then I sneak back to see if Sherry comes to get the things but she never does. It's always just some frightful-looking boy. I try to follow him but I always lose him before he can lead me to Sherry." She laughed ruefully. "The police say they're taking advantage of me, those kids, stealing, that even if Sherry's alive she's probably long gone from Berkeley by now, but I don't think so. I think she's still here. Don't you?"

It was somehow a serious question. Her eyes enlarged, as though to search out my concurrence with all their power. I struggled for an answer for so long that she spoke again before I had come up with one. "But you're not interested in Sherry, are you? You're here about Dianne."

I nodded, relieved that she had been the one to point that out.

"What do you want to know?"

"I suppose you've heard they arrested her husband," I began.

"Yes. I heard."

"Did it surprise you?"

"No." It was her first firm word.

"So you think Usser was capable of . . . that?"

"*Any* man is capable of that."

She seemed about to launch a tirade, so I tried to focus her. "Were they having problems? Did you see something like this coming?"

I regretted the question as soon as I'd asked it. Phyllis Misteen gave me a look that curled my toes. "If I had *seen this coming*, I would have killed the bastard myself. And I'd have done it the same way he did." The eyes that had been so murky when I arrived now blazed clear and hot.

"I'm sorry. I phrased that badly. But I think you know what I meant."

She nodded. "Have you ever spent much time with an intellectual, Mr. Tanner? I mean with a genuine, certified, grade A genius?"

She shoved her voice into a country twang. I shook my head, though the answer was not that simple. I've known some bright people in my day, but they weren't bright from top to bottom. Somewhere in the middle of each of them there had been a hole, and what had leaked out of it had been the reason I'd gotten to know them, the reason most of them were eventually put in jail or in an early grave.

"Well, Lawrence Usser was a genius," Phyllis Misteen was saying. "*Is* a genius. And if you didn't recognize that right away, he'd be sure to let you know it about two minutes into the conversation. Do you know the concept of battered wives, Mr. Tanner? The syndrome?"

"Sure."

"Well, Dianne Renzel was a battered wife, even though her husband never laid a hand on her, at least not until the night he killed her. What Lawrence beat her with was his mind. He used his brain like a club; he slapped her around with words and phrases, bludgeoned her with criticism and accusation. And I'll tell you something, Mr. Tanner. It hurt like hell. If you could get inside Dianne Renzel, you'd see her psyche was completely black and blue."

"Was it always like that between them?"

"I don't know. I mean, I moved here three years ago, so what was going on before that I don't know about. See, it's not as if Dianne saw it the way I did. She worshiped the ground the asshole walked on, at least she did till lately. Not as a person— she knew Larry was basically a jerk—but as a . . . paragon. A god. She thought Lawrence Usser was a Christmas gift to the downtrodden of the world, but she was in pain all the same. And it was getting worse."

"How about recently? Did she say anything that indicated there was a change in Usser's behavior? That he was doing things he'd never done before? Acting strangely? Anything?"

"I'd like to tell you there was something like that. Believe me. But I can't. Larry turned odd as hell *after* the murder, but not before, at least not that I heard."

"What was he doing after the murder?"

"Oh, wandering around the yard at all hours. Talking to himself. Calling out for Lisa. Calling me up to talk, then hanging up after three words."

"If he did do it, what do you think was his motive?"

"Another woman, probably."

"Why not just get a divorce?"

"Money. Lawrence liked to live high, liked nice things. He had a lot but he didn't have enough."

"Do you know of a specific woman he might have been in love with?"

"No. I heard there was someone at the law school, but I don't know who she was. Dianne knew he slept around, by the way. She didn't care, I guess. I don't know, we didn't talk about Larry all that much. She knew I didn't like him."

"How about Dianne? Was she bothered by anything recently? Afraid of anything? Or anyone?"

Phyllis Misteen's expression grew more tormented. "I don't know. All I know is that she tried to reach me four different times on the day she died. And I wasn't here for her. It's been hard to live with that, let me tell you, Mr. Tanner."

"Tried to reach you how?"

"By phone. I have this answering machine, because of Sherry. If Sherry calls, I want to know it. If she wants me to come and get her, I want her to be . . . well, I just want her to be able to say whatever she wants to say."

"So Dianne Renzel left a message on your machine?"

"Right. Four of them."

"What did they say?"

"Just to call her back. That it was important."

"Nothing else?"

"No."

"Do you still have the tape?"

She shook her head. "I erased it before I knew she . . . died."

"Do you have any idea at all what it might have been about?"

Phyllis Misteen clasped her hands in an unconscious prayer. "What I hope is that it was about Sherry. I hope Dianne saw her or heard something, and was trying to let me know."

"But it could have been that she was in trouble. That something had scared her. It could have been almost anything, right?"

I had splashed water on the fires of hope and it angered her. She rose halfway out of her chair, then sagged back into it and glared at me. "You're working for *them*, aren't you?"

"Who?"

"The Ussers. Mr. and Mrs. High-and-Mighty. They hired you to get him off, didn't they? Christ. I *thought* that was her car over there. Listen. I think I want you to leave. *Now*."

I shook my head and held up a placative hand. "They're not

my clients. And I'm not trying to get Usser off. I'm just trying to find out what happened."

"Then who did hire you?"

"I can't say. Really. So how about it? Was anything at all unusual going on in Dianne Renzel's life of late?"

Phyllis Misteen shrugged. "What we talked mostly about was her work. That was *always* unusual."

"What did she do, exactly?"

"She was a counselor at the Community Crisis Center, over by the campus. She saw it *all* over there, believe me."

"Where was her office?"

"On Bowditch, between Channing and Durant."

"Near the law school."

"Right. He used to walk right past her window when he was going off to lunch with one of his precious students. *Women* students, mostly. God, that man attracted a crowd. And all of them with dripping cunts, excuse my French."

"You think he slept with students?"

"Sure. I mean, I think he was capable of murder, so of course I think he was capable of screwing his students."

I smiled because I thought Phyllis expected it. I was wrong. She saw nothing funny in Lawrence Usser. "How about Dianne?" I asked. "Did she have a lover?"

Phyllis gave me an odd look. "I told the police I didn't know."

"Was it the truth?"

She looked at me, still deciding. "No. It wasn't. That man Kinn made me mad. He didn't want to hear *one word* about Sherry all the time he was over here."

"So who was her lover?" I asked, taking my own risk of making Phyllis mad by avoiding her daughter's plight.

"Pierce Richards. Her boss."

"How long were they together?"

"Not very. A few months. Like I said, Dianne finally saw Larry for what he was—an ambitious smart-ass who made his reputation putting lunatics out on the streets."

"Did Usser know about her affair?"

"I doubt it, but I really can't say."

"If he found out, do you think he'd react violently?"

"Maybe. He's a man, isn't he?" Her eyes widened with concern. She had clearly told me more than she'd planned, and wanted to think it over. "Listen," she said. "I got some things I've got to do, so . . ."

She stood up and I followed suit. "One last thing," I said as we walked toward the door. "How about Lisa? The daughter. What's the story on her?"

Phyllis Misteen stopped and turned to look at me. "Lisa. God. If Lawrence is a genius, then Lisa is genius squared. She's sixteen, but half her classes are upper division courses at the university. She played Mozart at six and gave up music entirely at ten, except for the punk stuff. She toys with people; her parents, her friends, everyone. Every day she's a different person. Half the time I thought Sherry was corrupting her, and half the time I thought it was the other way around. One day she brings me flowers from the garden, the next I see her sneaking into the house as I get home at six A.M., stoned out of her mind, babbling away about something or other. The past couple of months Lisa's hardly been home at all. She's totally and completely fucked up, if you want the truth. Dianne used to go on and on about her to me. But I'd screwed my own kid up so bad I wasn't much help." A tear appeared at the corner of her eye and she smeared it across her cheek.

"Were Lisa and your daughter friends?"

"On and off. Off, before Sherry ran away."

"Did you ever talk to Lisa about why Sherry left home?"

"I tried. Believe me. But talking to Lisa is even less satisfactory than talking to Lawrence. Not only wasn't she helpful, she seemed not to care. But then Dianne said lately Lisa didn't care about anything, even herself."

"Do you think Lisa knows why Usser killed her mother?"

"If you mean specifically, I doubt it. But even if she does know, you'll play hell getting it out of her."

"Can you give me some idea of how to approach her?"

Phyllis shook her head. "Lisa is a true schizoid, if you ask me. I have no idea how she'd react to anything. Sherry was the same way, though not as bad. I . . ."

She looked at the photograph once again, and once again it seemed to daze her. "Listen. If you're going to be wandering around Berkeley, asking questions and all, would you keep your ears open for anything about Sherry? And if someone mentions her name, would you try to find out where she is? And let me know? I'd really appreciate it. I'd try to pay you something, maybe monthly?"

"No problem," I said. "If I hear anything, I'll let you know."

"Thanks. You don't know what I . . . Thanks."

She was right. I didn't know and I was thankful for my ignorance.

I reached into my pocket for a business card, jotted my home number on it as well and gave it to her. "If you think of anything that might help explain what happened over at the Usser place, give me a call. Or if you just want to talk."

She smiled a sad smile and shook her head. "I can't tie up the phone just to talk," she said, then stuck my card under the edge of an ashtray and showed me to the door.

ELEVEN

left my car on Hillside Lane and set out on foot for the law school. It was a ten-minute trip. The way was lined with frat houses and apartment complexes, their windows filled with wine bottles or street signs, their lawns littered with beer kegs and broken furniture, their surfaces marred with graffiti or decay, their sidewalks swarming with students of every size and stripe, from preppies to punks, surfers to stoners, nerds to jocks. Despite all that, by the time I reached my destination I felt a spring in my step, a bounce to my stride, a whistle on my lips, but I was haunted by the suspicion that I was late for class and unprepared for the quiz in second period.

The Berkeley Law School was housed in a former University of California dormitory, a high-rise structure on Channing Way just south of the UC campus. As befitting its origins, the exterior was nondescript and austere, more a fortification than an educational institution. The view from the top floors must have been spectacular, but below that the windows revealed only the high stone wall that surrounded the place.

The walkway to the entrance was lined with bicycles and mopeds and students recumbent in the courtyard. The first-floor halls were dark and hollow, the offices opening off of them busy but exclusive, a warren of special interests: the Black American Law Students Association, the Asian Law Caucus, the

La Raza Law Students League, the Berkeley Law School Lesbian and Gay Alliance, Christians at Berkeley Law and the National Lawyers Guild.

The bulletin boards bore announcements for the *Women's Law Journal*, the *International Tax and Business Lawyer* and the *Ecology Law Quarterly*. Hand-lettered notices advertised upcoming speeches by Gary Hart and Barbara Jordan, an address by an anonymous someone entitled "Animals and the Law," and the opening of the Bay Area Sexual Harassment Clinic. A tiny note on the door of a phone booth requested a ride to Reno. A formal document proclaimed that all seniors must be finger-printed before they would be allowed to take the bar examination. Next to the phone booth at the end of the hall the wheels of a dozen bicycles were chained into concrete envelopes.

I went up two flights of stairs and found the administrative and faculty offices. The directory listed Lawrence Usser's office in room 328. I was looking for a clue to where that was when I noticed a small table next to the door to the dean's office, just below a shadowy oil portrait of some robed and ancient personage the school evidently had reason to be proud of. The man looked much too mean to do anything but teach. I bet myself his specialty was tax.

The sign dangling from the edge of the table read LAWRENCE USSER DEFENSE FUND. The young man sitting behind it looked young enough to be in grade school and mischievous enough to be doing something illegal with the money he collected. His shaggy blond hair was the brightest object I'd seen inside the building.

When I walked over to him, he looked up at me with an evangelist's fervor. "Faculty contributions are welcome, sir," he said.

"I'm just a visitor."

"Do you know Professor Usser?"

"A little. How about you?"

"I'm his junior research assistant." He announced the title with a nicely controlled pride that still managed to let me know that the position was something special.

"Then you must know him pretty well."

He shrugged. "Not really. Mostly I take my orders from Krista. Krista Hellgren, she's his senior assistant. Krista likes to keep the professor to herself." He knew the remark was catty, and he was a bit embarrassed by it, but all the same he left it dangling beside a boyish grin that denied his capacity for guile. I asked him his name.

"Danny Wilken. You go to school here, sir?"

I shook my head, flattered by being mistaken for someone who was pursuing knowledge rather than miscreants.

"Are you a lawyer?"

"Used to be," I said. "Not anymore."

"What do you do now? Business?"

"Sort of," I said, suddenly suspecting that Danny was setting me up for a plea for a summer job. "How are collections going?" I asked quickly.

His grin turned appropriately rueful, but I guessed he was not totally immobilized by his mentor's predicament. "Sort of slow, I guess. The thing is, no one around here can *believe* they arrested the professor. I think they all assume it's just a big mistake, cops hassling him because of the work he does and stuff, and that he'll be released any day. But Krista thinks we'd better be safe than sorry. So far we've got a hundred and fifty bucks. From what I hear, that'll buy Jake Hattie for thirty minutes."

The kid's expression indicated that his life's ambition was to get where Jake Hattie was. I couldn't blame him. If I'd been as good as Jake, I'd still be practicing law myself.

"Who are Usser's friends on the faculty?" I asked. "Maybe you should make a personal pitch to them."

"Well, he and Grunig were tight for a while, but I heard they had some kind of fight. The only other one I know of is Ms. Howson, but she, I don't know, *I* wouldn't want to be the one to hit her up for bread. She eats guys like me alive. And I got her for Advanced Alimony next term." Danny wriggled inside his numbered jersey, as though the gesture would dislodge her from his course schedule.

"What course is that?" I asked.

"Family Law 102."

I smiled. "Surely Usser has friends other than Ms. Howson around here."

"Well, if you go by what you hear, he has a *lot* of them, at least after dark." He gave me a crooked leer that italicized his meaning. "But I just work for the guy. He's not a god to me like he is to some of them. To me he's just another line on the résumé. That and an 84 average will get me to Wall Street."

Another student walked past the table and Danny waved at him, then glanced at his watch. "I got to get to class. So what do you say, sir? If what Krista thinks is true, the professor's going to run up legal fees the size of the federal deficit. How about making a contribution?"

Danny could have raised money for seal slaughterers. And would have if the pay was right. I wondered what tall tale he had told Usser to get himself hired to assist him.

I reached into my wallet and pulled out a twenty and gave it to the kid, more for my own sake than for Usser's. Danny Wilken's ersatz aspect might be of use to me somewhere down the line. Certainly it would be of use to him, masking as it did the skills that much lawyering demands—craft, cunning and a duplicity that comes as naturally as breath.

Danny thanked me and stuck the bill into the metal box on the table in front of him. I asked him how to get to Usser's office. He pointed the way, then looked at me and winked. "You won't find him in, though. Old Larry's new office has bars on it."

I left Danny Wilken chuckling at his own black wit and followed his directions to Usser's office. It was down a long narrow corridor, its walls an egg-yolk yellow, its floor an underwater green. Shelves of legal reporters and law reviews lined the path —the professors' private stock.

I read numbers until I read the one I wanted. The name on the door said simply USSER. The bulletin board next to it was posted with the grades to Criminal Procedure 201. Someone had gotten a 96. Someone else had gotten a 52. Below the grade list were a political cartoon that maligned the U.S. Supreme Court and a glowing review of Usser's latest book, excerpted from *The California Lawyer*. Below the review, someone had altered a snapshot of Usser so that it mimicked a mug shot.

I knocked on the door and listened for an answer. Surprisingly, I heard one. It told me to come in.

I opened the door and entered a small anteroom that was reminiscent of the one at my own office. A plain, somewhat startled woman sat behind the desk that protruded from a wall.

She eyed me with what looked like trepidation. A dishwater blonde, she was simply and inexpensively dressed, the light in her eyes a few watts short of adequate. "May I help you?" she asked in a voice that aped a sigh, a voice I'd heard over the telephone five days before.

I suddenly realized I didn't know what I'd come for. Usser wasn't there, and whomever I questioned about him would want some sort of reason to talk with me. As my mind spun toward a gambit, the woman across the desk seemed to shiver, my uncertainty augmenting her own.

"I was wondering," I began, "who is looking after Mr. Usser's academic affairs while he is, ah, away?"

She bit a lip and hesitated, so I prattled on. "There's a faculty meeting tomorrow, and I need to know if Professor Usser planned any input." I tried to assume an avuncular aspect, but it's not one of my best disguises.

She responded bravely. "I believe Ms. Howson has taken over Professor Usser's classes, with the help of Dr. Lonborg, and will give the final exam. Ms. Hellgren is in charge of his research projects, I think. I don't know of anything he prepared for the faculty." She closed her eyes as though she feared her response would provoke a scolding.

"How about the matters he consults in? Lawsuits and the like?"

"I believe you should speak with Dr. Lonborg about that."

"Is he here today?"

"I don't think so."

"Then . . ." I shrugged.

"Well, perhaps Mr. Grunig would know, though I'm not sure he . . ."

I nodded. "Yes, there was some trouble there, wasn't there? Silly business."

She nodded in return, apprehension still rising off her in almost visible clouds. She was probably attractive when she wasn't frightened, but I guessed she wasn't attractive often enough for her to count on it. I asked if she knew where I could find Ms. Hellgren, Usser's research assistant.

She frowned and glanced at the clock on the wall. "I believe she's in class till noon. She usually spends the rest of the day in the library. She has a carrel. Let's see." She looked at a sheet of paper that was taped to the top corner of her desk. "It's number 209."

I thanked her for the information. "Have you worked here long?" I asked, eyeing the nameplate on her desk, the one that read LAURA NIFTON. "I don't remember seeing you around the school before, but your name is familiar."

"Not too long," she murmured. "I . . . my brother . . . that is . . ."

She was about to get it straight and I was about to remember where I'd heard the name when the door behind me opened. The woman looking in at us was the opposite of the one behind the desk. Composed, coiffed, suited and svelte, she was an accomplished aggressor in every inch of her being and she was issuing orders before she got into the room. "Laura, I need—"

When she noticed me she stopped short. "What is this?"

Laura was frightened again, as though someone had thrown a switch. "A teacher, Ms. Howson. He—"

"He's not a teacher. At least not here. Who *is* he?"

The question wasn't aimed at me but I let it hit me anyway. "The name's Tanner. I'm a private investigator looking into the death of Dianne Renzel. I—"

"Grilling Laura won't tell you anything about that at *all*," the woman interrupted.

I smiled easily. "Then what will?"

She eyed me as though I sported sores. "I'm Elmira Howson. Come with me," she ordered, then turned her stare to Laura. "Professor Usser is under arrest, as you know. Thus a legal privilege may well attach to all of his affairs. Discuss them with no one, Laura. *No one.* Is that clear?"

"Yes, Ms. Howson."

"If someone persists in questioning you, call me immediately or send someone to find me. That Wilken boy or someone. *By no means* leave visitors alone in these offices. Understand?"

"Yes, Ms. Howson."

"It's possible the police will show up with a warrant. Thanks to those fascists on the court, the Fifth Amendment has been written out of the Constitution. Still, one must hold out for brighter days. If the police *do* appear, do not show them *anything* until you locate me. Or Dean Randolph. You know from your own experience how the police can be. Right, Laura?"

Laura nodded dumbly.

"Very well. Let's be sure they don't do it to Professor Usser, okay?"

"Yes, Ms. Howson. Ms. Howson?"

"Yes, Laura?"

"Dr. Lonborg has been calling to ask what the faculty is doing about Professor Usser. What should I tell him?"

"Tell him that as usual the faculty is doing nothing constructive. Tell him, in fact, that the faculty finally has Lawrence Usser exactly where they want him. But I'm sure he knows that already. Just tell Adam to talk to me. Is that all?"

"Yes, Ms. Howson."

The woman nodded curtly, pivoted like a sergeant major and marched out of the room without another word. I followed along as best I could, making a silent vow to try to talk with Laura Nifton once again, in a place less cowing than the bowels of the Berkeley Law School and the umbra of Elmira Howson's heavy stare.

TWELVE

Professor Howson was tall and trim, with a square jaw, a high cheek, a thin lip and an aquiline nose that hinted of royal genes. Her hair was short, with a slight wave that sent auburn streaks across her forehead in the style of a current vice-presidential candidate. Her eyes gleamed with a glint of purpose that I suspected was both perpetual and grandiose.

Her martinet's stride led me back to the main hallway, then to a narrow staircase, then to a small, militantly tidy office on the floor above. There were no windows, no skylights, no hint of the often lawless world that festered outside the book-lined walls. I guessed that was exactly the way she wanted it.

She sat behind her desk and pointed to my assigned seat. As I was getting comfortable her phone rang. She picked it up and spoke in short, sharp phrases, her side of the conversation an impatient rattle.

The subject seemed to be the spring graduation exercises. The speaker chosen by the senior class was not a lawyer or a judge but a comedian, best known for his late-night television appearances and his bawdy, manic chatter. He was not acceptable to the faculty. A student protest march was threatened, even a strike. Ms. Howson made it clear that she thought the faculty should reverse its stand. The person on the other end of the line disagreed, vehemently enough for me to hear the muffled moans. The conversation surged and waned, then surged again. I looked around the office.

The books were mostly about domestic relations matters. The diplomas were from Oberlin and Michigan Law. The certificates of admission were to the bar of the U.S. Supreme Court and the Ninth Circuit Court of Appeals. She was a member of the American Bar Association and the Association of Woman Law Professors. Her interest in art was nonexistent, and was any evidence that she had a personal life that included a spouse or a child. Which made her like a priest, a specialist in matters of the family who had no family of her own. The telephone debate raged onward, until Professor Howson hung up the phone as though she was trying to stun it into a permanent silence.

"This place is a zoo," she muttered. "A bureaucratic joke. It's so reactionary it makes Ed Meese look like Karl Marx." She shook her head with disgust. "*Bees* arrange themselves more sensibly than this. I'm Elmira Howson. I teach Family Law and related obsolescences."

"Marsh Tanner."

She nodded crisply. "In what capacity are you looking into the Usser case?"

It was a question I'd been dodging for what seemed like a year. I tried to dodge again. "I can't name my client at this time. All I can tell you is I'm trying to learn what happened and why."

She nodded and thought about it. "Since Larry's already in jail, it doesn't make sense that you'd be working against his interests. I mean, the police already have that side taken care of. My guess is it's the parents. Right?"

I gave off no more than a knowing smile, or so I hoped.

"Okay," she went on. "So the Ussers hired you to try to get Larry off. I don't have any problem with that. Or maybe you're working for Jake Hattie. It doesn't matter. What do you want to know? What have you found out? And what did Laura tell you back there?"

No one asks questions more expertly than law professors, and these were assembly-line products—precise, relentless, slick. I found myself sweating the way I had sweated a quarter century before, when the questions involved the requisites of a binding contract or the nuances of proximate cause, and seemed far beyond an answer. "Laura told me nothing," I began. "You got to her before I had a chance to pump her."

Ms. Howson frowned dubiously. "Are you sure? Laura's unfit for that job, of course. Larry hired her out of pity—she's the sister of one of his causes. He defended her brother in a murder case and got him acquitted on insanity grounds. When he got out of Napa he stopped by his sister's place to get his clothes and rip off all her money before he hit the streets. Larry gave her a job because he mistakenly feels responsible for his client's heartlessness. Laura's a harmless little waif, I suppose. But I should probably get her out of Larry's office before she gives away the store to the first cop who shows up."

"You mean you're afraid there's something incriminating in Usser's office?"

The professor groused as though I'd cited an irrelevant code section. "I'm not saying that at all. I'm just saying as a matter of principle the police shouldn't be allowed to walk into a law professor's office and ransack his private papers."

"Even a law professor who killed his wife?"

I thought it might get a rise out of her but all it got was a mild irritation. "Don't be ridiculous. Why would Larry do that?"

"I don't know. You tell me."

"Any problems Larry was having with Dianne could be resolved in a divorce court. There's no reason on earth why it should have led to more than that."

"Even if she was sleeping around on him? Even if she'd found a lover?"

She eyed me levelly and made me squirm. "I have reason to believe that whether Dianne did or did not have a lover was of no interest at all to Larry."

"Why? Because he had one of his own?"

She smiled lazily, incomprehensibly flirtatious, though only for an instant. "What makes you think that?"

"Hints. His sexuality seems to float over like a blimp every time his name is mentioned."

Elmira Howson touched her forefinger to her lips and considered me and my mission. "Do you really think the murder has something to do with Larry's sex life?" she asked after a moment. "Or Dianne's, for that matter?"

I shrugged. "She was nude, she was ready for seduction or appeared to be, her sexual organs were mutilated. It seems as good a line of inquiry as any."

She nodded twice, then shrugged. "I know nothing at all about his wife's behavior, carnal or otherwise."

"Okay. Let's stick to the professor. Was he sexually active outside the marriage?"

"Yes."

"Do you know that for certain?"

She paused. "Yes."

"Was it a recent thing or had it been going on for a long time?"

"For as long as I've known him. Or almost."

"Which is how long?"

"Eight years."

When I hesitated, Ms. Howson stood up and began to pace the room, circumambulating my chair as though I was a wagon train and she was a Comanche. "Do I sense disapproval, Mr. Tanner?" she asked archly. "Am I in the presence of a moralist? Or perhaps you're born again."

I shook my head. "I have no desire to pass judgment on Usser's conduct or anyone else's. Not yet, anyway. And my judgments never affect my work, they just affect my conscience."

"A conscience? How quaint. Do you find it of use to you in the modern world, Mr. Tanner?"

"Occasionally. You don't?"

She circled me once more, talking as she went. I suppressed an urge to trip her. "A conscience is excess baggage," she declared while she was somewhere at my back. "Ethics are of interest only to those who perceive themselves as definitively ethical and others as definitely not. So let's get back to Larry. There are men in the world who cannot be entirely satisfied with just one woman, Mr. Tanner."

"And vice versa?"

"Of course."

"Was Larry that kind of man?'

"I believe so. Definitely."

"And are you that kind of woman?"

She paused. "I seem to be claiming that distinction, don't I?"

"Would you like to talk about it?"

"About what?"

"You and Usser."

Her smile confirmed that she was getting a rather nonaca-
demic kick out of the subject matter. "What purpose would it
serve?"

"I don't know yet."

"I see none at all."

"You're taking a risk, aren't you?"

"How?"

"You might have information that would help clear him."

"I doubt it."

"I might be a better judge."

"You might; you might not. At this stage of the game I choose
to keep my own counsel."

"Just answer this," I insisted. "Are there any men who would
be incensed by your liaison with Lawrence Usser? A husband,
current or ex? A lover, current or former?"

She was shaking her head before I finished. "When I termi-
nate a relationship, I do it in a way that leaves the man without
the slightest desire to see me again. Believe me. In that sense I
am a truly monogamous being."

"Is your relationship with Usser current and continuing?"

She frowned. "It was until the murder. We have met only
formally since then. But I have no reason to believe it will not
resume once he is freed from this travesty the police have inflicted upon him."

She had closed one line so I tried another. "Had Usser been
acting strangely of late? Anything to indicate he was losing his
grip?"

"He was under a lot of tension, if that's what you mean. He
seemed to be drinking more. Losing his temper quite often. But
what does *that* have to do with anything? He didn't do it. A fact
which is proved by the marked *increase* in those tendencies *after*
his wife's death. He was devastated by it, Mr. Tanner. Not at all
relieved. I was quite surprised by his reaction, to tell you the
truth, given certain, ah, amatory outbursts he had made in my
presence over the past year or so."

"If he didn't do it, who did?"

She shook her head. "I haven't the faintest idea. I met Dianne
only a few times. She didn't like me, she didn't like the school. I

suppose she resented the time Larry spent here. She rarely attended faculty functions, not that I can blame her for that. Faculty parties have the approximate ambience of a poorly attended wake."

I decided to go for a bigger bite. "Who else around here was sleeping with Usser?"

"What makes you ask that?"

"I've heard rumors."

She shrugged casually. "Larry was an attractive man. He enjoyed the company of women. Naturally there were rumors."

I smiled. "Which ones of them were true?"

"I'm sure I don't know. I mean, I'd be the last to know, wouldn't I? Or next to last, at least."

"How about his research assistant?"

"Krista? They are very close. He relies on her a great deal. There are those who say she wrote every word of his books, every line of his briefs, every phrase of his speeches."

"Is it true?"

"I don't know. She is very intelligent. And very lovely." And very young, Elmira Howson thought but didn't have to say.

"Any other women around here Usser is close to?"

"I certainly hope not." For the first time a note of regret slipped into Elmira Howson's tone. "So many intellectuals have been satyrs as well. Odd, don't you think?" She had abstracted the subject, making it useless to me.

"How about the faculty?" I asked. "Is there a groundswell of support for Usser's release?"

"I'm afraid not. Larry was not . . . popular. The faculty is bitterly divided these days. Larry and I, plus a few others, are trying to break pedagogic patterns that have existed for fifty years. There is jealousy and there is a stark terror at what we are seeking in the way of change. I'm sure a majority of the faculty greeted news of Larry's incarceration with the first orgasm they've had in years."

"How about Grunig?"

"What about Grunig?"

"Why were he and Usser feuding?"

She shook her head wearily, as though the subject had already exhausted her. "Larry was Gus Grunig's protégé. Grunig teaches criminal law and procedure too. He and Larry soon split

over matters of social and political philosophy, but I'll give Gus
credit. That didn't turn him against Larry, not in the personal
sense. It was only when academic issues raised their ugly heads
that the split came. And when it came, it was a real thunder-
storm. Larry and Gus haven't spoken in a year without an inter-
mediary."

"What were the specific issues?"

"Why don't you talk to Gus? He's mounting a rather aggres-
sive campaign to be appointed dean of the law school when the
incumbent steps down next year. He'll therefore be in a position
to give you a totally biased account of the entire history of our
faculty contretemps. As biased as my own account would be."

"But why did their quarrel become so heated? Surely more
than pedagogic matters were involved."

Elmira Howson shrugged. "You know what they say. Academic wrangles are always so vicious because the stakes are always so small." Her smile was devoid of humor. "There *was*
something personal between them on top of the more esoteric
issues, but neither of them have ever talked about it and I don't
think I should tell you what it was. I'm the only one other than
Gus and Larry who knows, by the way, so don't waste your
breath asking questions in the hallways and the restrooms."

"Tell me a little more about the pressures Usser's been under
lately."

She looked at me for a long minute, then returned to her
desk. "Look, Mr. Tanner. I'm telling you this because you seem
to be an intelligent man and because *someone* involved in all this
ought to know what Larry's had to deal with lately. Let's start
with his teaching. It's fashionable in today's anti-intellectual
environment to make fun of academics—absentminded professors, naive innocents, impractical idealists, pointy-headed
intellectuals and all that. Plus we've all read the more or less
accurate reports of the current generation of students and their
fixation on wealth and materialistic success. But in the better
professional schools—and Berkeley Law, like Stanford and
Boalt Hall, is definitely one of those—there still exists, thank
the Lord, a hard core of students who truly want to change our
hapless world. To make it better not only for the calamari and
tax shelter set, but for the underclass as well. These students
are very demanding, Mr. Tanner, and it's a real challenge to

teach them. Not because they're not bright; on the contrary, some of them are brilliant. But because if you don't present the legal system to them in a way that admits to a degree of hope, a dash of optimism, *a place to go with their ethical instincts and their professional lives,* then we lose those kids entirely. They drop out and become poets or social workers or whatever, to the detriment of all of us who believe the law is at the cutting edge of social change. So that's pressure point number one, especially since Larry tried to turn *all* his students into selfless altruists. A Promethean task if there ever was one."

She looked to see that I was with her. After I nodded my understanding she continued.

"Pressure point number two was the faculty wrangle that Gus will describe for you ad nauseam. And pressure point number three—and in Larry's case the most painful one—was his trial practice. Larry began having doubts about his role in the larger scheme of things, he was becoming consumed by the tensions between madness and sanity, violence and police power, guilt and innocence, advocacy and truth, the whole spectrum of issues that the criminal system demands be addressed but so few practitioners really engage. Larry was haunted, from time to time, by the thought that instead of advancing the course of civilization he was in fact setting it back, that in defending and freeing his clients he was *contributing to* the crippling bestiality that rages in the streets and makes cowards of us all, the barbarism that he was so determined to eradicate by uplifting the condition of man, particularly the mentally unbalanced. He had these horrible *nightmares,* of madmen doing vicious, violent things and going unpunished for them."

"Things like the things that were done to his wife," I interjected.

She looked at me as though the connection had never occurred to her. "Yes. I suppose."

"And he was drinking a lot as a result of all this?"

"Some. Not a lot. Just more than before."

"What else?"

"Forgetfulness, perhaps. Increasing egotism and insensitivity. He tried to be solicitous of other people's needs. After his wife died he seemed to be less so, more caught up in his own requirements, more focused on himself."

"Did he ever threaten you? Hit you? Frighten you, Ms. Howson?"

Her back arched against the chair. Her glare was chilling and dismissive. "Larry? Me? Don't be ridiculous. You ask awfully strange questions, Mr. Tanner, for a man who's out to clear Larry Usser's name."

THIRTEEN

The law library was my next stop. It was guarded by a security system worthy of a prison. Somehow, I pushed through an aluminum bar, crossed an invisible eye and passed inspection by a skeptical librarian, all without setting off alarms.

On the glass door to the main reading room a sign had been taped at eye level:

CAUTION—THERE HAS BEEN A
RECENT RASH OF THEFTS
IN THIS LIBRARY. PLEASE BE ALERT.
KEEP PERSONAL BELONGINGS WITH YOU AT ALL TIMES.

I went in anyway, spotted a young woman shelving books and asked her how to get to carrel 209. She pointed to a blue metal staircase rising out of the middle of several rows of law reviews arrayed on metal shelves. I took the stairs, making noise, smelling mold, climbing into the stacks where only the serious students and the committed faculty ever dared.

The carrels were white metal booths attached to the back wall of the building, with built-in tables and shelves and straight-backed metal chairs. I found number 209 without any trouble. The person sitting in its egglike shell looked young enough to be below the age of legal consent. Her cheeks were appled and round, her nose pert, her eyes the color of the sky at morning. But despite her wholesome aspect she looked up at me beneath a frown designed to shove me on my way. I held my ground and asked if she was Krista Hellgren. She nodded impatiently and asked me what I wanted.

"I'd like to talk to you about Professor Usser."

She shook her head. "I'm not authorized to discuss his work. I can tell you that his article on the bifurcated trial will appear as scheduled in the next issue of *The Hastings Law Review*. If that's what you're interested in."

"It's not."

Our eyes met, then dodged. She was lovely in a bucolic way, flawless and unaffected, a way that had the impact of a nocturne, not a march. She wore Levi's and a sweatshirt that matched her eyes. She had ink smudges on her fingers and a gold band around her wrist. Her white-blond hair was disciplined by a coiled cloth headband. Her breasts roamed easily beneath her shirt as she twisted to look at me, and she caught me admiring them. My face must have reddened because she smiled a hardened smile that told me I was just what she expected me to be and I should be ashamed of it. "Are you from the police?" she asked.

I shook my head. "I'm a private investigator. I'm looking into the circumstances of Professor Usser's arrest. Can you give me a few minutes?"

She glanced quickly up and down the aisle, then looked at the books piled all around her. "No. Not now. Not here."

"Where and when?"

She ignored my question. "Are you telling me the truth? Are you really a private investigator?"

"That's not the kind of thing people usually brag about."

This time her smile meant what it said, which once would have been close to everything I ever wanted to hear. "But I don't *know* anything. Not about Mrs. Usser. I mean Ms. Renzel."

"That's all right. I just need some information about your boss."

"But why do you think . . . who have you been talking to?"

"Various people. Students. Faculty."

Her eyes widened into sapphires set in pearl. "What did they say about Professor Usser and me?"

"Just that the two of you worked very closely together."

Her look was pained. "They said more than that, didn't they?"

"Maybe a hint or two."

"*They don't know how it is. None* of them. They think they do but they don't." Her lips vibrated bitterly, and she wiped away a tear. Her emotions were complex enough to fill a book the size of the ones that lined her shelf. She sniffed, then wiped her nose. "If I talk to you, will it help him be found innocent?"

"It might." I decided it wasn't quite a lie.

"He is, you know. Innocent. He couldn't possibly be convicted. He's not . . . that way."

"What way is he?"

"Brilliant. Kind. Oh, I can't talk now or I'll start to cry. Come to my place tonight. I'll be home any time after nine. It's not safe to walk home from campus after nine, unless you use the escort service."

She added the last as though to explain her departure from her studies at such an early hour, then gave me her address and instructions how to find it. I told her I'd see her then, and went back to the staircase and made my way back to the faculty directory and looked up Gus Grunig, wondering all the while if Krista Hellgren's beauty was a trophy a man would kill to make his own.

Grunig's office was near Usser's. I retraced my steps, pausing at Usser's office to see if Laura Nifton was still there. The door was locked and no sounds came from inside, so I continued down the hall till I found the door marked GRUNIG.

The clippings on his bulletin board made obvious the differences between the men. Grunig's were from William Buckley and Thomas Sowell, and they railed against a host of fashionable liberal thought, from affirmative action to sex education to the current requirements for a legal search and seizure. I knocked on the door and was told it was open. When I went inside I found myself looking down upon a small, balding man who sat like a befuddled bear cub in the aftermath of a cyclone.

Gus Grunig was almost a dwarf, his limbs and hands no bigger than a boy's. In comparison, his office seemed oversized and overstocked, as though built to house an entire law firm and Grunig was the lone survivor.

When I approached his desk, Grunig was reading a case reported in the *Federal Supplement* and pecking some information into the Apple II on the corner of his desk. He heard me coming, put down the book, and scowled over the top of the monitor. "Is this about the faculty search committee?"

"No."

"Good," he growled. "That means whatever you're here about will be an improvement upon what I was expecting."

"I'm here about Lawrence Usser."

"I retract my statement." Grunig closed his eyes and bowed his head. The overhead light made his pate seem a peeled potato. After hibernating for another minute he raised his head and spoke. "Who are you?"

"My name's Marsh Tanner. I'm a detective."

"Police?"

"Private."

"Hired by whom?"

"I'm not at liberty to say."

"Then you have no power to compel me to respond to your questions."

"Only the power of the search for truth."

His smile was as dubious as mine. "Yes, well, that concept is an elusive one, isn't it. These days truth has become in the nature of a chattel, an object to be owned. He who owns the medium owns the message, or thereabouts. I may do an article on it one day, take up the mantle of Mr. McLuhan, so to speak. But I digress. What can I tell you about Lawrence, except that I wish him well?"

I was about to answer when a young man stuck his head in the door. His hair was of Prince Valiant, his beard of Vandyke. "Can I talk to you about my grade in Crimes sometime, Mr. Grunig?" he asked, clearly expecting a refusal.

"Of course."

His eyes widened. "When?"

Grunig looked at me. "Five minutes?"

"Ten," I said.

Grunig repeated the figure. The kid said "Great" and disappeared.

"He believes I disapprove of his hair and dress," Grunig said when the door had closed. "And he's right. He also believes that my feelings affect the way I mark his examinations. In that he is wrong. Actually, he's somewhat refreshing, in an odd sort of way. A throwback to the days when they all looked like him, the brighter the student, the more disheveled the aspect. Now they all look like IBM trainees and the bright ones are all divorced women over thirty who slave like hard-rock miners and want to work for banks. But I digress again." Grunig lowered a pair of spectacles from the top of his head to the bridge of his nose. "What can I tell you about Larry?"

"Whatever you know."

"At one time I could have told you much. Now I am not so sure I know anything at all." He tilted his chair away from me, until he was virtually horizontal. "You should understand that around here I am known as the Fossil. A dinosaur in miniature. I make my students work hard. I make them think, not merely regurgitate. I dispute both their values and their tastes. I have a host of principles of my own, developed over a period of time longer than most of my critics have been alive, and I demand that they be acknowledged, if not acceded to. I find almost all current trends appalling, the product of the total lack of rigor in our society. I see Berkeley Law as an important counter to such trends, as a bulwark, if you will. Thus I am didactic. Doctrinaire. Goebbels, some of them call me behind my back." He shrugged off the taint. "In any case, anything I tell you should be measured against this background."

I nodded, and waited for the disproportionately weighty voice to continue. Gus Grunig was staring at his computer, as though answers to the questions I would ask were merely mathematical, the product of data and device.

"Larry, needless to say, was precisely my opposite," Grunig said abruptly. "What he cheered, I bemoaned, and vice versa, whether the subject was legal, social or economic. Our disputes were legendary, yet despite our diverse perspectives I regarded Larry Usser as my surrogate sibling for many years. We were as close as two men can be in this day and age, when male friendship brings on whispers and snickers if it aspires to exceed the shallow. My regard extended to his family as well. I taught little Lisa how to ride a bike. I have been a regular contributor to the crisis center. In short, I loved Lawrence Usser, and I can say that about no other man of my acquaintance. Present or past."

Grunig's sigh was long and pained. I asked him what had happened between him and Usser.

He seemed to shrink even further, as though he wished to

disappear entirely. "These are difficult times for places such as this. Funds are diminishing. The profession itself is under fire and founders without clear vision. The society at large rages almost beyond our comprehension, the populace cowering in fear of violence, almost helpless. Still, here at Berkeley Law our ideals are for the most part fully developed: We know what we want to do, and that is to offer an excellent legal education to as many persons as are able to absorb it, and to as many as we are able to absorb. Some will carp about the path to excellence, others about what skills are encompassed by the term 'legal education,' about what ethical component should be included in the phrase, for example. But basically our problem is not definitional, it is practical. The pursuit of our ideals must necessarily take place in the reality of the age. We can only draw our students and our faculty from the world that is, not the world we might wish to exist."

"For example?" I prompted.

"Lawrence, Elmira Howson, others of their ilk, they look at the faculty and see only token numbers of blacks, women, other minorities. And they say that condition must change. Period. End of discussion. I and others insist that one more question needs be asked: Have we discriminated against minority applicants on bases unrelated to their teaching requirements? If we have, of course we must change. Invidious discrimination must be eradicated. Totally. The same with students. If we are keeping qualified minority students out, then of course we must act immediately to admit them. But if students or faculty are *not qualified,* if their admission into the Berkeley Law School would result in reduced levels of teaching and scholarship, in an inferior quality of graduates in terms of education and ability, then they *must not be hired or admitted.* We should encourage them to upgrade their skills and apply again, we should direct them to programs where this could happen, but we must not lower our standards. The minute we do so, we are threatened with total collapse, with anarchy, with an absence of excellence that will merely accelerate a similar trend in the society as a whole. That must not happen. I will oppose it with every fiber of my being."

Grunig stopped to gasp for air. His face had reddened with the force of his oration, from the Calvinist fires that burned inside him. It took a minute for the spell to break, then he

smiled at me sheepishly. "It all seems to outsiders like yourself
as such a simple difference of opinion. But believe me, its ram-
ifications in a place like this are enormous. Then of course there
is the problem of the curriculum."

"What problem is that?"

"Lawrence commissioned a study to determine where our
graduates were finding employment. The results were not surprising to me, but they were both surprising and disappointing
to him. It seems the brightest students at Berkeley Law over the
past five years have ended up in San Francisco working for the
large corporate law firms. The Pillsburys, the Morrison Forsters,
the Brobecks, et cetera. Larry saw this as an indictment of our
entire approach to teaching. He wanted a course list that would
result in the best and brightest ending up in the trenches, fo-
menting revolution. And he went further. He suggested that
those faculty members whose research aided the corporate firms
in achieving their ends, that promoted the establishment rather
than the outcasts, were undermining the entire thrust of the law
as he believed it should be, which was to oppose the status quo
and to undermine privilege wherever it existed. He attacked
some of our faculty with a vehemence more appropriate to
criminals or fascists, and of course there was an appropriate
reaction. What Lawrence *really* wants is to program our students
to do his bidding after they leave here. And several of us have
objections to that. A year ago, when he called me a monarchist
in print, Lawrence and I were cleaved irretrievably."

Grunig smiled wanly. I said the first thing that came to mind:
"I'm sorry."

Grunig shrugged. "If you ask questions around here for very
long, you will hear many accounts of our quarrels. Lawrence
and I disagreed over these and other subjects, and we did so
violently and publicly. He once threw a drink in my face. I once
called him a child. Our public pugilism lasted for about six
months, until we both were exhausted by it. It is not an epoch I
am proud of. Quite the opposite, in fact."

He stopped and looked at me closely. "I tell you this to put
my next comment in context: There is no way on earth that
Lawrence could have done to Dianne what the papers say was
done to her. He is capable of anger, of rage, of jealousy, of
insult. He is *not* capable of butchery. Unless there is evidence of

drug use of some pathogenic amount, there is no way Lawrence Usser is guilty of this crime."

Grunig paused for breath. His tiny body heaved like a bloated fish. "Having said that, I will also tell you that I am resisting all forms of student and/or faculty support for his defense. We are scholars here, not advocates. We must remain neutral on *all* issues of guilt or innocence. We defend principles, not people. It is the only way to maintain what integrity we still possess."

He came to a stop while I was still awash in his courage and his convictions. His eyes blazed until he heard a knock on his door. Then he glanced at the clock on the wall above my head and prepared to ask me to leave. "Just one more thing," I said quickly. "You mentioned that your dispute with Usser began a year ago. Did that correspond with a change in Usser's personality? Or with a psychological problem he might have developed at about that time?"

"With the onset of legal insanity, you mean?" Grunig's smile ridiculed my predictability. "The short answer is no. Lawrence was not insane or anything close to it. The more helpful answer is yes, over the past few months Lawrence became increasingly fractious, at least in my opinion. He increased the amounts of scholarship and consultation he engaged in to inhuman levels. He was always late, always behind schedule, always on the phone. He seemed to be engaged in some religious rite, if you want the truth, to be working to accomplish something that would compensate for his rather earthly sins. There was a strong element of fanaticism in his life, no doubt about it. I found it quite disturbing. I even suggested he see someone professionally. Someone besides his sidekick Lonborg." Grunig shook his head. "Lawrence laughed at me and accused me of wanting him put away. Now he is just that—away—and I am as sick at heart as I have ever been, save one instance. I must tell you, however, that I do and will continue to resist his return to the faculty in an active role until a final judgment of his guilt has been reached."

"You don't believe in the presumption of innocence?"

"I believe in it for the common man with all my heart. I believe, however, that those of us who endeavor to order the society—who teach students the concepts of right and wrong and suggest the processes through which such determinations should be reached—we must be held to a higher standard. Our lessons cannot be seen to spring from a desperate self-interest."

He seemed to be waiting for me to comment, but I had no idea what to say. His moral sense was so large it barely left me room enough to breathe, let alone debate.

"There is one thing more you should know," he said after a moment.

"What's that?"

"Five years ago I was engaged to be married to a fellow member of the faculty of this institution. You should know her name before you proceed with your investigation."

"Professor Howson?"

He tilted his head. "Very perceptive. Mutt and Jeff, they called us. I was very much in love, for the first time in twenty years. Elmira uttered similar sentiments, until Larry seduced her away from me. There are those who will tell you my differences with Larry stem entirely from that betrayal. They will be wrong—our friendship survived my heartache and my fury— but that will not stop them from talking. If ignorance were a muffler, the world would be as silent as a tomb."

I started to leave, convinced that Usser's purloining of Elmira Howson was the personal matter Ms. Howson had been referring to a short while earlier. But then I reconsidered. It didn't fit. It wasn't a secret, first of all, and the timing was all wrong. Usser's friendship with Grunig had continued for four more years. I settled back in my chair and ignored Grunig's hints that he was tired of talking to me. "I understand you're hoping to be appointed dean next year," I said to him.

"Yes. That's correct."

"Is part of your campaign an anti-Usser movement?"

"I suppose some would call it that."

"In what way?"

Grunig crossed his arms above his barrel chest. "The main change I will recommend upon my appointment is the abolition of all forms of consultation arrangements in litigation matters of the kind that Lawrence so frequently engages in. The imprimatur of this great school should not be lent to one side or the other in a courtroom dispute. No matter what the stakes."

Grunig's final words were quick hard bites of rage. I watched his granite eyes a moment, then asked my question. "There was something personal between you and Usser that you haven't mentioned yet, wasn't there? Something more serious than him calling you a monarchist?"

"Why do you say that?" Grunig's look was stricken.

"I've heard rumors. And I have hunches."

"What if there was?"

"It might help me put all this together if I could know what it involved."

"Put what together?"

"The reason Usser might have killed his wife."

"I've told you," Grunig insisted. "I cannot believe he did it."

"Then all the more reason for all the facts to come out. One of them might exculpate him, based on a connection no one but Usser can explain."

Grunig thought it over. Like most people I encounter, he was reluctant to trust me. Like many of them, he finally allowed himself to be persuaded to speak out anyway.

"The matter was kept from everyone at the time, Mr. Tanner. No one knows the truth except for Lawrence and myself and one other person who, though sworn to secrecy, would I'm sure divulge it immediately if she were at all persuaded it would help acquit Lawrence Usser. Which is why I'm telling it to you now."

"What's it all about?"

Grunig closed his eyes. "Two years ago a young man on this campus developed an obsessive attraction for a coed. He followed her everywhere, called her hourly, slept in her yard some nights, hounded her fiendishly, for months on end. She was progressively amused, annoyed and finally frightened by the devotions of the young man."

"I've heard a little about it," I said.

"Yes, I thought you might have. Well, one evening, the girl and the boy she *truly* cared for decided to torment the tormentor. While he was watching from his car, they began what used to be known as heavy petting. Rather than driving the suitor away, however, the tactic enraged him. He advanced to the porch where the couple was embracing and killed the girl with a single thrust of his knife, then fled down the street, leaving his car behind. He was later caught and tried for his crime. The killer's name was Ronald Nifton. The dead girl's name was Swanson."

"Right. I remember."

"Do you remember the name of the boy on the porch?"

"No."

"Few do. He was a witness at the trial, but the focus was on the maniacal young killer, of course. Well, to make a long story short, Lawrence Usser defended Nifton, won him an acquittal on the basis of insanity, and then was instrumental in seeing that Nifton was released from the state mental hospital shortly thereafter, to resume his place in the society of free men."

"Nifton," I repeated. "The girl in Usser's office is named Nifton."

"That's right. She is the sister of the murderous young man. But my point is not Ronald Nifton or his sister, it is the other boy. The real boyfriend of the dead girl. Do you know what happened to him?"

"No."

"He left Berkeley ultimately, haunted by the death of the girl and the thought that he should have somehow been able to prevent it. He wandered the West for several months, used drugs in increasing quantities, was arrested for shoplifting twice. Finally, a year ago and a year after the murder, he killed himself down in Big Sur. He jumped off a bridge on Highway 1 and was smashed on the rocks below."

"That's very sad."

"Yes. His name was Wendell Dainwright. He was the child of a couple that included his natural mother and the stepfather who adopted him. His birth was the product of an unfortunate if not calamitous marriage that ended in divorce many years ago. The marriage was mine. The boy was my son. Now he is dead, and thanks to Lawrence Usser the Nifton man appears before me regularly, amid the swirl of Telegraph Avenue, to remind me of my loss and of his own outrageous liberty."

FOURTEEN

By the time I found my way back to the car, it was pushing six and time to eat. I drove down Bancroft, circled left, and came back up Telegraph Avenue, where so many young people had marched for their own immoderate formulations of peace and freedom, where so many arms of the state resisted them, where the scars of those struggles still linger twenty years after the wounds first began to be inflicted.

Once a beacon to the world or at least a vocal portion of it, symbol of the ascendancy of youth and the assault on fixed ideas, Telegraph Avenue seemed to have no essence anymore, seemed to be trying to do too much for too many and as a consequence did too little for too few. Perhaps it's because society as a whole has no essence beyond a shriveled cinder, and Telegraph is merely its mirror. Or perhaps it's just that Berkeley's day has passed, its revolution come full circle so that it worships what it once reviled. Or perhaps, as I raced toward my fiftieth year of life, I was begging the past to be more momentous than it was, in a piteous attempt to augment my own lame history. I sighed. The traffic stopped and started. I stuttered my way along and studied the street more closely.

A few of the old stores remained—Moe's, Cody's, the Mediterraneum, Foley's Drugs, Larry Blake's, Nicole's. But in place of Robbie's and Fraser's and other landmarks of the past was a string of storefronts that marked the recent shift in Berkeley's passions—Blondie's Pizza, Yogi's Yogurt, Thomas Sweet Ice Cream, Mrs. Field's Cookies, and Ribs R Us. The Bank of America branch still loomed large, but now was windowless, shamelessly immune to riot and revolt. On the other hand, the view of Sather Gate was blocked not by a rank of state police but by a phalanx of falafel stands on wheels.

People still thronged the avenue in impressive numbers—more people walk Telegraph Avenue than walk Times Square—but they were not the same mix I'd seen in the mid-sixties, when all the world had seemed to stroll the street. Today's Telegraph was mostly given over to street people—vendors pushing everything from toys to ties to crystal amulets; aging foreign students jabbering in oddly warbled tongues; dingy transients with bedrolls on their backs and lunacy behind their eyes; disabled people in motored chariots scooting like a superior species through globs of plodding pedestrians, BMXers and skateboarders; street musicians exchanging riffs for tips; and more visible than all the other breeds the never-young kids displaying their erupting sexuality or their still-untested courage or their nuclear nihilism in the most impudent manner they could both imagine and afford.

By the time I reached Bancroft Way I had decided what was missing was the radiant spark that had arched across the avenue some twenty years ago, that electric sense that things were happening on Telegraph Avenue that had never happened before, not in Berkeley, not anywhere, things that would cleanse the world, bleach out its stains forever, perfect the heretofore imperfect march of man. Now Telegraph was merely bogus, to use Cal's term: stale, warmed over, tired, bizarre by necessity and not by choice, too weary to be worthy of its past. Still, by the time I turned left at Bancroft I sensed that I'd be back on Telegraph before the Renzel case had ended, looking for something or someone that would be very hard to find, and probably dangerous to seek. I turned right on Shattuck and a few blocks later settled for a hamburger at Oscar's, which had been in town long before anyone knew what falafel was.

I chewed my sandwich without enthusiasm and watched the clock tick its way toward seven. The imprecision of my errand still disturbed me. I was supposed to be finding proof that Law-

rence Usser was sane and had been when he killed his wife. So
far, I'd found nothing at all to indicate he wasn't, but nothing
much to indicate he was.

Arrayed against me was the very act for which he was imprisoned. Ladies and gentlemen of the jury, the prosecution
claims Professor Usser was sane on the night of the crime. Now
I ask you: Would a sane man have done what Lawrence Usser
did? Of course not, and thank you very much. Unfortunately
for the Renzels, at this point that argument might well prevail
against any evidence I could offer against it. I licked a dab of
mustard off my lip, got in my Buick and headed back the way
I'd come, this time toward the city of Piedmont, a little knoll of
wealth between Oakland and Berkeley, one that could hold its
own with any of the better-known enclaves of privilege that
ringed the bay.

Everything gets quiet in wealthy neighborhoods. The birds
seem stunned by their surroundings, the dogs cowed, the traffic
disciplined to be seen and not heard. Trucks are an endangered
species. The garbage probably comes in Styrofoam cans and is
picked up by a tribe of barefoot Indians, one to a customer. As
I wound my way up LaSalle, on Piedmont's most luscious hill, I
wished I'd put a higher octane in the tank.

The Ussers lived in oddly tasteless splendor behind a prickly
holly hedge that allowed only invited guests to see just how
wonderful life was treating them. I parked in the street, let
myself through the iron gate that broke the forbidding thicket
and advanced to the door feeling that someone would soon
suggest I use the tradesmen's entrance.

It took only two seconds for the door to open behind my
knock, which meant a security system had warned of my approach. The man who opened the door looked to be sixty and
was probably eighty. He wore black trousers and a light gray
jacket and was frail and stooped, just the way movies make them
out to be. I told him my name and that Mrs. Usser had told me
this was a convenient time to call. He showed me to a parlor off
the foyer, said he would be with me shortly, then shuffled out
of sight.

It took him longer than that, long enough for me to inspect
the little oils on the wall, the little porcelains on the mantel, the
little Wedgwood on the tables. I was admiring what purported

to be an original Corot when the old gentleman slid open the parlor door, looked at me and bowed.

"Mr. Usser, sir."

"Thank you, ah . . ." I raised my brow.

"Price, sir."

"Thank you, Price."

Price disappeared, leaving his employer in his stead.

He was large enough to fill the doorway, and angry enough to punch me in the nose. He advanced on me like an awkward robot, his oiled gray hair flapping from the vigor of his approach, his square jaw as sharp as a destroyer's prow. He wore a velvet smoking jacket and silk slippers, and carried a Malacca walking stick. When he spoke, his voice reverberated with authority, suggested my quick surrender.

"I'm Carlton Usser. My wife was somewhat incoherent about your business here. Something about you prowling around in my son's house this morning, for some mysterious purpose. So perhaps you can enlighten me, Mister, ah . . ."

"Tanner. John Marshall Tanner. I'm a private detective."

"And your business here? Specifically."

"I'm trying to find out why Dianne Renzel died."

"I see." He tapped his stick on the parquet floor. "The police believe she was murdered by my son. Do you agree with them?"

His hooded eyes challenged me to accuse his offspring, and threatened violent objection if I did. "It's too soon to believe anyone," I said. "I've only been on this for a day."

"Who's paying your fee?"

"That's confidential for now."

Usser paused and looked at me with calmer eyes than those he'd brought through the door. He searched my face for the kinds of clues all wheeler-dealers think reside there, then began to tap his stick again, faster and faster, accenting his frustration. The wildness in his eyes indicated that the arrest of his only son had been a bitter hint that his powers had badly faded.

"Oddly enough I was discussing this matter with my attorney only this morning," Usser remarked, suddenly affable, reaching some decision. "Clifton Daltry. Do you know him?"

I shook my head, which irritated him again.

"He suggested I might employ a detective myself, to help prove my son's innocence. What do you think of that?"

I shrugged. "Probably a good idea."

"Of course, if *you* are competent, and if you're as objective as you suggest, an additional investigator would be redundant."

I smiled at Usser's effort to save himself some money. "Maybe. On the other hand, I don't claim to be perfect. Another investigator might help out."

"So what do you recommend?"

"It's up to you. All I can tell you is, you're not my client. Our interests may or may not conflict. If I find evidence indicating your son did kill his wife, I'll almost certainly be asked to bring it out. If I find clear and convincing proof that he's innocent, I'll probably bring it out myself, without being asked. And if I don't find anything either way, I'll probably do whatever my client suggests."

Usser seemed not to be listening. "If I were to hire an investigator, whom would you recommend?"

"I'd recommend you use someone from over here, someone who knows the territory. But there are only three investigators I know well enough to suggest, and none of them are based in the East Bay. So I can't help you. Maybe your lawyer can."

"You're not very forthcoming."

"I am when I have something to come forth with. And when I have someone paying me to do it."

Usser scowled again and began to pace, his walking stick brandished more as a weapon than a crutch, his demeanor suggesting he was unused to indecision. "So what do you want from me?" he asked finally.

"The police are a little vague about the reason your son might have committed the crime. I thought maybe you could help me."

"The police are vague, sir, because there is no evidence that he did what they have accused him of. Lawrence is a brilliant, vibrant man. He has everything to live for. A limitless future. There was no conceivable reason for him to do what they say he did."

"Are you saying he's evolved beyond human emotion, Mr. Usser?"

"I don't know what you mean."

"I mean what if he learned his wife had taken a lover? Just for example."

"Don't be ridiculous. Dianne would have no reason to prefer another man to Lawrence. The world does not contain his equal."

Usser's soaring hyperbole momentarily silenced both of us. The cane stopped tapping, then started up again. I was conscious of time slipping away. From all of us. "You aren't really that naive, are you, Mr. Usser?"

He frowned. His face wrinkled to accommodate it. "No. I suppose not. But Dianne was not without her principles. She may have devoted her life to the spoiled and the lethargic, but she wouldn't do something as common as that. Lawrence influenced her at least that much, I'm sure."

If half the rumors I'd heard were true, Lawrence Usser's influence would have made his wife a courtesan. I refrained from pointing that out. Instead, I asked Usser if the police or the D.A. had told him anything about the case they had developed against his son.

He shook his head disgustedly. "No, except that they seem to be relying entirely on some poor, misguided . . . Well, never mind about that. When I insisted that I be given details, they refused. My attorney says nothing is made public until the preliminary hearing. And that *lawyer* Lawrence hired, that Hattie fellow, refuses to return my calls. I hope Lawrence hasn't made a horrible mistake in engaging him. Perhaps I should interfere."

I suppressed an urge to endorse Jake Hattie. "Tell me this, Mr. Usser. Did you see your son frequently over the past few months?"

Usser hesitated. "Once a week, at least. Unless he was away on a lecture tour or in a trial. Larry still values my advice," Usser added proudly, and perhaps a bit hopefully.

"Did you sense any change in his behavior of late?"

"How do you mean?"

"Did he do anything you felt was out of character in recent months? Did he surprise you in any way? Were you worried about him at all?"

Usser waved a hand impatiently. "No, no and no. The implication is absurd." Usser came to a stop in front of me. "Is there anything else?"

"Do you know how much your daughter-in-law's life was insured for?"

Usser's face turned scarlet. "I have no idea. Not that I would tell you if I did. I'll have Price show you to the door."

"Is your wife available? Perhaps I could speak with her again."

"She is not available. I'm sorry."

"How about Lisa? I'm interested in talking to her, too. Just for a minute."

Usser began to fidget, his martial aura crumbling for the first time. "Lisa isn't here."

"When will she be back?"

"I'm not sure, but it doesn't matter. She's not in any condition to speak about what happened. It's driven her . . ." Usser swallowed the word he was about to use. "It's upset her. She is still in a difficult stage of recovery. We are trying to get help for her, to convince her to talk with someone, to straighten out these wild ideas she has."

"What ideas are those?"

Usser's jaw jutted stubbornly. "They're no concern of yours."

"Who are you sending Lisa to?"

"Well, Lawrence's friend, Dr. Lonborg, has told us he would be happy to counsel Lisa. He's quite insistent about it, in fact, but Lisa refuses to commit herself. Apparently Lonborg was seeing her before Lawrence was, ah, arrested, and he wants to be sure there's no interruption in treatment. If only we could get Lisa to . . . well, that's no concern of yours either. Is there anything else? Or may I get back to my meal?"

I shook my head. "I hope you'll tell your wife I'd like a chance to speak with her sometime about all this."

"My wife knows nothing that would interest you," Usser said heavily. "Nothing at all."

"Maybe I'd be a better judge of that."

"You most certainly would not. That's an incredibly arrogant statement." Usser raised his stick as though to strike me, then looked at it as if it were an apparition.

I stood up. "I'll stop back in the morning and see if I can catch Lisa before she leaves for school. It won't take long. I'll make certain my questions don't upset her."

Usser assembled all his power and directed it to his voice. "Apparently I must make it clear that you are *not welcome here,* Mr. Tanner. Please leave us with our troubles, to resolve as we see fit. *Please.* I have been in business all my life; I am used to solving problems. I don't need your help, or anyone's. If you persist in trying to communicate with my family I shall call in the authorities."

We were almost nose to nose, teeth gritted, eyes locked, debating an assault with further words. The next sortie was about to be launched when Price appeared in the doorway. "Mr. Gable, sir."

Usser snapped out of his trance. "Thank you, Price. Show him in. Mr. Tanner was just leaving."

I stalled, hoping Howard Gable would want me to stay for the meeting. Assistant district attorneys seldom make house calls, not in my neighborhood at least, so the purpose of the visit might be of interest. I loitered until Gable came through the door, shepherded as I had been by the supercilious Price.

When he saw me Gable raised a brow. "This is Mr. Tanner," Usser said to him. "He says he's investigating the case, though in what capacity I'm not sure."

"I know," Gable said simply.

"You do?"

"Yep."

"And you approve?"

Gable shrugged. "Doesn't matter. Unless he interferes with us in some way, he can do what he wants."

"But he won't even disclose his client."

"Doesn't have to do that, either. Yet." Gable's smile was thin and just a bit sour. "Let's get at it, Mr. Usser," he went on. "You sounded a little frantic on the phone."

Usser looked at me. "I want you to leave."

I waited long enough for Gable to say something to counter the request. When he didn't, I walked toward the door. As I passed him Gable winked.

After I left the room, Carlton Usser shut the door. Price led the way toward the foyer. I lingered, then bent to tie my shoe and listened for anything I could hear. After a few seconds what I heard was Howard Gable's muffled burst of anger.

"What? You told me you'd keep *track* of her. God *damn* it."

Usser said something I couldn't hear, then Gable spoke again.

"I don't care about that, I care about the girl. . . . It's no business of yours *why* I want her. . . . What makes you think that?

. . . I'm sorry you feel that way, Mr. Usser. . . . If that's the way you want it, sure. . . . Okay, I'll take care of it. But for now I need to know *where the hell she is.* So I'd appreciate it if you'd tell me everything you know."

I was about to sneak closer to the door when Price turned and caught me. "This way, sir," he insisted. I didn't have the heart to resist.

It was a long walk to the car. When I got there, I thought up several reasons not to go anyplace for a while.

FIFTEEN

I was waiting for Howard Gable, but the first person I saw was Price. He had exchanged his butler's coat for a linen sports jacket and was strolling down the drive looking very dapper and very spry and very glad to be leaving the Ussers behind.

When he reached the street, I got out of the car and caught up to him. "Night off?" I asked, matching his stride.

"Yes, sir."

"Can I give you a ride someplace?"

"Oh, no, sir. Thank you very much."

"Been working for the Ussers long?"

"Twenty-seven years."

"You're kidding."

"No, sir. They underwrote my passage to this country."

"From where?"

"Southampton, sir. Originally."

"How'd you hook up with the Ussers?"

"They were traveling. My family has always been in service, and at that time I was offering myself as temporary assistance for those taking holiday in Britain. The Ussers were pleased with my work and offered to take me with them when they left for America. I accepted. Gratefully."

"Why?"

"It seemed to offer a better future."

Price's voice indicated that when his future finally arrived, it didn't shine as brightly as he'd planned. I started to imagine catering to other people's whims for twenty-seven years, but I couldn't do it and didn't want to. Then I wondered if it was that much different from what I did myself. "So you knew Lawrence Usser as a boy," I said.

"Yes, sir. Of course."

"Have you seen him often lately? I mean before the arrest?"

"Not recently, sir. Mr. Lawrence is very busy."

"His father told me they still saw each other regularly."

"Perhaps at Mr. Lawrence's home, sir."

"So Lawrence never came here?"

"On Christmas, sir. For the evening meal."

"That's all?"

"To my knowledge."

"Mr. Usser gave me the impression that he and his son were quite close."

Price risked a glance back at the Usser house, which by then was out of earshot. "Mr. Usser finds it convenient to take credit for many of Lawrence's accomplishments, sir," Price said softly.

"But Mr. Usser is quite successful in his own right, isn't he?"

"I believe the funds are hers, sir. Mrs. Usser, I'm speaking of. Her family once owned an airline, I believe."

I thought that over for a minute and decided it had no meaning. "Did Lawrence and his mother get along?"

"Oh yes, sir."

"Did he and his father ever quarrel?"

Price came to a stop when we reached the corner. "I really shouldn't be talking to you, sir. Not without Mr. Usser's permission."

"Just tell me about Lawrence, then. What was he like as a kid?"

"A very fine young man."

"Perfect?"

"Brilliant, sir."

"I know, I know. It seems to be the word of choice when it comes to dear little Lawrence." I thought over what I'd learned in the past few days, and took a shot in the dark. "Didn't he get in some trouble one time? With a girl?"

Price met my eyes. "I know of nothing of that nature, sir. Now, if you will excuse me."

"Just one more thing, Price. How about the professor's wife. Dianne. Were the Ussers happy with her?"

"I've never had the pleasure of meeting Ms. Renzel, sir."

"Really? She was never at the house? Not even at Christmas?"

"Not in my presence. I can't speak of other times."

"But you're always present, aren't you, Price?"

"I am not present now, sir."

I bowed and smiled. "Touché, Mr. Price. But why do you think she never visited the Ussers? Surely someone must have talked about it."

"I have only hearsay information, sir."

I put my hand on his shoulder. "If hearsay's all you've got, hearsay I'll accept."

I thought Price smiled. "It is my understanding that Ms. Renzel overheard Mr. Usser use a word in the presence of the daughter, Lisa, that Ms. Renzel felt was inappropriate. From that day on, she refused to come to the house or to allow her daughter to come here."

"What word did Usser use?"

"I believe the word was *nigger*, sir. Now I must truly move along. Please."

"One last question. I need to talk to Lisa. When's the best time to find her at home?"

"Miss Lisa is difficult to locate, sir. I can't be at all helpful in that regard."

"Come on, Price. Is she home now? What time does she go to bed? Is there a private phone line in her room?"

Price frowned and started to cross the street. I reached out a hand to stop him. "Please, sir," he insisted. "I must hurry to my bus. Please."

I had to let him go. He hurried away as though I were diseased. If boorishness is infectious, then I guess that's what I was.

I trudged back to my car, trying to decide what I knew if I knew anything at all. As I was walking across the driveway, the gate swung open and Howard Gable almost ran me down in his Accord. When he saw who it was, he grinned mischievously. I stood my ground and waved him to a stop. He rolled down the window and I asked him what was going on.

"What makes you think anything's going on, Tanner?"

"Your presence. I doubt that you're here to collect for the United Way."

Gable closed his eyes, then sighed. At the corner of his mouth a muscle began to twitch. "Okay. Since you're still stumbling around over here, you might as well know, so you can keep an eye out. The kid's missing."

"Lisa?"

"That's the one."

"Any idea where she went?"

Gable shrugged. "From what I hear she travels with a tough crowd. Street kids, most of them. Runaways. We'll find her in Berkeley sooner or later, in some crash pad, or maybe sleeping in People's Park or in line at the Food Project. I just hope it's soon enough."

"Soon enough for what? Why are you in on this, anyway? She hasn't even been gone twenty-four hours."

Gable eyed me thoughtfully, as though debating my credentials once again. "You could help me out on this if you would."

"How?"

"Help me find her."

"Why should I?"

"You're working for the Renzels, right?"

"Right."

"Well, the girl's my case." Gable seemed to shudder at the thought.

"You mean she told you her father killed her mother?"

"Yep. Hey. Don't look at me like that. She knew things about the scene she'd only know if she saw it all go down." Gable paused and raised his brows. "Still think our case is thin?"

I smiled. "It is if you don't find her."

"Don't I know it. And I need her by tomorrow morning."

"Why?"

"Arraignment. I need her to tell Judge Wu why her old man shouldn't be released on bail." Gable hardened his eyes, gave me another precative stare. "So if you stumble across the Usser girl tonight, your *very next move* is to call me. I better not hear that you could have helped me out on this and didn't, Tanner. I better not hear that at all." Gable's teeth ground audibly.

I avoided a cooperative response by asking a question. "What made her take off? Or maybe the question should be what made her move in with the Ussers in the first place? From what I hear, she's been running pretty wild lately."

Gable swore. "I think she may have set me up. When she showed up at my office to rat on her old man, I asked where she could go after we made the arrest. She mentioned the Ussers, so I had a black-and-white drop her off. Hell, I didn't know how wild she was. Not then I didn't. I *thought* I was doing everyone a favor."

"What happened?"

"She ripped them off this afternoon."

"She stole things?"

Gable nodded. "Usser claims the take was worth thousands, but he's a blowhard. Whatever, the girl cleaned out all her own stuff and the family jewels as well and hit the streets. Happened about four. What triggered it was old man Usser finding out his granddaughter was the chief witness against his pride and joy. I guess he went over my head, to the chief trial deputy, maybe to the D.A. himself. Anyway, when he learned what Lisa had told us about the murder, he called me up and said he wanted the girl taken away, given to the Youth Authority or whoever, said he wasn't about to shelter someone who had accused his son of murder, even if she happened to be his own flesh and blood. My guess is the girl overheard the conversation, and bye-bye. I imagine she's heard stories about the Youth Authority from some of her street buddies. Some of them might even have been true. Well, out of my way, Tanner. I got work to do."

Gable spun his tires and roared away. I went back to my car and started the engine, then let it idle. Lisa was suddenly the key, to my job as well as Gable's. The cops would be looking for her soon, and once they found her she'd be stashed away where I couldn't get at her. I had only once chance to beat them. Not by trying to penetrate the Berkeley street scene, as Gable had suggested, a scene I knew little about, but by returning to the scene of the crime. I put the car in gear.

By the time I was back in Berkeley it was almost dark. Lawrence Usser's house loomed like a thunderhead in the gray flannel sky as I eased my way up Hillside Lane. There was but a single light in the block, a stamp of gold on the side of Phyllis

Misteen's blue cantina, marking her vigil for her absent daughter. The other cantina was dark, the poetry reader doubtlessly
asleep, her dreams tormented by the fiendish schemes of a
coven of librarians.

I got out of the car and went up the Usser steps. The night
was quiet and cool, the house unfriendly and reluctant. I listened at the door and heard nothing. I peeked in a window and
saw only shape and shadow, all of it immobile, as dark as deep
despair. I waited for an idea to form, but they were out of
season.

My thoughtless mind and I were walking down the steps when
I heard a bump, a muffled thud somewhere at my back, somewhere in the house. I trotted back to the porch and tried the
door, but it was locked. Forced entry would require noise, and
noise might bring the cops. I walked around to the back yard
and went up the steps to the rear porch. I reached needlessly
for the knob—the door was already open. I listened at an omi-
nously heavy nothing, then went inside, making more noise
than I wanted to.

I moved quickly through the kitchen to the main hallway,
then listened again but heard only the slumbering wheezes of
the old house and my own old body. I inhaled, then moved
forward on a carpet of threadbare caution.

Halfway to the front of the house it occurred to me that the
intruder could be someone much more menacing than the teenage Lisa Usser. Without my bidding, my right hand drifted to
the pocket where I used to keep my gun. The pocket was empty,
for a variety of reasons, none of which seemed sufficient. I
made myself advance into the musty mildew of the hallway.

I'd found nothing by the time I reached the front stairs. If
Lisa was in there with me, she was likely in her room. I started
up, causing the treads to creak and my heart to skip. I saw her
in my mind. By now she would know someone was coming.
There was a gun in her father's dresser. I hoped she didn't
know about it. I hoped if she did know she would decide not to
use it. I hoped if she decided to use it she looked before she
opened fire.

It seemed to take a year to reach her room. I approached
cautiously, then stood in the doorway, my senses as alert as I
could make them. Nothing sounded, nothing moved, nothing

retrieved or returned my quivering vibrations. I went into the room and chanced turning on the light.

I flicked the switch and got a quick impression that nothing had changed from my visit earlier in the day. Then I heard the clattering sounds of footsteps from the floor below. There were two sets of them, at least, and they both broke into a run as I trotted down the steps in quick pursuit.

The rear door slammed open. I heard my quarry fleeing out the back as I reached the first floor and turned to dash after them. I surged toward a run, but my right foot struck the milk can beside the staircase and I went down in a heap of tin and umbrellas.

By the time I was on my feet again and had reached the back yard there was only time to hear the rapid rustle of the rear hedge and to see, in a pale veil of moonlight, a young girl, as frightened and as skittish as a faun, waiting her turn to crawl through the leafy green escape hatch. She heard me on the stairs, and for a moment she looked back at me in an open gasp of terror, mouth open, eyes so dark it seemed someone had removed them. I started for her. She ducked and disappeared. By the time I reached the hedge Lisa Usser and her companions had vanished, leaving me panting and alone.

I hurried around to the front of the house, got in my car and drove through the neighboring streets as rapidly as I could. I circled as many blocks as I could find, but the area was a scrambled maze of one-way alleys and dead-end lanes and I saw nothing suspicious, nothing that seemed to flee me, nothing to pursue. I drove back to the Usser house and went inside.

If any of the neighbors were inclined to do such things, the police must have already been called, so I sacrificed caution for speed, flipped on lights as I went and searched the house for reasons Lisa might have gone there after running away from her grandparents.

Lisa's room seemed only as disturbed as I had left it. Her parents' room was likewise untouched, the other second-floor areas similarly unremarkable. I trotted down the stairs. The living room bore what smelled like the musk of unwashed bodies, and I guessed that was where they had hidden while I tiptoed past them like a late-night drunk. I found nothing out of place until I reached the den.

I had almost given up before I noticed it, and I wouldn't have noticed it even then if I hadn't spent the past six months debating whether or not to buy myself a video recorder. Usser had one, camera and all, and I'd noticed earlier that day that one of the prerecorded tapes in his collection was *Reds*. It's my favorite film of the past few years, which was why I noticed it was missing.

I looked on the floor, behind the credenza, anywhere else that it might have accidentally strayed, but it was nowhere to be found. Which meant that either Bart Kinn had returned and taken it after I'd left him that morning, or Lisa and her friends had broken into the house just to steal that tape. When I couldn't think of a reason for either action, I left the Usser house behind and headed for my appointment with the professor's right-hand girl.

SIXTEEN

The address Krista Hellgren had given me was on Warring Street, which turned out to be only a couple of blocks down the hill from the Ussers'. It was a large brown-shingle structure as well, but it had been subdivided into multiple pouches of student housing and was suffering as a result. There was a dumpster in the drive, for no apparent reason. The ivy that obliterated the lawn gave off the smell of urine. A FOR SALE sign had been tacked below a window on the second floor. It looked like it had been there for a long time. The fraternity house next door emitted noises that had already become annoying by the time I got out of my car.

She had told me apartment 6. The bank of mailboxes included that number but gave no hint of where it was. I went into the building, climbed two flights of stairs, heard the muffled murmur of conversation behind one door and the flighty gallop of a flute behind another, but the apartment numbers only went to four. I retreated, then followed the path to the rear of the house.

The trail ended at a paved patio in back of the main building. It in turn was flanked by two smaller buildings, cabins bearing numbers 5 and 6. They were shingled to match the big house in front, and looked snug and romantic. Their roofs were matted with pine needles; their chimneys emitted silver threads of smoke. The frat-house frenzy that still despoiled the air was the only indication that I was not in some Sierra glade.

I made my way through the patio furnishings—a plastic recliner positioned to catch the sun, an empty easel, an exercise bicycle, a claw-footed bathtub that could be used for anything from cooling off to brewing beer—and knocked on the door to number 6. The knocker on the door was in the shape of lovers kissing. I allowed them two platonic pecks, then heard a scraping sound from inside the cabin. The door opened seconds later.

Her long gray gown was quilted and cut square above her breasts. Her hair was pinned on top of her head in a golden orb that exposed an elegant neck and sculpted shoulders and ears as delicate as blossoms. A gold heart dangled to the apex of her cleavage; a single pearl dripped below each lobe. The kitchen at her back, though spotless and precise, seemed grossly utilitarian compared to the woman who leased it.

"Hi," she said.

"Hi."

"Come in, please."

"Thank you."

I followed her through the kitchen into the living room which was on two levels, the lower containing cane and canvas furniture arranged before a fireplace, the upper containing a desk and bookshelves and other accoutrements of an office that were partially shielded by a free-standing, folding screen.

There was a small blaze in the fireplace. There was Mozart on the stereo. The air was noticeably warm and carried whiffs of baking bread. I grew suddenly suspicious that Krista Hellgren had entered my head and extracted all my passions and was turning them against me. She asked if I would like some wine.

"Sure."

"I have a zinfandel and a white Bordeaux. Or brandy, if you prefer. Or I can make some Irish coffee."

"I'll try the brandy."

"Cheese?"

"No, thanks."

"Crackers?"

"No. Nothing. But please help yourself."

She smiled as though no one had ever offered her that opportunity before, then excused herself. As she went off to the kitchen I noticed that her feet were bare. Given the scrubbed formality of the scene, that hint of sweet lubricity was an erotic, narcotic rush.

I watched the flames play tag among the split-birch logs until Krista returned and handed me a small snifter. Pretending, I swirled, inspected, sniffed and thanked her.

She asked me to sit down. I chose the butterfly chair beside the fire, so I could inspect Ms. Hellgren without a flickering distraction.

She took a seat on the couch along the wall opposite me and curled her legs up under her. As she leaned forward to place her wineglass on the floor, her bodice dropped forward to reveal the surge of flawless breasts. I was as aroused as I had ever been outside a bedroom, but my checkered history with women led me to wonder if she was displaying herself for reasons ulterior to ardor.

"Do you do this every night?" I asked, gesturing at the wine, the fire, the gown.

"Not every night, but sometimes. Life gets so . . . homely over at the law school, I like to remind myself that there are pleasures beyond a well-crafted opinion by Learned Hand or a welcome statute from the legislature. Is the brandy all right?"

"Fine."

"It's not expensive."

"Neither am I."

Her smile was an extravagant reward for my nonsense. "Would you prefer some other music?" she asked.

"The flute quartets are as good as music gets."

"You know Mozart."

"A little."

"Have you seen the film? *Amadeus*?"

"Not yet."

"It's flawed, but it gives an important hint of the vulnerability of genius, I believe."

From the pained look in her eyes I was certain she was talking about a genius more contemporary than Mozart. "Can I get you anything at all?" she asked me.

"No. It's all perfect. You don't need a roommate do you?"

I sent my little joke to her on the back of a grin, but she

sobered instead, looked momentarily stricken. I guessed she
had entertained the professor in just this way on more than one
occasion, had fantasized that he might become a permanent
fixture, and the thought that he might never be in a position to
enjoy her hospitality again was unbearable to her.

"You are investigating Ms. Renzel's death," she said, suddenly
bloodless, the academic.

I felt my fancy cool, and was only half happy that it had. I
confirmed her statement of my mission.

"But how can I help you? I only met her a few times. When
Lawrence had parties for the law review staff."

"Do you think the professor killed her?"

Firelight mottled her face, created shadows of frown or fear.
She crossed her arms and pressed her breasts until they swelled
above her bodice. "No. Of course I don't believe he killed her."

"Why not?"

She let her arms fall away from her chest, her hands fall to
her lap. "Because his life has been devoted to *saving* lives, not
taking them. And because killing someone is stupid, and Lawrence Usser is not stupid, he is quite the opposite. And because,
in spite of his uncommon life-style, he loved his wife. More
important than that, he admired her and the work she was
doing at the crisis center. He would never, *ever* kill her. No
matter *what* she might have done to him."

She looked at me so intensely that I imagined my soul was
stained a bleak and matching blue. If Usser was ever tried for
murder, Krista Hellgren was a walking, talking rope with which
Jake Hattie could hang his jury.

"It sounds as though you think his wife did do something to
him," I said.

"I think so. Yes."

"What was it?"

"I don't know. Lawrence wouldn't say. But he was very hurt
by it, whatever it was."

"When did all this happen?"

"Not long before Ms. Renzel died. Two weeks, perhaps. No
more than a month."

"What exactly did he say about it? Can you remember?"

She closed her eyes and began to sway, as though her efforts
were self-hypnotic. "We were here. Relaxing, the way you and I
are now. He had several glasses of wine, more than usual. He

said something like, 'If only she hadn't done it. I guess I should have known she would, but she promised me. She *swore* she would never do it. Now she's ruined everything. Marriage. Family. It may never be the same again. God, I don't know if I can live with that. I really don't.'" Krista opened her eyes. "That's all I can remember. It was as if he was talking to himself."

"So what do you think it was? Sex? His wife had a fling with someone?"

"It sounds that way, doesn't it? But I don't know. Really. And I'd prefer not to guess."

"Sounds like the professor observed a double standard."

Krista shook her head. "I don't know. I don't *want* to know."

I did her bidding and took my questions somewhere else. "You work with Usser every day, I imagine."

She nodded. "When he's in town."

"Research."

"Yes."

"Books and articles and speeches."

"Yes."

"Anything else?"

"Briefs, sometimes. Particularly when he's been designated amicus curiae."

"Does all of it involve legal insanity?"

"Yes. For the most part."

"Have any of your assignments been peculiar of late? Anything out of the ordinary?"

"How do you mean?"

"I mean did he have you do anything that wasn't obviously related to his academic or trial work?"

I was fishing for a sign that Usser had launched his research assistant on a search for a derangement he could persuasively adopt, a look at madness from a perspective different from the scope of his normal pursuits. But Krista Hellgren was shaking her head, offering nothing helpful.

"How long have you been his assistant?"

"Two years."

"So outside his immediate family, you must know him as well as anyone."

She lowered her eyes and squirmed. "I hope that is the case."

"So tell me. Is there any chance that Usser is insane?"

I expected a vehement rejection of the proposition, but instead I got a reflective stare. I thought back to what she had said about the Mozart film, and about its essay on the flaw of genius.

Her eyes were looking past me, at the center of the dancing fire. "I have considered that possibility," she said. "After I learned of the arrest I thought back over the months before his wife's death, to see if anything might have changed him, to see if anything had happened to force Lawrence across the chasm."

"What chasm?"

"It was what he called it, the skip into insanity that so many of his clients took: crossing the chasm between the sane and the insane."

"What does he think sends people there?"

"Do you really want to know?"

"Sure."

Krista leaned back against the couch, tilted her head against the wall and stared at the thick beams in the ceiling overhead. "What Lawrence thinks is that madness is a physical, not a psychological, disability, and thus is subject to eradication. Like polio and smallpox. He believes madness is triggered by biochemical changes in the brain, an alteration of the normal balances of the electrochemical processes that constitute both intelligence and consciousness, that govern mood and behavior as well as motor functions. For example, research indicates that much if not all schizophrenia results from an excess of dopamine transmission, which in turn causes a corresponding decrease in the activity of the neurotransmitters. Also, various depressive disorders have been found to correspond to a depletion of serotonin and norepinephrine, which results in turn from the activity of enzymes such as monoamine oxidase, plus related amino acids and peptides, the exact operation of which is yet to be understood by the neurochemists. Lawrence is confident that other mental illnesses admit to similar explanations, which will one day be discovered." She lowered her head and looked at me. "Okay so far?"

"I guess so."

She smiled a teacher's smile. "For Professor Usser's purposes, which are the purposes of criminal justice, it is the *origin* of those neurochemical changes that is important, the causative propulsion that send his clients across the chasm. Lawrence believes that mental illness is like cancer and heart disease in that certain life experiences—fear, anger, stress, frustration, the exposure to environmental pollutants—trigger chemical responses in both the mind and the body, and that ironically the legal system is therefore correct in its focus on the sociology of crime, although it is correct for outmoded reasons. Lawrence believes that certain objective stresses, combined with certain aberrant behavior, automatically mean madness given a finding of abnormal chemical responses, and that therefore madness should not be punished by the judicial system, no more than the disabilities resulting from multiple sclerosis or epilepsy should be punished by it. He believes that, in fact, madness is uniquely its own punishment. He also believes madness cannot be effectively treated except pharmacologically, by use of proven drugs such as the phenothiazines and the tricyclics, but he doesn't say that very often or very loud, for fear of alienating the alienists who continue to be essential in criminal prosecutions if not in therapeutic situations. He believes, in short, that the system is right in theory—the insane should not be punished—but wrong in practice—evidence of insanity is medical and chemical, not psychological. And that about sums it up. In a nutshell, so to speak."

Krista raised her brows and inspected me. Some of what she'd said made sense and some of it sounded naive and superficial. Possibly she'd tailored the digest for me, however, because she assumed I was naive and superficial myself. "Let's assume he's right," I said. "What stresses was he under just before the night his wife was killed?"

"Well, there were the usual things. His workload was enormous. He was having trouble with the last chapter of his new book, and the publisher was pressing him to complete it. He was doing more administratively than he should have been, advising the law review on top of all the rest. And the usual faculty wrangles. I believe there was pressure on him to try for the deanship, in opposition to Professor Grunig. Also he was considering joining the defense team for that mass murderer up in Washington State, the one that killed those prostitutes."

"Not a popular cause, I imagine."

"No, but Lawrence feels it is exactly the most hideous of crimes that demands assertion of the insanity defense. Of course there was the usual pressure on him to keep out of it, that it would be bad publicity for the school, that the alumni would use his work as an excuse to cut back contributions and like that. Also, one of his former clients, a man named Nifton who had been acquitted on insanity grounds and treated for a short time and then released, was back in Berkeley causing problems for his sister and all kinds of other people. Lawrence was feeling pretty responsible for that, although there was no reason why he should."

She finally stopped. "That's quite a list," I said.

She shook her head sadly. "People see only the success, the power, the display; they never see what all that cost him in terms of his energy and his compassion. He would come over here sometimes and literally collapse from exhaustion. That was the basis of our relationship, actually, that Lawrence could relax with me, that I put no pressure on him. None. Ever."

"If he was subject to all those stresses, what was the aberrant behavior that resulted?"

She shook her head. "That's just it. There was none. Not before his wife died. I mean, Lawrence got depressed from time to time, deeply depressed, but . . ."

"Why? Most people would say he had everything."

"He worried that he was doing more harm than good, that he didn't understand madness, not really, that his conclusions were all wrong. But after a few days he'd snap out of it and go on about his business."

"Did he take drugs?"

"No. Never. I offered him marijuana one night and he shoved me away from him. It was the only time he ever struck me."

I realized she had begun to speak of Usser as though he were dead. And I realized I was sorry for her because of it. "You say there was nothing strange about his behavior, but from what I hear, he was sleeping with all kinds of women besides his wife and he didn't seem to mind that everyone knew it. I find that a little aberrant, don't you? Particularly if he loved her, as you say?"

Pain skewed her face. "That's what you came here for, isn't it? To talk about sex."

"I'm too old to get my kicks hearing about other people's sex lives, Ms. Hellgren. Usser seems to have been promiscuous. Which means he must have left some heartache in his wake.

And where there's heartache, there's motive, and *that's* what I'm looking for. So. Will you help me out?"

She got up and went into the kitchen and came back with both brandy and Bordeaux. She poured without being asked, then curled up on the couch. "How can I help?"

"First of all, was there any change in your relationship with Usser recently?"

"No."

"It was sexual, right? In part?"

"Yes."

"Did you know there were other women in his life?"

"Of course."

"Did he talk to you about them?"

"Occasionally."

"Did he tell the others about you?"

"I don't know. It doesn't matter if he did."

"So you weren't jealous."

"No."

"Were any of the others jealous of you?"

"I don't know. They had no reason to be."

"Why not? Most women like to feel they give their man everything he needs, don't they?"

"I don't know. I'm not every woman. I gave him things he didn't get from the others, and that was enough for me."

"What kind of things?"

She met my eyes. "You don't need to know, but I'll tell you anyway. They were things of the flesh, and things of the soul as well. Our relationship was entirely one-sided. I wanted nothing from Professor Usser, except to give him whatever it was *he* wanted. Mostly what he wanted was my mind. I'm an intelligent woman. I was proud when Lawrence put his name on my work and published it as his own. I was proud to see my work quoted and cited, even though no one knew it was mine. And I was proud, Mr. Tanner, to give Lawrence my body when he wanted that as well. It wasn't that often, actually. But whenever he needed me, I was there for him. He knew it because I told him so."

"It's hard to believe you were satisfied with such a one-way relationship, Ms. Hellgren."

"Different people are satisfied with different things. I have studied eastern philosophy and religion. There the tradition is to serve, to erase the self, to please yourself by pleasing others. I was satisfied by helping Lawrence Usser be everything he could be, which was far more than I could ever be on my own."

"You don't sound like a disciple of women's lib."

She shrugged. "I don't know if I am or not. I'm satisfied with my job but I'm not dependent on it, so in that sense I *am* truly liberated. I also know that one day Lawrence will want neither my body *nor* my mind. He will have absorbed all my ideas and he will move on to those of someone else. I will be sad, but I will not be devastated. And I will move on to someone else as well, though I suspect my movement in that sense will inevitably be downhill."

Her blind devotion made me furious. It reminded me of the religious cultists who equate nirvana with the absence of thought and the acceptance of absurdity. It also reminded me that I was no longer young enough to court a woman like Krista Hellgren, and perhaps that's why my fury stirred.

When I spoke again it was with a bitter bite. "You're writing off the rest of your life before you've begun to live it."

"Don't feel that way, Mr. Tanner. I don't. Some people never get to the top of the mountain at all."

She leaned back and drank her wine, as content and enduring as a slug. I was still determined to poke holes in her bubble of rapture. "So nothing at all bothered you about your relationship with Usser?"

"Only that I might give him less than he needed."

"What about what you were doing to his wife? What about *her* feelings when she learned you were sleeping with her husband?"

Krista lowered her head. "It wasn't Dianne that I was concerned about. It was Lisa."

"Why Lisa?"

"Because she was very upset by our relationship. She didn't understand it at all."

"How do you know?"

"Lawrence hinted at it. And once shortly before he was arrested he and I were having dinner at a place on Telegraph. Lisa walked by and saw us through the window. I thought she was going to have a fit. I felt terrible about her pain."

"But not bad enough to leave her old man alone."

I was still ashamed of my remark when the telephone rang and broke the tension that had curdled the air between us. Krista excused herself and went up to the desk to answer it. I turned around and jiggled the fire with a poker, wishing that what I poked was Krista's wrap of self-delusion and my own reaction to it.

I couldn't help hearing her side of the conversation. "Hi, Danny. . . . That's all right. . . . Good. I'll look it over in the morning and give you a memo by the end of the day. . . . No. . . . Yes. . . . No, I can't. Come on, Danny; don't do this to me again. . . . Yes. . . . Okay, I forgive you. . . . Sure. See you then. . . . It's okay. Good night."

She hung up and came back down to the living area. "Business," she explained.

I nodded and tried to apologize for my earlier insult. Krista waved it away, then tried to stifle a yawn but couldn't. Then, as though she remembered the lines her role required, she curled herself at my feet and rested her hand on my knee and her cheek on my thigh. She smelled of lilacs. I patted her hair. It was as soft as sable.

"You think I'm strange, don't you?" she asked sleepily.

"A little."

"You wouldn't if you knew more about me."

"Maybe you'll tell me more about you sometime."

"Maybe I will. Maybe I'll do more than that."

"You don't have to, you know."

"Don't have to what?"

"Sleep with me to help your boss."

She stiffened, but kept her place. "I wouldn't do that."

"Sure you would. But it wouldn't work. Believe me. Not that I wouldn't do it, you understand. Just that it wouldn't make any difference."

"I see."

"Good."

"I might want to anyway, someday."

"Good."

"But not till Lawrence is free."

"That might take a long time. And I might be helping to see to it that it does."

SEVENTEEN

was tired, and more than a little depressed by my conversation with Krista Hellgren, and I wanted to go home and sleep it off. But if I was going to get anywhere with the Renzel case I needed to catch up to Lisa Usser, and there was one place I might be able to do it even at this time of night. I found my car and drifted down the hill toward Telegraph Avenue, made two right turns, and lucked into a parking place on Haste Street, just opposite the undeveloped parcel of real estate that has become known as People's Park.

It's a cheerless place these days, a park in name and symbol only, but for a decade or so people marched and chanted and fought to keep the block unoccupied by the owner, the University of California, and its project, a multilevel parking lot. The Berkeley *Barb* had been the first to sniff out the university's plan, and in April of 1969 it had summoned the faithful to act before the school could implement its parking plan. A park of sorts was built in a day, with sod and plantings and the other trappings of urban nature, at a happening of the sort that occurred periodically in those days in response to joy or jeopardy.

On that first day, the *Barb* people had gotten their way without opposition. Beautification of the park continued for a month. But the university administration decided that a statement of its rights was needed, a symbol of its affirmation of the concept of the private ownership of land, and it awarded a contract to erect a steel fence around the property. On May 15, while a small contingent of Berkeley police occupied the property, the president of the university's student body exhorted a noon rally to "take the park." The confrontation was on, and it turned violent immediately.

The students tossed bricks and bottles and worse; the police retaliated with tear gas. The violence escalated, as violence does, and when the county sheriff's deputies arrived they began to fire their weapons. A bystander observing the action from the comparative safety of a rooftop was killed by a sheriff's shotgun, and another student was blinded by a similar weapon. Six police officers were injured, and more than sixty students as well. By nightfall the National Guard had been called in, and People's Park had become a legend and a cause.

Conflict continued for several days in the form of skirmishes and demonstrations. A National Guard helicopter "bombed" protesters with tear gas as they approached the chancellor's residence, and on May 22 almost five hundred demonstrators were arrested, ending the violence for a time. The university eventually removed the fence, and only halfheartedly proposed to utilize the area over the next decade. A few weeks ago, I had read that the Berkeley Landmarks Preservation Committee had declared People's Park an official city landmark, because of its "unique place" in the city's history. But the scruffy, scrambled plot of ground I was looking at seemed appropriate only to lament the dead and the forgotten.

The east end of the park was a grove of evergreens in various stages of maturity. Some high pines swayed in the night wind; some small firs looked abused and neglected. From where I sat I could see only shapes and shadows within the grove, moving blobs of black that congregated around a small bonfire at the center of the stand of trees.

The central portion of the park was an open field, its grasses worn away in paths that crisscrossed the block in dusty shortcuts. The only structure I could see was a flat stage, raised some three feet off the ground, sprayed with graffiti, suitable for rock bands or orators if oratory was still in style. On the stage a couple was copulating under a grimy blanket, or giving a good imitation of the act. Elsewhere in the field, isolated individuals lay prone or sat hunched over, heads bowed, backs bent, consciousness erased by sleep or drugs or the cumulative catastrophe of their lives. Oblivious to it all, a preppie couple strolled hand in hand across one of the shortcuts, in the blithe certainty that none of the despair around them was worthy of concern or even a moment's glance.

The west end of the park was subdivided into little garden plots, most of which looked stricken by a viral blight. A valiant bamboo bush tried to eke out a life in the middle of it all. Beside it, an overstuffed couch and a grocery shopping cart constituted someone's worldly possessions. The someone was asleep on the ground beside his chrome container, his sockless ankles glowing in the moonlight like the tusks of a jungle beast.

Surrounding the park, both in front of my car and behind it, was a string of vehicles, tires flat, windows smashed, paint eroded, fenders ripped or dimpled. I assumed them to be abandoned until I saw a face appear above the dashboard of the Pinto directly across the street from me. It was a young but battered boy, surely not yet twenty. He scrubbed at his eyes, looked sleepily at his surroundings, saw nothing promising or dangerous, then returned to his burrow. When a car door slammed shut behind me, I turned in time to see a girl hop out of a dented Datsun, carry a plastic bag full of garbage over to an abandoned pickup truck, toss the bag into the bed of the truck, then trot back to the Datsun and drive away with her hairy mate, both of them smiling at their creative solid waste disposal.

What I was looking for was Lisa Usser, but from where I sat I couldn't see her. The only possibility was that Lisa and her mates might be among those gathered in what looked like celebration around the glowing ember in the center of the pocket forest at the top of the park. I got out of my car and went up to take a look, alert for an encounter with a crazed inhabitant of the little unwalled city the people still claimed for themselves.

Keeping to the sidewalk, I walked around three sides of the grove, slowly, carefully, but I couldn't see anything from that distance. I took a deep breath, crossed my fingers and edged my way into the dark, dank stand of trees.

The group around the fire seemed to number five or six. At least two of them were women. Their voices cackled in manic gaiety, indicating a high artificially induced for the occasion. The dance they did was tribal, the purpose unclear. I was still not close enough to focus on a face, so I penetrated farther, hiding behind one bush and then another, moving closer to the fire, feeling like a kid playing war and winning.

As I was about to move to the next vantage point, I stepped on something round and soft. I heard a mumbled curse and felt something slap my leg. I looked down, muttered an apology at the heap of rags that slept there and moved on, inhaling only belatedly the stink of cheap booze and rotten wool. A minute later I had gone as far as I could if I wanted to keep my presence secret. I knelt behind a young Scotch pine that had somehow survived as lush, and looked closely at the twirling celebrants.

There might have been some bodies snuggled in the cape of darkness beyond the fire's gold reach, but the only ones I could see were five in number, three men and two women. All but one of them looked young and overly thrilled by whatever enlightenment they thought they were experiencing. They were dressed in the baggy ugliness of the street, their dominant features the hairstyles that seemed crafted with pinking shears and the glittering accessories that suggested either death or a variety of enslavement.

The exception was the man who stood apart from the dancers in the manner of a commandant. He was tall but stooped, dressed in an army field jacket and the jungle fatigues that had been originally issued to the kids who went to Vietnam but now are worn by kids who have never heard of the place or who think it lies somewhere south of Florida.

His head was a scruffy thicket, his eyes were hidden behind mirrored sunglasses; he chewed gum in lazy movements of his jaw. He circled the fire in slow, mincing steps, his arms hanging stiffly at his sides, his hands twitching nervously. He wore jungle boots and a bandanna around his neck, and his legs were wrapped with knotted strips of rags that ringed them at ten-inch intervals, from ankle to crotch. The only other people I knew of who did that were Viet Cong sappers. The rags acted as tourniquets when they were hit, enabling them to fight much longer before they bled to death.

As I watched the dance, one girl separated herself from the group and drifted toward the older man. She was young, thin, sad-eyed, a waif wearing the same knee-length boots and skin-

tight jeans I had seen her in just before she had ducked through
the hedge behind the Usser house a couple of hours before.

She seemed more in control than the others, less given over
to the drugs, more aware of both herself and her leader, the
guy in the wardrobe out of *Taxi Driver*. As the others began to
circle the fire again and to sing a song about what sounded like
money, the girl, Lisa, drifted to the leader's side.

He draped an arm across her shoulders and kissed her. She
kissed him back. They embraced, then danced a few steps.
When he twirled unsteadily his back was to me for an instant
and I saw two things, a word emblazoned on the back of his
jacket in white paint and a stubby, pearl-handled pistol stuffed
into the back pocket of his fatigues. The word on the jacket was
MANIAC. As I shuddered with a psychic chill, one of the dancers
stumbled into the fire, almost fell, put a hand into the flames to
right herself, then drew it out slowly, looking quizzically at its
sooty sear, laughing.

I tried to decide what to do. As my mind gave off a series of
bad ideas, Lisa pulled something from the pocket of her bulky
canvas jacket and held it up to the firelight, then asked the
Maniac a question. He nodded and pointed to the ground beneath the tallest tree in the grove. Lisa walked to the spot and
began to dig. When she had a hole the size of a basketball she
put the object into it, then took something else out of her pocket
and tossed it in the hole as well, then covered them up, tamped
the earth flat with her foot and pulled a half-burned log to the
place to mark it and keep it hidden. Her task completed, she
brushed off her hands and returned to the Maniac's side and
looked up at him in sedated awe, praying for approval.

He bent to kiss her again, and this time they were body to
body. His hands went to her buttocks and pressed her pelvis
into his. Her hands edged between them so she could fondle his
sex. He raised her off the ground and swung her in a circle. She
laughed and whispered something in his ear, and he laughed,
too, and ground his hips on hers. She slid down his body till she
was on her knees, then pressed her face into his crotch. He
grasped her head with both hands, moved it back and forth,
masturbating against her lips. Smiling, Lisa reached for his fly.
The dancers at her back seemed to sing her praises and to urge
her on.

I was about to step forward when a shout sounded from

somewhere behind me, fearful, cautionary. Everyone froze, including me. Lisa got to her feet. A cry went out again: "Cops!"

I looked behind me and saw a line of four uniformed men moving into the grove from the sidewalk. I looked back at Lisa. She and the group were already running, following the Maniac out of the grove, sprinting for the street opposite the one the cops were coming from, heading for the scramble of commercial buildings on the next block.

I had started after them when someone yelled at my back, "Halt! Police! Don't move, buster. Hold it right there."

I stopped and turned and waited while they approached. One of them had his gun out, the others moved warily past me at his signal and followed after the Maniac and his clique. In the undergrowth around me I could hear the scurrying sounds of the park's other occupants making their escapes. The cops didn't seem to mind. I thought about making a break myself, but the one with his gun out looked able and willing to shoot me. I stayed put and watched while a confident smile and a matching swagger brought him to me.

He was young, blond, image-perfect. "What's your name?" he demanded, holstering his weapon.

"Tanner."

"What are you doing here?"

"Looking."

"At what?"

I smiled my friendly smile. "Am I under arrest?"

"Damn right."

"For what?"

"Trespassing, for a start."

"I thought this was a park."

"This is university property."

"I thought the university gave up on that idea back in 1969."

"Like hell," the cop said, but he shifted uneasily at the prospect that I might know something about the situation that he didn't. In 1969 he would have been still wetting the bed and playing with toy trucks.

"I think this is private property only when it's convenient for you to call it that," I went on. "I think my case will be tossed out of court on the ground of discriminatory prosecution. What do you think?"

"I don't think, pal. I just bring them in. You and the rest of the punks."

"You're after Lisa Usser, aren't you?"

His eyes narrowed with a suddenly specific suspicion. "What do you know about her?"

"I know she was here a few minutes ago. I know she took off. I know from the look on those guys' faces that she got away."

I gestured toward the policemen that were trudging back to where we stood, unaccompanied by suspects. The cop who'd been grilling me asked me where Lisa went.

"I have no idea," I said. "Is Howard Gable here? Or Bart Kinn?"

The cop frowned. "You know Kinn?"

I nodded. "Tell him who I am. Tell him I'm looking for Lisa, too. Tell him if he lets me go I might have a shot at finding her."

"Where?"

"I don't know yet. If you take me in I never will."

The cop thought it over. "Wait here," he said finally, then told one of the other officers to keep an eye on me and trotted out of the grove to an unmarked car that was double-parked on Bowditch, the street that bordered the east end of the park.

He leaned in the window and said something to whoever was inside, nodded, then trotted back. "You can go," he grumbled. "Kinn says he wants to know the minute you find anything. I don't know how well you know Kinn, buster, but when he tells people to do something their lives are a lot easier if they do it."

I nodded and moved away from the police and toward my car. My plan was to wait till the cops had finished poking around in the now-vacant pine grove, then go back and dig up whatever it was that Lisa Usser had buried by the fire. But my plan was amended by the hand that grabbed my shoulder as I passed the derelict pickup that served as the local landfill.

"It was Lisa, wasn't it?" he asked, his voice high and frightened.

"Hello, Cal."

"They want her, don't they? I heard them talking. Will she be put in the Youth Authority?"

"I don't think so, Cal. I think they just want her as a witness."

"A witness to what?"

"Her mother's murder."

"That's lame. She doesn't know anything about it," Cal blurted, then looked sorry that he had.

"How do you know?"

"She . . . ah, hell. She was with the Maniac, right?"

"Right."

"Piss on her, then. Just piss on her." Cal's hands congealed into fists and he punched the pickup hard enough to hurt himself. As he rubbed his hand he kicked at a bourbon bottle that lay in the gutter. The bottle skittered across the street like a fleeing rat. When it reached the opposite curb it shattered.

Cal started to walk away. I put out a hand to stop him. "What did Lisa tell you about her mother's murder, Cal?" I asked.

"Nothing. Zero. Now let me go."

"You'd be helping her if you tell me."

"So who wants to help her? She just lies to me, man. All lies."

"Lies how?"

"She told me she'd leave the Maniac alone. Stop taking drugs. Quit hanging around the avenue. But they were just there, weren't they? She and that fucking psychotic. What were they doing, anyway?"

Cal was so hyped on jealousy his eyes glittered in the moonlight as though they'd just been glazed. I fought with the image of Lisa's face pressed against the Maniac's bulging crotch, with the sodden, sultry smile she'd worn as she reached eagerly for his fly. I fought with it until I could keep it secret from Cal and anyone. "They were just smoking some dope and dancing around the fire," I said instead. "Do you have any idea where they went?"

"Naw. Who gives a shit, anyway?"

"I do. You do, too."

I looked at him. He looked back. He stopped tugging against my grip so I released him. He ran a hand through his hair and sighed. His eyes shone enough for me to think he was close to crying. "The Maniac has this place he crashes, with his sister somewhere. I never been there. Neither has Lisa, I don't think. But there's this other place they go sometimes. Hell House, they call it. Down on Blake, couple blocks above Shattuck. It's this old apartment house where the trippers crash till the cops come roust them every week or so. They might go there."

"What's the address?"

"I don't know the number. I'll have to show you."

"Let's go."

Cal came with me to the car. I followed his directions, which led me around the traffic barriers that so frazzled strangers to the city, and got me where we were going with a minimum of detours.

The house had once been white, a square, two-story box of Mediterranean design, once-removed from Italy or Spain. Now it was suitable only for destruction. The walls were stained from rust and weather, the windows cracked or missing altogether, the door teetering on a single hinge, the shutters flapping periodically in the wind like sets of fractured wings. The front steps were rotted and collapsed, the stucco facade was pitted and pockmarked, the grass dead and tangled beneath a glaze of litter that included mounds of broken roof tiles. I circled the block without finding a vacant slot, so I pulled into the Hell House driveway and stopped the car.

Subdued, Cal looked past me at the building. "I hate to think of her in there," he said. "You wouldn't believe what goes down in there sometimes."

We got out of the car and went up the steps, careful not to fall through the spongy wood. The door didn't need opening. The lower hallway smelled of feces and dog food. As I walked its length I peeked in doorways, hoping I wouldn't be able to see anything familiar.

The first room was empty; the second sheltered a group of sleeping bundles similar to those I'd seen in People's Park, except one of these bundles was crying. In the room at the back a women was suckling a child beside the stub of a candle. The soft gold glow wasn't nearly enough to make the scene maternal, given the sores on the mother's face and the bruise on the baby's back and the terrible silence that bound them to each other.

In the only other room on the first floor, six young kids were gathered around a kerosene lantern smoking cigarettes so reverently they could only have been joints. Cal stopped in the doorway and asked if they had seen the Maniac.

One of the six told him to fuck off. I couldn't tell which one had spoken. From the nodding listlessness they all possessed, I doubted they could be of help. I had started to move on down the hall when I felt something fly past my face and strike the wall behind me. "Fucking narc," one of them muttered. I thought I saw the glimmer of a knife blade as I looked to see which of them had assaulted me. I debated going in after him, but Cal was tugging me away. I let him succeed with less reluctance than I would have had five years before.

We went upstairs. For several minutes the only sounds came from the scrape of our shoes on the gritty dirt that salted the floor and the creaking floorboards that suffered our search. All the rooms looked empty, all the shelves looked bare. I had reached the back of the building and was starting to retrace my steps when I heard a moan from the far wall of the apartment numbered 5. I went inside the room, squinted, tried to see who it was, saw what I thought was human. I turned on my pencil flash to make sure.

It was a girl, lying on the floor, dressed in the lumpy linens of the street people, her feet and arms bare, her body curled against itself. I knelt beside her. As I was reaching for her wrist to take a pulse, she opened a single eye. "I need a hit bad," she breathed. "You carrying?"

I shook my head.

"Who are you? A cop?" Her voice was high, a child's.

"No, I'm not a cop."

"Are you from Daddy? Did Daddy send you after me?"

"No. I don't know your daddy."

"Daddy wants me to come home. He sends people to find me but they never can."

She groaned again and I asked her if she was all right.

"I don't think so," she said, strangely objective. "I think I got some bad shit."

"What did you take?"

"I take whatever they'll give me," she said. "Ow. It hurts in there."

"Where?"

"My gut. Do you know where Sherry is, mister? Sherry takes care of me. Sherry can tell me what to do."

"Sherry Misteen?"

"Sherry. Yeah. Do you know where she is?"

"No."

"But have you *seen* her? She's been gone so long, no one's even *seen* her lately."

"I haven't seen her. No."

"The Maniac says she's dead. She isn't dead, is she, mister? If Sherry's dead, then everyone I know is dead."

Her singsong voice, drugged and pained, compelled me to stay with her. "Do you need something? Food? Water? Anything?"

"I need some dope, man." She giggled. "Shit, skag, speed, snow; crystal, coke, crank. Anything. What have you got?"

"I don't have any dope, but I can call an ambulance to take you to a hospital."

"No." Her body arched and stiffened. "No hospital. They'll lock me up if I go there. Ah, Christ. I *hurt,* man. Maybe I'm dying. Like Sherry. You think I'm dying, mister?"

I was trying to decide what I could do for her when Cal came into the room and tugged at my shoulder. "Come on," he said, the words rough and peremptory. "The Maniac's out back. I just heard someone call out to him."

"This girl's in trouble," I said. "We should do something."

Cal looked down at her and sneered, his expression hardened beyond anything I'd ever seen on his face. "You can't help her," he muttered. "Everyone in Berkeley's tried to help Needles, and it don't do no good. She don't want help, she just wants people to want to try."

"She might be dying."

"She'll be better off if she does," Cal declared. "So will the world."

EIGHTEEN

It's not what we do that disturbs our dreams, it's what we don't do. Action admits of ambiguity; inaction is absolute. We embrace the rationale that inertia is for the best. In the long run. All things considered. Given the circumstances. But the undone deed seldom admits to such evasion, and we live lives shadowed by the consequences of timidity.

I was about to acquire another such shadow myself, since I was about to leave the anonymous addict lying where she was, as she was, what she was. Because Cal was urging me to come with him. Because there was nothing obvious to be done for her. Because the Chinese say that if you save a life, you are responsible for that person forever. I wondered what the Chinese had to say if you let a life expire. I stood up with a grunt and left everything behind me but an image needled into my brain like a loser's bleak tattoo.

Cal led me out of the apartment building through the rear exit, onto the concrete slab in the back. The parking area was occupied by a VW van and a Toyota pickup with a homemade camper unit built into the bed. The sides of the camper were cedar shakes, the roof a peaked chalet. Smoke was drifting from a crooked smokestack, so I assumed the fairy-tale conveyance was where Cal was taking me, but he trotted past the pickup and headed for a small square guest cottage that was hidden behind some boxwood bushes on the far side of the parking area.

The cottage looked in better shape than the main building, less battered and bruised. Cal trotted up the steps. I expected him to plunge inside, but he stopped short and knocked at the door in an incongruous burst of etiquette. "This is the Maniac's place," he told me. "I mean, he crashes here sometimes. He's got a whole bunch of places he hangs out, but I don't know where all of them are."

"Looks like he's a good housekeeper," I said.

"His women keep it up for him. And even the stoners and the blood know better than to fuck with the Maniac's pad."

Cal started to knock on the door again but I put out a hand to stop him. "Hold on a second. Who was the girl we left back in the apartment building?"

Cal tried to shrug away the subject. "She goes by Needles. I don't know her real name."

"She mentioned another girl to me."

"Who? Lisa?"

I shook my head. "Sherry."

"Sherry who?"

"Sherry Misteen. Do you know her, Cal?"

Cal labored to look blank and blasé. "Sherry. Yeah. She and Lisa were real tight for a while."

"What happened between them?"

"Who knows?" His shrug was comprehensive.

"Where's Sherry now?"

"Who knows?"

"Needles says she's dead."

Cal jerked as though I'd slapped him, then examined me to see if I knew anything or was just making guesses. "Is she right, Cal?" I went on. "Is Sherry Misteen dead?"

Cal's face cast off its initial wrinkle of concern. "That's what they say."

"Who says?"

"I don't know. People, you know? You hear stuff on the street. Half the time it's bogus, anyway. I mean, all kinds of people are supposed to be dead, and aren't right? Paul Mc-Cartney? All them guys."

"How does the street say she died, Cal?"

"I don't know, man," Cal muttered with exasperation. "Probably the same way Needles is going to die."

"Do they say someone killed her, Cal?"

"Naw. Nothing like that." Cal's eyes rolled. "Now come on. Needles and Sherry are stale. Lisa's in here."

Cal knocked on the door again, and he must have heard something because he nodded briskly, turned the knob and opened the door. "Come on," he urged, then paused and eyed me speculatively. "You got a gun?"

"No."

"Good."

"Why?"

"The Maniac don't like guns."

"You mean except his own."

Cal frowned. "Maybe you better wait out here. You know, till I check it out. If Lisa's there, I'll bring her out."

When I didn't respond, Cal disappeared inside the little bungalow. After several seconds I followed along.

The narrow foyer was dark and empty. From the sharp smell I guessed it had recently served as a cat's boudoir. The first door off the foyer opened onto a small kitchen, with sink and counter and cupboards, but no appliances and no furniture. One of the girls I'd seen earlier in People's Park was standing at the counter, her back to me, struggling in the dim glow from a candle stub to open a canned ham. On the counter beside the ham were two bricks of cheese and two bottles of red wine. I wondered if they were bought or stolen. Cal didn't pause at the kitchen, but went straight to the other room, which took up the entire remainder of the cottage but for the bathroom that smoldered in vandalized putrescence next to the kitchen.

The living room was a hazy cave of light and shadows, furnished in makeshift fashion—the couch a vinyl car seat, the table an empty spool of phone cable, the chairs a ripped-off park bench and several mounds of fabric bound with twine into bulbous pillows. The only light came from a dozen or so candles arranged around a bowl of something dark and fluid in a way that looked symbolic.

A tape deck played a repetitive, mechanical rhythm in the style of Philip Glass. All but two of the occupants lay along the walls, smoking dope, oblivious of me and of each other, invisible in the shadows but for the hot dots of their reefers and the milky marbles of their sleepy eyes. But none of those were the eyes that Cal and I had come to see. Lisa's eyes, like the rest of her, were snug beside the Maniac.

They were sprawled on the car-seat couch, arms across each other's shoulders, heads inclined and touching, slumped so that they were lying, chins on chests, rather than sitting. Lisa looked uneasy when she saw us coming, but it was Cal she was watching, not me. The Maniac, on the other hand, gave me his entire attention as he huddled like an armadillo in the soft shell of his field jacket, his eyes red and active, his breath rapid, his lips smacking noisily, his foot vibrating like a safety valve to the man's compulsive devilment.

As I approached, the Maniac released Lisa's hand and slid his own behind his back, slowly, so as not to alarm me. I pretended not to notice that when it emerged again it was curled around a pistol. He didn't point it at me, but nestled it between his legs and left it there.

His face was large and square, framed by bangs of dirt-brown hair that crossed his forehead like a tattered hem. His eyes were small, tucked behind a protective squint. He seemed much bigger than he had in the park, more powerful and more threatening, yet it was a man-child's menace, sporadic and unpredictable. Either that or he used his deranged expressions and his manic gestures as a ploy, to gain the psychological upper hand. If that was his game, it wasn't entirely ineffective.

"Hi, Lisa," Cal said, trying to keep the hurt and worry from his voice, trying to keep his cool. But his roiling body and his halting voice betrayed him, so obviously that the Maniac emitted a burst of wild, belittling laughter.

Lisa barely reacted to Cal's greeting, barely managed a brief, high "Hi." The Maniac noted her reserve, nodded approvingly, and squeezed her more snugly to his flank.

"Can I talk to you outside for a minute?" Cal went on, undaunted by the Maniac's thick glare.

"Am I invisible?" the Maniac blurted. Like his face, the words were bloated, melodramatic, angry. "Do I not exist?"

"Hello, Maniac," Cal managed.

"I am often not where I seem to be," the Maniac said mysteriously. "I am often where I am least expected."

Cal didn't know what to say to that, so he looked at Lisa again. "Lisa? Can we rap?"

The Maniac interrupted again. "What brings you to me? Do you need help? Are you like the rest? Like this one? Do you need me as your instrument: to oust the beasts that feast upon your soul?"

"I just want to talk to Lisa, Maniac."

"Ha. Then like the others who seek her out you must not have heard."

"Heard what?"

"Of Lisa's vow."

"What vow?"

The Maniac's grin of glee was followed immediately by a frown of caution. I still had no idea whether he was playing or was truly addled. He might not have known himself.

"Lisa talks only to *me*," the Maniac continued. "As always, I am her instrument. To speak to her you must speak through me. I am Papa Bell. I reach out and clutch someone."

Cal gulped air as though it was an upper. "Come on, Lisa. This guy doesn't own you. Please? Just come outside for a minute."

She dared only a flick of her eyes; to the Maniac, then back to Cal. I wanted to help Cal out, but I had no idea how to do it, so I just stayed quiet and kept my eye on the pistol.

The Maniac finally broke the silence. "So. It appears the lines have all gone dead. So why don't you get out of here before I have to *hang you up*?"

The final words were dense and leaden, unmistakably a threat, shoved forth by a gristly lump of tongue. The Maniac's free hand drifted to his weapon. Cal took a quick step back, and for the first time noticed me. He made a silent plea for help, but I wasn't certain I was going to be able to give him any.

The scene was taking on the trappings of an Elizabethan farce, with Cal and me the jesters, the Maniac the insanely jealous monarch. I didn't want to leave it that way for long, but I was interested in whether Cal and Lisa were going to work it out. I was pretty sure Cal would come up empty, but I owed him the chance to make it happen.

My presence gave Cal the heart to try once more. "Lisa? You know I'm your friend, Lisa. Just talk to me for a while. That's all. That can't do any harm, can it?"

Cal's words fell into an empty world. Lisa was beyond en-treaty, knew only the Maniac, obeyed only his erratic will. I sensed it had become my turn.

I hadn't much more to ask than Cal had asked, and I had no reason to expect a better result, so I tried a different tack, one which had as its chief stratagem the effort to keep the Maniac talking until he said something I could use. He looked like an obsessive type, and obsessives like to hear their own voices, probably so their obsessions won't be complicated by dissent or by the always scrambled truth.

"You're Ronald Nifton, aren't you?" I began.

He left his gun between his legs and clasped his hands behind his head and regarded me peacefully. "Who are you?"

"Tanner."

"More."

"A private investigator. I'm looking into the death of Lisa's mother."

"Death. I look into death quite often." He uttered a staccato giggle. "What I get off on is when Death looks back." His smile became both mad and maddening. His foot was a blur of move-ment.

"I've come for information," I said. "From Lisa."

"I can think of no reason for her to give you any."

"There's been one murder. And maybe two."

"There are many murders. Bodies, minds, spirits, all are mur-dered by this world. As *The Astral Light* discloses, humanity must disgorge its diseased members. What has this to do with me?"

"You're connected to the murders I'm talking about."

The Maniac rolled his eyes and opened his mouth. His tongue flopped forward briefly, a reptile trying to escape its cage.

"Connected? Of course I am connected to murder. I am a murderer. Aren't I, Lisa?"

"Yes, Maniac." Her voice was as small as Cal's slim hopes. She seemed not at all revolted by the Maniac's grotesque expres-sions.

"I'm talking about the murder of Lisa's mother," I persisted. "You know Lisa, and you know her father, too."

The Maniac closed his eyes. "I know too much. I know more than they believe, more than they will ever allow me to say."

"I think you know of another murder too. Her name was Sherry. Sherry Misteen."

For the first time since I'd started talking, Lisa Usser did more than listen with an alert passivity. Her eyes locked on mine with sudden sharp ferocity. I felt both hatred and apprehension in her stare.

"Sherry." The Maniac seemed truly puzzled, as if the name were new to him. Then Lisa whispered in his ear, and he smiled and nodded. "We knew her as Lady Lancelot."

"Then she really is dead?"

"We are all dead," the Maniac said with finality. "Death before Disappointment is the teaching of the modern world. Right, Lisa? We die so that we may live."

Lisa seemed to accept his nonsense, which was the most worrisome thing I'd seen her do since I'd arrived. Before the Maniac could dismiss me the way he had dismissed Cal, I tried to keep him going.

"You're the Nifton who killed that student a couple of years ago, right?"

He frowned. "I am what I wish to be. My past is what others wish it was."

"When did you change your name?"

His eyes gleamed to match the candles. "My identity was disclosed to me by a box of men. They recognized what I am, and they labled me so that I would not forget. I am grateful for the revelation."

"You mean your trial."

He raised his brows. "You know of it?"

"You enjoy a certain fame in legal circles."

"Legal circles make you dizzy." Once again, Nifton's tongue slipped from his mouth and dangled like a limp, soft sock. His thoughts seem to drift beyond the room, only to return a moment later. *I am a maniac,* Nifton declared, emphasizing each word. "Officially adjudged and decreed. I am also officially without responsibility for my actions. Which leaves open an interesting question, don't you think?"

"You mean if not you, then who?"

"Exactly. I occasionally suggest to the tiresome Christians who accost me along the avenue that according to their tenets the answer must necessarily be God. They do not seem comfortable with the suggestion. But I am merely pointing toward salvation. A 'comfortable Christian' is an oxymoron, is it not?"

"I wouldn't know."

"You are not a believer?"

"I have my own theology, I suppose."

"Does it posit a supreme being?"

"More like a supreme obligation," I said, then hurried to shift the focus from my own ideas and onto his. "How about yourself? How do you see the subject?"

"*The Astral Light* is the one true food for all our souls. You feel the same way, don't you, Lisa?"

The Maniac gave her a proprietary pat. Lisa nodded, but halfheartedly. I sensed she was coming off whatever downer she'd been on, was regaining or reasserting a portion of her will. If she was as brilliant as her father, then a large portion of her devotion to the Maniac must have been self-induced, even self-inflicted. I guessed she used drugs to maintain the stance. And I guessed that even drugs weren't always enough to live with the charade.

"Tell me more about the trial," I urged. "Who was your lawyer?"

"I had an army of them. They understood nothing, but those opposed to me understood even less."

"Was Lawrence Usser one of them?"

I glanced at Lisa to see if her father's name would provoke a reaction. It did, but it was beyond interpretation. Her narrow face was squeezed to a numb rigidity; her eyes seemed to search for something safe but fail to find it.

"I know the name," the Maniac said calmly. "I know the face. I know the mind."

"Have you seen Usser lately?"

"Why would I? I know all I wish to know about him. He is an intensely selfish man, and the consequence is here beside me." He patted Lisa once again.

"I heard he helped your sister, Laura, find a job."

For the first time I provoked him. He sat up straight and momentarily brandished the gun. "*Never* say her name again. She has nothing to do with me. The Maniac has no sister. No mother, father, no one. The Maniac is sui generis, sprung from the ear of Ebenezer, the cunt of Cassiopeia."

The Maniac was a fool but not a stupid one. I kept at it, still hoping something would anger him enough to reveal a trail I could follow. "It seems like Lawrence Usser's got a pretty strong tie to you," I said. "Getting you off a murder charge; giving your sister a job; letting you take his daughter away from him. He's done a lot for you."

"For me? Or to me?"

"Well," I said, gesturing at the room, "this isn't much but it's better than jail."

"Jail means nothing," the Maniac boasted. "They cannot jail the mind of a maniac."

"They can scramble it up a bit."

"Impossible. A maniac's mind is prescrambled and pre-shrunk." His glazed eyes focused again. "Why are you here?"

"I'm a friend of Professor Usser's. I'm trying to find out why his wife died."

"You think I killed her?"

"I don't know. Did you?"

His smile was easy. "I doubt it. It doesn't seem to be my style."

"You've killed a woman before."

"Only because I loved her."

"Did you love Mrs. Usser?"

"I don't believe so. I don't believe I loved her at all." He gave Lisa a chilling glance, then reached into his pocket and took something out and popped it into his mouth. Whatever it was would probably take him even further from me than he was already.

"Did you know her?" I persisted.

"In what sense?"

"In any sense."

"Perhaps unconsciously. Perhaps in the fifth dimension. Perhaps in a former life."

"How about the here and now?"

"I am more familiar with the there and later."

I sighed and plunged ahead. "If you didn't know her mother, how did you meet Lisa?"

"She came to me. As they have all come to me."

"Why?"

"For understanding."

"Of what?"

"Of how the dead can become alive."

"How is that?"

"By doing what I tell them to do. By doing what I *let* them do."

"What do you let them do?"

"Accept their desires; dare the forbidden." Nifton smiled smugly. "When they learn I have killed the one who denied my passion, killed and yet walk free, they know I tell the truth, risk the truth, *am* the truth."

Nifton's soliloquy was followed by a reverential silence, as frightening as it was real. I couldn't help thinking about the Manson clan, about what black thoughts must have been hatched during mad meanderings of the sort Nifton had just engaged in. I shuddered inside my clothes and looked at the girl at Nifton's side. "I'm looking for some truth myself," I said quietly. "I think Lisa knows the truth I need. So why don't you let me talk to her?"

"She would talk to you if she wished. But she does not. She has nothing to say to any of you, do you, Lisa?"

Lisa shook her head and lowered her eyes. "What are you afraid of?" I asked, my question directed at Nifton but my hopes directed at the girl.

Nifton opened his mouth. I assumed another barrage of psycho-babble was on the way, but nothing happened. Time seemed to take a nap; the world to miss a turn.

Nifton groaned, then suddenly stiffened, his arms locked at his sides, his legs thrust forward, as stiff as crutches. His jaw clamped shut on his lolling tongue; his eyes rolled up until the sockets were two white holes. His body twitched and jerked, flopping off the couch in the process. Blood gushed from his tongue and down his cheek. His body bucked more violently with each mad thrust, the throes of a mortal wound.

I hurried to his side but Lisa beat me to him. When I knelt beside her, she reached out and shoved me away. "It's just a fit. He does it all the time. We can handle it."

"How can I help?"

"You can't. Just leave. Take Cal with you."

I couldn't take my eyes off Nifton. "You should pry open his mouth. Then be sure he doesn't swallow his tongue."

"I *know* what I should do," Lisa said impatiently. "I've done it a thousand times."

"Is he an epileptic?"

"Sort of. It's too complicated to explain right now. Will you please get *out* of here?"

Her voice maintained an icy calm. She turned away from me and bent over the Maniac and worked at loosening his jaw. Two other people roused themselves from their stupors and moved wordlessly to Lisa's side and held Nifton's arms and legs so Lisa could more easily free his tongue.

I glanced at Cal. He had retreated in horror at the scene, and stood with his back against the wall like a candidate for a firing squad. I was startled myself, but also amazed at the calm with which the young people worked over the Maniac's thrashing body, as though they had staffed an emergency room for years and had seen life in all its strange mutations long before this night.

"Should I call an ambulance?" I asked, conscious that I was asking the question for the second time that night, conscious that I was among people who concocted cures themselves or chose to do without.

"We can handle it, I said." Lisa glanced at me quickly. "Please go. Come to my house tomorrow. I may be there, if I can get away."

Before I could ask what time I should be there she turned back to Nifton, patted his field jacket pockets until she felt what she was looking for, then unsnapped the pocket and removed a small brown bottle. She held it to the light, unscrewed the cap and extracted a glass eyedropper, filled it, and squirted its contents into Nifton's open mouth. Moments later his spasms seemed to slacken. Lisa began to stroke his brow and croon in low, soft sounds.

I looked at Cal again.

"Fuck it," he said. "I'm splitting. Lisa's all yours. Yours and the Maniac's. Hope you like her."

Cal headed for the door. I decided I owed him a share of his retreat. Before I joined him, I looked back at Lisa. "Your father's being arraigned tomorrow. In Berkeley Municipal Court. The D.A. wants you there. If you're not, your father will probably be released on bail. I think maybe you don't want that to happen. I'll be there too. I'd like to talk to you about the murder. And about Sherry Misteen." I paused. "Also, the Renzels are worried about you. They want you to come and live with them instead of with the Ussers. If I were you, I'd take them up on the invitation."

Lisa had no reaction to any of it. I turned and followed Cal out the door.

NINETEEN

By the time I was outside, Cal was trotting far ahead of me, a furtive shadow in the meek light from the distant street-lamp. I called out to ask if he wanted a ride, but he shook his head and kept running away from the girl who had hocked his heart. I went to my car, got inside and drove back up the hill, till I was once again on Haste Street, across from People's Park.

My plan was to retrieve whatever it was that Lisa Usser had buried there, but I was going to have to wait. When I was half-way into the grove of trees I could see that another cluster of people had occupied the site, this time a group of tattered transients who had built their own fire and were passing around a bottle wrapped in a brown bag while swearing drunkenly at each other and the world. One of them was curled into a fetal ball on the exact spot where Lisa had dug her hole and buried her treasures. I waited for a few minutes, but it was clear it would take many more pulls at the bottle to blot out enough inflamed consciousness to allow any of them to sleep. I walked back to my car, but halfway there I detoured toward a phone booth.

I looked up the number of the Berkeley police and called it. Bart Kinn wasn't in. I left a message that I had seen Lisa Usser at the Blake Street place they call Hell House less than thirty minutes before. I tried to make it sound like no big deal. The woman on the other end said she'd get the message to Kinn.

From her tone it sounded like it wouldn't reach him till he was pulling down his pension, which suited me just fine. Still, I hung up feeling less than sterling for having fulfilled my part of the bargain I'd made with the authorities in the persons of Bart Kinn and Howard Gable.

I started to leave the phone booth but there was no exit, not yet, not until I fished out another dime and looked up the number for an ambulance service, dialed it and told the woman who answered that there was a girl in pretty bad shape at a house on Blake, drug problems, probably, and she needed help. I gave the woman the street number and started to tell her how to find the place. "I know it," the woman said wearily. "I probably even know the girl."

"They call her Needles."

"Yeah. Needles. Well, here's the way it is, pal. The last time we took Needles in, no one paid the bill. So this time she's on her own."

The phone died quickly in my ear. I considered making another call, to someone whose compassion was less shrunken by the steamy laws of economics, but in the end I didn't. It was the kind of situation where intervention can bring more trouble than it prevents. Or so I was believing as I hung up the receiver and noticed the sign scrawled on the coin box with a Magic Marker: THE GODDESS WILL BE CALLING YOU. I didn't know what that meant. I didn't know what much of anything meant in Berkeley, so I got in my car and drove home.

When I got to my apartment, my phone was ringing. It was Ingrid Renzel. I was trying to decide what to tell her about my investigation, such as it was, when she interrupted me. "We have received another call."

"What did it say?"

"That there is something happening in court tomorrow. That Lawrence may be set free when it is over. Can that be true, Mr. Tanner?"

I took a deep breath. "Tomorrow's the arraignment, Mrs. Renzel. It doesn't have anything to do with Lawrence Usser's guilt or innocence, it's just the time when he hears the charges that have been filed against him and has a chance to enter a plea. He'll undoubtedly plead not guilty. There may also be a bail hearing. Do you know what bail is?"

"Where they pay money and go free?"

"Yes, but only temporarily. Till the trial starts."

"So Lawrence will be free tomorrow." She made it sound like Doomsday.

"Not necessarily. Bail isn't automatic in this state anymore. For a serious offense, a hearing is held and the judge can deny bail if there is a substantial likelihood that the person's release would result in bodily harm to another, or if the defendant has made a threat to another person and there's a substantial likelihood that the threat would be carried out."

"So. Has Lawrence made such a threat?"

I started to tell her no, because it seemed so unlikely, but then I thought about it more carefully. "I think he may have," I said after a minute. "I think he may have done just that."

"Who? Who has he threatened?"

"I'm not sure, but I think he may have threatened his daughter."

Mrs. Renzel's breath hissed in an astonished gasp. "Lisa? He has threatened Lisa? When? How?"

"I don't know any details. I just think the district attorney expects her to testify to something like that at the arraignment. The problem is, Lisa ran away from the Ussers' place tonight. So the D.A. won't be able to present her testimony at the bail hearing, not if they don't find her before morning. And without Lisa's testimony my guess is Usser will be released pending trial. If he isn't, I'm sure his lawyer will go for a writ of habeas corpus to try to spring him that way."

Ingrid Renzel's voice was grave. "Gunther will not like it if Lawrence is released."

"But it's only temporary," I said again. "He hasn't been convicted of anything yet, you know. He's innocent until proven guilty, so bail is simply imposed to make sure he appears for his trial. Do you want me to talk to your husband about it? To explain some of these things to him?"

"Gunther is not here. He is drinking schnapps and playing euchre."

"Maybe you'd better not tell him about all this till he's sober."

"Yes."

"Is there anything else you can tell me about the phone call, Mrs. Renzel?"

"No. Only that it was the same man as before."

"Was he trying to disguise his voice?"

She took time to think about it. "It's possible. The sound was muffled. The words were spoken slowly."

"Okay. I'm going to the arraignment in the morning, and I'll let you know how it comes out. Do you still want me to work on the case?"

"Of course we do. Yes. But tell me. What have you found out? Was Lawrence sane? Was he in his right mind when he murdered our Dianne?"

"I don't know, Mrs. Renzel. All I can tell you is I haven't found any evidence that says he wasn't."

"That is good. That is very good."

I wasn't sure I agreed with her.

I tossed and turned with the Usser case all night. It was amorphous, a turbulent cloud, as variable and varied as one of Berkeley's demonstrations. I was traveling in no direction, was taking no ground, was learning a lot about the Usser family but nothing at all about why Dianne Renzel had been murdered. The key was clearly Lisa, but getting her away from the Maniac would be difficult. If she was inclined to separate herself from him voluntarily, I should know it at the arraignment. But if she didn't show up, I'd have to track her down, possibly by finding her at her house as she had suggested, but probably by pursuing the Maniac to another lair.

The first thing in the morning I was on my way back to Berkeley. The arraignment would be in the Municipal Court, a cheaply constructed blue and beige building next to the old city hall. I circled the block several times before finding a place to park on McKinley Avenue, across from the Hall of Justice building which housed the police department and the municipal jail, where Usser was undoubtedly being held pending arraignment. My parking slot was next to an abandoned apartment building that seemed stuffed full of bicycles. I was about to get out of my car when I saw the rear door to the Hall of Justice open and a line of men file out.

They were handcuffed to waist chains and joined to each other by the chain that passed through their leg hobbles. Two policemen watched over them casually, as though the chances of escape were nil. All of the men were black except one. The one was Lawrence Usser. From where I sat, Usser looked serene, almost happy, his eyes bright, his lips parted in a half-smile. It was exactly the opposite of what I would expect, which made it the first sign I'd uncovered that Lawrence Usser might actually have lost his mind.

The line of men crossed the parking area and disappeared through the back door to the courthouse. I hurried through the parking lot between the police and fire stations and ran around to the front door of the courthouse and went inside.

The only offices on the first floor were down a narrow hallway to my right. A court calendar was pinned to a bulletin board at the head of the hall, and it indicated that felony arraignments were in Department One, second floor. The fifth name on the list was *People* v. *Usser.* I trotted up the stairs and joined the crowd of people outside the door to Department One.

Most of the people I'd talked to over the past few days were there—Kinn and Gable, of course. And Lonborg. And Professor Howson and Krista Hellgren and Danny Wilken. And Carlton Usser, behind a cocky knot of news reporters. And, trotting up the stairs behind me, clutching a monogrammed calfskin portfolio, the great Jake Hattie.

Jake nodded a greeting that was less friendly than I anticipated and went inside the courtroom. When Howard Gable noticed Jake's arrival he followed him inside. The rest of us stayed in the hallway and tried to ignore each other.

Krista Hellgren caught my eye and smiled sadly. She didn't look in a mood to talk. Danny Wilken whispered something to her and put his hand on her shoulder. She quickly shrugged it off. Professor Howson wore a disdainful grimace that indicated she found the entire proceeding unseemly. Adam Lonborg stared out the window, his back to me and everyone. Carlton Usser started to join me, then decided not to. The parents and friends of the other men in the chained line looked either sorrowful or enraged. I drifted to the wall and leaned against it.

After a minute Bart Kinn joined me. "Ever catch up to Lisa Usser?" I asked.

"Nope. You?"

"Nope. I went home and went to bed."

"With Krista Hellgren?" Kinn smiled a lurid implication.

"What makes you think that?"

"Because after you left her place, she called the station to see

if anyone had heard of you, and if you were who you claimed
you were. Luckily I was there to back you up."

"Thanks. I think."

Kinn shut down. I had never seen a man so at ease with
silence. I asked him if there was anything new in the case. He
shook his head. I asked if Gable was going to oppose bail for
Usser. He nodded. I asked if he thought Gable would prevail.
He shrugged disinterestedly. "Might help if the guy was running loose," Kinn added after a minute.

I was about to ask him what he meant when the crowd began
to move toward the door. I glanced inside and saw the judge
standing behind the high wood bench, waiting beneath bright
squares of fluorescent light for the spectators to take their seats.

The blond wood furnishings of the courtroom were surrounded by sections of milk-chocolate paneling. The curved-
back theater seats were sufficiently numerous to accommodate
maybe thirty spectators, but we were an overflow crowd. The
bailiff eyed us warily, waited while we found our seats, then
instructed the standees to arrange themselves along a side wall.

When the din had subsided, the judge banged his gavel. "You
may stay seated," he said, then took his own seat high above us,
satisfied that the crowd was as comfortable as he could make it.
The sign in front of him said his name was Wu. He looked
impossibly young to be a judge of his own behavior, let alone of
anyone else's.

The line of men I'd seen in the parking lot were now seated
in the jury box, shoulder to shoulder, glum, sullen, motionless.
Lawrence Usser's former good humor had deserted him. Now
he stared forward in an unblinking daze, his hair splayed and
tangled, his clothes limp and wrinkled, his eyes locked on anything but the faces of the friends who had come to root for him
and the foes who wished him jailed.

The judge eyed the spectators one last time, frowned briefly
as his glance encompassed the cluster of reporters who sat in
the front row with their pens poised above their pads and their
feet on the bar of the court, then turned his attention to the
men in the jury box. Most of them didn't look back, even after
the judge began to speak to them. Most of them looked like they
had been there before. All of them, Lawrence Usser included,
somehow managed to look guilty as hell, if not of what they

were charged with then at least of something that would make flogging appropriate.

"This morning we have six arraignments," the judge began. "You have all been charged with a criminal offense, and today you will all have a chance to hear the charges that have been made against you, and to enter a plea to those charges. You have certain rights in this proceeding. Each of you has the right to an attorney. If you cannot afford an attorney, one will be provided for you. A deputy public defender is in court, and can advise those of you who do not have private counsel of your rights and options. Ultimately, each of you will have the right to confront the witnesses against you, and to a jury trial of the issues raised by the charges filed against you. You may or may not be entitled to bail. Your attorney can advise you on that matter, and will make an appropriate bail motion when the time comes. Now. The clerk will call the calendar."

The judge pulled a file toward him and the clerk consulted his list and called the first case. The charge was armed robbery, the defendant was indigent, the public defender was appointed to represent him and he entered a plea of not guilty on behalf of the defendant. Bail was set at fifty thousand dollars. The public defender objected, stating that the defendant had a job, had lived in Berkeley for nine years, was married and had never been convicted of a crime before. The prosecutor pointed out that the defendant was armed with a weapon both at the time he allegedly committed the crime and at the time of his arrest. Bail reduction was denied, and someone in the rear of the courtroom began to cry. The defendant was led out of the room by a sheriff's deputy, on his way to a bus that would deliver him to the Santa Rita Prison Farm, where he would stay until he was tried or until bail was reduced to an amount he could pay.

The second matter was a burglary, with much the same result, though without the tears. The third, an assault with intent to commit rape; the fourth, malicious mischief. The fifth matter was *People* v. *Usser*.

The professor and Jake Hattie met at the defense counsel's table, shook hands, exchanged smiles, one spare and wan, the other hearty and encouraging. Howard Gable stepped to the second table, laid a file folder on its varnished top and crossed his arms and eyed his adversaries with cool suspicion. *"People* versus *Lawrence Smithfield Usser,"* the judge announced. "Number CR 84-2601. Is that your true name, Mr. Usser?"

Usser nodded. "Yes, Your Honor."

The judge ruffled some papers. "The charge is murder in the first degree, as defined in Penal Code Section 189, with special circumstances as defined in P.C. 190.2, subdivisions 14 and 18. That is a capital offense, Mr. Usser. Thus you are required to be represented by counsel in all stages of the proceedings against you. Are you able to engage your own attorney?"

"Yes, Your Honor."

"And have you engaged such an attorney?"

"Yes."

Usser gestured to Jake Hattie. Jake stood as straight as a saluting solider. The judge began to smile. "Mr. Hattie, are you Mr. Usser's counsel in this matter?"

"I have that privilege, Your Honor."

"It's a pleasure to see you again, Mr. Hattie."

"Thank you, Your Honor. It's a pleasure to see one of my former law clerks serving the judiciary of this great state."

Judge Wu seemed momentarily embarrassed. "Thank you, Mr. Hattie. Now, since this is a capital case there are certain additional duties imposed upon you pursuant to Section 1240.1 of the Penal Code concerning the certification of the record on appeal following trial. Are you aware of those duties and do you agree to abide by them?"

"I am and I will, Your Honor."

"Very well. Do you waive reading of the indictment?"

"We do, Judge, subject of course to a later motion to set it aside as being improperly rendered."

"And is the defendant prepared to enter a plea to the indictment in this case?"

Jake nodded. "He is, Your Honor."

"And what is your plea, Mr. Usser?"

"I plead that I am not guilty of the offense charged." Usser's voice was barely audible to those of us in the back. Jake patted him on the back and whispered something in his ear.

"Very well," Judge Wu said. "Your plea has been entered on the minutes of the court."

"Your Honor?" Howard Gable's voice caused every head to turn his way.

"Yes, Mr. Gable?"

"May the people know whether there will be a motion pursuant to Section 1367 that the defendant is not competent to stand trial in this case?"

The judge started to speak but Jake Hattie raised a hand to stop him. "The people will know when and if such a motion is made, Mr. Gable. And the people may be assured that it will be made in a timely manner."

Gable returned Jake Hattie's grin. "Such a motion might bear upon the issue of bail, Your Honor."

"Bail," the judge repeated. "Mr. Hattie, what are your thoughts on the issue of bail? As if I didn't know."

Jake grasped his lapels with his pudgy hands and leaned against the counsel table. "Defendant requests release on his own recognizance, Your Honor. He is a respected member of the community and of the legal profession. The possibility that he would fail to appear for his trial is nonexistent. I am prepared to offer testimony from his colleagues as to Professor Usser's unimpeachable moral probity and reliability."

The judge nodded and swiveled in his chair. "Mr. Gable? What's your view on the matter?"

Howard Gable cleared his throat and shifted from foot to foot. "The defendant is charged with a serious offense. Bail is therefore not automatic. The district attorney's office is informed and believes that Mr. Usser has made threats to a major witness in the case. On that ground, we ask that bail be denied."

Jake Hattie seemed to have grown six inches in the last six seconds. His voice threatened to shatter the lights that bathed him in a holy glow. "The recent amendment to Article I of the California Constitution requires *proof* that such a threat was made, Your Honor. I hear only Mr. Gable's naked offer of a double-hearsay assertion of a preposterous event. Where is the proof? Where is the witness? In the absence of either, I request the defendant's immediate release."

"Mr. Gable? Are you prepared to prove the constitutional requirement?" the judge asked softly.

Gable hung his head. "Not at the moment, Your Honor. The witness is temporarily unavailable. However, I expect the witness to be located momentarily. Furthermore, this is a capital case. The people will seek the death penalty upon conviction.

In view of the heinous nature of the crime, and of the recent amendment concerning public safety bail, release of the defendant would be inappropriate regardless of the amount of bail."

"Your Honor!" Jake Hattie thundered. "Mr. Gable is apparently determined to try Professor Usser in the media, which is represented in force at this proceeding, as Mr. Gable well knows. Bail is a right unless specifically restricted. Section 1268(a) provides that bail is inappropriate in a capital case only, and I quote, 'where the proof is evident or the presumption thereof great.' Neither of those circumstances is present in this case. Professor Usser will appear at his trial, and he will be acquitted of all charges against him. At that point he may have charges of his *own* to file, against the law enforcement officials who have conspired to persecute him in this manner because of his valiant defense of the rights of the psychologically disabled persons in this society, persons whom Mr. Gable and his cohorts would clearly prefer to see locked away in dungeons, out of sight and out of mind, regardless of the mens rea component of the criminal law, an element of willfulness that has been a hallmark of civilized societies since the thirteenth century. Therefore, I object strenuously to—"

"That's enough, Mr. Hattie," the judge interrupted. "Bail will be set at five hundred thousand dollars, subject as usual to a petition for reduction or withdrawal. Now . . ."

"Your Honor?"

"Yes, Mr. Gable."

"May the people know whether defendant contemplates a change of plea prior to trial? Specifically, may we know whether Mr. Usser intends to plead not guilty by reason of insanity? If he does, then the court's appointment of psychiatrists pursuant to Section 1027 could go forward immediately, and the evaluation of defendant's mental state could be performed at a time as near as possible to the date the offense was committed."

Jake Hattie seemed about to explode. "The defendant will move for an amended plea when and if he chooses to do so. For the district attorney to attempt to force the issue is an outrageous—"

Lawrence Usser said something but nobody could hear what it was, not at first. He coughed and tried again, and this time every ear could hear the words. "I do plead insanity, Your

Honor. If I did in fact kill my wife, Dianne, it was because I was insane."

Jake Hattie frowned and pulled Usser toward him and whispered something urgent in his ear. Usser shook his head and leaned away. Howard Gable smiled. Jake Hattie looked up at the judge. "The plea at this time is against my advice, Your Honor. I ask that it be withdrawn."

"It is clearly the defendant's wish," Howard Gable insisted. "The plea should stand."

Judge Wu was frowning. Finally he shrugged. "This is a matter for the Superior Court. For now, both pleas will be entered. Preliminary hearing is set for November 19. Call the next case please, Mr. Clerk."

Both Hattie and Gable opened their mouths to object, then both thought better of it. I glanced at Carlton Usser. He already had his checkbook out. The man next to him looked more like a banker than a bail bondsman, but in either case I had no doubt that Lawrence Usser would be on the street by noon.

The majority of spectators stood up and filed toward the hallway. The next defendant stood silently by his chair as the courtroom cleared, eyes closed, head bowed, thankful for anything that would delay for even an instant what life now had in store for him.

TWENTY

joined the line of Usser's supporters that was heading for the exit. Behind me, Jake Hattie was huddling with Lawrence Usser and his father, arranging the mechanics of the bail deposit with the banker/bondsman and the clerk of the court.

In line directly in front of me was a tall, slim man, forty or so, with long hair and arms that seemed to hang to his knees. His jacket and slacks were of unmatched corduroy, his shoes the kind they used to call desert boots. Because he seemed a part of Berkeley's past rather than its present, I tapped him on the shoulder.

He must have assumed it was accidental because he ignored me and kept moving toward the door. I tapped again. By this time we were out in the hall, buffeted by the rest of the crowd. The tall man glanced back at me, then stopped and turned. "Yes?" he said. "Do you want something?"

His words were as soft as chamois. "Is your name Pierce Richards?"

"Yes."

"Can I talk to you for a minute?" I gestured toward the window to a place out of everyone's way.

"Well, I . . ."

"It's about the Renzel case. About Dianne Renzel, in particular."

"I see." He twisted uncomfortably, obviously reluctant.

"You were her boss, weren't you?"

"Actually we were co-directors. You're not from the police, are you?"

"No."

"Are you a lawyer?"

"No. A private investigator."

"Working for Professor Usser?"

"No."

He was bothered by my reticence, but his chiseled cheeks supported kindly eyes and he was too much the gentleman to refuse me. He shrugged and walked to the window and waited for me to join him. I was squeezing through one last group of spectators when I noticed that one of them was Danny Wilken. When he saw me, he smiled his surfer's smile. I asked him how collections were going.

"About the same," he said cheerfully, eyes casting beyond me to a target I guessed was Krista Hellgren. "Do you want to make another contribution?"

I shook my head and thought about his phone call to Krista Hellgren, and about the phone booth next to the bike racks at the law school, and about the ticking sound that bicycles make when you push them. I put my hand on his shoulder in a comradely fashion. "I want to talk to you for a minute," I said, and started to guide him toward the wall. When Danny began to resist, I squeezed the trapezius muscle until it hurt him.

"Hey. What's this all about?" The surfer's grin was replaced by wide-eyed disbelief.

"Just this," I said, and shoved him toward an unoccupied space. Danny lost his balance and had to use his hands to keep from crashing into the wall. By the time he had turned back toward me I had my finger in his face.

"Someone's been making phone calls to the Renzels," I said with my most sinister sizzle.

"Yeah? So?" Danny had retrieved a portion of his courage, but his failure to ask who the Renzels were augmented my filmy hunch.

"The calls are coming from someone who knows quite a bit about criminal procedure," I said. "And they're coming from someone who's more concerned about Lawrence Usser staying in jail than about whether or not he killed his wife."

"Hey. I don't know what the fuck you're talking about, man."

"I think you do, Danny. I think you're the one who's been making those calls, in the hope that Usser will be held in jail from now till his trial, and then be found guilty and imprisoned for a long time after that."

"Why the hell would I care whether he's in jail or not?" Danny protested, his voice high and whistling.

"Because if he's in jail you'll have a better chance to make a move on Krista Hellgren. I know you've been trying to get her to go out with you, and I know she won't do it. I don't give a damn about that, but I do give a damn about the Renzels. They've got enough to worry about without you messing with their minds. So the phone calls stop. Right now. No more scare tactics; no more scenarios that suggest Usser will get off without being punished for murdering their daughter."

Danny's top lip curled. "Yeah, well, look at what just happened in there. He *is* getting off, isn't he?"

I pressed Danny against the wall. "You'd better get back to the law school and learn a little more about the system, Danny. Usser hasn't gotten away with anything. Not yet, he hasn't. Pretrial detention's a tool of dictators. Instead of making phone calls to frightened old ladies why don't you take some time and learn why that is."

When I took my hand away, Danny Wilken stumbled toward the stairs. He looked back at me once, muttered a defiant oath, but he kept going until he had disappeared down the stairwell.

I turned back to Pierce Richards, who was glancing at his watch and fretting about being late for something. I joined him at the window. Down in the parking lot the line of chained men was returning to the Hall of Justice. This time every one of them was black.

I told Richards I was sorry for the delay. He told me it was okay. His blue eyes were clear and trusting. His narrow neck wobbled as he spoke, and his long, thin fingers slipped in and out of his jacket pocket, as though they'd been ousted from their former home and were looking for a new one. "I'm looking into Mrs. Usser's death," I began. "I—"

"I'd prefer you refer to her as Ms. Renzel. It was the name I knew her by; the name she preferred."

Richards' voice was deep and clinging, not easily ignored. "I understand you and she were close," I said.

"We worked together closely, if that's what you mean."

"I mean closer than that."

I let the phrase lie there by itself, hoping Richards would give it meaning, but he merely nodded abstractedly, as though I had commented about the weather.

"I was wondering if you had any idea why Usser killed her?" I asked bluntly.

Richards' eyes squeezed into a pained squint. "No. Why would I?"

"I thought maybe you could tell me if Usser was jealous."

"Of whom?"

"Of you."

"But why . . . ?"

"Because of your relationship with his wife."

"Who suggested I had a relationship with her? Other than a professional one, of course."

"The suggestion was made by someone in a position to know."

"I see." Richards' back stiffened and his jaw set. "Well, Dianne is dead. Her private life is no business of yours, nor of anyone's. I have a staff meeting at the center, so if you'll excuse me I'll be going."

"I'll tell you something that might interest you, Mr. Richards," I said quickly. "The police may have arrested Lawrence Usser and charged him with the murder, but they don't have the faintest idea why he did it."

"So?"

"So juries like to know why. If no one tells them why, they frequently decide that if there was no reason for the guy to do it then maybe he actually *didn't* do it. And they let him go. It would be a shame if that happened in this case, Mr. Richards, particularly if there was someone around who *knew* why. Someone like you, for instance."

Richards sighed heavily and turned to look out the window. Whatever he thought made him shudder. He turned back to me and wiped his brow with his spidery hand. "What do you want to know?"

"I want to know whether Usser ever made any comment about your affair with Dianne Renzel, to you or to his wife."

"You mean threats of some sort?"

"Yes. Or anything else that indicated he knew what was going on."

"Oh, he knew."

"How?"

"Dianne told him."

"Why?"

"I'm not sure. She was mad at him for some reason."

"What happened?"

"Nothing, as far as I know. Lawrence had his own women, of course. He always had. Now Dianne had someone too. Usser told her he was happy for her."

"Did she ask for a divorce?

"No."

"Why not?"

"Because she loved him." Richards closed his eyes against the fact his words established.

"Did you want her to divorce him?"

"Of course."

"Did you and Usser have a confrontation over it?"

"No. I rarely saw him. When I did, he seemed always to be laughing at me. Of course, that was before Dianne gave in to my advances."

"You sound as though you didn't have much use for Usser."

"I hated him," Richards said simply. "Because of the way he treated her."

"Even though his mistreatment ultimately drove her to you?"

"I . . ." Richards fumbled with his thoughts.

"How about Dianne? Did you hate her, too, when she wouldn't leave Usser and live with you?"

"I was upset. Yes. But I had hopes she would change her mind."

"Upset enough to kill her?"

It was a silly question, but Richards' reaction was deadly serious. "The murderer is in that courtroom, with his high-priced lawyer and his fat-cat father, and he's going to get away with what he did. I know that as well as I know that I will never be as happy as I was the four short weeks before Dianne died."

"Your affair only lasted a month?"

"Yes."

Richards twisted away from me and lurched toward the stairs, half blinded by a scrim of tears. "Can I come see you at the crisis center?" I called after him. "To talk about Ms. Renzel's work?"

Richards seemed to nod, though perhaps he was only urging his body to flee from me even faster than it was already.

I was still thinking about Pierce Richards and Dianne Renzel when the door to the courtroom opened and Adam Lonborg, Usser's psychiatrist friend, came into the hallway. When he saw me, he marched my way as though he suspected I had slandered him. "I thought that was you in there," Lonborg said as he approached. "Why are you still poking around in Larry's life?"

"Because I'm getting paid for it."

Lonborg tugged at the lapels of his blue blazer. The gold crest over the pocket exactly matched his hair and was doubtlessly significant to the millions more enlightened than I. "Did you persuade the police to arrest Larry?" he asked suddenly.

"Why would I do that?"

"I thought maybe you'd come up with some ridiculous Sam Spade theory as to why he must have done it."

I shook my head. "I was as surprised as anyone when they charged him."

Lonborg inspected me to see if I was telling the truth. "Then tell me this, Tanner. Now that Larry's been arrested, why aren't the Renzels satisfied? Or do they want a private pound of flesh as well?"

"I think what they want is to see that Usser doesn't get away with it."

"Get away with it?" Lonborg frowned. "How would he do that?"

"By having a psychiatrist like you take the stand and say he was suffering from an acute associative amalgamation or some such horror, aggravated by a manic delusive occlusion, so the jury will decide he was legally insane and let him off. Then, after he's committed for treatment, those same shrinks will line up to proclaim him miraculously cured, praise to Jung, and swear that he can be released from the mental ward without the slightest risk to either himself or the rest of us."

"Those terms you used make no sense. Neither does your forecast of the future."

"Nevertheless, that's what the Renzels are afraid of. Can you suggest any recent history that proves they're foolish?"

Lonborg smiled easily but ignored my request. "If that's what they're afraid of, how do you think you're going to stop it?"

"I'm not sure. Any suggestions?"

"Not really." Lonborg shrugged. "Except perhaps for you to go back to San Francisco and forget all about Lawrence Usser."

"Why should I do that?"

"Because he's a disturbed young man." Lonborg's eyes bored into mine. "Brilliant, but disturbed. His rehabilitation will be long and difficult. It won't be helped by you poking and prying into the far corners of his past, reminding him of the pressures that converged to cause the problem in the first place. You see, your usual mode of operation has no meaning in this case, Mr. Tanner. Whether he did it and why he did it and how he did it, the usual focus of a criminal investigation, is irrelevant here. Lawrence Usser is mentally ill. He is not capable of forming the usual indicia of criminal conduct. He is not guilty of anything, in any sense that is commonly understood within these walls."

"You mean they should just let him go and forget about it?"

"Not forget about it. Merely see to it that Larry receives appropriate treatment."

"From you, I suppose."

"Not necessarily, though now that Dianne is dead, I do know Larry better than anyone else. I believe I could put that knowledge to use therapeutically."

"What do you think is wrong with him?"

Lonborg smiled another flash of neon tolerance. "I have ideas, and I'm certain my ideas are correct. But this is neither the time nor the place to discuss them. I suggest you tell your clients that their sense of vengeance is misplaced, Mr. Tanner. They would as appropriately be enraged at the weapon he used or the clothes he wore. Neither Larry nor the weapon nor his clothing could help what happened that night, because none of them possessed a will strong enough to prevent it. So go home, Mr. Tanner. Go home and leave us to our little tragedy. To do with as we will."

"Let me ask you something, Lonborg."

"Yes?"

"There's something I don't understand. Your patient Lisa Usser tells the police her father murdered her mother, and tells them he's threatened her as well. Yet here you are, spouting a sob story about Usser's problems and why everyone should go away and leave poor Larry alone. Isn't there a conflict of interest there, Doctor?"

Lonborg's lips curled. "I don't need you to tell me my ethical responsibilities, Tanner. I am treating Lisa when I can, and I will continue to do so. Her statements to the police indicate she has regressed dramatically, to an infantile primitivism. The fact that I am sympathetic to her father's dilemma has no bearing on her treatment."

"When's the last time you saw Lisa?"

"Why?"

"Because she's a little hard to locate these days. I thought maybe you could tell me how you go about it."

"I can tell you nothing, Mr. Tanner. About Lisa or Lawrence, either one."

"Oh, you've told me one thing, Lonborg."

"What's that?"

"You've told me that you think your buddy killed his wife."

Lonborg shook his head then strolled away, his soft shoes silent as bare feet as he crossed the empty hallway.

I stayed behind, gazing out the window at the rear wall of the police station, wondering what it had been like for a man like Lawrence Usser to spend the weekend within its walls, wondering why the case made less sense the more I learned about the participants in it, wondering if I should call the Renzels and, as Lonborg had suggested, remove myself from charting Usser's fall. After a few more minutes I shrugged my mind and started to leave the way all the others had left.

"Tanner."

The voice was gruff and dictatorial. I turned and faced the scowl of Jake Hattie. As usual he was strutting like a bantam rooster and was about to bust his buttons. "What the hell are you doing here, Tanner?"

"Just looking, Jake."

"Well, you're not working for me, and you're not working for my client, so I can only assume you're on the other side. Am I right?"

"To tell you the truth, I don't know."

"What the hell does that mean? You represent the Renzels, I know that much. Usser just told me. What I can't figure out is what more your clients want. They've arrested Usser and charged him with, first-degree murder, and they're going for the death penalty. The Renzels want to pull the switch themselves?"

"They haven't executed anyone in this state since 1967, Jake. There are almost two hundred people on Death Row."

"Tell me about it. And tell me what it's going to do for my reputation if the first one to take the pipe in twenty years is *my fucking client*."

I tried to suppress a smile. "The Renzels are just afraid he's going to walk, Jake. They're afraid he's going to win on a bogus insanity plea. From the look of what just happened in the courtroom, it seems that's just what Usser's got in mind."

Jake frowned and shook his head. "He shot his mouth off when he shouldn't have. If he listens to me he'll withdraw that fucking insanity thing at the preliminary hearing and stick to a simple 'not guilty.' "

"I don't think he's going to listen to you, Jake. I really don't."

"Shit. This case doesn't have anything to do with insanity; this case has to do with innocence. Usser didn't do it, it's as simple as that. If he lets me have my way I won't even have to put on a case. The thing stinks of reasonable doubt."

"I don't know, Jake. Gable's no fool. Why would he file if his case was so thin?"

"The daughter, that's why. You want to know what this case is about, you go find out why the fuck the silly little bitch is so pissed off at her old man she wants to see him take a fall for murder."

"Maybe it's because she thinks he killed her mother."

"Maybe. And maybe it's because of what Freud and the boys say makes the world go round. Oedipus and Electra and all that shit." Jake scraped his hand through his hair. "He wants to see you."

"Usser?"

"Yeah."

"When?"

"Now."

"Where?"

"Jury room down the hall. He'll be with you as soon as this bail business gets settled. Shouldn't be more than half an hour. He won't let me sit in, so if he says anything stupid, you tell me about it."

TWENTY-ONE

I waited for him for twenty minutes. The jury room was bright but depressing, haunted by the transparent husks of a thousand guilty verdicts that had been rendered there.

More than a million and a half arrests were made in California last year. At the other end of the pipeline, more than fifteen thousand people were committed to the state prison over that same period. The remaining million plus were disposed of in less drastic fashion—county jail, probation, fine, community service, tongue lashing, dismissal, even acquittal. It's a system that's overloaded, and it's despised by virtually everyone connected with it. As with most inadequate institutions, the most obvious remedy is money. But criminals don't make up much of a political constituency, and prisoners can't vote, so the likelihood of significant reform is close to nil.

I leaned back in one of the twelve chairs, put my feet up on the table and began thinking about the time some fifteen years ago when I'd spent six months in the San Francisco County Jail at San Bruno, serving a sentence for contempt of court. The nights had seemed endless, the very early mornings the loneliest, most vacant moments of my life. As Lawerence Usser joined me in the jury room, I was trying to remember exactly how the county jail had smelled. I wasn't having any luck, though at the time I was certain I'd never forget it. I guess those scientists who claim you can't remember smells are right.

Usser took a seat across the table, collapsed into the chair, sighed, removed his glasses, lowered his face into his hands. His clothing was rumpled, his hair a gob of paste, his skin oiled and off-color. He emitted the stale sour scent of confinement, which was a component part of the stink I'd just been trying to remember.

When he raised his head from his hands, he apologized for being late and thanked me for waiting for him. I told him it was all right. He replaced his glasses. Behind his wire-rim lenses his eyes were fogged with the same miserable smear as the first time I'd seen him.

I asked if he'd posted bail.

He nodded slowly. "I'm afraid I have totally and thankfully taken advantage of my family's wealth."

"What's wrong with that?"

"What's wrong is that ninety-nine percent of the people in this country, if charged with what I have been charged with, would still be over in that horrid jail."

"That bothers you?"

"Of course it bothers me, though obviously not enough for me to waive bail and return to my cell. Doesn't it bother you?" Usser looked as though he dared me to deny it.

"It used to," I admitted. "I'm not sure it does anymore."

"Why not?"

I shrugged. "I guess because outrage at economic disparity implies that all problems admit to economic solutions. We seem to be building a world where money is the measure of everything. Everything has a price tag; everything is measured by its financial aspect. I read the other day that a student decided not to go to medical school because it wouldn't be a good return on investment. That seems a little off the track."

"Well," Usser said slowly, "maybe you're right, though I have my doubts. The benefits of letting the economic chips fall where they may are seldom recognized by those who don't have many of those chips to play with." He managed a weary grin. "In any event, if I weren't so exhausted, I'd enjoy debating the proposition with you."

I shook my head. "It wouldn't be much fun. I can't defend my position with anything more than a hunch. And I doubt that

I can establish that being in jail is in any circumstance better than being out of it."

Usser nodded, then closed his eyes and seemed to close his pugnacity as well. "It would be difficult to convince me of the proposition, I can tell you that. If there is a system of punishment more certain to breed brutal, remorseless criminals than the one in effect in this country, I'm sure no one has thought of it."

"Was it bad for you in there?"

"Bad enough. The hint of incipient violence was as heavy as a shroud. I was choked by it, literally. I quickly came to believe that anything was possible in that place. Anything at all."

"You were probably right."

"Yes. I probably was." Usser seemed still terrified by the ordeal. If he was like me, the experience would stay with him for years. "It's not going to make it any easier for me to see any of my future clients sentenced to prison, I can tell you that," he added. "If I have any future clients."

The conversation melted into Usser's silent envisioning of his destiny. I let him muse for a moment, then asked him what he wanted to speak to me about.

"I want to ask a favor of you," he answered simply, looking here and there, at everything but me.

"What favor?"

"I want you to quit investigating the murder of my wife. I want you to leave all of it alone; to call and tell the Renzels you are resigning your commission."

"And why should I do that?"

Usser met my eye. "There are reasons. Good ones. Reasons that would satisfy the Renzels if they knew them."

"Like what?"

Usser hesitated. "Let's just say the reason is that I'm guilty. Do you understand? I'm admitting it, right here, so that you can tell them. I'm guilty and I've been arrested and I will go to trial. So there's no need for you to investigate any longer, no need for them to waste their money."

"I already told them that. They didn't buy it then; I doubt they'll buy it now."

"But why not?"

"Because the first thing they're going to think of is that if I withdraw from the case, it will be that much easier for you to make your insanity defense hold up."

"But that's nonsense. *You* can't play a part in the resolution of that issue. It's a medical question, not a factual question."

"I told them that, too. But I don't think I'll tell them again."

"Why not?"

"Because I don't think I'm wasting my time in this case. Not anymore."

Usser gave me a twisted grin. "Is it that you don't accept the concept of criminal responsibility, Mr. Tanner? Is it that you disagree with the suggestion of Professor Kadish that the abolition of the insanity defense would, and I quote, 'open to the condemnation of a criminal conviction a class of persons who, on any common sense notion of justice, are beyond blaming and ought not to be punished'? Do you deny the wisdom of Justice Holmes, who noted that even a dog distinguishes between being stumbled over and being kicked?"

"It's not that, I—"

"Do you really think it fair to treat everyone the same?" Usser interrupted, the opaque sheen across his eyes now burned away, replaced by sparkling crystal. "Think of the infinite variety of mental aberration, Mr. Tanner. Think of the ones who mindlessly hurt others and the ones who similarly hurt themselves, of the ones who never speak and the ones who can't stop speaking, the ones who think they're rabbits and the ones who think they're Christ, the ones who feel superior and the ones who feel inferior, the ones who hear and see nothing and the ones who hear and see things that are never there, the ones who feel no pain and the ones who feel pain perpetually, and the ones who feel no guilt and the ones who are paralyzed by it. Are we to lump them all together, Mr. Tanner? Grind them through the system and toss them in a cell with the truly evil ones who prey on us with full faculties?"

"I'm not saying that, Professor. I'm just saying that the system needs repair."

Usser waived at my objection with a hand. "The insanity plea isn't all that common, you know. Ninety-five percent of all criminal cases are plea-bargained out, as I'm sure you know. And of the five percent that go to trial, only one to two percent involve the insanity defense. That's one tenth of one percent of the total number. You and the other critics are making a mountain out of a molehill."

"But when it happens it tends to be dramatic," I said. "Like this case, for example."

Usser smiled a bleak crease. "I suppose so. But we punish people as a deterrent, do we not? To affect the conduct of others? Surely you see that punishment of one insane person will have no effect at all on the behavior of other insane persons. One in the grip of an insane delusion is not likely to consider the fate of schizophrenics past."

"Maybe. But there's always revenge," I said, suddenly the devil's advocate, suddenly enjoying myself.

"Do we take revenge on paraplegics because they can't walk? Do we take revenge on children because they run into the street? No. We make allowances."

I smiled. "What kind of allowances do you want them to make for you, Professor?"

Usser paused, took a deep breath, then expelled it with a ghostly whistle. When he spoke again, it was no longer as a fevered sophist but as a puzzled commoner. I couldn't tell if he was addressing my question or one of his own. "Do you ever wake up in the night, Mr. Tanner? In a cold sweat? Your breathing labored, your heart pounding, your mind racing because you believe—no, you *know*—that something you have done will have absolutely *disastrous* results, for you or for someone else? Does that ever happen to you?"

"Fairly often, as a matter of fact."

"What do you do about it?"

"I get up and fix myself a drink."

"And if that doesn't work?"

"I fix myself another drink."

Usser didn't smile. His eyes were dull again, and his thoughts had wandered far beyond the room.

"Is that what this is about?" I asked when he didn't speak. "Did your wife accuse you of doing something that caused needless harm to someone? Did it have something to do with the release of the Maniac, by any chance?"

Usser blinked his eyes and frowned. "Who?"

"His name is Ronald Nifton. He used to be your client."

Usser nodded with less reaction than I expected. "A troubled man. And a troubling one. Why do you mention him?"

"Because I saw him last night."

"Really? Where?"

"Here. In Berkeley. At a place the street kids call Hell House."

Usser was still uninterested. "I've heard of it," he said absently.

"He was with your daughter."

The statement broke the spell, and Usser seemed to levitate. "What?"

"Nifton was with Lisa. She seems to see him as her designated savior. She seems to owe him something and to be willing to do about anything to repay the debt."

Usser was clearly stunned. His hand rose to his face and tried to rub away the information. "My God. Then it's true. I . . . Was Lisa all right?"

"She was drugged to the eyeballs," I said bluntly, with a touch of exaggeration. "And rather determinedly self-destructive. She wouldn't have anything to do with me or with a kid named Cal who used to be her boyfriend and who wants to get her away from the Maniac and his entourage."

"Maniac. Why do you call him that?"

"Because that's what he calls himself."

Usser's eyes had collected tears. He removed his glasses and swiped at them with the back of his hand. When he spoke again his voice was small and bewildered. "I was afraid of something like this."

"Why?"

"Lisa rejected me, us, so thoroughly she was bound to find some outrageous substitute, a surrogate parent who would be certain to provoke Dianne and me, if not frighten us."

"Nifton's frightening all right," I agreed. "His face is like Silly Putty, contorting this way and that. He can't stay still. His tongue keeps flopping out of his mouth. Is all that part of his mental problems?"

Usser shook his head. "I'm afraid all that is part of the cure. I've seen Ronald a few times since he was released, though only from a distance. Still, I'm certain he suffers from tardive dyskinesia, the symptoms being as you described. It's brought on by overmedication of the chlorpromazine derivatives. The result of such mistreatment is permanent brain injury." Usser sighed. "I'm a believer in psychoactive medication, but I'm afraid these days it's all too often characterized by over-optimistic claims of drug companies and overprescribing by the physicians in the field. I'm confident that one day biochemistry will provide most of the answers, but unfortunately that day is still not here."

When Usser paused, I changed the subject. "What happened at your place two months ago, Professor?"

He ended his reverie and frowned.

"What do you mean?"

"Two months ago—a month before your wife was murdered —your daughter flipped out and took to drugs and to the streets, your wife began having an affair with her boss, and you began being insensitive to your colleagues at the law school and drinking more than usual. What made all that happen? Did it have something to do with Nifton?"

Usser shook his head. "No. I . . . nothing. *Nothing* happened."

His words were a tortured lie. Usser knew I knew it, but he also knew there was nothing I could do about it. I was still thinking of where to take the conversation next when Usser spoke in a thoughtful drone. "Adam Lonborg says I shouldn't go back to teaching even after I'm released. He says I should find Lisa and enter psychotherapy with her and spend my time putting our lives and our relationship back together."

"Doesn't sound like a bad idea," I said. "But it's not going to be easy."

"To find Lisa?"

"That may be the easy part. The hard part will be to convince her that you're worthy of the effort to patch things up."

"You mean because she's told the police I killed Dianne?"

"That's part of it."

"But I'm being punished for that, and I will be punished even more. I'll either be in prison or in a mental hospital once the trial is over. Surely that will be enough to satisfy her. If not to make her love me, at least to make her return to a normal life away from people like that madman Nifton."

" Maybe. Maybe not."

Usser fell silent again, this time not the criminal but the parent, thinking of ways to rescue his daughter from the dangers she was drifting toward, dangers that could sink her. After a minute he looked at me again. "So you're going to keep on the case?"

"Unless my clients ask me to drop it."

"Will you let me know if you see Lisa again? Will you tell me where to find her?"

I shrugged. "If it seems right. I can't promise anything."

"But why not? What harm would it do to tell me where my daughter is?"

"It has to do with why I want to stay on this case. I haven't liked this thing since the first day. It didn't make sense; I kept thinking up excuses to get out of it. But while I was waiting for you to get here I finally figured out why it's always seemed so screwy."

Usser frowned. "I don't understand."

"I talked to Jake Hattie for a minute before coming down here. He doesn't want you to plead insanity, you know."

"I know. He told me he'll withdraw as my counsel if I persist. But what does that have to do with anything?"

"Jake told me the reason he didn't want you to plead insanity was because you're not guilty, and he wants to prove it and get you off."

"He's wrong."

"That's what I assumed until I started thinking about it. And what I finally decided was that Jake's exactly right. You *aren't* guilty. And you aren't insane and you weren't on the night your wife was killed."

Usser leaned forward and grasped my forearm. "You're *wrong*, Mr. Tanner. I'm going to withdraw my not-guilty plea after the preliminary hearing and I'm arraigned again in Superior Court. My only plea will be insanity. By doing that I'll be admitting that I committed the offense, that I murdered Dianne." His final words were hollow, as though desperation had eaten away their content.

"I know that's what you're going to do, Professor. But you're not going to do it because you actually killed your wife. The fact is you didn't kill her. That's the only thing that makes sense."

"Then why would I be doing this?"

"That's a good question. And I think I've got an answer. You're doing this because you're protecting someone else. You think you can sell your insanity plea to a jury and then talk your way out of the state hospital in a short time and return to a normal life, and in the meantime the police won't go after the person who really killed your wife."

"What person is that?"

"I'm not sure, but I know who *you* think did it."

"Who?"

"Your daughter. You think Lisa killed her mother and you're willing to risk your own incarceration to keep her from being tried for the crime."

Usser was shaking his head vigorously, as though to disgorge something horrible that had entered it. "You're very wrong, Tanner. You're totally mistaken. *I'm* guilty. *I* did it. Why won't you believe that?"

I leaned back in my chair and crossed my arms. "I'll tell you what, Professor. I'll believe it if you can pass a little quiz."

"What quiz?" Usser frowned nervously.

I smiled. "They found the murder weapon yesterday."

"Really? The scissors? I didn't know. No one told me."

"The way I see it, if you really killed your wife, you ought to be able to tell me where they found them. Right? I mean, you're the one who hid them, after all."

"I . . ."

"Well, go ahead. Convince me. Tell me where you stashed the weapon."

Usser started to say something, then stopped. My smile broadened. He bowed his head. "Jake Hattie told me not to discuss the case with you," he managed finally.

"I'll bet he did," I said. "But I don't think you could discuss this case with me even if you wanted to. The only thing you can do is make up some nifty little symptoms and mimic some psychotic ramblings you've picked up along the way, and use them to convince a jury that you're nuts."

Usser started to protest, then reconsidered. After another minute he leaned back in his chair and smiled, suddenly confident. "It doesn't really matter, though, does it?"

"What doesn't matter?"

"Whether you believe me or not."

"I suppose it doesn't," I agreed.

"It's going to work no matter what you do. Do you know why?

Because psychiatry is such an infinitely absorbing discipline. Anything and everything is grist for its mill."

"How do you mean?"

Usser's chuckle was a dry scrape. "You accuse me of planning to manufacture the symptoms of mental illness, to prevail at my trial by feigning insanity. Well, did you know that since 1898 the impersonation of mental illness by a prisoner awaiting trial has been known as the Ganser Syndrome? And that some psychiatrists consider such an impersonation *in and of itself* to be a manifestation of psychosis?"

I shook my head, amazed and amused. "So you can't lose. Even if they show you're faking, the faking itself may get you off."

Usser smiled but remained silent.

I stood up. "One last question."

"Yes?"

"What film do you watch most frequently on your VCR at home?"

"You mean commercial film?"

"Yes."

Usser frowned. "What does this have to do with anything?"

"Humor me."

"Well, I . . . *Reds,* I suppose. I watch it once a month or so. Why?"

"I don't know," I said truthfully.

TWENTY-TWO

I left the courthouse and headed for my car. In the park across the street a line of vans and buses—all old, all piled high with bedding and camping gear, all stuffed with people dressed in the flowing, flowery garb of the hippies of yesteryear —were spilling their occupants into the park. The mood was festive and communal. I stood and watched and wondered what was going on. When I noticed a street cop walking my way, I decided to ask him.

He looked over at the park and grinned. "Dead Heads," he said.

"What's that?"

"Fans of the Grateful Dead. The rock group? See, the Dead's giving a concert in the Community Theater on Halloween, and the faithful are starting to gather. By Halloween night the park will be full of them. Some of them follow the Dead all across the country, coast to coast." The cop paused. "Reminds me of the old days," he went on thoughtfully. "Too bad, in a way. Not much that's nice goes on in the streets anymore. Just the heavy stuff—drugs, muggings, trashings, like that. Hardly ever come across a crowd just having fun. Me, I wish the Dead would play here every week."

The cop saluted me and moved on down the street. I found my car and drove to another park, the one laid claim to in the name of the people back in 1969.

It was pushing noon. The stand of pine trees in which the Maniac and his dancers had gamboled the night before was now devoid of homesteaders. Daylight revealed unwelcome truths—that the ground was littered and parched, the flora anemic and forlorn, the atmosphere pathetic and obsolete, the odor heavy and cloying. I wandered in and out of the little grove for several minutes, making sure the nighttime denizens had all withdrawn, then made my way to the log that marked the hole where Lisa Usser had hidden her mysterious horde.

I rolled the log aside and began to dig with my bare hands. It was easy going. The dirt was dry as dust, a lumpy loam of pine needles and twigs and leaves, plus the occasional bits of broken bottles, plastic wrappers, aluminum cans and the other nondegradable artifacts of modern urban life. The smell of decaying garbage enveloped me like a tent. At the bottom of the hole I found two things.

The first was the videotape cassette of *Reds*. I picked it up and dusted it off and held it to the light. There didn't seem to be anything at all unusual about it. I took out the cartridge and confirmed that's all it was, then replaced it in its case. I still couldn't figure it, unless what was wound onto the cassette reel wasn't *Reds* at all but something else; something, perhaps, that identified Dianne Renzel's killer.

The second item was the little cedar box that Lisa's grandmother had retrieved for her at the Usser house the day before, the box containing the decorated fingernails that Bart Kinn had laughed at so disdainfully. I opened the lid. The nails were still there, painted in black and orange, silver and purple, the ominous colorations of mystics and the occult. I couldn't figure the fingernails, either. I put the box and the cassette tape aside and pawed around in the dirt for several seconds longer, until I was certain nothing else of interest was buried there, then filled in the hole and took the booty to my car.

The thing to do was find a video recorder and take a look at *Reds*. Peggy, my secretary, had one, but she lived in the city and it would take a couple of hours to drive over there and arrange to use it. I thought I'd seen a recorder somewhere at the law school, in Elmira Howson's office, if memory served. She'd grouse about my using it, but the only other alternative was to go back to Usser's house, wait for him to get home if he wasn't

there already and watch the tape with him. That one I didn't
like so well, since I had a feeling what appeared on the screen
wouldn't be nearly as cute as Warren Beatty. But before all that
there was someone I wanted to talk to.

I stuck the box and the tape under the front seat, locked the
car and walked back to Bowditch Street and headed two blocks
north, to the yellow stucco duplex that housed the Berkeley
Community Crisis Center.

Students swarmed around me, arms cradling books, faces
bright and cheerful, clothing clean and neat and new. A throwback to the fifties, in attitude as well as fashion. They say the
only thing they're interested in is making money. No public
service, no Peace Corps, no crusade for the right to anything
more than a Volvo and an Apple and a sure supply of sushi.
But the kid in front of me wasn't one of those. He had a Mo-
hawk haircut and a chicken bone through his nose. The sign on
the back of his leather jacket read IF VOTING CHANGED ANYTHING
IT WOULD BE ILLEGAL. As I trotted up the steps to the crisis
center the kid looked back at me and shook his head. "*They* can't
stop it, man. No one can stop it."

"Stop what?"

"The Holocaust. *That's* the crisis, man. In another year we'll
all be Day-Glo cinders. So get high and fly, man. *Morituri te
salutamus.*"

The kid waved and trotted off, not obviously anxious over
the prospect of nuclear annihilation. I wasn't sure I was all that
bothered by it myself. The vulnerability is democratic, at least,
as opposed to Vietnam, where we paid the blacks and the country boys a few hundred bucks a month to do the dying for the
rest of us. I opened the door and went inside, wondering how
Dianne Renzel had managed to fall victim to a crisis when she
was an expert at resolving them.

The waiting area was sparsely furnished and empty but for a
single woman sitting in the corner, whimpering, her face buried
in her hands. The only other person in view was the receptionist, a woman of graduate student age sitting behind a simple
plywood counter while she managed to talk on the phone and
type at the same time.

I looked for Pierce Richards' office but I didn't see it. Two
doors led off the waiting area, but they were closed and un-

marked. While I waited for the receptionist to give me directions I looked through the leaflets on the counter. They advised
the center's clients on everything from the legal rights of battered women to the free food at the Berkeley Emergency Food
Project and the free lodging at the Berkeley Support Services
Emergency Shelter.

The receptionist laughed a nice laugh into the telephone. Her
typing was stark and dreadful, reminding me somehow of the
young boy's forecast of atomic incineration. I was oddly relieved
when she stopped typing and hung up the phone and looked at
me critically, as if to gauge what particular crisis this old guy
was suffering from. Before she could dismay me with a guess, I
told her my name and that I was there to see Mr. Richards.

"He's with someone right now," she replied. "Can *I* help you?"

I shook my head. "I'll wait. It's a personal matter."

I started to take a seat in the waiting area, then remembered
the whimpering woman and stayed where I was and read another leaflet. The receptionist gave me an inquiring look. Her
name tag labeled her as Sandra. She wore her brown hair
straight, her cotton clothing simple, her ears pierced by silver
hoops. She was surrounded by forms and files and a Rolodex
the size of a tire, and she was still trying to figure me out. I had
a hunch that if I gave her another hour she'd come up with
something more fundamental than anything I'd managed to
find in the forty years I'd been working at it.

"I was wondering," I said when the silence became embarrassing. "Do you keep records of everyone who comes in to the
center?"

The girl smiled. "We try. We're pretty good if they stay long
enough to receive counseling. The hard ones are the in-and-
outers. They run in, complain about something or someone,
then run out before we can complete the intake record, let alone
do anything for them. Those we don't have anything on. Unless
they're regulars. Some people show up every time the rent is
due, or their period comes, or the moon is full. Around here a
full moon means a full house. Do you believe in astrology?"

I shook my head.

"What's your sign?"

"Cancer."

"Hmmm."

I laughed. "What's *that* mean?"

Her eyes twinkled back. "Nothing. Just hmmmm. You're here on some kind of business, aren't you?"

"Yep."

"Is Mr. Richards in trouble?"

"I don't know. Is he?"

She shrugged and flipped her long brown mane with a twitch of her head and neck. "I hope not. He's a wonderful man. A saint, really, don't you think?"

I tried to remember whether I knew of any saints who had slept with another man's wife. When I couldn't think of one, I asked Sandra why she thought Richards might be in trouble.

"I don't know. He's just so honest, you know? I figure one of these days all that honesty is going to get him busted."

"That's a little cynical, isn't it?"

Sandra glanced around the office. "You spend much time here, and see what life does to people, what *people* do to people, and it's hard *not* to get cynical. But I fight it."

"How?"

"By listening to people like Mr. Richards. And Ms. Renzel, before she died. Do you know about that?"

I nodded.

"Anyway, they're the greatest. Really. I mean, they do so much for others and hardly get any money at all for doing it, and hardly any thanks, either. I mean, I think they're the *real* Christians, don't you? Instead of those TV preachers who try to get you to believe that God wants you to be *rich* or something? Don't you think?"

I did and I told her so. Sandra went back to her typing. I looked around the office and tried to decide what kind of information she might be able to give me. "If I wanted to know if someone had ever been counseled at the center," I said finally, "where would those records be kept? Here? Or somewhere else?"

"They're over—" But she caught herself before she'd done any more than swirl a hundred and eighty degrees in her steno chair. "I'm not supposed to say anything about our records. They're confidential. Mr. Richards is a bear about that. So . . . you're not from the police, are you?"

"Nope. I'm a friend of the Renzels'. Dianne's parents."

"Poor Dianne." The pity seemed real. "And poor street people. Next to Mr. Richards, she was the best thing that ever happened to them. I just can't believe she's gone."

"Can you believe her husband killed her?"

Sandra frowned. "I don't know. I never met him, but I suppose so. I mean, the marriage thing gets pretty intense sometimes, don't you think? My folks fought a lot. So, *you* know."

"Did you know Dianne very well?"

"Not really. I mean, she'd counsel me sometimes. About my personal life. Working here, I mean, it gives you some weird ideas, you know? You start looking at people funny. Wondering what they *really* do for kicks. Guys and stuff, you know? I kind of have trouble keeping any kind of relationship going."

I'd had that trouble for thirty years but I didn't tell her that. Instead, I started to make another try for the records or at least the ones Dianne Renzel had kept on the people she'd counseled. But before I could get my question asked, Sandra's phone squealed as though someone had stepped on it.

Sandra picked it up, mumbled something I didn't get, then said my name, then listened. A few seconds later she replaced the receiver. "You can go in now. Second door on the right." She looked beyond me. "Mrs. Randall? It will be a few more minutes."

"What's her problem?" I whispered.

"Her Rolfer ran off with all her money."

"Her what?"

"Her Rolfer. That's a massage technique, kind of, except it treats your psychic pains as well as your physiological ones." I looked to see if she was serious. She evidently was. "But this guy wasn't a *certified* Rolfer," Sandra went on. "He was just a phony Rolfer. You've got to watch out for those healer types, don't you think?"

I didn't know but I could guess. I said good-bye to Sandra and went through the second door to my right and found Pierce Richards.

He was still dressed in his mismatched cords and still wore the ecclesiastical aspect of the saint his receptionist had just declared him to be. His office was appropriately ascetic, spare and unadorned but for a map of Berkeley tacked to the wall and a snapshot of a smiling Dianne Renzel that was preserved in a gold frame on the far corner of his government-surplus desk.

Richards saw me notice the photograph. "It wasn't there when she was alive," he said, softly yet proudly, as though he was grateful that death had made her his property.

I sat in the chair reserved for clients in crisis. Richards perched on the corner of his desk and looked down on me with a focused frown. "I still don't know what it is you're trying to do," he said. "I'm afraid I wasn't paying much attention back at the courthouse. There was too much else to think about. Too much to try to understand." He smiled weakly. "Too much to try to forgive."

"One thing I'm trying to do is get a better picture of Dianne Renzel. She's still fuzzy to me. Now that her husband's been arrested, you seem to be the best source of information."

Richards rested his chin in his palm. "Dianne was, well, the single most important thing about her was that she was always trying to do what was *right*. I mean, we all try to do that, I suppose, but Dianne *agonized* over it. Take abortion. Some people see it as a simple matter—murder, or free choice. But it's not that simple, really, and Dianne knew it and was tortured by it. She lost some friends by refusing to come out with a doctrinaire position, but . . ." Richards grimaced at the memory.

"She had a husband who slept with everything that moved," I said. "Yet she stayed with him. How do you explain that?"

"I struggled with that for a long time. I mean, I first asked Dianne to marry me more than three years ago. She refused. She loved him, is what it amounted to, and she was willing to overlook almost anything to fulfill her vows." Richards shook his head as though he still couldn't understand it. "She wanted nothing for herself. I gave her a present once and she scolded me for not donating the money to the center. She made me take it back. I told her I did, but I kept it." Richards began to cry but he spoke through his tears. "She was an excellent counselor because she had no ego. Nothing her clients said threatened her in any way. I mean psychologically. She was completely open, completely secure, completely genuine. Thus her husband's infidelity didn't hurt her the way it hurts most women. She was more concerned with Lisa and her husband than she was with herself. I . . . That's just the way she was. It sounds corny, but it's true. And it used to drive me crazy, sometimes."

"But eventually she slept with you. What I want to know is why."

"Why she began an affair?"

"Right."

"Well, I'm not sure. I didn't ask . . . a gift horse and all that."

"But something must have happened, don't you agree?"

He thought about it. "Possibly. I just don't know."

"How about enemies? Did she have any you know of?"

"No. None." He made it seem against the laws of nature.

"How about other lovers?"

"No. Impossible. No."

"Any close woman friends besides her neighbor, Phyllis Misteen?"

"Not especially. Not that I know of." Richards dried his eyes on his sleeve and frowned again. "Look. What are you getting at, Tanner? I still don't know where you're going with all this."

I smiled. "That's okay. When I saw you at the courthouse, I didn't know where I was going myself. But now I do."

"I don't understand. What . . . ?"

I held up a hand. "I'm going to be honest with you, Mr. Richards. I'm working for the Renzels, Dianne's parents. Do you know them?"

He shook his head. "Only through Dianne's descriptions. She admired them very much. Particularly her mother."

"Well, at first the Renzels hired me to find the killer. Then, after Usser was arrested, they wanted me to make sure he didn't try to get off on a phony insanity plea. I—"

"My God," Richards interrupted, his voice a startled squawk. "Of *course* that's what he plans. I should have seen it before now. What a diabolical man he must be."

Richards closed his eyes and bowed his head. "Wait a minute," I said quickly. "After I saw you in court I had a chance to do some thinking. And what I decided was, number one, Usser didn't do it. Even though he told me he did. And number two, the case doesn't have anything to do with all the love affairs Professor Usser *et ux* managed to accumulate over the past few years, including the one you were a willing participant in."

Richards had opened his eyes and was squinting in confusion. "But why would Usser say he did it if he didn't?"

"Because he's trying to protect someone."

"But who?"

"I think it's his daughter. So my next question for you is, what was going on between Lisa and Dianne? Were they fighting, and if so, why? And how serious was it?"

Richards clasped his hands around a knee and began to rock back and forth as he tried to form his answer. "I want to help you, of course. If matters are truly as you say, and Usser is innocent, then of course. . . . But I can't *believe* the police would—"

"The police aren't used to guys like Usser admitting to crimes they haven't committed."

Usser hadn't confessed anything to the cops, not as far as I knew, but he hadn't done anything to exculpate himself, either. All I cared about was getting Richards to think about someone other than Usser as the killer. "Lisa and Dianne," I prompted. "What was going on there?"

Richards hesitated. "I just don't know what I can ethically tell you, is the problem. Dianne spoke to me in confidence about her family. I'm not sure I could—"

"She wasn't a client, Richards. She was a friend. Someone murdered her. Something she said to you might ultimately identify her killer. I can't think of any reason for you not to come forward in those circumstances."

"But—"

"Morality is nice, Richards, except when it furthers immorality."

He finally surrendered, though not without some qualms. "Lisa went through a rather radical change in personality a few months ago," Richards began slowly, his words weighted with reluctance. "She began to do poorly at school, although all her achievement and basic skills tests register her as genius level. She began to skip classes and roam the streets, usually with a tough crowd. She took drugs and made little attempt to hide the fact. She flaunted it, almost, as though she was trying to punish the people who loved her. Dianne was extremely upset, needless to say. But it is often true that those who effectively counsel others are rather inept at ordering their own lives. That seemed to be true here. Lisa and Dianne fought bitterly. One or the other would frequently end up in tears. And the situation just got worse. They took Lisa out of Berkeley High. And Lawrence put her back in therapy with a psychiatrist named Lonborg, but none of it seemed to help."

"What caused all this? Did Dianne have any idea? Was it just adolescent weirdness?"

Richard shook his head. "She thought it was more than that, but I don't think she knew exactly what it was." Richards paused. "She thought it had something to do with her husband. Apparently Lisa had worshiped her father for years, and then suddenly turned on him, began behaving in ways that were calculated to destroy their relationship."

I thought for a minute, then voiced an idea that had been tugging at me ever since I'd met with Usser at the courthouse. "Usser's highly sexed," I said. "He's having affairs with half a dozen women, probably."

"Yes. So?"

"So I was wondering if there was any chance he abused Lisa. Molested her sexually."

Richards froze in place. The passage of time helped my suggestion grow increasingly probable. "Surely that's impossible," he said finally. "Surely a man like that couldn't—"

"Come on, Richards. Perversion isn't limited to the ignorant and the poor."

He bowed his head. "Yes, of course."

"Did Dianne ever consider that possibility?"

"No. I'm sure she didn't. She loved him, as I told you."

"If that really was the problem, and Dianne found out about it, that would give Usser a hell of a motive for killing her. For doing, in other words, what I just told you I didn't think he'd done."

Richards nodded silently, still reeling from my speculations. "But let's put that aside for a minute," I went on.

"But the authorities," Richards blurted. "You should notify them, do *something*. He should be charged with assault. I mean, he's *out* there again, and so is Lisa."

"I don't know if Usser's done anything like that or not. The only one who does is Lisa. When I leave here, I'm going to try to find her. She told the police that Usser killed her mother.

Maybe that's why she said it, to pay him back for what he did to her. But let's assume none of that happened, and Usser really is innocent. Then the killer might be someone Dianne met here at the center. Someone she angered because of something she said or did in the course of her work."

"I don't think that's possible," Richards protested meekly. "Dianne was a skilled counselor."

"She was killed in a brutal, savage manner, Richards. The police photos upset an assistant D.A. I know, and she's been looking at murder victims for twenty years. So talk to me. Some loonies must roll in here from time to time. Did any of them have a mad on for Ms. Renzel?"

"No. I can think of no one."

"Then let's look at the records."

"What?"

"Her records. She made notes, right? Of the people she counseled? Let's check the logs for the month before she died, and get the files of any repeat visitors and see what she had to say about them. See if there were any threats, see if she was frightened, see what was going on."

"No." The word was the first cruel utterance I'd heard from him.

"You're kidding."

"No. Absolutely not. You're talking about our official records now, patient records, not my private conversations with Dianne. I can't disclose those to you. The center's credibility would be totally destroyed if I did that. Our clients rely on our discretion. Without it we will *have* no clients."

"I think I can persuade the cops to get a court order."

"I'd fight it with every breath in my body. And even if they won, it wouldn't do them any good."

"Why not?"

"Because our counselors make their notations in code. A code known only to them. It's a device I suggested just to avoid intrusions such as the one you are suggesting."

"Code? But how does anyone else read them?"

"They don't."

"So if someone leaves, like Dianne, the new counselor has to start from scratch with all the carry-over patients?"

"Yes, unfortunately. It's the price we pay to preserve our

rights that the Fourth Amendment secured before the current court began to render it a nullity."

"Okay," I said. "Just the names, then. No files. Just a list of the repeaters over the past few months."

"No."

"Okay, tell me this. Did Ms. Renzel ever talk to you about a guy named Nifton? He calls himself the Maniac."

"I know Nifton."

"Lisa Usser has joined his merry band. Did Dianne know that?"

"Yes."

"Was she worried about it?"

"Of course. Nifton was not a stable individual."

"Did she try to put a stop to it? Try to keep Lisa from seeing him?"

"I'm not sure. My impression was, now that I think about it, that Dianne felt Nifton was protecting Lisa in some way, that if she was determined to live on the street, then it was good that Nifton was looking after her."

"Did you or Dianne counsel Nifton professionally?"

"I can't tell you that."

"Just let me check her records. I won't disclose anything I learn. I'm good at keeping my mouth shut, Richards. It's part of the job description. So . . ."

"No. You will have no access to records of any kind. Now if you'll excuse me, there's a rather pathetic woman waiting for me to tell her how she's going to survive without her life savings."

"What are you going to tell her?"

"I haven't the faintest idea."

TWENTY-THREE

Richards followed me into the waiting room. Behind me, I could hear him introduce himself to the weeping woman and invite her into his office. I found reasons to linger until the two of them had disappeared, then went back to the counter and leaned on it.

Sandra was still pecking at her typewriter. Six seconds after I started staring at her she looked up. "Do you need something?"

"Do you know a guy named Nifton? He's twenty-five or so, big." Sandra's look was blank. "He calls himself the Maniac."

She smiled and nodded. "The Maniac. Sure. What a strange guy."

"He comes in here once in a while, doesn't he?"

"Sometimes. Why?"

"Did he come to see Ms. Renzel?"

"No. Not especially. I mean, he hardly ever talks to anyone. Anyone in particular, I mean. Usually he just talks to whoever's sitting over there." She gestured toward where the weeping woman had been sitting.

"What does he say to them?"

"Crazy stuff, mostly. He likes to see who's in trouble, especially the young ones. Then he tries to get them to come to *him* for help, instead of us. He tells them to come over to the park, that he'll show them how to find life after death. That's what he always says—'death before life.' "

"Does he ever get violent?"

"Not really. He's scary, sometimes, when he starts ranting and raving. But he never actually does anything."

"And he never met privately with Ms. Renzel?"

Sandra shook her head. "Not as far as I know."

"Were you working the day Dianne Renzel died?"

"That was a Friday, wasn't it?"

I nodded.

She shook her head. "I don't work Fridays. I'm in seminar all day."

"How about Dianne's daughter, Lisa? Did the Maniac ever mention her?"

"I don't think so. The one who always asks about Lisa is Cal. Do you know him?"

I nodded. "So he comes in a lot?"

Sandra nodded again. "Ms. Renzel always talked to him, tried to calm him down. I think she was kind of a mother to Cal. I think he was more her child than Lisa was, in some ways."

"How about a girl named Sherry Misteen? Did she ever come in for counseling?"

"I don't think so."

"Did Lisa Usser come in?"

"Only once, I think. She was with this doctor. I think he was a psychiatrist."

"Lonborg?"

"I think. I can't remember. They weren't here for long. Lisa didn't look very happy about being here at all."

"How about Lawrence Usser? Did he come around much?"

Sandra frowned and shook her head. "I've never seen him before in my life, except for his picture in the papers. If he killed Dianne the way they said, then they should hang him, don't you think?" She put her hand over her mouth. "Mr. Richards wouldn't like to hear me say that. He thinks capital punishment is evil."

"And he thought Dianne Renzel was pretty special, didn't he?"

Sandra opened her mouth to answer, then changed her mind. "I don't think I better talk about that. I mean, I like my job, you know?"

I started to ask another question, but Sandra noticed something behind me and quickly lowered her head and began to type. What was behind me was Pierce Richards. What he had in mind was getting me out of his center. The way he did it was to ask me politely to leave.

It was only three long blocks from the center to the law school. I trotted back to my car, fed the meter, grabbed the *Reds* cassette from beneath the seat, then walked back up the hill and entered the Berkeley Law School behind an animated group of students who were discussing the merits of the doctrine of comparative negligence. I followed them to the second floor, then went to Lawrence Usser's office and knocked on the door.

When no one answered I knocked again and waited, but Usser didn't answer and neither did the person I wanted to see —his secretary, Laura Nifton. I went back to the main hall and was about to wend my way to Elmira Howson's office when I saw her standing beside the entrance to the library, exchanging heated words with Gus Grunig.

"It's despicable that you want Dean Randolph to bar him from the school," Professor Howson was saying as I approached, hands on her hips, her jaw thrust like a cudgel.

Her ex-lover was at least six inches shorter than she was, but he was the calmer of the two, in control of himself and the situation. "He is a criminal defendant, Elmira," Grunig said patiently, as though he spoke to a child.

"He is accused; he is *not guilty.*"

"If he remains not guilty after the trial has concluded, I will be the first to welcome him back to the classroom. But until then we should not ignore reality."

Elmira Howson swore. "The *reality* is that you want Larry dismissed from the faculty and since there are no legitimate grounds for discharge you're seizing on this ridiculous murder charge to do what you can't accomplish otherwise."

Her charge fazed Grunig not at all. "I understand he pleaded insanity, Elmira. Can that be true? And if it is, can you possibly suggest he be allowed to instruct law students as long as he assumes that posture?"

"I—" Ms. Howson noticed me for the first time, and cut off her rejoinder. "I saw you in court. What are you doing here?"

"I'd like to talk to you for a minute."

"Did you see Larry at all? Did you talk to him after the arraignment?" She was so eager it was embarrassing to both Grunig and myself.

I nodded.

"How is he? That prima donna Hattie wouldn't let me get near him."

"He's okay," I said. "He didn't like jail much, but I've never talked to anyone who did. The bail thing got worked out, so he could well be home by now." I hesitated, and looked at Grunig. "Your discussion may be moot," I went on. "He's thinking about staying away from here till the trial's over, spending his time with his daughter instead of his criminal procedure students. She's been hanging around with a guy named Nifton who calls himself the Maniac. Sleeping in the streets, taking drugs, possibly becoming promiscuous. Usser's worried about her."

I kept my eyes on Grunig. It was my intention to blunt his enmity for Usser by showing they shared a vulnerability to the Maniac's obsessions, but Grunig didn't seem to have heard a word. He dropped his arms to his sides and stomped off as though I'd somehow insulted him.

"I'm going to try to call Larry," Elmira Howson said, and started for her office.

"Do you have a video recorder up there?" I called after her.

"Yes. What about it?"

"Is it beta?"

"Yes."

"May I use it for a minute?"

She smiled malevolently. "Do you have some sweaty little porno number you picked up down on Telegraph? And you can't wait till you get home to see all those bodies slither in and out of each other?"

I ignored her slur with difficulty. "I have a tape that says *Reds* on the outside. It used to be in Lawrence Usser's study. His daughter took it out of there and buried it in People's Park. I want to find out why."

Elmira Howson still wasn't as apprehensive as I was. "She did what? I don't understand."

"I don't understand either. Let's go watch the tape."

She started to ask another question, but held it and turned and led me to her office.

The recorder was where I remembered it being, on a shelf

beside a thirteen-inch Panasonic television set, next to a row of BNA and CCH binders. I looked over the machine, pressed the *on* button, pulled the cassette out of the jacket and pushed it into the slot.

The machine absorbed the tape with a mechanical whir. "You have to turn on the set separately," Elmira Howson instructed. "Then press channel four."

I did, and the lines and shadows of the cassette began to stream across the screen, black and white, suggestive of nothing but technology. I waited, but even after several seconds I couldn't tell what was on the tape. It certainly wasn't *Reds*, or any other professionally recorded film. I waited longer. The stream of shadows finally stopped, abruptly, but the dissolve didn't clear things up. If anything the images were blurred even more, blobs of light and dark, jerky streams of movement from one shape to another, all of it indecipherable. My guess was that someone was trying to photograph something with a hand-held video camera, and wasn't using enough light, and didn't have enough experience. Behind me, Elmira Howson dialed a number on her phone.

I picked the remote control unit off the top of the TV set and went to the nearest chair and sat down. As I did so, a face appeared on the screen, a face I didn't know. It mugged in close-up, stuck out its tongue, then disappeared. What followed was more darkness, bits of light in liquid streaks, all accompanied by the harsh white noise of nothingness. I began to think I was wasting my time. To my right, Elmira Howson had begun to leaf through an issue of the Supreme Court advance sheets as she pressed the phone to her ear, no longer interested in what I was doing.

I punched the speed search button on the remote control. The abstractions quickened their pace, as though they were being chased. Then the diffused and senseless imagery dissolved and I thought I saw a coherent object. When I realized what it was, I pressed the *stop* button and the *off* button and turned to Elmira Howson. "If you don't want your life to get real complicated over the next few days, I suggest you find something to do somewhere else."

She looked up, frowning. "Larry isn't home," she said as she replaced the telephone. "What on earth are you talking about?"

"I think this tape is going to be evidence in a murder case. If you don't want to spend a lot of time telling the police how I happened to be here and what you happen to know about what's on this tape, then I suggest you get out of here for about twenty minutes. If anyone asks, tell them I asked to use your VCR, you told me where it was and how to use it, and you don't know any more than that."

"But—"

"You don't want to see what's on this tape, Ms. Howson. Really, you don't."

"Does it have something to do with Larry?"

"I think so."

"Does it mean he's guilty?"

"I don't know yet."

"I think I should stay."

"I don't."

"But . . ." Her voice trailed away to silence. She thought about it for so long I thought she was going to stay just to spite me, or to prove she was as brave as I was.

It took thirty seconds to decide, but she finally gathered an armful of journals and stood up and headed for the door. "I'll be in the faculty lounge if you need me," she said without looking back. "Which I'm sure you won't." When the door closed I advanced the tape on speed search and watched it till I was certain the production had ended, then rewound and watched at normal speed.

The first few minutes were static, the next section some sort of unsteady experiment, as though someone was trying to figure out how to use the camera. Then came a section that was so underexposed I could make out nothing but vague shapes— human, it looked like—but so faint the forms and faces were anonymous. Then came another blank section, followed by the portion of the tape that had caused me to ask the professor to leave the room.

To remedy the exposure problem, someone had found some flashlights to light the scene. After being aimed at by the lights, the camera zoomed onto a flickering image, one that made me sit up straight and rub my eyes for a clearer view, one that made me wonder what the whole thing meant.

It was a body, a woman, naked, lying on what I finally decided was bare ground. She didn't move, and though it was what I expected, no one joined her for erotic foreplay or sadistic stunts. Shapes moved about her, swooping, bowing, but none of them were captured clearly by the flashlights. They remained mysterious attendants, a band of shrouded lechers.

At first I thought what I'd found was a homemade stag film, something Usser had shot for kicks, probably using one of his willing law students as his star. But when the woman still hadn't moved two minutes later, I looked more closely and decided she was dead.

I could see no wound, no scar, no deep dark seep of blood, but I was certain I was looking at a corpse. Even on film the dead look strangely empty—hollow eggs that lack the churning stuff of life—and this bone-white woman was as soulless as any cadaver I'd ever seen.

The camera continued its march around the body. For a moment I assumed the woman was Dianne Renzel, the tape a trophy for her killer. But by the time the camera reached the decedent's head and peered down from above like some mercenary mourner I could see that I was wrong.

The face that had stared happily at me from the pages of the newspapers that had reported her murder was not the face that stared at the heavens in the smudged and grainy videotape. This face was younger, ravaged by more than its demise, old beyond its years, abused. I was still struggling to determine who it was when the shadowy forms surrounding her began tossing dirt atop the body. Then I realized that the woman lay in a shallow grave and the camera was there to prove her burial.

They had placed her on a sheet of plastic. After the first ceremonial handfuls of dirt, the attendants draped the plastic around the body before covering her completely. Handful by handful, clods and clumps defiled the head and torso until the flesh had disappeared beneath a soft black blanket and the camera panned the sky and caught the ghoulish, peeping face of the Mortician in the Moon.

By the time it panned back to the grave, someone had scrawled various symbols in the dirt, crypto-religious scratchings that presumably warned of calamity or protected from defilement. One was a swastika, another a fish, a third what looked to be an erotic illustration out of the *Kama Sutra*. The camera made one final sweep across the grave, zoomed onto a pair of human hands clasped in prayerful penance, then faded to black at the instant I realized who the dead woman was.

I rewound the tape, ejected it from the recorder and left the office. I got out of the law school as quickly as I could, then jogged back to the car and put the tape back under the seat and took out the little cedar box and opened it. As I suspected, the outlandish fingernails weren't fake at all. Their backsides were caked with tiny crusts of blood and flesh, their painted sides scarred by the pliers that were used to pull them off the fingers of the dead woman in the film. I put the box back under the seat, locked the car and walked to where I was certain the interment had taken place.

It was still too early for the regulars to gather in the park. They were still out scrounging, pawing through dumpsters, begging for change, scavenging aluminum cans, plying the derelict's universal trade. I went back to where I'd found the buried tape and looked around.

The ground seemed uniformly firm and flat but for the place where I'd uncovered the box and the tape. I got down on my knees, probed the ground in various places, traced the outline of what seemed to be its softest spot and began to dig.

Again the earth came free in crumbling clumps of dust and litter. Again it took only a few minutes to duplicate the hole I had dug two hours earlier. This time I kept going, pawing like a dog for a bone. The smell I'd thought was garbage now was suspect. Two feet beneath the surface I came across the plastic shroud, and the smell of rotting flesh seared a passage to my brain.

I broadened the hole, convincing myself that I was pursuing an accurate identification rather than an unhealthy curiosity. I worked my way quickly to the head. I was careful, considerate, dainty, but when I brushed away the dirt and peeled away the plastic I wasn't certain I was looking at the girl I thought it was, the one whose mother clung so desperately to the false hope of her existence.

The body had begun to decompose, the stench its defensive weapon. Flesh had changed its color and contour, had yielded space to bone. When a maggot crawled from behind an eye, it was more than I could stand.

I was trying to replace the shroud when I noticed the single black incisor peering at me from above an obscenely drooping lip. The discoloration duplicated that in the photograph that Phyllis Misteen so fiercely cherished. I redraped the face and went to the corner and called Bart Kinn.

TWENTY-FOUR

Kinn got there in twenty minutes. I spent the interval warding off wanderers disposed to share the grove with me. I succeeded with all but one, a grizzled transient who, like a virus which thrives on penicillin, took my baleful gaze and donned it like a nightshirt as he made a comfortable cabin for himself beneath the lowest bows of a spreading spruce. By the time Bart Kinn arrived the transient was noisily asleep, an empty bottle of Night Train cradled in his palms like a badly damaged bird.

Kinn and another plainclothes officer got out of an unmarked car and strolled into the grove with professional intensity. When they got to the grave they circled twice, once looking down into the pit, the second time looking at the surroundings, which included me.

The initial inspection finished, Kinn said something to the second man that sent him back toward the car. When he got there, I could hear the squawk of his radio as he called for a technical crew to come and tell him exactly what he'd found.

In the meantime, Bart Kinn trudged toward me, his jaw bulging, his lips tightened into twin thin cords in his effort to control his anger. I wondered whether he was more angry at me than at the crime.

"How long ago did you dig that up?" The question was gruff and mean.

"Just before I called you."

"You look inside the plastic?"

"Yes."

"You got any idea who's in there?"

"Yes."

Kinn didn't bother to ask the question. "I think it's a girl named Sherry Misteen," I said.

Kinn frowned. "Who's that?"

I was certain he'd heard the name before, and almost certain he knew exactly who she was and so was testing the limits of my own knowledge before he questioned me further.

"A girl about eighteen," I told him. "Disappeared about two months ago."

"How long's she been dead?"

"No idea. A while," I added.

"How'd you happen to come across her body?"

"I smelled it."

"Shit." Kinn crossed his arms across his barrel chest. His hands looked big enough to palm a basketball, and strong enough to crush it till it popped. "It's foul but not that foul. How'd you know where to sniff?"

"If it's who I think it is, she lived across the street from the Usser place. Her mother was a good friend of Dianne Renzel's. I talked to her after I saw you and Mrs. Usser, and she asked me if I'd keep my eyes open for her daughter while I was fooling around with the Renzel thing. So that's what I did."

"This have anything to do with the Renzel murder?"

"Not as far as I know." It was the truth as things stood then, but it might not be the truth for too much longer.

"I suppose you know who killed her."

Kinn's sarcasm was heavy, even for him. He'd probably never had an outsider solve a case for him, probably never had to fit such kismet into his delicate self-image. When I told him I didn't know who'd killed the girl, he seemed relieved, and his next question was both easy and earnest.

"How about taking a guess?"

I shook my head. "I can't even do that. I don't know how she died, or where, or why. I just stumbled across her body while I was looking for something else."

"Here?" Kinn gestured at the park, as though only a lunatic

could expect to find anything of value within its tattered boundaries.

"Here and there," I said.

"This have anything to do with you being over here the other night? Checking out the Maniac and his crew?"

Kinn was getting close to bone. I had always felt he was reticent about the Usser case, was for his own reasons pursuing it with less than normal energy. But if I told him everything I knew, he'd intensify the search for Lisa Usser. If he found her before I did, she'd be instantly incommunicado. I wanted at least one real conversation with her, away from the Maniac and the cops and her father and her drugs and anything else that might warp her response to my questions. I looked at Kinn and tried to barter a little lie for a little block of time.

"Listen," I said. "I've got an appointment in downtown Oakland in an hour. I don't want to break it, so I'll offer you a deal."

Kinn eyed me skeptically. "What deal?"

"You let me go now, and in return I'll stop on the way and tell Mrs. Misteen her daughter's dead. That way you won't have to do it. Then I'll come by your office at four or so and we can talk some more about the case. I'll tell you whatever else you want to know."

"If you've got any firm leads to this killing, I need to know them now."

I shook my head. "I don't know any more than I've already told you. The only people in Berkeley I know anything about are connected to the Renzel case, not this one."

"You better not be shitting me, Tanner."

"I'm not. The most likely prospect is that she was killed because of some street scam. Her mother gets phone calls from time to time, saying Sherry needs clothes or money, telling her where to drop them off. She'd always try to follow whoever came to pick the stuff up, but she always lost them. Sherry herself never showed up at the drop point. Maybe it's because she's been dead all the time. Maybe someone killed Sherry so she wouldn't go back home and the guy could keep bleeding her mother dry."

Kinn thought it over. While he did so, the medical examiner arrived with his satchel, walked to the grave, bent down, and did something in its depths that Kinn and I couldn't see. "Doc?" Kinn called out to him. "How long's she been dead?"

"How'd you know it's a she?"

"Never mind. Just tell me if she's fresh or stale."

The sound of rippling plastic was followed by a muffled curse. "She's been down here a long time," the M.E. called back. "More than a month; less than six. God *damn* she's putrid."

"How'd she die?"

"Can't tell yet."

"She in shape to be identified?"

"Not from her looks, she isn't, unless her kin's got a Teflon stomach. Charts on this one."

Kinn grumbled to himself and looked at me. "Okay. You can take off. Tell the Misteen woman we'll be in touch after we finish up here. Tell her she can claim the body after the autopsy's been done. Tonight or tomorrow. Probably tomorrow."

I nodded.

"And I'll see *you* at the station at four sharp."

"Right."

I got out of there as quickly as I could, before Bart Kinn changed his mind.

It took four minutes to get to Hillside Lane. When she saw who had rung her doorbell and what expression he wore on his face, Phyllis Misteen flinched and then recoiled. "Is it about Sherry?"

I nodded.

"Is it bad?"

"Maybe I should come inside."

She stopped retreating and held her ground. "She's dead."

The words were firm, rehearsed, the dire conclusion somehow a balm to her. Instead of collapsing into a wayward grief, Phyllis Misteen straightened her back and blinked here eyes clear of sleep and sloth. "Would you come in and tell me how you know?"

"Sure."

I followed her inside. It was still dark and dreary, but the first thing she did was open the shades and invite in as much sunlight as would come. The bright splash was like a new piece of furniture. Phyllis admired it for a moment, then picked up some newspapers and magazines, coffee cups and cigarette wrappers, and stashed them out of sight. "Would you care for coffee? Or a drink?"

"No, thanks. Nothing."

"Then would you excuse me for a moment?"

"Of course."

She went off, her sweat clothes flapping, her hair a spidery tangle, her hands clenched white against the threatened mugging of despair. Her daughter stared at me from within her silver frame. I stared back and tried to decide why she was dead, and whether she knew what she had done to convince someone they had to kill her.

I heard some kitchen sounds, and a bathroom flush, then nothing. I stared at Sherry, hoping she would send me signals. When she hadn't in the next five minutes, I realized her mother had been gone too long. I began to worry that she'd fled, or collapsed, or done something to herself. As I stood up to go look for her, she materialized in front of me.

"I'm sorry I took so long. Are you sure you won't have anything?"

Her smile was as bright as the swatch of daylight on the wall. Her hair was combed and pinned, her body proud in tailored slacks and a silk print blouse. Her hands fluttered before her in lithe and elegant positions.

I told her I was fine. She took a seat across from mine and crossed her legs and placed her hands on her upraised knee. Her composure seemed genuine, not a fragile crutch, further proof that the aftermath of death is as various and unpredictable as its cause.

"When you were here before I told you I was certain Sherry was still alive," she said, her voice now modulated by intelligence, not longing. "I was lying. To you. To myself. I have known, somehow, for quite a while that Sherry was gone to me." She met my eyes. "I assume there's no doubt about it."

"No. But formal identification may require her dental records."

She trembled, then regained control. "Where was she found?"

"In People's Park. Buried."

"My God. How long has she been dead?"

"Apparently for at least a month. My guess is it's more like two. The police want an autopsy. Then you can claim the body. They'll probably be over here in a while, after they finish at the scene."

"She was murdered?"

"Yes."

"By whom?"

"I don't know. The police don't, either."

"Will they try to find out?"

"Yes."

"Even if I don't want them to?"

"I'm afraid so."

"I see."

The silence was all-consuming. Phyllis Misteen bathed in it, found solace in its cleansing powers. "Do you have any idea who might have killed your daughter?" I asked.

"No. None."

"She was apparently killed even before Dianne Renzel. Was there a connection there that might have been a motive for someone to kill them both?"

She shook her head slowly. "Dianne knew Sherry, of course. And vice versa. But they were only neighbors, as far as I know. Of course Lisa and Sherry were friends, so Sherry spent lots of time over there. But that was before."

"Before what?"

"I don't know. Before they quarreled."

"You really don't know what happened between them?"

"No. The breach was bitter and complete. But I have no idea what caused it. You know teenage girls."

"Could it have been jealousy? Over a boy named Cal, perhaps?"

"Cal?" Phyllis considered it, then shook her head. "Sherry knew Cal; he was around here quite a lot. But she was never interested in him emotionally, not that I know of. He was a bit too bland for Sherry."

"He didn't look so bland the last time I saw him."

"Not on the outside, maybe. But inside he was . . . what word did she use? Yogurt. That's what Sherry said. Cal was just plain yogurt."

I tried again. "How about a guy named Nifton? No one would confuse him with yogurt. He also goes by the name of the Maniac."

She frowned. "Nifton. The name seems familiar, but I . . ."

"You probably saw it in the papers. He killed a girl a couple of years ago. Lawrence Usser defended him. Pleaded insanity and was acquitted. Now he's out and collecting a little harem of girls who are more cooperative than the one he knifed. They seem willing to do anything to keep him happy."

"Lord. I certainly hope Sherry wasn't involved with someone like that. But I have to admit she might have been. Teenagers are so determined to keep their lives secret from their parents. I think they *need* to feel their problems are unique and momentous. They seem offended by the idea that their parents were ever young themselves, and so might be able to help. I don't know anything specifically. I'm sorry. I don't think Sherry ever mentioned him."

"Needles? Does that name mean anything?"

"No. Nothing."

"Did Sherry have a drug problem before she left home? A serious one?"

Phyllis Misteen shrugged. "She experimented, I'm sure. But I don't think she was a regular user. I looked, of course. For all those signs they talk about? But I don't know. They're always surprised, aren't they, the parents of the ones who go bad? As though they never had a clue. But that's impossible, don't you think? There's always *some*thing. There's a blindness there; both ways."

She drifted into a nostalgic silence. I let it settle for a while, then said what was on my mind. "I have to tell you, Mrs. Misteen, I think Sherry's murder has something to do with the murder of Dianne Renzel. It seems likely they were killed by the same person. So while I can understand your reluctance to explore the last weeks of Sherry's life, that information might lead to other evidence that would explain the Renzel case. So I'm going to be—"

"*Wait* a minute," she interrupted. "*Lawrence* killed Dianne. Are you saying he killed Sherry too?"

"I'm saying I don't think he killed either one of them."

"But the police—"

"Are wrong sometimes."

"But if Lawrence didn't kill Dianne, then who did?"

"I don't know. That's why I need to do one more thing before I go."

"What?"

"Look at Sherry's room."

"Why?"

"To see if there's anything in it that explains why she and Lisa quarreled, or why she left home, or was killed. Do you mind?"

She lowered her eyes and sighed. "Not if I don't have to go with you. It's down the hall, first door on the left. I've already looked for those things, you know. Things that would let me understand why Sherry did what she did. But I didn't find anything. Anything but me."

She paused, and I started to get up, but she began to speak again. "She used to be upstairs, the room next to mine. But that was too intimate for her all of a sudden, too violative of her privacy. So she moved downstairs. I hardly ever saw her after I started working nights. I worried I wasn't being a good mother. Dianne and I spent hours and hours talking about our responsibilities—to our families, our community, our sex, our world. We never quite figured it out. I mean, something always took a back seat. I tried to convince Dianne that *we* were the neglected ones, that everyone took from us but no one gave anything back. She didn't believe it. But then she had Larry and then Pierce Richards and I didn't have anyone. Anyone but Sherry."

Her smile was sad, resigned to truth and to the unbroken horizon of her future. I left her and went to look over her daughter's private things.

Sherry's room was much like her ex-friend Lisa's. Clothing and music were the passions, though Sherry's tastes in both were even more bizarre than those I'd encountered across the street. There were strong hints of sadism and bondage in the clothing accessories and the pictures on the record albums. A poster on the wall read LIFE IS HARD. THEN YOU DIE. A stuffed teddy bear on top of the dresser had a pencil through his heart. A rosebud had been dipped in black enamel and made to seem macabre.

Everything else was similarly fierce or homely; nothing was attractive or serene. The air itself seemed angry and resentful. The strangest thing of all was that the door to the room was missing.

I had no idea what I was searching for, but there was no point looking in the obvious places. Anything of interest would be under, above, behind, or inside something else. A hiding place, a secret stash, a private trove. All kids have them, though these days they're likely to contain an illegal substance or a lethal weapon instead of a dirty book or a pack of Camels or a pressed corsage.

The desk contained the tools of art and literature, a collection of psychedelic stickers, pens imprinted with revolutionary slogans, a ball of string. The dresser drawers were so full that clothing leaped onto the floor when I opened them. There was nothing unusual under the mattress or behind the reproduction of Picasso's *Demoiselles*. I looked inside shoes, aerosol can lids, blue jean pockets, pillowcases, lampshades, album jackets, even a sealskin muff. I looked everywhere I could think to look, until there was but one place left.

There weren't many volumes in the little walnut bookcase. I gave them a quick once-over, trying to guess which pages might compress a secret. Not the books for school—dictionaries, *Elements of Style,* thesaurus. Not *Gatsby, Jane Eyre,* or *Pamela;* such novels don't excite a youthful passion for intrigue. Not the art books or the biographies of Lennon, Joplin and the Rolling Stones. Maybe the poets.

I tried Plath. Nothing. Then Sexton. When I riffled through the pages, something fell out. I picked it up, a Polaroid snapshot of a young man, naked and unfamiliar, with an erection he displayed like a fresh-caught fish. I replaced the erotica and tried Browning, Maya Angelou and Virginia Woolf. Then *Living at the Movies* by Jim Carroll. Something drifted to the floor again.

This was a photograph as well, of Sherry, taken at school beneath a banner for Berkeley High. This time Sherry was smiling, but someone had taken red and black grease pencils and added a rather realistic bullet hole to her forehead and a slender thread of blood across her nose and down her cheek. I looked on the back but there was no message beyond the graphic wound. I put that one back as well.

In the living room I asked Phyllis why there was no door on Sherry's room.

She sighed. "She used to slam it all the time. After we had a fight? It was usually after I ordered her to clean her room before she left the house. So I told her if she did it again, I was going to take the door off for a month. She did, and I did, too. That was a month before she left. I guess I'll keep it off. Hell, maybe I'll take them *all* off. I've got no one to hide from anymore. And no one's left to hide from me."

TWENTY-FIVE

I needed more than ever to talk to Lisa Usser, and the best place to start looking for her was right across the street. Freed from the maze of Phyllis Misteen's grief, I trotted up the now-familiar steps and knocked on the door.

The police notice had been removed, but the house still seemed hollow, of historical interest only. I knocked again but heard nothing that resembled an occupant. I wondered if Lawrence Usser was away or was merely hiding, struggling to find an attitude from which to endure the days until a jury of his peers declared his guilt or innocence, his sanity or lack thereof, while all around him everyone assumed the worst. I started to return to my car, then decided to look in one more place.

The rear yard was as I'd seen it last, down to the recumbent garbage can that Cal had overturned in his dash to evade my capture. I stood in the center of the patio and looked back at the house. No one peered through windows, no curtains slid suspiciously aside to make way for spying eyes. The wind chimes played a piece that might have been by Hindemith—atonal, eerie, portentous.

I walked toward the far corner of the yard. Cal had said he'd lived for a time in the potting shed at the rear of the lot, so maybe it was a nook where Lisa hid as well. I approached warily and felt ridiculous for doing so, since the little hut made me think of Hansel and Gretel.

The little door was closed, but the padlock dangled by its shackle from the eye of an open hasp. I walked to the side of the shed and tried to look through the window but it was too filthy to reveal anything. I returned to the front, grasped the knob and eased open the door. Daylight entered tentatively, as though the darkness charged admission.

She didn't move, didn't even seem to breathe. I got down on my knees and leaned over her till I was certain she was alive, then sat back and curled my legs under me and watched her sleep. Suddenly soothing, the wind chimes blended with the whistling cadence of her measured breaths.

She wore a man's blue work shirt, sleeves rolled to doughnuts at her elbows, tails flapping freely down her sides. Beneath the work shirt was a thin cotton undershirt, also a man's, in the old strap style. Her slacks were a baggy burlap, gathered tightly at the ankle by elastic and at the waist by a knotted necktie. Her shoes were chartreuse canvas high-tops, laced halfway.

She was lying on a foam camp pad. A flannel-lined sleeping bag, unzipped, was bunched below her feet. As I tried to decide how to get her in shape to talk to me, Lisa moaned and raised a hand to her face to shield it from the light that poured like a waterfall through the open door. I waited. As she slipped back into a purring slumber I closed the door so her face was in shadow, then inspected her cluttered lair.

She and Cal had rigged it like a tent, with camping equipment they had doubtlessly pilfered from their parents' stores. Above her head, a Coleman lantern dangled from a nail in the ceiling joist, its unlit mantles shining like the product of two imprisoned spiders. A second sleeping bag was rolled and stuffed along the wall that Lisa curled against. A half-full bag of peat moss had been molded into a makeshift chair. Beside it was a pile of science fiction novels, an empty bag of Cheetos and an empty can of Sprite. The rest of the shed's contents were mostly garden supplies—tools and hoses, buckets and pots, chemicals to make things grow or die. The smell of fertilizer combined with the fumes from the gas in the Lawn Boy to create a surprisingly nostalgic fragrance.

As time drifted away from us, I began to hear things that lurked outside—birds, sirens, traffic. Suddenly I was certain Lawrence Usser was approaching across the lawn, but when I peeked out the door it turned out to be a dog, heading down toward town, crossing the yard from east to west. A few minutes later I was remembering how meticulous my father had been about our yard back home, how he'd made me mow it every Saturday morning before I did anything else, how I had to hand-trim the edges and pull all the foxtail and the water-grass and sharpen the blades on the hand mower with a file.

The lawn mower had broken down, and I was hiking toward the highway, barefoot, with the blade reel in my hand, when Lisa Usser coughed, groaned, rolled from one side to another and woke us both up. Our eyes opened simultaneously, our senses returned at matching rates. "Who . . . ? Where . . . ? Who are you, anyway?" She wasn't as frightened as she should have been, was used to waking beside a stranger.

"My name's Tanner. I saw you down at Hell House last night. I was there with Cal."

"Oh. Yeah." She rubbed her hand along her brow and scraped her hair away from her face. "Jesus, my head hurts."

"I need to talk to you, Lisa."

"Yeah? About what? How'd you know I was here, anyway?"

"Just a guess. Cal told me he used to stay back here some-times."

"Cal. Poor fucking Cal. He thinks I'm still a kid. If he knew what I *really* was, he'd . . . ." She shrugged away Cal's innocence and her own transgressions. "Is that why you're here? To find me for Cal?"

"I'm here for lots of reasons. One of them is to talk to you about Sherry Misteen."

Her thin face narrowed even more. "Sherry? What about her?"

Her voice, formerly hard and dismissive, was for the first time timorous. "She's dead," I said.

"They've been saying that for weeks. It's just talk. No one knows *where* she is." There was a wishful thinness in her final words.

"They do now."

"Huh?"

"They found her body. In People's Park. Where you and your buddies buried it."

She leaned away from me. "Hey. Jesus Christ. What are you trying to pull here, anyway?"

"I'm just trying to learn the truth before the police do. About Sherry. And about your mother."

"My mother? She's . . . Oh. I get it. I heard they let my old man out. Does he know I'm back here? Did he send you out to get me?"

"As far as I know he doesn't know where you are. Do you want me to go tell him?"

"Shit, no. The bastard. I'm just waiting till I can get in the house and boost some stuff to hock. I'm a little short of bread, you know?" She eyed me closely. "You got any?"

"Some."

"You pay me if I talk to you? Like they do on TV?"

"Maybe. If you tell me the truth."

Her eyes grew slim and calculating. "Yeah, well, first I need a bath. And some chow. You up for that?"

"If that's what it takes. Where do you want to go? In the house? I don't think anyone's there."

"Hell, no. He might come back."

"Your grandmother's?"

She laughed contemptuously. "You got a car?"

"Yes."

"Let's go. I'll show you on the way."

She scrambled to her feet and grabbed a backpack that had been buried beneath the clump of sleeping bag and crawled out of the shed. "Come on," she urged. "Let's get out of here before anyone sees me."

She began running toward the front of the house. I hurried after her, afraid I'd just offered candy to a baby, for purposes not entirely proper.

She scrambled into the car, and I drove away from Hillside Lane. After she'd directed me back to Dwight Way, then left onto Warring and left again onto Derby I was certain we were headed back to Piedmont, to her grandparents' mansion. But three minutes later, as I was climbing Ashby on my way toward the freeway that stretched to Piedmont and East Oakland, Lisa suddenly reached out and grabbed by shoulder. "Here. Turn left. Hurry, before you get caught in traffic."

I wrenched the wheel to the left, frightened an approaching

Subaru, bounced over the curb and came to a stop beside a small
white building that blocked the road. The security guard inside
leaned out his window and I rolled mine down. "Are you checking in, sir?" he asked.

I didn't know what he was talking about. Beside me, Lisa
Usser nudged my ribs. "Tell him yes."

"I guess we are," I said to the guard.

"Straight ahead; follow the signs. We hope you enjoy your
stay at the Claremont."

I remained disoriented until he uttered his final word. As I
put the car in gear I leaned forward and looked up the hill.
There it was, sure enough. The Claremont Hotel, doyenne of
Berkeley's hostelries, a huge white structure that gazed down
over Berkeley, then out across the bay and fixed its haughty
stare on distant San Francisco, as though to assert its equal
elegance. The row of dormers across its top and its gaily
trimmed facade gave the structure a festive, resortish feel, as
though it had been designed by a pastry chef rather than an
architect.

I took a parking ticket from the machine, passed through the
barrier and drove slowly up the drive, glancing at Lisa Usser
when I could. "What are we doing here?" I asked as I swung
left toward the main entrance.

"Checking in, like I said."

"Why?"

"So I can eat. And take a bath. And we can have that talk you
want so bad."

The last was said with a taunting roughness, a whore's dis-
dain, as though in Lisa's world it was talk, not sex, that was a
mortal sin.

I almost convinced myself that I was asking for trouble if I
agreed to Lisa's plan, but at bottom it seemed worth the risk.
Two were dead, and more might die if the Usser case did not
unscramble. And I was as close to that as I knew how to get.

I parked near the front entrance, beneath a massive awning.
Lisa and I got out of the car as a doorman rushed to assist us.
"Baggage, sir?"

His face betrayed no doubt of our propriety, no hint that he
took exception to my sharing a hotel room with a girl less than
half my age. I couldn't say the same for me. From within a

nervous blush I told him I had only a tote bag, and that I'd get it later. The doorman nodded. When he reached for Lisa's backpack she turned away and told him she'd take it in herself. I had reached the front desk before it occurred to me that people might mercifully assume that Lisa was my daughter, whom I was treating to a break from school.

The check-in was uneventful, the desk clerk barely noticing the girl standing to my rear like a domesticated pet that was swaddled in a burlap bag. We shared the elevator with a smirking bellhop who kept his eye on Lisa's breasts. By the time we got to our floor Lisa was laughing audibly at my discomfiture.

The bellhop turned on the lights and the air conditioner and lingered for his tip. I gave him a five, in a hopeless attempt to buy discretion.

When he'd gone Lisa turned to me, hands on hips. "I'm hungry."

"Okay. There's the Presto Café downstairs. Let's—"

"Room service."

She opened drawers and pulled out a menu from the third one she tried and glanced down it quickly. "I want the salmon, with artichoke hearts to start, and the spinach salad."

I shook my head. "A sandwich is plenty, if you expect me to pay for it. Then, if we have a nice long talk, you can have dessert."

"Tightwad."

"Right."

She pouted for a second, then looked back at the menu. "Club sandwich and a Coke, plus a side order of fries."

"Okay. Call it in."

"You want something?"

"No."

She picked up the phone and asked for room service. "Hi. This is room 319. Mr. Tanner's room. Send me the large filet, medium rare, with the works. The chocolate mousse. And a bottle of your best Cabernet. And make it quick."

She dropped the phone onto the cradle and laughed delightedly, then reached for the buttons to her shirt. "I'm taking a bath. Don't you dare come in or I'll scream rape. Do you have to piss first?"

I shook my head. She kicked off her shoes, peeled off the

oversize shirt and stepped out of the billowy slacks, which left her in cotton briefs and undershirt. She looked like a boy, the nudge of her breasts and the arc of her hips the sole marks of her sex, marks her clothing seemed designed to hide.

She gathered up her clothes and trotted into the bathroom and shut the door. In a moment the roar of water filled the room. I called room service and amended Lisa's order, then flipped on the TV and lay back on the bed and watched whatever came on, which happened to be a rerun of *Mannix*. His secretary was a Peggy, too. Someone had kidnapped her son. Mannix saved the day, and I was into the opening credits of *Hart to Hart* before Lisa came out. When she did she was dripping wet and naked.

"Hi," she said, with the lilt of the practiced flirt.

"Hi."

She eyed me impudently. "Well? Let's get at it." She walked to the bed, climbed onto it and knelt at its foot. "You don't mind me all wet, do you?" she asked, rubbing her hands along her flanks. "I'll just have to wash you off me when you're done, so there's no sense drying off. I hate it when come keeps dripping out of me all day, you know? Besides, it makes weird noises when you're wet."

I didn't say anything. Lisa lifted her hands off her hips, looked at them, then dried them on the bedspread. When she looked at me again she frowned. "Come on. I can't stay here forever." She paused. "You still want to ball me, don't you?"

"What makes you think that?"

She laughed, forcing a bawdy pose. "*All* you old guys want to fuck young chicks. Take a guess how many times a day I get hit on by wheezy old professor-types along the avenue. Huh? So how do you want me, belly or back?"

She flopped down on the bed and rolled over, then back again, leaving spots of water that were as dark as smears of blood. "Just get dressed," I told her.

"Hey. It's okay. I owe you for the room and food and stuff. You're not the first guy I've paid off in the rack, believe me."

I tried very hard to believe it was a bluff. "It's on the house this time."

My reticence was making her mad. "What's the matter, I'm not stacked enough? I make up for it, Mr. Detective, don't think

I don't. So what do you want to do to me? Go ahead. Name your perversion. I've let guys do all *kinds* of stuff to me."

"Why?"

"Why not? It's the way of the world. I learned it from my old man. Sex with anyone, anytime. You married?"

"Nope."

"Too bad. I like to imagine what the wives look like when they find out, you know? I like to think about their faces when their old man tells them all the stuff I did. So you want to get it on, or what?" Lisa hopped off the bed and went over to her backpack and fished around inside and came up with a little bag tied at the top with a string. "I got some hellacious grass here. It'll make it real nice for you. Bet you've never got laid while you were stoned, have you? Bet you've never gotten stoned, period. You're so straight you need help to tie your shoes."

"Tell me about Sherry, Lisa. Tell me what happened between you two. Why you weren't friends anymore."

Lisa twirled the Baggie like a pinwheel. "Sherry. I don't know nothing about Sherry. I mean, she lived across the street, then she split, and now you claim she's dead. Which I doubt."

"But what happened between you?"

"Who says something happened?"

"I hear things."

"Well, hear this." She flipped her middle finger at me, then rummaged in her pack again and brought out a cigarette, lit it and perched on the edge of the dresser, legs drawn up, chin on her knees, looking like an ad for a Warhol film or a brand of new cologne.

She took a deep drag and blew smoke at the ceiling. "One guy tried to burn me with a cigarette. You into that? Sadism and stuff?"

"Did Sherry try to beat your time with the Maniac? Is that what happened?"

She tapped her cigarette angrily. The ash drifted to the carpet like a dehydrated tear. "Sherry? You must be nuts. Me and the Maniac are into stuff Sherry never even *heard* about, let alone did. Not sex, either."

"What else?"

"Stuff. Just stuff. You're a jerk, you know that? You want to fuck me or not?"

"No. So you can put your clothes on."

Her grin was as close to evil as she could shove it. "What's the matter? You don't like my twat smiling at you?"

She swirled so she could see herself in the mirror at her back. "I think it's kind of cute." She twirled back at me and spread her legs. Her pubic hair was thin and straight, like a clump of new spring grass.

"Who killed Sherry?" I demanded.

"Who knows? Who cares?"

"Who took the videotape of her funeral in the park?"

That one jarred her out of her burlesque vamp and into a frightened stare. "I don't know what you're talking about."

"The videotape you took from your father's study and buried in the park, along with Sherry's fingernails."

"You know about that?"

I nodded. "And when I leave here the police will too. Then they'll be on you like a new tattoo. You won't see the street for days. Longer than that if they can tie you to the murder. The only way you can keep that from happening is to talk to me. If I know exactly what went down, maybe I can point the cops in the right direction and away from you."

"Shit. Am I supposed to think you give a damn about me? Well, I don't."

"All the conspirators to a crime are as guilty as the one who actually did the deed, Lisa. From the looks of that tape, I'd say Sherry's murder was a group effort. There were several people dancing around that grave, and if they can show you were one of them you're in big trouble. Maybe bigger than I can get you out of. But if you're as smart as they say you are, you'll give me a chance to try."

"I don't know anything about it. Now shut up. Just *shut up*. I don't want to *hear* any more about Sherry."

She was on the border of hysteria. I could see no point in pushing her over it, so I backed off, hoping she could discard this mood as easily as she did the others. "Let's talk about your mother," I said easily.

She closed her eyes and squeezed a tear from each of them, then shook her head. "Jesus. Why don't we talk about Auschwitz, too? And maybe Jonestown for a while. And Cambodia and Ethiopia and all those other good places. I mean, you want to talk about dead people, why limit it to one or two?"

"Why did you tell the police your father killed her?"

"Because he fucking *did*."

"I don't think so."

"Oh, no? What makes you such an authority?"

"My business."

"If Daddy didn't kill her, who did?"

"I don't know. But I think you do."

"Like hell."

"Was it the Maniac? Did he kill Sherry and your mother?"

"No, no, a thousand times, no. Will you let up, you bastard? Just because the Maniac killed the sorority prick teaser doesn't make him a mass murderer, for Christ's sake. He's better now, anyway."

"He didn't seem much better the other night."

"Yeah, well, maybe you didn't see him before, you know? Besides, that was just his medicine. He doesn't keep track, sometimes."

She started to pace the room, still heedless of her nudity, still contemptuous of my effort to understand why the two women closest to her were dead. "Sherry I can understand, maybe," I said softly. "A street thing. She ripped someone off. Or squealed to the cops. Maybe she had it coming, like the other girl. But my problem is, I can't figure out why the Maniac would kill your mom."

She put out her hands and leaned against the wall. "He *didn't*. Really. You've got to believe that."

She pushed away from the wall and went over to her pack and pulled out some baggy shorts and a T-shirt and put them on. Somehow she looked more naked than before. I went over to her and put my hands on her shoulders. They were as thin and fragile as a doll's. She wouldn't meet my eyes.

"I'm going to ask you something, Lisa," I said. "And before I do I want you to realize that there are people who can help you with the problem. Who can make sure it never, ever happens again."

She gave me a puzzled look, then went into the bathroom and got the slacks and shirt she'd taken off to bathe and came back and stuffed them in her pack, along with her underwear. "What the hell are you talking about?"

"Did your father ever abuse you sexually, Lisa? Did he force you to have intercourse with him?"

She dropped her pack to the floor and stared at me. "You're a fucking *pervert*, you know that? You don't know anything about *anything*. Now let me alone. I mean it!" She was crying, and was enraged at herself because of it.

Her denial was so vehement and immediate I tended to believe her. Which put me back to square one. Sexual abuse would have explained a lot, including the personality changes that each member of the Usser household had experienced a month before Dianne Renzel had been murdered. I decided to try an even longer shot, a second possibility that had crept into my mind sometime that morning. I was about to ask the question that posed it when someone knocked on the door.

I opened it to the room service waiter. He pushed his metal cart into the room, uncovered the sandwich and the fries, opened the bottle of wine that I had forgotten to cancel along with the steak. I tipped him and he vanished, then I invited Lisa to eat her dinner.

She didn't move for a moment, remained curled in a fetal ball on the floor beside the bed. I was about to help her up when she uncoiled and went to the cart and wolfed down the sandwich in three gulps and took a slug of wine straight from the bottle. After a second swallow she offered the bottle to me. I hesitated, then matched her lack of couth. The moment of hobo fellowship was oddly pleasurable. I gave the bottle back to Lisa and she took another swig as I asked my question.

"What was the relationship between your father and Dr. Lonborg?"

I had intended to ease toward my hunch with a certain subtlety, but Lisa vaulted there immediately. "You mean are they gay? Christ. My *father*? Sure he screws anything that moves, but it has to have a cunt. I mean, come *on*. Are you on *dust* or something? Get real."

"Okay," I said. "I guess I'm off base."

"Twice," she reminded.

I apologized but she waved me off. "*You're* the one like Lonborg," she accused. "Every time I turn around there he *is,* always coming up with these *explanations* for everything. Well, some things don't *have* explanations, you know? Some things just happen." Her eyes declared that what had happened to her had been infinitely sad.

I told her I agreed with her. "I'll give up on the wild theories, Lisa. But maybe it would help if you would tell me some things about your mother. About her relationship with your father, and with you."

"Why should I?" Lisa groused.

"Because she's dead. And no one knows why."

Lisa sank back to the floor and leaned against the bed. Long seconds passed. She drank absently from the wine bottle, staring straight ahead, slipping into some postnarcotic daze.

When she spoke her words were flat and unaffected. "Why did it have to be her? That's what I want to know. If it had to be someone why wasn't it him?"

"Your father?"

She nodded. "He's vomit. A total jerk."

"Why?"

"It doesn't matter. It doesn't have anything to do with anything important." She took a long pull at the Cabernet, draining the bottle and tossing it aside. "You got any hard booze on you?" she asked halfheartedly, as though she had pledged to get bombed and was willing to honor it even though she didn't want to.

I shook my head. Lisa shrugged, still in a fog. "Mom's a jerk, too, sometimes," she said suddenly, her tense as confused as the rest of her. "People think she's so great, you know? Doing so much for the city and all that? Well, she did a lot more for *them* than she did for *us*. She was always down at that fucking *crisis* center, listening to the bullshit artists. Or if she wasn't down there she was on the phone, *counseling* someone. What garbage. Poor little junkie, poor little schizoid, poor little whore. Why didn't she pay attention to *us* once in a while? Huh? Answer me that."

"Was there a special problem you needed her help with, Lisa?"

"Nah. I didn't need her near as much as Daddy did."

"How do you mean?"

Lisa lowered her head. "Aw, just that he wouldn't have done the shit he did if she'd given him what he needed, right? He wouldn't have gone out sniffing up all those skirts if he had a good thing going for him at home, would he? I mean, it's *her* fault he—" She bit off her final words.

"He what?"

"Nothing. He's a void. They both were voids. Now I got to get out of here. Take me back to the avenue."

"Lisa?"

"Huh?"

"Your father thinks *you* killed her."

"Dianne?"

"Yes."

"When did he say that?"

"He didn't say it. But I know that's what he thinks."

Lisa's eyes betrayed a swift alarm. "So are the cops after me?"

"No. And they probably won't be."

"Why not?"

"Your father is going to confess to the murder himself. He's going to admit he did it and then he's going to plead insanity."

"He's doing that for me?"

I nodded.

"Jesus." She shook her head in wonder.

"You didn't see him do it, did you? You lied to the police when you told them you did."

She paused, then nodded.

"And he didn't threaten you, did he? That's why you weren't at the arraignment, because you were afraid they'd learn you were lying if you showed up in court."

She nodded again.

"Do you know anything at all about your mother's death?"

She shook her head, only half listening. "Just what Cal told me."

It was my turn to be surprised. "Cal? What does Cal know about it?"

"I don't know. Listen. I got to think. I'm not talking to you anymore, so there's no use asking questions. I got to get out of here. Now. You can come or stay, it doesn't matter."

She grabbed her pack and left the room. I retrieved her bag of pot and hurried after her, as relieved as if I'd broken out of jail.

TWENTY-SIX

I t was after six when we left the hotel. I'd missed my appointment with Bart Kinn, but if Lisa Usser didn't decide to be honest with me it wouldn't matter if Kinn ordered me off the case. Lisa was all I had to go on, and if she didn't change her mind and tell me everything she knew about the storm that struck the Usser house some two months earlier, I wasn't going very far.

Within a few minutes were were coasting down Ashby, heading back toward the campus. Lisa was huddled against the far door, gazing out the window, lost in thoughts that must have included murder if she knew what I thought she knew.

At the Tanglewood intersection I asked her where she wanted to go. The encounter in the hotel room had embarrassed us both, so badly that we wanted out of each other's way regardless of the consequences. "Take me back to my old man's place," she mumbled. "There's still some stuff I got to get."

"If you need a place to stay, I can make a suggestion."

"Where?" she sneered. "With you?"

"No. With—"

She waved off my offer of the Renzels' home with an insolent twitch. "I don't want to hear it. I don't want to hear anything else you got to say."

"You're supposed to be smart, Lisa. But you're not acting very

smart. You keep on this way and you're going to end up in jail.
Or worse. Whoever killed Sherry and your mother might decide
you know too much to let you stay alive."

The dome light on my car flashed on. I slowed down. "You
keep up that shit and I'll jump out right here," Lisa threatened.
"I mean it."

"Okay, okay. Shut the door. I just want you to be careful.
Okay?"

The light went off. Lisa sulked in silence. I kept my promise
as I took Claremont, then Warring, then Dwight Way, and approached the entrance to Hillside Lane. "Go slow," Lisa ordered
as I started to make the turn. "I want to make sure my old man's
not around."

I eased into Lisa's street and drove slowly through the dogleg.
There weren't any lights on in the Usser house, and no car out
front. I drove to the end of the street, turned around and
parked in front of her house.

Lisa reconnoitered. "He's probably down at his precious law
school," she said bitterly, "getting stroked by the little lady lawyers."

I thought of the mixed reception that was awaiting Usser at
the law school and I smiled. Lisa saw me. Her lip curled angrily.
"You think it's funny, huh? You think it's just some fucking
sport, don't you? Like rugby or something. You're pathetic, you
know that? You make me sick. All of you."

Lisa kicked open the door and scrambled out of the car and
started up the steps to her house, her long thin legs as white as
birch trees in the dusk. I reached behind me and grabbed her
backpack off the rear seat and got out on my side and called out
to her. "Wait, Lisa. If I was like that, I'd have taken you up on
your invitation back at the hotel. Right? Come back and get your
pack."

She stopped, turned, looked down on me like a dark and
dubious archangel, then trudged back down the steps. When
she reached out her hand for her pack, she kept her mouth
shut, which was as close as she could come to an apology. I
wasn't certain she owed me one.

Instead of giving her the pack I put it on the sidewalk and
took out my wallet and got out a business card. Then I took out
a twenty and handed the bill and the card to Lisa. "Here's where

you can reach me if you want to talk," I said. "If you want to stay out of the Youth Authority, I think it's pretty important for you to tell someone all you know, and do it soon. Me or the police. If you decide to go to the cops, the guy to see is Bart Kinn. He's tough, but he's smart and he's fair."

"Fat chance," Lisa said, then held up the twenty. "What's this for? You change your mind and want to buy a quick blow job in the back seat?"

"That's for you to buy yourself a meal."

"Meal, hell. Soon as I find the Maniac, I'll buy myself a couple of lines. The Berkeley Hills Diet, don't you know?"

Lisa laughed at me with a seamless contempt. Our discussion had so focused my senses I hadn't noticed the car that had turned into the street and crawled ahead, lights off, until it was almost opposite mine. It was too dark to identify the driver even after he got out of the car and started for us.

Lisa was tugging on her pack straps, preparing to throw it onto her shoulder, when the man spoke to her.

"Hi, Lisa."

Lisa dropped her pack and spun toward him. "You."

Her eyes were bright in the evening shadows, as though she saw something she didn't believe existed. I squinted and looked again. The man was Lisa's father, dressed the way I'd seen him in court that morning, slouching, hands in pockets, his shoes scraping on the street as he approached, looking more like a prisoner than the men who had been led away in chains.

"Are you coming home, Lisa? I hope so." Usser's voice was shy, a bashful plea.

"Never," Lisa blurted. "I'll *never* come back to you."

"Please? Can we just talk about it? Then if you still want to leave I'll take you. Wherever you want to go."

"I won't go *anywhere* with you, don't you get it? I can't stand the *sight* of you."

"Mr. Tanner can come, too, if you want. If it bothers you that much to be alone with me."

"It bothers me to *look* at you. It bothers me to *smell* you. It bothers me to know you're alive."

Usser retreated from her assault, stumbled down the curb, had to grab the fender of my car to keep from falling. When he stepped back up onto the sidewalk, he wore the empty aspect of the penitent. "I'm your father, Lisa. I know you can't believe this now, but I love you very much. I love you enough to do whatever you want me to do to make things the way they used to be with us. Anything. I've just been to see Dr. Lonborg. He's made some suggestions about how I can . . . improve my behavior, toward you and toward the people I work with. I'm going to try to change, Lisa. I *promise* you I am. So will you give me a chance? Please?"

Usser clasped his hands. I thought he was going to sink to his knees but he just stood there, open to his daughter and the world. I felt a twinge of sympathy, but I also wondered what he'd done to distance his daughter from him.

"You still don't get it, do you?" Lisa was saying.

"Get what?"

"That I will never forgive you for what you did. *Never*. Till the day I die, which I hope like hell is *soon*."

Lisa reached for her pack again and swung it over her shoulder. With a final, cutting curse she started down the street, shoving her father out of her way, silencing me with a glance of white-hot hatred.

Usser looked at me helplessly. "I don't think there's any point going after her," I told him. "If she's going to come around, she's going to have to do it on her own. It's not something you can force on her."

"I suppose not." I could barely hear his voice.

"I need to know something," I said.

"What?"

"What made you think Lisa killed her mother? Was it some argument they had, or did you find something at the scene that incriminated her?"

"I . . . I'd better not talk about it. Jake Hattie said I shouldn't."

"They've found another body, Usser. Killed by the same person who killed your wife."

"Who?"

"Sherry Misteen."

Usser's face seemed to empty of all but disbelief. I followed his eyes as they looked imploringly at the house across the street, as though he prayed that Sherry would magically appear and render me a liar. Behind me, I sensed Lisa had stopped to listen. "Who . . . What happened to her?" Usser stammered.

"She was murdered a couple of months ago. Sometime later she was buried in People's Park. Whoever did it recorded the burial on videotape and put the tape in the *Reds* cartridge in your study so you'd come across it by accident. Why would someone do that to you?"

Usser pressed his ears as though what he'd heard had injured them. "I don't know. I don't have any idea."

"Come on, Usser," I said. "Your little game is getting dangerous. Tell me why you thought Lisa killed your wife."

He lowered his hands and met my eyes. "I found a book."

"What book?"

"It's called *The Astral Light.* I noticed Lisa carrying it around after she started running wild."

"Where did you find it?"

"Under Dianne's body. It was terrible. It was soaked in her blood. I got it all over my hands but I couldn't just leave it there, I had to hide it. God, I was sick. To think that Lisa could do something like that, my own flesh and blood, I . . . If Adam Lonborg hadn't helped me see that I could eventually *save* Lisa, I think I would have killed myself."

I thought back to my search of Usser's house. "I saw the book on your shelf, didn't I? Why didn't you toss it out?"

"I was afraid the police would find it, no matter what I did. Then somehow I hoped it might eventually exculpate Lisa. . . . I was irrational, is what it comes down to."

"Is that why you cleaned up the mirror, too? Because you thought Lisa had written all the slogans?"

Usser shook his head. "The police asked me that. I didn't know what they were talking about. I still don't."

Usser fell silent. The evening breeze sighed high above us, saddened by what had been visited upon the little dead-end street. As I was looking to see where Lisa was a shot rang out, a faraway explosion that shattered the silence of the street the instant before it shattered the windshield of my car.

Bits of glass flew over Usser and me, as though it was raining chips of ice. Twenty yards in front of us, Lisa Usser screamed. I thought for a moment she'd been wounded, but she just stood motionless, stunned, her senses shut.

Usser said, "My God," and looked to the end of the street where the gun sounds had originated. I yelled for him to get down, but he ignored me. I ran to Lisa's side and slipped my

arm around her waist and carried her back behind the car.
Another shot rang out as I dumped her to the ground and
tackled her awestruck father. This round struck something far
behind us.

We waited, looking at each other nervously, measuring our
safety and our courage. The air still seemed pregnant with the
brief explosions, to be charged with echoes and excitement.

Lisa began to cry. Her father put a hand on her shoulder but
she shrugged it off with a violent twist. Usser's glasses aimed
reflected light at me. "Who was it?"

I shrugged. "I don't know. The only gun I've seen in this case
belonged to the Maniac."

"Who?"

"Nifton. Your former client. I told you about him this morning. He and Lisa are soulmates."

It came out more disparaging than I intended. Lisa swore,
sniffed, and swore again.

"But why would he try to kill her?" Usser asked.

"To keep her quiet." I looked at Lisa. "Right?"

"You don't know *who* it was. You're just trying to scare me."

She was right. Although I had no indication who had been
the target, I thought if Lisa was convinced that someone was
trying to kill her she'd decide to talk to me. But even attempted
murder didn't shake her. She started to stand up. I reached for
her arm and held her down. "He could still be down there. Let
me go first. I get paid to do this stuff."

I curled my legs under me, preparing to make a dash for
Usser's car, the first stop in working my way toward the shrubbery that must have hidden the shooter. I took a deep breath
and had begun a pagan prayer when I heard a door open somewhere behind me. "Are you all right?" a voice called out. *"Please.
Are you all right out there?"*

I knew who it was. The poetry reader, who had some bones
to pick with the local librarian. "Please call the police!" I yelled
back.

"I have already done that. I have told them it is an emergency
condition. Was I in error?"

"You were exactly right."

"Good. You will pardon me if I don't come out of doors until
they arrive." The door slammed shut.

I smiled to myself as a siren sounded in the distance. From

the end of the street I heard a car door slam and an engine fire, then fade away after a squeal of tires. It might have been the errant assassin, it might have been a chemistry major on the way to the lab to check his latest titration.

I stood up cautiously and peered down the street. Nothing moved, nothing took a shot at me, nothing but my windshield seemed changed at all by the fact that one of us had nearly died a small moment earlier.

I was about to do something brave and slightly foolish when a police car turned into the street and raced to where we stood, then screeched to a stop. Two uniformed men got out, revolvers drawn, and crouched behind their car doors. "Throw down your guns," one of them called out. "Then put your hands on your heads."

"We're unarmed," I yelled back. "We're the ones he shot at."

Another car careened around the corner and came to a stop behind the blue-and-white. Bart Kinn got out slowly, as though he was in the Safeway lot and needed a loaf of rye. He strolled to the crouching policemen, talked to the one on the driver's side, then strolled down the street toward us. I walked to meet him, feeling like the Saturday heroes of my youth.

Kinn's smile was his usual display—aloof, mocking, a challenge to my every preconception. "You shoot somebody?" he asked.

"Got shot at. Along with Lawrence Usser and his daughter."

"Anyone hit?"

"Only my car."

"Where'd it come from?"

"The bushes down there, I think." I pointed toward them. Kinn turned and yelled for the uniforms to go down and check it out. Then he looked back at me. "Any idea who did it?"

"Not really."

"Any idea why?"

"Not really."

"Any idea which one of you he was shooting at?"

I thought about it. "It's just possible he wanted to kill us all."

"Who?" Kinn asked again.

"It's just a guess," I replied. "I haven't got a shred of proof, but I think it must have been Nifton, the Maniac."

Kinn looked at me. "Why do you say that?"

"Because he's the only one that fits all the parts of the puzzle.

He knew Sherry Misteen, he knew Mrs. Usser, and he was crazy enough that motive wasn't necessary."

Kinn's smile had broadened with my every word. "You know, when I first saw you I was afraid you were good," he said. "I thought you were going to show me up, solve my case for me, make me look like a big dumb nigger. But you're not gonna do that, are you, Mr. Tanner? You're not going to embarrass me at all."

"Am I supposed to know what you're talking about?"

Compared to his usual disposition, Kinn's enjoyment knew no bounds. "You say you think the Maniac did it, right? Well, just before your call came in we got word the Maniac's as dead as yesterday's cigar."

I suppressed a curse. "Where?"

"His sister's place. At least twenty minutes from here. I'm on my way to check it out. Want to come?"

"Sure."

"Just let me go see Usser for a minute. Don't want to give him any less law enforcement than the average citizen, just because he's a fucking wife-killer. Plus I better take the girl in case Gable still wants her."

"I still think that part of it's wrong, Kinn."

"Yeah, well, you thought it was the Maniac down in those bushes, didn't you? Hell, you probably think Mondale's gonna win the election."

Kinn chuckled heavily, then walked over to my car. I trailed behind, trying to sort it out. I wasn't even close to anything that worked when I got to where Kinn and Usser were standing.

They were arguing heatedly. "The girl took off," Kinn said to me. "He let her get away."

"I didn't let her get away," Usser protested. "I just wasn't prepared to use force to restrain her. She's angry enough at me as it is."

"Why?" I asked.

Usser fidgeted, glanced across the street and back at Kinn, then looked at me. "I think that should remain our secret."

Kinn was about to say something castigating when I spoke. "I think you're making a mistake, Usser. Your secret may get someone else killed. Kinn says the person who shot at us wasn't the Maniac after all."

"How does he know?"

"The Maniac's dead."

Usser's eyes widened. "Nifton? You mean Ronald Nifton?"

"The same. That's three deaths," I said. "You'd better take a long, hard look at the little game you're playing. You'd better think about telling someone what you know."

It was the same lecture I'd given his daughter only minutes before, but his response was slightly different. "I don't know anything," he said. "I don't know anything at all." The fact seemed to both puzzle and frighten him. He leaned against my car and wiped his eyes.

Kinn put his finger on Usser's chest. "I'll be back later to talk to you about the shooting. Stay out here till the officers take your statement, then stay home till I get back. Got it?"

"Yes."

"If you want your lawyer, you better go call him."

"Okay."

"You see your daughter around you give me a call. Gable's got a bench warrant out for her."

This time Usser didn't say anything. Kinn inspected him for a moment, then turned away as though Usser were unworthy of his time. "You coming, Tanner?"

I told him I was.

Kinn looked at my car. "Can you see anything through that windshield?"

"I think so."

"It might cave in on you."

"I'll go slow," I said. "Where is it?"

"Chestnut Street. That's north of University, just west of Sacramento." He gave me the number.

"That's Laura's house," Usser blurted when he heard it. "Why are you going there?"

"That's where the body is," Kinn said, and strolled off toward his car.

"Did she kill him?" Usser asked, but Kinn was too far off to hear. Usser sank slowly to the curb and lowered his head to his hands, as though he despaired that everyone in his world had become an executioner.

I started to open my car door, then turned away and trotted over to the far cantina and rang the doorbell. When the little old lady answered, I thanked her for calling the police.

"I know my duty, young man. And I do it."

"You might have saved a life."

"It's nice of you to say that, even if it's untrue."

"It's truer than you think," I said. "Your neighbor, Mrs. Misteen, got some bad news tonight. Her daughter has been found dead."

"How awful."

"She might like some company."

"Of course. I'll go right over. Is there anyone else I should call?"

I thought about it, then shook my head, then thought suddenly of Needles. "I think everyone she knows is dead."

I started down the steps. "I doubt that you're a librarian, young man," she called after me. "I doubt that very much indeed."

My battered Buick took me out of Hillside Lane, and I got to Laura Nifton's house without being lacerated by my windshield.

The door to the green bungalow was open. Laura Nifton stood in the center of the living room, her housecoat pulled tight around her body, looking disconsolate and befuddled, frowning, trying to answer Bart Kinn's questions. Her brother lay on the couch behind her, his blood blotting out the bright print flowers that had enlivened the upholstered cushions, his head buried beneath a brocade pillow. A man in a safari coat was leaning over Nifton's body, measuring things.

"He was exhausted," Laura Nifton said in her feathery voice. "He told me he hadn't slept for three days. He got like that, sometimes, his brain kept *feeding* things to him, forcing him to think, to remember, to scheme and plan. He heard voices a lot. He would bang his head on the wall to get them to stop taunting him. Once he hit himself with a shoe. Again and again. He only stopped when I started screaming. I always wished there was a switch on him, so I could turn him off."

A single tear slipped down her cheek. She glanced my way but didn't seem to know me. I started to say something, but she wasn't finished. "When it got real bad, he'd come here and let me calm him down. Sometimes I could, sometimes I couldn't. When I could, he'd sleep for hours. Days. When I couldn't, he'd hit me, or destroy things, and rant and rave about 'death before life.' " She stopped and sniffed. "This time I got through to him. He was asleep when it happened."

"Tell me about it," Kinn said.

Laura Nifton nodded, her tone still an emotionless dirge. "This man rang the bell. I answered it. He asked if Ronald was here. I said he was, but he was sleeping. I guess he could see Ronald behind me. He pushed past me and went over to the couch. He reached down and shook Ronald till he woke up. I kept asking him what he thought he was doing, but he ignored me. At first I thought he was from the police, but he seemed awfully short for a policeman. Then I recognized who it was."

"Grunig," I said.

She nodded. "He started talking to Ronald, berating him, really, with that *voice*. He had such a powerful voice for a small man. It was like a dentist's drill or something; Ronald seemed to feel every word. The professor just kept *at* him, telling him he was an animal, a wild beast who was a threat to everything good in the world, telling Ronald he had ruined a dozen lives, telling him he was going to be locked away for good this time, for what he was doing to someone named Lisa, that Grunig was going to petition to commit Ronald to Napa, that no one would help get him out, that even Professor Usser wouldn't help him anymore. Then he started talking about the state hospital, and what would happen to Ronald when he was sent back there. The . . . perversions. I could see Ronald remembering. He was almost raped up there the last time. I could see from Ronald's face that he remembered it vividly. I could see he was terrified. Everyone was afraid of Ronald, but really it was Ronald who was afraid. The little man went on and on, until Ronald turned away, reached back, and pulled out a gun and shoved it into his mouth and pulled the trigger."

Kinn looked at me. I spoke into the silent reverberations of a violent death. "Grunig's a professor at the law school. He used to be Usser's best friend. Grunig's son was the boyfriend of the girl the Maniac killed a couple of years ago. The boy committed suicide himself about a year afterward, because he hadn't been able to stop Nifton from knifing his girlfriend. Grunig was there when I was telling another professor about Nifton and Usser's daughter, how she had started following him around, taking drugs and all that. Grunig used to be close to the Ussers. I guess he decided to put a stop to Nifton's charm, once and for all."

"You think Grunig's the same guy who killed Dianne Renzel? Or the Misteen girl?" Kinn asked.

"No chance at all," I said, and turned away.

"Where are you going?"

"Home," I said. "I've had enough of Berkeley for one day." I looked back at Kinn. "Are you going to charge him?"

"Grunig?"

I nodded.

"What with?"

I shrugged. "Psychological homicide? Scaring Nifton to death?"

"Shit," Bart Kinn said. "This may be Berkeley but this ain't Halloween."

TWENTY-SEVEN

The case would have to come to me; I could no longer go to it. That was both my consolation and my concern as I puttered through the evening, straightening my cobwebbed apartment while I tried to straighten my cobwebbed mind.

I had thought I had the answer, and that the answer was Ronald Nifton—that he had killed both Dianne Renzel and Sherry Misteen, for reasons rational only to him. Now Nifton himself was dead, and someone else had shot at me or at the Ussers. Which meant my suspect might well have been what a jury had once declared him to be—innocent of all but madness.

The case stretched before me like a trackless plain. If I was going to stay on it I would have to start from scratch, retrace my steps, resift everything I'd learned. I didn't want to do it, but if the Renzels insisted I probably would. It was still unimaginable to say no to them. I finished off my novel and went to bed early, after a nightcap of Courvoisier and *Nachtmusik*.

I thought sleep would be a problem, but the day had worn me down. As a result, the phone labored long and hard to awaken me at 4:04. As I struggled to find my ear with the receiver, I still thought I was dreaming, that if I just waited for a minute more the dream would end and I could slip back into the snug and bristly black of sleep.

"Mr. Tanner? Are you there? Hello . . . ? I think I got a wrong number. Let me see the card again."

The final words were faint, said to someone else. The silence let me gather my wits and wonder why she was calling at that hour. "Hello," I managed finally. "Who is this?"

"Mr. Tanner?"

"Yes."

"This is Lisa. Lisa Usser."

"Are you all right? Has something happened?"

"No, nothing's happened. It's just—I been talking to Cal, you know? And . . ."

"What?"

"Could I . . . we . . . talk to you?"

"Sure. Shoot."

"In person, I mean."

"Okay. When?"

"Well, whenever."

I looked at the digital glow beside my bed. "I could be there by six. Is that okay?"

"Sure. I guess."

"I'll try to make it sooner. Where are you?"

"Well . . . What street is this?"

"Who's with you, Lisa?"

"Cal. I'm with Cal. We're crashing in his van. It's on Fifth Street, just off Virginia. They call it the Rainbow Village."

"I'll find it," I said. "What's his van look like?"

"It's a black Econoline, but it's fixed up, you know? Like, there's this painting of a flag on the side, with a picture of a joint on it? And underneath it says PEOPLE'S REPUBLIC OF BERKE-LEY. And, oh yeah, it's got two flat tires."

"I think I can find it, Lisa. I'll see you at six, or a little earlier. And do me a favor."

"What?" Her voice took on that protective wariness I'd become accustomed to.

"If you really want to talk, don't ta¹   my more drugs."

"I . . ."

"I'm not telling you how to live your life, Lisa. I'm just telling you that if you want my help then I've got to get the straight story from you, not PCP paranoia. Okay?"

"Okay. I'm straight now. I guess I can stay that way for a while longer. Cal's been on me to stay off the stuff anyway."

"Good. Keep listening to him. Is he still around?"

"Yeah."

"Can I talk to him a second?"

"Hi," Cal said after a moment.

"Is this on the level, Cal? Is she going to open up to me?"

"I think so. Yeah."

"Is she scared?"

"Yeah. A bunch. She doesn't know what to do. She heard the Maniac got killed. Is that right?"

"Yes."

"We heard the cops ambushed him."

"That's wrong, Cal. Nifton shot himself after a confrontation with a man named Grunig. Grunig thought the Maniac had caused the death of his son, indirectly, a year ago. He threatened to have Nifton committed again. Nifton flipped and blew his brains out. That's all there is to it. No cops; no conspiracy. Okay?"

"I guess."

"See you in a while."

I hung up the phone and stumbled through the motions of getting dressed. On my way out of town I stopped for coffee and eggs at Zorba's. Zorba opens early, to accommodate the guys who work the docks and the farmers' market, and the girls who work the streets.

He waved at me from behind the grill. I told him I'd have the usual. Then I read the latest excerpt from the *Iliad* that Zorba had printed up by hand and tacked above the coffee machine. Then I settled into a booth with the late edition of the *Examiner* and read about the Niners' latest win. The columnists were talking Super Bowl already. I hoped it happened. In '81 I'd gotten a lot of business tracking down witnesses against those people who had celebrated the victory by beating someone to a pulp.

I finished breakfast in a hurry, fended off a bawdy invitation from a woman wearing fishnet stockings and red vinyl shorts, and stepped outside. The morning chill was slap enough to get me sufficiently awake to keep my car on the bridge. My shattered windshield made the world seem broken, in need of glue. When I took the University Avenue exit it was five-thirty in the morning.

Fifth Street was less than a half mile from the bayfront, which in Berkeley was a neglected mud flat that had remained in limbo for years while the city and the landowner engaged in a waltz of

inverse condemnation litigation. Near the Virginia cross street
the neighborhood was a mix of industrial buildings, renovated
apartment clusters and a peculiar collection of Victorian houses
that had been bleached by the sea breeze, abandoned, herded
behind a Cyclone fence, posted as the property of the Berkeley
Redevelopment Agency, and raised onto jacks and support tim-
bers as though someone was about to haul the whole horde of
them away. I looped across University and around to Fifth, then
followed it to the Rainbow Village.

There were fifteen of them, maybe, a colorful gaggle of
homes on wheels that had gathered along a single block of a
mostly residential neighborhood and claimed it for their own.
A few were old schoolbuses, their Blue Bird bodies a faded,
crumpled yellow, their windows painted in psychedelic swaths
or masked by heavy curtains. One was the pickup truck with the
camper unit I'd seen behind the Hell House, its chimney still
spewing a straw of smoke. There was even an ancient Trailways,
a full-sized cruiser that had doubtless roamed from coast to
coast and now sported hand-painted slogans such as SPEED KILLS
and THINGS GO BETTER WITH COKE.

I drove through the block and turned around. All the resi-
dents of the mobile village seemed to be asleep. No light came
through windows, no music masked the hum of the freeway
that sliced through the night only a few blocks away.

Some trash barrels had been overturned by a marauding dog.
A VW bug had been similarly overturned, for reasons more
obscure, as helpless as a similarly situated turtle. I pulled up
behind Cal's van and got out of the car.

Across the street, a man was sitting on the front stoop of a
board-and batten bungalow, shirtless, something that might
have been a shotgun lying across his knees. We looked at each
other for a time, then I went to the back of the van and knocked.
The metal panel hurt my knuckles. The sounds I made seemed
distant, echoing, reminding me of the submarine movies of my
youth, the enemy overhead, the sub maneuvering desperately
to evade its sonar.

Cal finally pushed the door open. "Come on in. Thanks for
coming."

He was wearing pinstripe denims and a Harvard sweatshirt.
Behind him, the van radiated the rich hues and heavy scents of

a desert caravansary. The floor and the walls were lined with oriental rugs. The pillows were wrapped in batik cottons; the blankets were multicolored afghans and sheepskin robes. The music was slippery and sensual. Incense thickened the air, made it almost nauseating. Cal backed away and allowed me to climb in.

There was no room to stand, but there was room to sit like Buddha on one of the pillows, which is what I did. Cal lowered himself to the one beside me, and we both looked at Lisa Usser.

She was reclining like an odalisque on a sheepskin rug, leaning against a pillow propped against the wall, nibbling on a stick of stiff brown jerky. She had changed back to the baggy slacks and workman's shirt. In her reluctant agitation she seemed a victim of white slavery, compelled to audition for the sultan's harem.

I wriggled my way to comfort and waited for someone to say something. Cal kept looking at Lisa, urging her to begin. "I'm cold, Cal," she said.

Cal dug though a heap of clothing on the floor behind him and came up with a cardigan sweater which he tossed Lisa's way. She struggled into it. The warmth seemed to thaw her thoughts.

"I'm sorry I woke you up," she said, timid, bashful, not at all the drug-brave hussy I'd catered to the previous evening. "It's just when I came off my high I got real scared, you know? And with the Maniac dead, and someone shooting at us and everything, well, I just . . ." She shrugged her way to silence.

"I know," I said. "I was scared too. Don't worry about it. You haven't seen anyone following you around, have you?"

She shook her head. "Do you know who it was? That shot at us?"

"No. Do you?"

"No."

"But you know why, don't you?"

She shook her head.

"Sure you do. He shot because he was afraid at least one of us knows who killed your mother."

"But I *don't,*" Lisa protested.

"I think you do. You just don't realize it. If you tell me everything, maybe I can put it all together."

Lisa didn't say anything, she just glanced at Cal, then took another nibble on her jerky.

"It's time you talked to me, Lisa. The Maniac's dead. You don't need to protect him anymore. You'll be better off if you get it off your chest. Murder's a heavy load to carry around."

Lisa closed her eyes. Cal crawled over to where she was lying and put his arm around her. "Come on, Lisa. You said you'd talk to him. Why don't you just get it over with? Then we can split. Go down to Santa Cruz or something. Hang out on the beach and forget about Berkeley for a while."

The police might have other plans for Lisa, depending on what she told me, but I didn't point that out. Instead, I let Cal do my work for me. He lowered his voice and murmured words I couldn't hear, and stroked Lisa's flank to the rhythm of the Persian music. "Okay, okay," Lisa said finally. "Just don't push me; okay, Cal? Just let me do it my way."

Lisa sat up and wrapped her arms across her chest and began to rock, up and back, eyes closed again, head lowered, breaths deep and labored. Cal and I just watched her. "Okay," she said after a minute, meeting my eyes. "Here's the way it went down. But this is everything I know. I mean, just let me tell it, okay? No questions; no comments. Just let me tell it and then do what you have to do. Okay?"

"Okay," I said.

"Will you tell the cops?"

"Probably."

"Okay. I know you have to. I just, well, tell them I didn't know what to do, you know? Maybe I could have stopped some of it, but I didn't know how. That's all I can say. I just didn't know what to do." She began to cry. Cal started to comfort her but she shrugged him away.

She sniffed back her tears and wiped her eyes and looked at me, suddenly a child who was far too young to know what she knew, to have done what she'd done. A million parents must look at their children and have the same reaction.

"Okay," Lisa began. "First, the Maniac killed Sherry. Okay? Sherry Misteen. He killed her, and buried her in the park and took a tape of it and gave it to me. Okay?"

I nodded.

"But I didn't know any of this till after, okay? I mean, I didn't know he actually *did* it. He *said* he was going to, but I didn't believe him, not till he gave me her *fingernails*. God. It was so gross. I mean, back then I didn't know . . . I didn't know he really *was* crazy, that he actually *did* the stuff he was always talking about, like killing that girl and everything. I didn't even remember Daddy had been his lawyer. I didn't put any of that together at all, till after he killed Sherry."

"That's true," Cal interjected, but Lisa silenced him with a frown.

"Most guys are just blowing smoke, you know?" Lisa went on, her monotone a match to the music. "They rap about drugs and sex and all this low-life crap, but it's all mind games, trying to get to your cunt by going through your brain. But not the Maniac. He really wanted to blow you into another mind zone. To make you see things in a different way, hear the voices he heard, and like that. He—I don't know—he was weird but he wasn't all bad, you know? He did things for me. Talked to me. Listened. Understood. When I went down to him, I was ready to kill myself, and he made me decide to stay alive. I owe him for that, you know?"

I nodded.

Lisa sagged back against the pillow once again, and I let her rest for a minute while I caught up to what she'd been saying and got a fix on what else I needed to know. I'd pretty much guessed that the Maniac had killed Sherry Misteen, but what I hadn't guessed was why it happened, so that's what I asked her.

"My old man," Lisa answered simply. "That's how the whole thing started. With my goddamned old man."

"What did he do to you?"

"He's such a bastard," Lisa said between clenched teeth. "I still can't believe he did it. I can't fucking *believe* it, you know?"

"What did he do? Molest you?"

"He fucked Sherry. He stuck his dick in my best friend."

Her final words were a scream that seemed to shred her voice. When she spoke again she was a stranger who had aged and sickened in the past few seconds. "He couldn't leave them alone. *Any* of them. All those law students, I used to hear him *brag* about it to her, how he'd banged some sweet young thing. So why did he have to do it to Sherry? Huh? That's what I don't get. She was *my age*, you know? He might as well have been fucking *me*."

A Freudian might have worked for years with her final phrase, and Lisa might have been the better for it. But I do my

business on the surface—action and reaction, deed and consequence, crime and punishment. Only after it was over, and all
the pieces were fit into the puzzle and all the strings were
tied, could I lie back in my recliner and sip a little Dewar's and
delve into the depths of the unconscious regions of the minds
I had encountered, to try to take it back to where it
started.

But this one wasn't over yet; this puzzle was still scattered
across the floor. "So that's why you ran away," I said. "You
found out Sherry and your father had an affair so you hit the
streets and hooked up with the Maniac. Right?"

Lisa nodded.

"How did you find out about them?"

"Sherry told me. She got mad when I wouldn't let her wear
my jellies."

"You told the Maniac all about it, right? About how angry you
were at both of them? How you wished they both were dead?
Or was it only Sherry?"

She nodded once again. "Sherry."

"And the Maniac took you seriously. You said you wanted
Sherry dead, so he decided to do it. Maybe to pay back your
father for getting him off the murder charge, in some perverted
way, by helping you. That was the beast he was talking about
over at Hell House. The one that was feeding on your soul. He
killed Sherry as a favor to you."

"Yes. God. I . . . I started doing more drugs to forget about
it, you know? To keep it out of my head, that he actually *murdered* Sherry because I was so pissed at her."

"So did he kill your mother, too? Was that part of the favor?"

Lisa was shaking her head. "That's the thing. I don't think he
killed Dianne. I really don't. He never talked about it or anything, and I think he would have if he'd done it. Plus, he and
my father, you know, had this relationship. Because Daddy defended him and all that? I don't think he would have done that
to Daddy."

"Sometimes we start to hate the ones who help us, Lisa. Sometimes we can't deal with the obligation."

"I know, but . . ."

"Did the Maniac put the tape in your father's study or did
you?"

"I did."

"So your father would see it by accident sometime? See what had happened to the girl he'd betrayed you with?"

She nodded.

"And when you saw him last week with Krista Hellgren you decided he was up to his old tricks again, so you told the police he'd killed your mother."

"Yes."

"And threatened you."

"Yes."

"And you still hate him, don't you?"

"Yes. *Yes.*"

"So you put the scissors in his plant, to frame him."

She shook her head vigorously. "No, I didn't do that. I don't know anything about any scissors."

That stumped me. My mind groped for a new answer.

"That was me," Cal said suddenly. I looked at him in surprise. "*You* put the scissors in the plant?"

He nodded.

"What else did you do?"

"I was there, see?" he said, his eyes eager and innocent. "Just after Dianne was killed. I was looking for that stash I told you about. Hell, I didn't even think anyone was home. Then I'm walking down the hall upstairs, and I glance into the Ussers' bedroom, and wow. There she was, blood all over the place, the room totally trashed. I almost barfed. I still get nightmares, man. I got this blood on me and it won't come off."

"You thought the Maniac had done it, right? Just like he did to Sherry."

Cal nodded.

"And you were afraid Lisa would be arrested too, for helping him or something, so you cleaned up the place so it would look like a more normal thing, not something crazy."

"Yeah. It was bizarro in there, man. Stuff ripped up. Writing on the walls. *Piss.* He pissed on her body, man. Sorry, Lisa. But it was total splatter. *Friday the Thirteenth—Part Ninety-nine.* I tried to straighten it up but there wasn't much time. When I heard someone coming, I grabbed the scissors and took off. That day you caught me behind the house, I was in there putting the scissors in Usser's fucking plant. Even if he didn't kill Dianne,

what he did to Lisa was lame enough to stick him with the death
penalty, right?"

"Wrong," I said.

"Come on. He was a child-fucker."

"But not a murderer, Cal. Was there anything in the bedroom
that indicated who the murderer really was? Anything at all?"

"Naw. Just a big scramble, was what it was."

"Did you take anything away but the scissors?"

"No."

"And you're each telling me you don't know who killed
Dianne Renzel?"

They looked at each other and nodded.

"Do you think your father could have done it, Lisa? In all
honesty?"

Lisa didn't move. From her look she was thinking thoughts
she didn't want to deal with. Finally she shook her head. "No. I
don't think Daddy did it."

"Okay. Let me think a minute."

I closed my eyes and drifted with the information I'd just
acquired. Three people were dead. One suicide and one murder were explained. The most important one, the one I'd been
hired to solve, was still a mystery. I tried to link it up, but I kept
floating back to the beginning, the most obvious possibility a
stoned junkie who entered the Usser family's battlefield by accident.

I looked at Cal. "You didn't plant a book in there, did you?
Or leave one behind by accident?"

Cal frowned. "What book?"

"It's called *The Astral Light*."

He shook his head. "Never heard of it."

"That's the Maniac's book," Lisa said. "He carried it around
all the time. He called it his Bible."

"But he loaned it to you, didn't he?"

Lisa nodded. "So what?"

"It was found beneath your mother's body."

Lisa's protest was immediate. "But I didn't—"

"I know," I interrupted. "You loaned the book to someone,
didn't you?"

Lisa frowned, then shook her head. "I lost it. I don't know
where. The Maniac was pissed at me."

"Okay Lisa. Now think about this carefully. Did you tell anyone what the Maniac claimed he was going to do for you? Did you tell anyone at all that Nifton was bragging how he was going to kill Sherry Misteen? Before it happened?"

Lisa closed her eyes, then nodded. "Sure. Sure I did." She opened her eyes and looked at me and named him. "Was it him? Is he the one who killed my mom?"

I told her I'd let her know when I was certain.

TWENTY-EIGHT

"Hello?"

"My name is Tanner. We met—"

"I remember. What can I do for you?"

"Perhaps you remember you expressed surprise when I mentioned I was a member of the bar."

"Yes. What of it?"

"Being a lawyer comes in handy sometimes. This looks like one of them."

"Am I supposed to understand this?"

"I'd like to talk to you about a case. A lawsuit."

"I'm afraid I can't discuss pending litigation, Mr. Tanner. For obvious reasons."

"I'm not talking about a pending case, I'm talking about an old one."

"Which one?"

"Tarasoff versus *The Regents of the University of California."*

"But I wasn't involved in that case."

"Not personally, no. But I'm sure you're familiar with the rule of law it established for people like yourself."

"Of course. But I still don't understand what you're driving at."

"I believe the rule of *Tarasoff* explains why you murdered Dianne Renzel."

"What? Are you out of your mind?"

"No, but you might be. But then you'd know better than I, wouldn't you?"

"Where are you, Mr. Tanner?"

"In a phone booth on Telegraph Avenue."

"Have you gone to the police with this nonsense?"

"Not yet."

"Do you realize what it would do to me if I'm charged with that crime? Even if I'm ultimately declared innocent?"

"I imagine it will be quite similar to what's been happening to Lawrence Usser."

He paused. "Perhaps. The charge itself would ruin me, even if I'm eventually exonerated. Surely you can see that."

"Sure. I can see that just fine."

"Well, don't you think I deserve a chance to persuade you that you're wrong? As a matter of professional courtesy, if nothing more?"

"I don't know."

"Surely you can't be *completely* convinced of your speculations. If there was any hard evidence of what you suggest, the police would have already arrested me."

"What do you have in mind?"

"I have to be at the Greek Theater in thirty minutes. It's a rather unique form of therapy I conduct, for some of my pro bono patients. Perhaps I could meet you there. At ten o'clock? Then, if you feel the same way after we've talked, you'll be free to take your suspicions to the police. Well?"

"I suppose you deserve that much."

"Thank you. I'll see you shortly. I trust you'll be alone."

He hung up before I could respond.

I was being foolish in delaying giving the whole thing to Bart Kinn, but Kinn had taken a lot of pleasure in my mistake the night before, too much pleasure for me to go to him with anything less than a fact. Plus, I agreed to meet him because he was right. I wasn't completely confident of my hunch, not beyond a reasonable doubt I wasn't, and tangible evidence to support it might never be found. The only person who could provide the proof that would convince me to a moral certainty was Dr. A. Adam Lonborg himself.

I hung up the receiver. The telephone in the booth rang almost immediately, while I still huddled inside. I started to ignore it, but as I pulled open the door I noticed a young man in a dashiki and a yarmulke standing on the sidewalk, grinning, daring me to answer. I picked up the receiver to prove something, I wasn't sure quite what.

"This is the Goddess speaking." The voice was a sensual contralto. "Were you waiting for my call?"

"Not exactly. I was just here."

"That's fine. Thank you for answering the phone. You must be in need. Are you?"

"Presumably."

"Have I spoken to you before?"

"No."

"Good. I welcome new friends. Are you all right? Physically, I mean?"

"I think so."

"So you don't need emergency treatment."

"No."

"How about food? Clothing? Shelter?"

"Nope. None of those."

"I see. Good. I speak with many who lack the most basic items. It's difficult to go beyond the rudiments when the rudiments themselves are absent. No?"

"Yes."

"So perhaps you lack companionship. Are you alone?"

"From time to time."

"I know people who will entertain you. Do you want me to arrange a meeting?"

"No. Not now. Thanks, anyway."

"Are you sure? You sound lonely to me. You sound like you haven't spoken from your heart in a very long time."

"Look, I've got to—"

"The subject embarrasses you. I understand. Perfectly. I have one last question, then you may ask me what you will and I will answer truthfully, to the extent the truth is known. Okay?"

"Okay."

"What is the state of your spirit, sir? Is there truth and beauty in your life?"

"Lots of truth; not much beauty," I said, and then I said good-bye. The kid in the dashiki was still grinning at me as I walked back to my car.

I drove to Bowditch Street and double-parked in front of the Community Crisis Center. Sandra was behind her typewriter and there was still someone weeping in the waiting room, though this time it was a man. "I have to talk to Richards for a minute," I said to Sandra. "It'll only take a second."

"But—"

"Just ask him. Please. It's very important."

She pressed a button on her telephone console and in a moment Pierce Richards emerged from his office. The only change since the day before was the color of his cords. "What do you want?" he asked impatiently.

"Did Dianne Renzel keep a log of all her phone calls?"

"Yes," Richards said. "The entire staff does. Why?"

"Would you tell me if there's a particular name on hers? On the day she died? Just one name, and he's not a patient."

"I thought we'd been over this, Mr. Tanner. The records are confidential."

"It's Lonborg," I said. "Adam Lonborg, the shrink. It's important for me to know if Dianne Renzel talked to him that Friday. There's nothing confidential about that information, Mr. Richards. Nothing at all."

"I—"

"I'm close to naming her killer, Richards. This information could make the difference."

"Just a minute."

Richards went over to a gray metal file cabinet and pulled out the top drawer and thumbed through some papers. After a few seconds he stopped, then read for a moment, then looked over at me. "Yes," he said. "She called him twice. At 1:15, and then at 3:05."

"She called Phyllis Misteen several times in between, didn't she?"

He glanced back at the file. "Yes. And that's all I'm going to say. I'm sorry."

"Okay," I said. "Sometime today I want you to go through Ms. Renzel's treatment files, and anything else she might have written on the day she died, and see if she indicated what the calls to Lonborg were about. I also want you to see if there's any indication that she saw Ronald Nifton that morning, at any time before 1:15."

Richards shook his head. "He is a client, more or less. His records will not be revealed."

"He's dead, Richards. He killed himself last night."

Richards' jaw dropped. He reached for the file cabinet to steady himself. "I didn't know. What a . . . tragedy, is all I can think of. That boy's entire life was a tragedy, inflicted on him and others by his mental illness. Do they know why he did it?"

"A man named Grunig pushed him toward the edge. I guess he decided to jump off."

"But why?"

"Nifton screwed up Grunig's son a few years back."

"More than one parent could say that about the Maniac, I'm afraid," Richards said sadly. "Dianne was very upset that her husband and Dr. Lonborg had acted to put Nifton back on the street and away from custodial therapy. They had a quarrel about it, at least once."

"Probably more often that that," I said. "The police will be here later, probably, to see those phone records and whatever else you have on Lonborg and the Maniac for the day Ms. Renzel died. Do everyone a favor and don't make trouble about disclosing them."

"I'll have to think about it. I'll—"

"While you're thinking, think about how much longer you want Dianne Renzel's killer to go without being caught and punished."

"But who did it?" Richards said, frowning, "The Maniac? How can he be punished if he's dead?"

It didn't seem the time to bring up Dante. "I'll talk to you later," I said. "I've got an appointment in Epidaurus."

"Where?"

"It's a Greek city. There's a theater there. I was paraphrasing John O'Hara."

"I still don't understand."

"It's all right. At this point there's nothing to understand except that I haven't had enough sleep."

I left the crisis center, climbed in my car and drove up the hill to Piedmont Avenue, then left onto Gayley Road. The Greek Theater was just north of the football stadium and the intra-mural fields, a gray stone and concrete amphitheater sheltered in a eucalyptus grove, donated to the school in 1903 by William

Randolph Hearst, a forum for everything from graduation exercises to rock concerts. The last time I'd been there it was to see Miles Davis and Gil Evans. The time before that—Bobby Kennedy, a few months before he died.

I parked my car in a shaded lot just to the south of the theater and walked up the steps to the side entrance. An iron gate was partially open, and there were no signs forbidding entrance. I felt slightly cheered when I saw a maintenance truck parked beside the gate. But there was no one in sight, and no sounds beyond the wafting breeze that rustled the eucalyptus leaves, and the unbroken rumble from the traffic that streamed past on the road below. I went through the gate and entered the theater and looked around.

It was larger than I remembered, perhaps seeming so because it was empty. A semicircle of concrete risers had been built into the hillside, tier upon tier of simple slabs of seats, the legacy of a plan first formed three hundred years before the birth of Christ. At the foot of the seats was an orchestra area of perhaps thirty yards across, complete with a stone altar that mimicked those the Greeks had dedicated to Dionysus. Ten feet above the orchestra stretched a rectangular slab that was bordered on each end by high stone blockhouses and at the back by a sounding board ornamented with a line of Doric columns, their spare square capitals rising thirty feet above the stage on which three people stood talking. From where I stood they looked too small to be real, insignificant in all but voice. By some magic of acoustics, I was able to hear every word they said.

The one in the middle was Lonborg. He was flanked by two women and he was asking them how they felt, what they'd been doing, if they were ready to begin. Lonborg wore his usual jogging suit, rust this time, with navy trim, but though he labored to be fashionably compelling, the women were far more intriguing.

One was tall, so thin and stiff her body seemed possessed of only five bones—four limbs attached to a slightly thicker torso. The other woman was her opposite—obese, an alarming heap of flesh encased in the plastic, elastic slacks such women always wore, slacks that promoted the world's aversion. Above her slacks was a middy blouse that must have come from a maternity shop.

Other opposites prevailed as well. The thin one was blond, the other brown. The large one was voluble and animated, the other still and silent, a Giacometti statue. The portly woman seemed gay and eager, the other morose and mournful. Lonborg stood between them, as though to moderate their vast extremes.

As I started down the stairway to the orchestra area the fat one cried out, "My turn, my turn!" Lonborg patted her on the shoulder, handed her a book, then stepped out from between the women. The large one began to read, her voice clear and surprisingly skilled, her eyes skipping from the page to the other girl, then back again.

"Not marble, nor the gilded monuments
Of princes, shall outlive this powerful rhyme;
But you shall shine more bright in these contents
Than unswept stone, besmear'd with sluttish time.
When wasteful war shall statues overturn,
And broils root out the work of masonry,
Nor Mars his sword nor war's quick fire shall burn
The living record of your memory.
'Gainst death and all-oblivious enmity
Shall you pace forth; your praise shall still find room,
Even in the eyes of all posterity
That wear this world out to the ending doom.
So, till the judgment that yourself arise,
You live in this, and dwell in lovers' eyes."

By the time she was finished I was standing in the orchestra pit, looking up at the stage that spread across the amphitheater some ten feet above me. "Can I do another? Please? Cassie wants another."

The large girl trembled from head to toe with the fervor of her request. Lonborg glanced around the theater as if to judge the mood of the invisible audience. When he noticed me he frowned, then nodded to the girl. She turned a page and began a second sonnet. As she had been doing since I arrived, the thin girl stood stock still.

Lonborg hopped down to where I was and motioned for me to join him on the row of marble chairs just beyond the pit. We became an audience of two as Shakespeare's miracles soared above us, to the back row of seats and into the oblivious world beyond.

I gestured toward the girls. "Who are they?"

Lonborg smiled. "Cassandra and Leandra. Thin and fat, respectively."

"Are they twins?"

"Very perceptive. They are former Siamese twins, severed shortly after birth, and shortly after their parents disappeared and left behind the ignominy they believed the event entailed."

"How old are they?"

"Nineteen. They live in a foster home that caters to children with mental disturbances. They are, unfortunately, quite mad, though in entirely different ways. As you can see, their genetic codes have gone spectacularly awry. Cassandra has never uttered a word. Leandra is talking all the time and usually repeats everything she says, as though she speaks for two. Cassandra is capable of violent emotional swings—laughter to despair in seconds. She has attempted suicide at least three times. Leandra, on the other hand, is invariably euphoric. If I slit your throat this minute, she would continue to babbly merrily away, as happy as a lark, just the way she is now." Lonborg unzipped his Dior jacket and turned to look at me. "The subject of murder brings us, I believe, to the reason for our meeting. You mentioned *Tarasoff*."

I nodded. "I've been over here for almost a week, Doctor, poking around in the Renzel case. It's been a frustrating experience, because in all that time I didn't come up with anything resembling a motive for Dianne Renzel's murder. But fortunately, with what I learned this morning, that's no longer true. *Tarasoff* gives you a motive that will stand up in court just fine."

"Please explain. If you can."

I matched his glacial grin. "I think you know what I'm getting at, Doctor, but I'll lay it out for you anyway. A couple of months ago, Lisa Usser suddenly had reason to be very angry at two people—her father and a neighbor girl named Sherry Misteen, who had up to that point been Lisa's best friend. Do I need to tell you why Lisa was mad at them?"

Lonborg shook his head. "Lawrence and the girl had a brief but devastating affair. Lawrence is . . . ungovernable when it comes to matters of the flesh. Lisa told me initially, then Lawrence came to me shortly afterward, confessed all, and asked what he should do. But by then Lisa had allied herself with a man named Nifton, and wasn't at home much, so Lawrence could do nothing very effective in terms of repairing the psychological damage he'd inflicted."

"When Usser came to you, he asked you to go out in the streets and look for Lisa, didn't he? To convince her to come back home and stay."

"Something like that."

"And one night you found her, didn't you? Down at Hell House. Because you'd treated her before, you were able to convince Lisa to talk to you. Away from the Maniac and the other street people she was living with. And when you talked to her you learned something."

"Learned what?"

"That her pal the Maniac was telling Lisa he was going to kill Sherry Misteen, as a favor to Lisa, because Sherry had slept with her father and Lisa hated her for doing it. You'd treated the Maniac, too, at least before his trial a year ago, maybe even after that. You knew or should have known what he was capable of. You knew or should have known that Sherry Misteen was in a great deal of danger. And that brings us right to *Tarasoff*, doesn't it?"

Lonborg stayed silent, so I continued.

"In *Tarasoff* versus *The Regents*, the Supreme Court of this state ruled that a psychotherapist has a duty to warn anyone he has reason to believe is in danger from one of his patients. If the psychotherapist doesn't give such a warning he can be held civilly liable for whatever damages his patient ultimately causes. Even wrongful death, if the victim dies."

"Go on," Lonborg said softly.

"Dianne Renzel learned that you had known before it happened that the Maniac was going to kill Sherry. I think the Maniac dropped by the crisis center on the day she died and told Dianne that he had killed Sherry and that you knew beforehand that he was going to. He might even have told Lisa to tell you what he planned, to test you, maybe even to set you up for a *Tarasoff* suit, maybe just to see if you'd have the guts to try to recommit him to Napa after you and Usser had worked so hard after his trial to convince the authorities he could be let out. My guess is he was bragging to Dianne Renzel that even you couldn't stop him from realizing his destiny or some such rot, his 'death before life' routine. Anyway, after she learned that, Dianne called you up and told you she was going to inform Phyllis Misteen that her daughter was dead and also tell her that she had a cause of action against you for not acting to prevent it. She was already irritated at you and Usser for turning mental cases out into the streets and causing problems for other people, problems she saw every day at the crisis center. This was the last straw. Unfortunately, before she could reach Phyllis Misteen and tell her what she knew, you killed her."

Lonborg still seemed unaffected by my essay. "You're mad," he said calmly. "Quite obviously mad."

"What did you do, climb up the back trellis, the way Lisa told you she used to do when she was running around with Cal? Did you surprise Dianne in bed? Did you kill her before she even knew why she was dying?"

Lonborg didn't answer.

"You got a bad break, didn't you?" I went on. "After you killed Dianne, you tried to frame the Maniac for the murder. He'd done it once before, after all, so he was a perfect candidate. So you cut Dianne to pieces, scrawled a bunch of nonsense on the walls and mirror, trashed the bedroom, masturbated on her, and left the book Lisa had left behind in your office as a specific piece of evidence pointing straight to the Maniac. Unluckily for you, a kid named Cal was the first to find the body. He erased the traces of insanity you'd so carefully manufactured, because he was afraid that if they led the cops to the Maniac they'd also lead them to Lisa Usser, and Cal was in love with Lisa and had been for a long time. Then Usser himself came along, and took the book you'd planted because he was afraid it implicated his daughter."

"This is too bizarre for words, Tanner. I'm shocked, to tell you the truth."

"What shocked you was that your attempt to frame Nifton evaporated. So you came up with another plan. At some point Usser told you he was afraid his daughter had done it. My guess is you convinced Usser that he could protect Lisa best by confessing himself, then pleading insanity, and in effect get away with murder. You may have even found Lisa again and persuaded her to tell the cops that her father killed her mother, just to make sure Usser was arrested before the police could look into the case too closely. Then, last night, you tried to kill Lisa and me to shut us up. You probably went looking for the Maniac, too, but someone beat you to it."

Lonborg looked puzzled for the first time. "I don't know what you're talking about," he said. "I was in Palo Alto last night, and I can prove it."

I shrugged and tried not to show how much that bothered me. "You'll get your chance to prove anything you want. I recommend you hire Jake Hattie to defend you."

"That's ridiculous. You haven't thought this out very well at all, Mr. Tanner. For instance, why would I refrain from warning the Misteen girl she was in danger?"

"Because to warn her you'd have to warn her mother, and in the process she would find out that Usser had had sex with Sherry. If she made a stink, it might ruin Usser's reputation, and tarnish yours as well. Also, if it came out that Nifton was threatening another murder, you'd be damaged when it came out that you were one of the ones who claimed he could be released because he wasn't a danger to anyone. I imagine what you did, instead of warning Sherry and her mother, was try to stop Nifton from committing the crime. But you were too late."

"If Nifton's second murder would tarnish me so much, then why would I try to frame him?"

"Because by then he'd *already* killed again. You couldn't do anything about that, and you had to assume it would come out sometime. At least by framing him for Dianne Renzel's murder you'd stay out of jail yourself."

Lonborg fell silent. After a moment he put his hand on my arm. In the environment in which we sat, his next question took on an unreal aura, the stuff of magic and melodrama: "Is there anything I can do to keep you from taking your insane delusions to the police?"

I shook my head. "I don't think so."

"I see."

Above us, the steady stream of verse fell silent, leaving Lonborg and me alone with a lyric echo tarnished by my prosaic allegations.

TWENTY-NINE

Lonborg seemed lost in thought, more wistful than unnerved at my disclosures. Since I wasn't certain how to nudge him toward confession, I gestured toward the stage. "Why the Shakespeare?"

Lonborg started, then looked away from the treetops and focused on the two performers. "The human mind is a peculiar contraption, as you know. Among its oddities is an often startling combination of ability and disability coexisting within a single brain. The two-year-old Mozart hears a pig squeal and calls out 'G-sharp.' An autistic child masters Rubik's Cube in minutes. A chess grand master is virtually a sociopath in other areas of his life.

"Twins are particularly prone to stunning feats. In one renowned set, each twin has an IQ of sixty, yet they are calendar calculators who, by performing an unconscious algorithm, are able to tell you the date on which Easter will fall for the next eighty thousand years. Their memory of their own personal history is so precise they can tell you what the weather was for any day since the age of two. They can also calculate prime numbers to twenty places. It's incredible, literally." Lonborg shook his head, then looked to see if I was with him.

"You mean the girls are geniuses of some kind?"

He shook his head. "No, not at all. But in Cassandra, up

there, you have a person who reacts to almost no spoken words, who seems to understand almost nothing that is said to her. She reacts, when she does react, almost exclusively to visual stimuli. But by accident one day, the BBC production of *As You Like It* was running in the background while I was conducting a session with her, and I gradually realized that somehow—because of the sounds, the rhythms, perhaps even through a miracle of reincarnation—the language of the Bard was instantly comprehensible to Cassandra. She reacted to every nuance, laughed and cried on cue, the perfect audience. As part of her therapy I began to read Shakespeare to her. Then I recruited other readers. Her sister, in particular, reads love sonnets. They have a symbiotic relationship, needless to say. Their foster parents suspect a sexual component as well. I doubt that, but if it exists, frankly, I see no harm. No harm at all."

We looked up to the stage. The girls were smiling and holding hands, gazing fondly at each other. "I got into psychiatry because I wanted everyone to be like me," Lonborg said suddenly, chuckling at the childish candor of his statement. "It sounds pitifully narcissistic to put it that way, I know, but it's true. I always knew I was special, that I could do anything I put my mind to, that I lacked the complexes and neuroses that seemed to shackle so many of my peers. I saw myself as a liberator, a savior. And I believe I have done a lot of good over the years. I really do. Of course I must believe that or it would be impossible to go on. And of course I must go on. So many people need my help."

"Dianne Renzel threatened to put a stop to it, didn't she?"

Lonborg responded only indirectly. "I've always been hypersensitive to incompetence. I can't abide it in others so of course I can't tolerate it in myself. For some reason, I am terrified of the consequences of personal inadequacy. The *public* consequences, that is. If only I know of my failures, it is endurable. When others know, it is abominable. Fortunately, with Larry's help I was able to know almost unbroken success. I am the foremost forensic psychiatrist on the West Coast."

Given the circumstances, I found his self-aggrandizement chilling. "That's great for you," I said. "I'm not sure it's all that great for the West Coast."

Lonborg laughed sadly. "You tease me, Mr. Tanner. You

hope to provoke an attack or an enraged confession. I assure you, I am sanguine. I am in control."

We fell silent again. On stage the twins were skipping in a circle, hands clasped, the large one trilling a nonsense song. Suddenly Lonborg left my side and crossed the pit and vaulted onto the stage and motioned for me to follow.

"My turn," he said to Leandra as I clambered up on the platform. She handed her book to him and clapped. "Oh, good; oh, good."

Lonborg flipped some pages, then began to read:

"O, lest the world should task you to recite
What merit liv'd in me, that you should love
After my death,—dear love, forget me quite,
For you in me can nothing worthy prove;
Unless you would devise some virtuous lie,
To do more for me than mine own desert,
And hang more praise upon deceased I
Than niggard truth would willingly impart:
O, lest your true love may seem false in this,
That you for love speak well of me untrue,
My name be buried where my body is,
And live for no more to shame nor me nor you.
For I am sham'd by that which I bring forth,
And so should you, to love things nothing worth."

By the time Lonborg had finished his recital Cassandra was sobbing, tears as thick as lava streaming through mascara and down her cheeks, above her groans of heartbreak. She made no move to stem her grief, and Lonborg made no move to stem it for her. Leandra was still her opposite, hopping up and down, calling, "What's wrong? What's wrong?" as her jellied flesh trembled beneath her slacks and flowing shirt.

Lonborg smiled and put the book on the floor. "What's wrong, Dr. Lonborg?" Leandra asked again. "What's wrong?"

Lonborg pointed to me. "He's going to kill me. I'll be dead, just like Shakespeare said. Do you understand, Cassandra? 'The earthy and cold hand of death lies on my tongue.'"

Lonborg looked expectantly at the slender girl. Cassandra just kept crying.

"Why, Doctor? Why?" Leandra pleaded, as jolly as she'd been when I first laid eyes on her, her words at total odds with her surface mood.

Lonborg went to the back of the stage and reached into a nylon sports bag he had placed there and pulled out two objects wrapped in towels and brought them back toward the three of us. I couldn't identify the objects until he unwrapped them and held them out, offering one to each of the girls. "Here. Take them. If you want to let me live, if you want him not to murder me, you must use these weapons. You must stab him. Again and again. *Stab* him. *Save* me, Cassandra. Save my life. 'I am done to death by his slanderous tongue.' "

Each of the girls took the climber's axe that Lonborg offered, looked at it, then looked at me. Without another word they separated, raised the axes to the assault position, and advanced on me from my flanks, as though they'd been drilled in such maneuvers. Leandra couldn't suppress a giggle; her sister still spewed forth her tears.

I looked at Lonborg. "For God's sake," I said. "You can't be serious. You can't want them to kill me."

Lonborg only smiled a plastic smile and admired the results of his instructions. I wanted to strike out at him, but I was afraid to turn my back.

Cassandra was the closest and the most dangerous. Still wordless, still in tears, she extended her axe to within a foot of my crotch, adze forward, and made a slashing, ripping motion, calculated to castrate. I backed away and glanced at the other one. She was grinning in moronic ecstasy, her axe upraised as well, her big body blocking my most direct escape. I circled, keeping them to my front, until my back was to the orchestra and the seats empty of help or even witnesses.

"I'll have to hurt them, Lonborg," I said, fear a black acid eating at my throat. "Call them off. Come on. This is absurd."

Lonborg laughed. "I seriously doubt that you can hurt them, Tanner. They are immensely strong. Their foster parents work them like mules and beat them for the slightest infraction. They think pain is an inevitable part of life; I doubt they will even notice."

We continued our ballet, each of us edging toward what we perceived as our advantage, one of us enjoying it, one of us more frightened by the minute, and one of us beyond intelligible emotion.

"Think of what you're doing to them, Lonborg, for Christ's sake. You're turning them into criminals."

"That's not true," Lonborg said mildly from somewhere near my back. "There's no court in the land that would find either one of them competent to stand trial. I may not know much that is certain in my field, but I know that."

"Now, Dr. Lonborg?" Leandra bubbled to my left. "Should I stick him now?"

"Yes, *now!*" Lonborg screamed, suddenly the savage. "Attack! Both of you."

Leandra lunged straight for me, her giant body advancing as relentlessly as a locomotive. I leaped to the side to avoid her thrust. At the same instant, Cassandra glided to my rear and circled my throat with an arm that was as hard and crushing as a cable on a winch. I tried to throw her off by twisting from side to side, but she held on like a mongoose, cinching my throat more tightly with each of my writhing movements. When I stopped to gasp for breath I saw her axe high over my right shoulder, pick down, poised to descend. I raised a wrist to block it. At the same time Leandra attacked from my other side.

I leaned back against Cassandra, until my weight was resting on her chest, then kicked out at Leandra's axe. The serendipity of violence let me strike her fist with the toe of my boot. The axe flew out of her hand and skittered across the stage. "Oh, no! Oh, no!" Leandra cried through her perpetual smile.

"I'll get it," Lonborg said soothingly. "Don't worry, Leandra."

Leandra came to a stop and waited obediently for Lonborg to fetch her weapon. For the moment it was one on one, as good as the sides were going to get. I curled forward suddenly, and reached behind my head and grasped Cassandra behind the neck and tried to flip her forward. But she held fast to my throat, cried out in a bobcat's scream and plunged the spike end of her axe deep into my side.

I groaned and sank to one knee. The pressure on my throat tightened. I tried to pry her arm free with my fingers but my vision blurred, my head grew light and empty, as though my mind had stepped beyond my reach.

My chest surged to draw air. My hands clawed at Cassandra's stringy arm. I tried to jab an elbow at her ribs but she was too thin to get at. A thick wet snake of blood crawled slowly down my leg, fleeing the white-hot fire that ate into my side.

I tried to stand, but the pain kept me where I was. Cassandra's breath was a torch beside my ear. I tilted one way, then rolled the other, trying to dislodge my wiry, crazed assailant. From somewhere above us Leandra laughed, as though her sister and I were playing horsey.

My weight was enough to topple us both to the floor. I twisted as we fell, and banged Cassandra's elbow on the concrete stage so hard she loosed her grip around my neck and grunted from the ache. I gasped a quart of air, shrugged her to my side, then strained to wrestle her to my front while I waited for my head to clear. After a second breath I twisted the opposite way all of a sudden, and her strength betrayed her and we were face to face, locked in a grim embrace.

The pain in my side flashed once more. My concentration broke and Cassandra knocked me to my back. Above me, her axe glinted in the morning sun. I reached for the hand that brandished it, and got a firm hold on a wrist that was as slick and solid as a bat handle.

In the movies they parry like that for hours. In real life, with a weapon such as Cassandra's, a fractional twist of the wrist can place the pick on the opponent's forearm and puncture it till it bleeds. I grunted and held on. Blood flowed down my arm to my elbow, then dripped onto my face.

In desperation I drove my other hand at Cassandra's sternum. She anticipated me and turned away, so that my stiffened fingers compressed only a bony cage of ribs. Behind me, Lonborg called out again: "*Now,* Leandra. Jump! Do it!"

The weight of a boulder slammed down onto my hips and thighs, crushing me against the stage, numbing everything below my waist. An instant later the nerves recovered, and the pain from my genitals reached my brain and stunned it. I passed out for the period of time in which my life was saved.

When I came to, a dark Othello was standing over me, his black face blotting out the sun, his crooked smile descending from a height that made me dizzy. "You okay?" he asked.

"Not yet."

"An ambulance is on the way. I got a compress tied around your waist, but you've lost a lot of blood and it ain't quit yet."

"Thanks."

"Sorry I couldn't keep her off your gonads. Your sex life may be a little tame for a while."

I tried to smile. "So what else is new?"

Bart Kinn grinned, then got down on a knee and adjusted the compress on my side. When he was finished he looked at me. "Lonborg sic them on you?"

"Right."

"The Renzel thing?"

I nodded.

"You know why?"

"I think so."

"The Misteen girl too?"

I shook my head. "The Maniac did that one."

"Anything I should do right now?" Kinn asked after he thought it over.

I coughed. My voice felt sanded, as though I'd swallowed gravel. "What evidence there is against Lonborg is at the Community Crisis Center. Have someone talk to Pierce Richards, the director. Have him show you what I told him to dig out of his records. It might be worth making another pass at the Usser place, to try to tie Lonborg into the bedroom."

"You got any other suggestions about how I can do my job?" This time the jab was gentle.

"Sorry," I said, and coughed again. "Did he get away?"

Kinn shook his head. "He looks better than he runs. But he ain't talking."

"How about the girls?"

"Had to cold-cock the skinny one to get her off you. The fat one's out there acting like she's on a trip to Disneyland."

"I'm not pressing charges against them," I said.

"Be a waste," Kinn agreed after a moment.

I breathed deeply in the silence, the eucalyptus fragrance a medicinal inhalant. "So how'd you know I was here?" I asked after a moment.

Kinn grinned once more. "You better get that windshield fixed, Tanner. Before someone gives you a ticket."

THIRTY

"Mrs. Renzel?"

"Yes?"

"This is Marsh Tanner. I've got some good news for you."

"Oh. Well. I . . . what is it?"

"The police have just arrested the man who killed your daughter."

"But I thought—"

"I know. So did the police. But Usser didn't do it. It was a man named Lonborg. A psychiatrist."

"Lisa went to a psychiatrist. Was he the one?"

"Yes."

"But why? Why would he do such a thing?"

"It's kind of complicated. He made a mistake, and your daughter was going to make it public. If she did, it would cost Lonborg some of his money and all of his reputation. He decided to try to keep that from happening."

"You make it sound so . . . normal."

"Oh, it wasn't normal. Not at all."

"Then he was an evil man?"

"I don't know. Fortunately, that's not for me to decide. I just think life got too much for him. He got very frightened. He didn't think it was possible for him to live any way but the way he had always lived. He didn't think he had a choice. But there's always a choice, Mrs. Renzel. It just doesn't seem that way sometimes. Does that make any sense to you?"

"Yes. I think so. Gunther and I were so afraid during the war, it turned us inside out. We did not recognize ourselves, not for many years. What about Lisa, Mr. Tanner? What will happen to her?"

"Well, her father's going to try to mend their relationship. If Lisa gives him a chance, I think she'll be all right. You might get in touch with Usser, Mrs. Renzel. He can use all the help he can get."

"Yes. Of course. I will. Right away."

"There's one more thing."

"Yes?"

"Your husband took a shot at Usser last night. He missed, but you'd better tell him to knock it off before someone gets hurt. In fact, you'd better tell him to stay out of Berkeley altogether. If he hangs around over there too much, it's going to drive him crazy."

The defendant has been found guilty of the crime of murder. It is now your function to determine the issue raised by the defendant's plea of "not guilty by reason of insanity." Such plea now places before you the issue as to whether he was legally sane or legally insane at the time of the commission of the crime. This is the sole issue for you to determine at this proceeding.

Although you may consider evidence of his mental condition both before and after the time of the commission of the crime, such evidence is to be considered for the purpose of throwing light upon the defendant's mental condition as it was when the crime was committed.

A person is legally insane when he was incapable of knowing or understanding the nature and quality of his act and incapable of distinguishing right from wrong at the time of the commission of the offense.

The defendant has the burden of proving his legal insanity at the time of the commission of the crime by a preponderance of the evidence.

By a preponderance of the evidence is meant such evidence as, when weighed with that opposed to it, has more convincing force and greater probability of truth.

California Jury Instruction 4.00 (1982 revision), for offenses committed after June 9, 1982

ABOUT THE AUTHOR

STEPHEN GREENLEAF was born in Washington D.C., and grew up in Centerville, Iowa. He has received degrees from Carleton College, Northfield, Minnesota, and from Boalt Hall School of Law of the University of California, Berkeley. After serving two years in the army, including a year in Vietnam, he practiced law for five years before beginning to write fiction. Four of his five previous books feature private detective John Marshall Tanner of San Francisco. His fifth book, *The Ditto List,* was Mr. Greenleaf's first nonmystery novel. Mr. Greenleaf lives in Oregon with his wife, Ann, an author of children's books, and his son, Aaron. He is currently working on another Tanner mystery.